P9-EDN-140

matatá

matatá

Malcolm McConnell

NEW YORK / THE VIKING PRESS

First published in 1971 by The Viking Press, Inc.
625 Madison Avenue, New York, N.Y. 10022
Published simultaneously in Canada by
The Macmillan Company of Canada Limited.
SBN 670-46219-5
Library of Congress catalog card number: 70-155660
Printed in U.S.A. by Vail-Ballou Press, Inc.

ACKNOWLEDGMENT

Screen Gems-Columbia Music, Inc.: *We Gotta Get Out
of This Place*. Words and music by Barry Mann and
Cynthia Weil. Copyrighted © 1965 by Screen Gems-
Columbia Music, Inc., N.Y., N.Y. Used by permission.
Reproduction prohibited.

FOR CAROL

matatá (mä-tä-tä′), *n.* Swahili. **1.** trouble **2.** confusion **3.** complication; difficulty.

N

CENTRAL
AFRICAN REPUBLIC

SUDAN

GABON

REPUBLIC OF
CONGO–BRAZZAVILLE

ORIENTALE

EQUATEUR

Coquilhatville

Stanleyville

EQUATOR

UGANDA

Goma

RWANDA

Brazzaville

Léopoldville

LÉOPOLDVILLE

KASAI

Luluabourg

Bakwanga

Bukavu

KIVU

BURUNDI

Albertville

TANZANIA

ANGOLA

Kamina

KATANGA

Elizabethville

DEMOCRATIC REPUBLIC
of CONGO

Miles
0   100   200   300

ZAMBIA

A. Karl / B. Kennedy

matatá

PART I **steve**

CHAPTER **1**

At dawn on Christmas Day, 1965, Léopoldville was blanketed by a low overcast that covered the city from the suburbs of Djelo Binza to the hills of elephant grass across the brown expanse of the Congo River. By midmorning the sky was still gray, unusual during the rainy season when normally the thunderheads stood like monoliths in a field of tropical blue. The cloud deck matched the holiday lethargy of the city's inhabitants, black and white alike, bringing an unexpected respite from the malignant sun. It was after eleven o'clock when the overcast broke and the first blinding columns of sunlight poured down on the tin roofs of the African *cité* and the mildewing European apartment complexes along the Boulevard du Trente Juin.

This was a very happy Christmas. In even the most crowded tribal households in the *cité* there was an uncle or cousin with an extra hundred francs for beer or palm wine. To the whites, with their generous hardship allowances, the long holiday weekend provided a welcome diversion in the monotonous heat of the rainy season. The scale and intensity of this year's reveling, however, far outstripped any of the previous five Christmases since the Independence of the Congo. The people of Léopoldville had reason to celebrate. For the first time since 1960 there was no rebellion, tribal war, or suicidal political infighting to menace the existence of the country. The last pocket of resistance of the *Muléliste* rebels had been surrounded in the Kivu mountains a thousand miles to the east. The Armée Nationale Congolaise under General Mobutu had staged a *coup d'état* a month before, successfully neutralizing the corrupt political superstructure that had mushroomed since Independence and rendered the government impotent to act in the face of turmoil and secession.

The Democratic Republic of the Congo was neither democratic nor a republic, but at last it was the Congo—one country, again officially under the control of a national government and, in principle, master of its own destiny. On this Christmas morning neither the Congo's past nor its future held much interest for the occupants of the "American Embassy ghetto" in the Royal Apartment Building on the Boulevard. Most of them were either still asleep or tottering about with prize-winning hangovers from the Christmas Eve parties that had shaken the building until sunrise.

Steve Sherman lay awake in the bedroom of his apartment on the fifth floor. His wife, Lisa, lay asleep next to him in the big double bed. They were both sweating heavily. The bedroom drapes were drawn apart and the sliding glass doors were wide open. When they had stumbled drunkenly into bed in the misty overcast after dawn, this had been a sensible compromise to make, considering they needed fresh air and the bedroom air conditioner was once again *en panne* with a blown fuse—the tenth that week. At dawn there had been an almost cooling breeze moving across the city. Now the overcast had broken and the full weight of the sun filled the bedroom.

After the frantic round of Christmas Eve party-hopping Steve was badly hung over. Normally he did not suffer much from the heat. He and Lisa had spent twenty-one months as Peace Corps volunteers in southern Morocco where air conditioning was unheard of and the electrical supply was even less regular than in Léopoldville. But with a queasy wine-and-champagne hangover the heat in the bedroom was intolerable. As a young trainee, the most junior Foreign Service officer in the Embassy, he had considered himself lucky to have been assigned an apartment in the

Royal. With the three big air conditioners purring, the five-room unit was usually pleasantly chill, but on this Christmas morning the bedroom was like a bread oven.

The heat, though, was not the cause of Steve's discomfort but only a part of it. His problem was that he wanted Lisa. He did not want to make love to her, carefully rousing her from sleep and displaying his growing repertoire of sexual skills; he wanted a "hangover quickie." Over their four years of marriage, and increasingly during their six months in the Congo, he had awakened from a few hours' drunken tossing, dry-mouthed and thickheaded, to lie painfully awake, unable to sleep again until he had quickly mounted Lisa and experienced a premature but intensely satisfying orgasm. This was a "hangover quickie," a matter of two minutes' quick friction, after which his body was filled with a tired peacefulness and he was able to slip once more into anesthetizing sleep. Given the unending official receptions and cocktail parties they were obliged to attend, together with the hectic swimming pool and apartment parties among the American community, Steve had resorted to this primitive sexual hangover therapy with growing regularity.

Unfortunately for Steve, Lisa had become more resistant to his morning demands as the frequency of their hangovers increased. She had recently pointed out to him with sweet determination that, although it might do him a world of good, allowing him to sleep off the worst of the morning, she was invariably left wide-awake, blinking on her back, to suffer alone with the added burden of sexual frustration. He had successfully resisted this temptation throughout December in spite of some disastrously hung-over mornings. Now he was determined to get one.

He knew, though, that he could not do it in this heat. They would either have to stumble onto the couch in the air-conditioned living room, a possibility he dismissed out of hand, or he would be obliged to go into the kitchen, get the box of fuses, nurse the bedroom air conditioner back to life, and wait until the room was sufficiently cooled before he could pull off the raid on Lisa's body. He lay shielding his eyes from the sun glare, trying to decide if simply closing the drapes would cool the room sufficiently. He knew that it would not. Despite his sick dizziness he would have to walk all the way to the kitchen, change the fuse, and draw the drapes before getting his reward. By the time he had done all this he might be so fully awake that he could not sleep again. He ran his tongue over his cracked lips, weighing the risks against the possible rewards. He belched, tasting cognac heartburn and garlic cheese spread. Lisa lay breathing softly on her stomach, her long body burned a wooden brown from hours at the pool, her bikini tan line rosy across her back, and her buttocks taut white.

"What a perfect body," he whispered to himself, rising on his elbow to stroke her back lightly and continue down to tickle the firm muscle inside her thigh. Lisa murmured in her sleep. It's worth it, he thought. Besides, I'm not all that hung over—tired mainly, didn't get enough sleep. Too damn many parties lately. O.K., boy, go to it.

He rose gingerly, rolling his head from shoulder to shoulder to test his equilibrium. He slid the glass doors together quietly and drew the drapes, darkening the room to a softly lighted cave. When he returned from the kitchen with the fuses and a screwdriver, he tripped the circuit breaker in the hallway and knelt to open the white galvanized fuse box above the baseboard. He removed the burnt-out fuse and held it in his palm as he stared at it with a thick-witted hangover thoroughness. In the dim light he saw something glimmering inside the fuse box.

"Jesus Christ!" he said softly. "There's a loose wire in there. No wonder the fuses were always blowing. Stupid *Belge* electrician didn't even see it the last time. What a country—no wonder the poor Congolese are so fucked up. They've been trained by jerks like that guy." Using the screwdriver, he tightened the loose wire at the base of the socket, replaced the fuse, and started the air conditioner. The switch clicked dryly, but the machine remained silent.

"Circuit breaker," he exclaimed, slapping his forehead lightly. "Now who's the jerk?"

The air conditioner surged to life as the hall switch was thrown. Steve stood triumphantly at the foot of the bed, feeling the sweet cold draft flow from the vents.

"Congratulations, baby," Lisa said, sitting up in bed. "You fixed it."

Steve turned to face her. She sat twining a strand of her long sandy-colored hair in her fingers. She smiled at him. "Do you always talk to yourself that way?"

"Beats me," he said. "Sometimes, I guess, when I've got a problem."

"Well, you've solved one problem, but you've still got another."

"What problem, honey?"

"Look," she said, pointing slyly at his still erect penis. "Come here," she said. "You deserve a nice reward for fixing the air conditioner."

"Oh, Steve," Lisa murmured, "that was beautiful. What a nice surprise. You know how long it's been since it's been so nice for me?"

He was still arched above her, trembling slightly as he waited, supporting himself on his outstretched arms. He shook his head in answer to her question.

"Such a nice surprise," she repeated, "and with a quickie, too. I must have been having sexy dreams." Her voice was languid, soft with encroaching sleep. "Hasn't been at all so good lately. Not for me at least, not with all these parties. I know it doesn't make that much difference for a man, Steve, that you can always manage it, but for a girl it's different. You've got to feel in the mood. That's hard when we get so drunk all the time. You've got to feel . . . close . . . you know, really in *contact*. Not just physically like it's been this last month or so, but this morning I really could *feel* you inside of me. It was wonderful."

"I know, Lisa," Steve whispered, "I know. I could tell. I'm glad it was so good for you. That's the way I want it to be for you always. . . ." He cleared his throat, being careful not to breathe rancid-mouth party dregs into Lisa's face. His arms were trembling badly now.

"You O.K. Lisa? Do you want to rest, or should I keep going? I'm almost there."

"Poor Steve," she said. "This was supposed to be your treat. Yes, baby, keep going. What do you want me to do? Should I put my legs down?"

"No, this is fine," Steve said, picking up the rhythm.

Lisa lay back, smiling at him as she played her fingertips lightly up and down his spine. "Won't be long now," she said happily. "That's for sure," Steve panted.

The metallic buzz of the doorbell echoed loudly down the hallway.

"Oh, damn," Lisa said.

Steve craned his neck to glare at the open bedroom door. The buzzing continued in short, irritatingly persistent bursts. He sagged, then rose again to his rhythm in a vain attempt to ignore the bell, finally collapsing beside her.

"Did you come?" she whispered.

Lips set in a scowl, he silently shook his head. The buzzing continued.

Lisa rose from the bed, grabbing her thin cotton wrapper. "Wait," she said. "I'll get rid of whoever it is and come right back." The ringing echoed louder. "For God's sake," she said angrily, "all right."

She was back at the bedroom door in a moment. "Steve," she said, "I'm sorry, honey, but there's a UN policeman from downstairs and some other people there. I can't make out what they want."

"Shit," Steve said. He jumped to his feet, slipping dizzily on the waxed tile floor. He looked vaguely about the room for his bathrobe and, not seeing it, snatched up a rumpled pair of Bermuda shorts and struggled into them, painfully bending his erection as he did so. The ringing continued. "Goddamn it," he yelled. "Knock it off."

He strode down the hallway, fumbled with the chain lock, and threw the door open with a bang. "What the hell do you think—" he began angrily, but stopped in mid-sentence, subdued by the group in the doorway. There were four Africans filling the little square landing that separated their apartment from 58C. They ranged in size from the bulky Nigerian in the starched tropical shorts of the United Nations Police to the nervous Congolese Boy Scout in a clean but threadbare uniform, replete with a bright neckerchief. Next to the Nigerian constable stood a little Congolese policeman wearing an oversized white helmet liner. The fourth member of the group was grotesquely deformed, a barefoot hunchback who stood grinning at Steve with a sightless and, as Steve discovered with a shock, *eyeless* face.

Steve felt his anger dissolve. After a moment an embarrassed smile formed on his face.

"Dey come now fo Christmas dash, mastah," the Nigerian said, his voice a guttural rumbling from deep in his throat. "Sergeant Major he say deese Congolais men no come building sept wid security police. I go escort dem and dis one go come too. Dis one and me we escort. Deese boys go come fo Christmas dash."

Steve had only limited contact with the Nigerian police, nodding to them as he drove past the United Nations checkpoint entering the Royal compound. The constable's pidgin English made little sense to him. "I'm sorry," he said, "I don't understand what it is you want exactly."

"Dey go come fo Christmas dash, sah," the constable repeated, frowning.

The Boy Scout jerked forward, making the three-fingered Scout salute, and breaking into a hopeful smile, he handed Steve a greasy scrap of a card. "The Boy Scout Council of the Congo wishes you a Merry Christmas and a Happy New Year," was badly printed on the card in French, English, and Flemish. Steve read the card slowly and looked up at the Scout. The boy thrust out an open school notebook on which lines had been carelessly drawn with a leaky ball-point pen. A loose pile of fifty- and one-hundred-franc notes lay in the crack of the book. Steve could see that he was expected to add to the pile and fill in one of the blank spaces on the page with his name and the amount given. He tried to read the smeared writing to discern how much others had contributed. It was an impossible task through his hangover dullness. He handed the book back to the Boy Scout. *"S'il vous plaît, patron,"* the child whined. *"C'est pour les Scouts."*

The blind hunchback now jammed his collection book into Steve's stomach, waving an equally greasy card before him with the other hand. "The Congolese Association of the Christian Blind wish you a Merry Christmas and a Happy New Year," Steve read in French. He shot a quick look at the man's horrific face and then turned away.

"Hang on a second," he said in English, closing the door.

"S'il vous plaît, patron," the Scout and the blind man chimed naggingly.

"Hey, Lisa," Steve called down to the bedroom, "got any change? It's a Boy Scout and a blind guy for a Christmas donation."

"Look in the kitchen, on the counter by the stove. There should be some change in my little purse."

Steve walked unsteadily into the kitchen and stood before the counter. He moved spice jars and cookbooks aside, searching for the purse. The doorbell jangled again, loudly, just above his head on the kichen wall. "Hey," he yelled, "hang on. You'll get your money. Just wait a second."

The counter was crowded with jars and bottles. The bell pounded away again. He found no money. "Lisa," he yelled over the noise of the doorbell, "where the hell is it, anyway?"

She could not hear him. Then he saw Lisa's leather change purse had slipped down behind the tin bread box. As he reached for it, his elbow knocked over the big apothecary jar in which Lisa kept brown sugar, spilling the contents across the counter and sending the thick glass lid shattering to the tile floor.

"Son of a bitch!" he swore. The doorbell rang louder. He trembled with anger as he flung the door open again, grabbing and savagely twisting the Boy Scout's skinny fingers away from the doorbell button. "I told you to knock that shit off," he said. The boy shrank away from him.

"He no good, no way," the Nigerian rumbled. "He go fo ring dat bell too much, too much."

Steve broke open the change purse, removing two tattered fifty-franc notes. He dropped one into the Scout's notebook and gently slid the other into the blindman's open hand which closed like a steel trap at the touch of the bill.

"O.K.," Steve grumbled, beginning to close the door. "Merry Christmas."

"Patron," the Congolese policeman said gravely, *"c'est moi, le policier.* I'm the policeman."

Steve blinked at the Congolese.

"You go dash dis one too, mastah," the Nigerian said, smiling.

"S'il vous plaît, patron," the policeman continued. *"C'est pour la police."*

Steve dug once more into the change purse, removing another fifty francs. "Here," he said, dropping the money into the little policeman's cupped hands and slamming the door. He was halfway to the bedroom when the doorbell buzzed again.

"What the hell do you want now?" he snarled at the smiling Nigerian.

The African's expression changed once more to an injured frown. "You go dash deese boys too much, mastah, but you no dash me no way."

Steve ran his fingers down his stubbly face, swaying slightly with the headache. "O.K., O.K.," he said, emptying a handful of ten-franc coins into the constable's huge palm. "Anything else?"

The constable stared quizzically back at him. "Sah?"

"Forget it," Steve said tiredly. "Merry Christmas, *bonne fête,* good-bye." He closed and chain-locked the door. As he shuffled back down the hallway, he saw a bright red smear on the tiles and, examining the sole of his right foot, discovered a long slash cut by a shard from the broken jar lid.

"Wonderful," he muttered. "Now I'll get the sheets all bloody."

Lisa lay seductively on her side with one leg drawn up against her breast and the other thrust out gracefully over the edge of the mattress. Steve pulled off his shorts and stood storklike to examine his cut foot.

"Oh, baby," Lisa said, "you're all small again. What's wrong with your foot?"

"Cut it on some broken glass in the kitchen. Listen, I'm going to take a shower and put a band-aid on my foot. Why don't you get the picnic stuff together and we can go to the pool right away?"

"Don't you want to finish making love?"

Steve felt the tight anger at the Congolese and heard the nagging buzz of the doorbell still echoing in his head. He sighed. "Why don't we just go to the pool now and come back early this afternoon? I'm really not in the mood any more."

"Did I do something wrong, Steve?"

"No, honey. It's just that I'm hung over and I got kind of upset with those guys. I'll be O.K. Let's just go to the pool now and swim before it gets too crowded."

Lisa took his hand, attempting to pull him down to the bed. But the image of the hunchback's eyeless face floated in Steve's mind and he tugged away from her.

"Steve," she whispered, "please come back to bed. That was . . . so good for me . . . I want it to be good for you too."

He was painfully aware of the sticky wetness where his cut foot touched the floor tile.

"Baby," Lisa continued, "please. It isn't always good like that. I mean honestly, I get sort of depressed sometimes after we make love because it's almost become a mechanical thing. I don't mean all the time, but now, since we came to the Congo. You're so tired at night and we drink so much at those silly parties. No, really, please don't get mad. I'm not saying it's *your* fault, baby. It's just that I hardly ever come any more. That's why it was so beautiful this morning, not just the coming. I really felt . . . that I was close to you, closer than I've been for a long time. You've been so preoccupied lately, you seem to be brooding on things so. The only time I can really feel close to you is when we make love. Please come back now and let me make *you* come nice."

"Oh, I do O.K. for myself, Lisa," he said, laughing uncomfortably. "I'm not exactly starving for affection, you know."

Lisa sat up in bed and reached out slowly to take his arm again. "Steve," she said, "I'm serious. Making love has always been something special for us. It's always been so good."

"It's good for a lot of people, Lisa. I don't want to sound crude or anything and you know damn well how much I love you, but the fact is that two perfect strangers can meet at a party and hop into bed and screw all night and it can be beautiful for them . . . physically, I mean. I suppose just as good as what we have."

"No!" Lisa protested. "It's not just screwing for us, Steve. I know people can have something purely physical, but for us it's really *important*. It's how we help each other get over the things that bother us."

"That's only one of the ways," he said, carefully choosing his words as he stood there resisting the pull of Lisa's hand on his arm. His thoughts jumped ahead through his hangover thickness, searching for a rebuttal to her argument, then he suddenly saw that she was right. When things got bad and one of them, usually Steve, was tense and unable to cope with it all, they would make love with long, passionate abandon, often spending a full twenty-four hours together in bed, and when they emerged things would be better. They had *helped* each other. He clearly remembered that last nightmare year at college when they were married and broke and his scholarship depended on an *A* in the American Political Institutions final, but his morning milk delivery route and his evening janitor's job kept him from a final cramming session at the library. It was a foul Wisconsin January and he had seen little of Lisa for weeks, she being completely absorbed in her own exhausting schedule of classes, study, and part-time jobs. Only at night in their bed did they find the time to unwind from the day and wordlessly salve each other with sexual love. They *did* help each other, too. The Sunday before the important exam they spent the entire day and night in their creaking secondhand double-bed-on-bricks. They hardly spoke. The FM radio provided an innocuous background of instrumental show tunes, and outside the icy branches scratched against the windows of the drafty wooden apartment house. "I really have to get up and study, Lisa," he repeated. "I've got to ace this baby, I've just got to." But they stayed in bed, and through the long afternoon they made love and dozed and made love again, and then it was midnight and they were both ravenous and they called out for pizza, no anchovies, but heavy on the cheese and sausage, and they made love again and again that night and they hardly spoke ten words that whole day and night. When Steve walked into the examination hall at eight-forty-five the next morning, his head was clear and he was calm inside, and he sat down and filled four and a half blue books with concise, well-organized answers which his instructor called more typical of a Ph.D. candidate than an undergraduate. And he got his *A* and his scholarship and senior honors too. And Lisa *had* helped him. She had done it with her body.

"What's wrong, baby?" Lisa asked, tightening her grip on his arm.

"Nothing," he said, shaking his head. "I was just thinking about

the way we used to be able to spend a whole weekend in bed."
Like that time in Morocco, he thought, the memories rushing up
again, when those clods at the Peace Corps Rep's office in Rabat
wanted me to do that irrigation survey that the French Army had
already done in '54, just worthless, bureaucratic make-work because they were scared of the Ministry and the Embassy and their
own fucking shadows, and I was going to throw the whole thing in
and quit, and then we took the jeep and the tent and went up to
the mountains and camped that weekend, and we hardly got out of
our sleeping bag and Lisa was so good and loving and we were
able to talk, that time we *talked* all the time we were making love
and it *all* came out, all the things that were bugging us, and, Jesus,
she was such a loving *woman,* and after that nothing was there to
bug me any more. All that mattered was that Lisa loved me. The
rest of it was just small change.

"You're right, Lisa," he finally said. "It'd be so nice just to
have a whole weekend together in bed to relax and make love and
talk, talk like we did on that camping trip up in the cedar forest
above Azrou."

"That's exactly what I mean by feeling close," Lisa whispered.
"That's why it's so important now. Since we've been down here
with the Embassy we haven't once talked that way, the way we
used to be able to. I *know* things are bothering you here, Steve.
That's why we have to work at getting close again. Things are
bothering me too. I've got things I want to tell you, but I just can't
blurt them out during one of those stupid receptions. We have to
get close again. . . ."

Steve clawed momentarily at the razor line of heat rash where
the collar of his office shirt always rubbed. "You're right, Lisa. It
has become sort of a mechanical thing. I'm sorry. I guess I am
brooding on things. We'll make love nice and slowly this afternoon, O. K.? I'm just a little upset right now.

"Wear some clogs or something when you go into the kitchen,"
he said. "I broke the lid to the goddamn sugar jar."

"Steve," Lisa said, "we don't *have* to go to the pool. You're
going to be gone all next week, and when you get back it'll be
New Year's and another whole round of parties. Why don't we
just stay here, at home? You've got the air conditioner fixed now,

and we can have our picnic right here in bed. I hardly ever see you alone any more, baby, and you'll be gone almost a week on that stupid trip."

"Why is the trip suddenly so stupid?" Steve said coldly.

"That's what *you* were saying last night, Steve."

"The *training* part of it's stupid—ridiculous, really. But the trip itself will do me a lot of good. I never said the trip itself was stupid, Lisa. The report that they expect me to write is the stupidest thing I've ever heard of, just like the rest of this Mickey Mouse stuff they've got me doing. They send all the trainees upcountry sometime during their first year. We're supposed to write a report that will 'indicate the quality of the junior officer's political and economic perceptivity' or some crap like that. That sounds wonderful, but I know damn well nobody will ever read the report."

"If you think the trip's going to be that bad, that's all the more reason we should stay home today and talk about things. I know you, Steve, you let things get under your skin and build up pressure. You hold things inside yourself. If things bother you, baby, you've got to tell me."

Steve straightened abruptly, again breaking Lisa's grasp. "We'll talk this afternoon, Lisa. Right now I'd really like to go to the pool and just relax in the sun before it gets too hot."

"Are you sure you're not mad at me for something?" Lisa called after him as he walked toward the bathroom.

"No!" he snapped. "I'm just all sweaty and hung over and I want to go to the pool. Get the picnic things packed, O.K.?"

"Whatever you want, baby," Lisa said sweetly.

CHAPTER **2**

Driving up the concrete ramp from the Royal's basement garage, Steve stalled the engine of their Volkswagen. He applied the hand brake and twisted the key to the start position. The starter whined faintly and then began clicking. The red light on the dashboard blinked out. "Damn!" Steve said. "It's the generator again."

The car sat at a steep angle on the ramp with the now brilliant noon sun blasting through the windshield. Lisa sat beside him in a short-skirted sundress, a foam picnic jug of gin and tonic on her lap. "I'll have to roll back down in reverse and start it with the clutch," Steve said, squinting back over his shoulder into the dim entrance of the basement garage. He sighed, shaking off his sunglasses. "Can't see a thing down there," he muttered. "You want to get out and guide me down? I've got to roll fast enough so that the motor will catch when I pop the clutch."

As Lisa opened the door, a Nigerian policeman walked toward them down the ramp.

"Battery's dead," Steve said to the constable. "Can you guide me around the curve down there if I roll back?"

The Nigerian glared at Steve and folded his hands behind his back. He was a big chocolate-brown man, out of character in his uniform shorts and knee socks.

"I've got to go back down to start the motor," Steve said. "Will you stand down at the curve and guide me around?"

"No good stay here, mistah," the Nigerian said. "Sergeant Major he say no good cars park dis ramp. Dey go stop garage fo otha cars."

"Shit," Steve said between his teeth. "Go on down there and guide me, will you, Lisa? This guy's hopeless."

Lisa went down the steep ramp, swinging the little foam jug. The faint tinkle of ice cubes aggravated Steve's swelling thirst and headache. He smelled the sweet stench of the uncollected holiday garbage wafting up from the basement rubbish bins. Twisted uncomfortably in his seat, he saw Lisa wave to him through the dusty sun glare on the rear window. He released the brake and rolled backwards, picking up speed quickly on the steep slope. Still looking over his shoulder, he engaged the clutch, shifted into reverse, and switched on the key. Out of the corner of his eye he caught a flash of gray cloth and, as he turned his head for a moment, saw the Nigerian policeman running alongside the car.

"No good, mistah," the African yelled. "Dis be 'up' ramp, you go use 'down' ramp if you go park garage."

"Get out of the way," Steve yelled, but it was too late. The big policeman had blocked the curve. Steve braked hard, but the tires slid on a patch of grease and the car slammed into the ramp wall with a snapping of metal and shattering pop of taillight glass. Steve sagged in his seat, his gut trembling with anger. The garbage smell was overpowering. His fresh sports shirt was sweated through. Lisa walked up the ramp, biting her lip sheepishly.

"I tried to warn you, honey—didn't you hear me?"

The Nigerian policeman's heavy boots echoed on the concrete. "Now we go make accident report one time," he called down. "I go fo de papers."

"Screw you, you black monkey," Steve said when the policeman was out of earshot.

He inspected the damage to the rear of the car. The right exhaust pipe and taillight had absorbed the shock. "Have to get it pulled up now," he said with tired resignation. "Too steep to try and push it up."

Lisa leaned into the car to deposit the picnic jug. "Look," she said, "the little red light's on now."

Steve started the motor on the first try. "Must have jarred something back in place. Come on, Lisa, let's get out of here before that monkey comes back."

As they bounced off the top of the ramp, they met the Nigerian policeman, who had been joined by two of his colleagues. The constable carried a clipboard thick with printed forms.

"You go write accident report, one time, mistah," he called as Steve sped past him and out the compound's open gate, then accelerated down the empty boulevard.

"God*damn* these people," he said. "They're as bad as the fucking Congolese."

Lisa glanced at him, reaching over his chest to open the window vent so that a breeze played over his sweating red face. She rested her fingers lightly on his bare knee but did not speak, preferring to wait until his anger had abated.

"Whole damn country's full of them—all they know is what some white man told them years ago. Don't know the reason for anything, they're just like robots. 'Up' ramp and 'down' ramp. Shit! That's O.K. for New York. Accident report, Christ! Did you see that pile of forms he had with him? Start filling out those in triplicate and we'd be there all morning. What a fucking country. The

Nigerians are supposed to be training the poor goddamn Congolese! Jesus!"

Lisa still remained silent. She wiped Steve's sunglasses clean and handed them to him. Then she reached back for two plastic glasses from the picnic basket and poured him a tall gin and tonic. He drank the icy drink down in three long pulls as he drove. Lisa refilled the glass and lit him a cigarette.

As he drove up the Avenue de la Huitième Armée, he relaxed in his seat, tapping his fingers on the steering wheel. "Well," he said, "the car had to go in the garage this week anyway for the six months' checkup. You'd better take it in early Monday morning so we have it for the New Year's weekend. I'll be gone all week, so I guess it's as good a time as any to be in the garage. You won't need the car much while I'm gone, will you, honey?"

"No," Lisa said, "I can always get a ride from one of the ladies in the building if I have to go anywhere. . . . Steve," she added, speaking very slowly, "last night you were saying that you might want to postpone the trip, that you were tired. How do you feel about it now?"

"It sounds stupid, but I really can't decide what I want to do." He laughed. "Right now I'd like to put a padlock on the front door and pull the telephone out by the roots and just sleep for a week."

Lisa smiled, touching Steve's leg. "I think that would be nice, honey. You *are* tired. Why don't you just forget the trip and stay home with me? We could have a grand time now that you've fixed the air conditioner in the bedroom." She tugged playfully at the sun-bleached hair of his leg, slipping her fingers coolly up beneath the edge of his swimming trunks. Steve jerked his thigh irritably.

"Ah, I think it would be better if I got out of Léo for a while. I'm tired, but it's not from working too hard. I haven't done any real work since we got here. I've sure spent a lot of time at the Embassy, though, and gone to a hell of a lot of stupid receptions and cocktails. I think it will do me some good to get out of this phony town and see what Africa really looks like."

They turned onto the Avenue Valke and drove in the shade of lofty tung-oil trees. On the root-twisted sidewalk four poorly dressed, barefoot Congolese carried a sick child toward the Danish hospital on an improvised litter. They stopped to gaze hopefully at the young white couple as the Volkswagen sped past.

"That's not being fair to yourself, Steve," Lisa said quietly. "You've been working very hard lately, especially since the coup. You're there at the Embassy at eight o'clock every morning and sometimes we have three receptions on the same night and don't get home until midnight. I call that hard work."

Steve looked away from the road and searched for the right words. The cold pine-needle effervescence of the drink was clearing his head. He turned to face Lisa, an embarrassed smile forming on his face. "Remember how excited I was when my training cycle got changed and they put me in the Political Section?"

Lisa nodded, studying his face.

"Yeah, well, I've got a little confession to make, baby," he said quickly. "I'm really not doing any of those things I said I was. You know, drafting cables for the Ambassador and going over to the Foreign Ministry. I sit there at a little toy desk that they gave me in the corner and I type up the Bio File. In the morning and at night I'm supposed to read the telegraphic reading file so that I'm *familiar* with the situation. Big deal. Real high-level diplomacy. It's tiring, all right, but you can't call it work."

"Well, you're a trainee, Steve. You've got to start at the bottom and work your way up."

"Yeah, well, Pete Joyce isn't a trainee. He's thirty years old. He's already had two posts in Africa. You know what *he* does all day?"

Lisa shook her head.

"He writes up the WEEKA. That's all he's been doing for a year."

"What's the WEEKA?"

"It's this stupid report that the Embassy cables to the Department each week. It has a couple paragraphs on the local situation as seen by the various sections . . . Pol, Econ, Military Attachés, like that. The thing is that Pete doesn't really write it. He just takes the reports from the guys in other sections and condenses them into telegraphese. That's all he does all week."

"Pete's nice, so is Doris."

"Sure, they're all nice, Lisa. That's not the point."

"Well, I'm sure that the WEEKA report is important or they wouldn't put somebody as experienced as Pete on it."

"You've got more faith in the Government than I do. Do you seriously think anybody bothers to read the WEEKAs that come in from all over the world? Remember when I was in training at the Department before we came out? A guy in the Bureau told me not to waste my time reading the WEEKAs because anything really important rated a separate cable. So there you are. It's the same with the Bio File I'm typing."

"It doesn't seem like the same thing at all."

"I know what I'm talking about, honey. Nobody bothers to read the Political Section Bio File. The CIA spooks in Poli II have the *real* one. If the Ambassador or the DCM wants to get the low-down on some Congolese politician, he just picks up the phone and calls down to George White or one of those other guys. I'm just sitting there treading water in front of my air conditioner. Like you say, that's not so bad because I'm a new boy and need to get the feel of things. But, Christ, Lisa, I look across the bull pen at Pete Joyce and realize that in about four years that's where I'll be sitting."

"Somebody's got to do it, baby."

Steve shrugged his shoulders and drained his second gin and tonic. "I know somebody's got to do it, Lisa. But, Jesus, you look at all the more important things that need to be done in this country, at the schools and the hospitals that have to be rebuilt and the way the whole interior has been just ruined by the rebellion, and then you look at the way we live down here with our make-work jobs and all these stupid parties night after night, and you wonder what the hell it's all about."

"You sound so pessimistic, Steve."

"Well, I guess it's all just so different than I thought it would be. I thought we were coming down here to *help* people."

"Things are never the way you think they'll be, are they?"

"I guess you're right," Steve said.

The parking lot in front of the Athénée Club swimming pool was already crowded with cars. Steve slowed, turning onto the rutted mud of the lot, and cruised slowly in the feathery shade of the jacaranda trees, searching for a parking space. "I guess I'd better park down at the end there in case the generator goes on the blink again and we have to push it. Too many cars here . . . the pool's crowded already." He handed Lisa his empty glass as they jolted over the ruts. As he maneuvered between the parked Simcas and Citroëns, a loose throng of barefoot Congolese urchins trailed after the car, calling hopefully to Steve as they indicated vacant parking places. They were ragged little street boys ranging in age from seven to twelve. All wore the tattered remnants of khaki shorts, and a few possessed patched cotton shirts or singlets. Slowed by the ruts, the car was soon surrounded by a cloying mob of children.

"*Moi, patron,*" they sang out. "*Prends-moi, je garde ta voiture.*"

A skinny waif of six or seven, dressed in a discolored sack that had once been an adult's white shirt, thrust a wilted bouquet of frangipani through the open car window at Lisa. "*Des fleurs, madame, pour Noël,*" he begged. "*S'il te plaît. . . .*"

Steve sounded the car horn to clear the clot of urchins from the parking place he had chosen next to the chain metal fence surrounding the swimming-pool grounds. He forced open the car door against the press of six children, who scrambled, shifting position to be near him. "*Moi, patron,*" they chanted. "*Prends-moi, c'est moi qui garde, je garde la voiture.*"

Steve bent back into the car to remove the picnic basket, uncomfortably aware of the children's spindly legs brushing against his own. On the other side of the Volkswagen Lisa was equally beseiged, surrounded by four little boys with their pitiful bouquets of bougainvillaea and frangipani filched before dawn from the gardens of the European villas in Kalina. Despite his sunglasses and the jacaranda shade, the noon sun blinded Steve painfully, compounding his sick headache.

"Hey," he said in English to the boys. "Take it easy, you *all* can't guard the car."

He wrestled the picnic basket out of the back seat and stood swaying slightly with the car door still open as the children surged in at him. On the clipped lawn of the club, Belgian families had arranged their blankets and canvas chairs. Their children dashed about in the dappled sunlight, savagely competing for their sleepy parents' attention with a splendid variety of new plastic Christmas toys. Steve slammed the car door shut and, doing so, almost smashed the fingers of an especially frail child who had been pushed up against the front fender by the stronger boys. The child flinched back onto the hot metal of the fender.

"Steve," Lisa cried painfully, "these kids are terrible—they're pulling at me so."

Steve grabbed the largest of the boys, a child of twelve, his big splay feet coated red with dry mud. *"Toi,"* Steve said, jamming a twenty-franc coin into the child's hand, "you're the *gardien*— twenty francs now and twenty later. The rest of you beat it. *Allez, va-t'en."*

Beaming, the successful candidate swept the smaller boys aside so that Steve could pass. He strode around the front of the car to rescue Lisa. On the lawn Steve could see several pudgy Belgians watching his predicament with undisguised amusement. As he reached forward to disperse the circle of boys closing around his wife, the skinny child who had escaped the slamming door dashed up to grab the handles of the picnic basket.

"Moi," he cried, *"j'apporte ton panier."* The child sagged beneath the weight of the basket, heavy with wine bottles.

"Hey," Lisa shouted, "stop that!"

The flower venders were literally clawing at her now that she had removed her change purse to search for small change to appease them. One particularly unattractive boy, his head a cap of ringworm and his pipestem arms girdled with scabs, clung beseechingly to her wrist. Steve stepped forward to break his grip on Lisa. The other child still held one handle of the picnic basket. With a rattling clatter the contents of the basket, two cold bottles of rosé and plastic refrigerator containers of sliced salami and potato salad, cascaded into the mud. The children stood frozen in horror-struck fascination.

"You little bastard," Steve said, swinging the empty basket with the child still grasping it. The boy's emaciated body slapped against the door of the car and he dropped hard to the mud. The impact had knocked the wind out of him, and as he sucked frantically for breath, he stared up at Steve with an expression of uncomprehending animal fear.

"Oh, Steve," Lisa said, "he's hurt."

Steve reached down to comfort the child, but the boy made a hoarse, sputtering sound and bounded off in a panic between Steve and Lisa to join his fleeing companions.

"Bravo les Américains," a red-faced Belgian called mockingly from his blanket on the lawn of the pool club.

"Go fuck yourself, you fat-assed frog!" Steve yelled back through his headache.

"It's O.K., honey," Lisa said. She bent to pick up the picnic lunch. "They were just kids. They wanted something for Christmas and they got too excited. Let's not let it spoil our day."

Steve stood with his fists clenched, glaring at the Belgian. "Yeah," he said bitterly, "it's a beautiful day, all right. A real fucking Grandma Moses Christmas. . . ."

CHAPTER **3**

Four hours later, the bedroom drapes drawn tightly against the afternoon sun, they lay again locked together in the mechanical wind of the air conditioner, Lisa partially on her side as Steve thrust away. She had enjoyed a quick, vaguely disappointing orgasm stimulated by a long session of foreplay. He was hot and wetly smooth on top of her, and she knew it would not be long. Closing her eyes against the heat of his shoulder, she rode with him. He was swelling inside of her, he was almost there.

"Come, baby," she said. "Come nice."

She heard the telephone jangling above the noise of the air conditioner.

"Shit!" he said, sagging. "Not again."

"Don't stop, baby, don't stop." She curled her legs up over his and pulled him back. And then very sharply, with a sudden pounding heat, it was over and she padded naked down the hall.

"Lisa, is that you?" It was Robert Henderson.

"Yes," she whispered.

"I'm sorry to disturb you. Were you taking a siesta?"

"We were making love," she said.

"Oh. I'm very sorry," he murmured. "You can talk, then, I take it?"

"Yes," she said, "Steve's in the bedroom cooling off."

"What did he decide? Is he going on the trip? I'd like to know so I can plan things for next week."

Lisa turned, holding the receiver so that she could look down the long hallway to see the bedroom door. "He's acting kind of funny. I think he drank too much at the pool. He was talking very pessimistically about his job. I think he's just in one of his moods. He'll go on the trip, all right. Everyone at the Embassy expects him to."

"Look," Henderson said, "you're going to the Reeds' for dinner, aren't you? So am I. Why don't you and Steve come up to my place for a drink around six-fifteen? I'm having a few people over. I think I can convince Steve to go on the trip. He seems to listen to me."

"Yes," she said, "he always listens to older men. He's got a thing about that."

"Fine. I'll see you in an hour or so, then."

"Fine, Robert."

"Lisa?"

"Yes?"

"It should be a very nice week. Do you still want to go through with it?"

Lisa could see a dull patch on the tile floor where the houseboy had missed with the wax. She turned back toward the living room, taking in the sterile uniformity of the government-owned furniture offset by their few Moroccan *objets:* a Middle-Atlas Berber rug and the painted cedar chest from Marrakesh. She had a flash of the week ahead in the empty apartment, alone with the old houseboy plodding soundlessly through his chores. She saw the empty nights in the chill bedroom, sitting up in bed alone with a mystery and a stack of records on the portable.

"Yes," she said. "I very much want to be with you next week."

"Good. You know how I feel about it. It should be nice. I've got a few things to do with the Italians on the oil refinery negotiations, but I should be finished by Wednesday and we can have the rest of the week free. I wish Tony Blackpool were still here with his Beechcraft—we could buzz down to Luanda."

"That would be very nice," she said.

"We'll have a fine time just the same, though. I'll see you both a little later, then."

"Bye-bye, Robert."

She paused before the full-length mirror next to the door of the powder room. Perhaps, she thought, I'll be able to even out my tan if Robert takes me out on the river again and we can swim nude like we did last month. That had been exciting. Just the two of them, water-skiing across the flat sheet of Stanley Pool, the river wide and swift with the lime-green rafts of water hyacinth rushing past, and Robert absolutely naked before her in the boat, watching as she bounded across the wake, her hair streaming out behind her in the wind, her body caressed so roughly by the hot air. It had been all speed and sunlight, so excitingly evil, naked in the middle of a Thursday afternoon out there on the river.

It had been so reckless, so typical of Robert. This was why he excited her so. He *did* the things he wanted to do, regardless of the consequences. The islands of the Stanley Pool were a favorite picnic and water-skiing preserve of Léopoldville's European busi-nessmen and the Diplomatic Corps. At any moment as the boat smacked along, rounding the points of the multiple islands, they could have come upon a business picnic, even a group from the American Embassy. Robert had gunned the twin outboard engines and laughed wildly in the sunlight, and Lisa had loved it. She'd drunk three quick gin and tonics on the boat ride out from the yacht club, and she reveled in the brazenness of their situation.

They had anchored the boat against the steady current of the river, and then he had had her in the shade of a steep-banked sand island. They were up to their waists in the clear water as he worked away above her, much taller and bulkier than Steve. It had been so good and so forbidden, reminiscent of class-cutting in bed with Steve in his funny little apartment in Madison before they were married.

She had been with another man, and Steve had been less than two miles away in the cement-and-aluminum cage of the Embassy, wandering about with his silly little cards, noting down pertinent facts about obscure Congolese politicians. She and Robert had been there in the river together and she had loved it.

She stood before the mirror, gently kneading the flesh of her hips. If she tanned *there,* Steve would notice it at once, and she could never explain where she had found the privacy to sun-bathe naked, and then he would know. She had to be very careful. That was the thing she really hated about this affair: the need to lie and to deceive Steve. Steve was more than her husband, he was really her best friend. It seemed that they had always been together, always been married.

Lisa could not imagine a life that did not include Steve. But that was, she realized, exactly what the affair with Robert represented for her, a life without Steve, something she could do by herself, where she became more than simply Lisa Sherman, Steve's wife. There was more to it than just that, she knew. It was difficult for her to define, even to herself, what it was exactly that attracted her so strongly to Robert Henderson. She stood very still in the long hallway, letting her mind move slowly around the riddle. When the answer suddenly came to her, she felt a sharp sadness. This affair *did* involve Steve; it wasn't just Robert and her. Steve was involved *in absentia.* It wasn't just Henderson's money or his looks or his sophistication that attracted her. He wasn't a particularly talented lover. It was his brazenness, the reckless manner in which he lived. It was this same brash, self-directed quality in Steve that had first drawn her to him during her freshman year at the university.

In those days Steve did exactly what he wanted. . . . That Sunday afternoon in the balcony of the student union movie theater, right in the middle of that sexy Swedish film, Steve took her by the hand up to the back row in the shadows near the projection booth and they made love with their clothes on and it had been so good. It was the danger that made it good.

That's the way Steve was then. Her parents had been furious with him when he took off on that Freedom Ride to Mississippi six days before their wedding, skipping the rehearsals and the bachelor dinner, arriving back in town dirty and unshaven only three hours before the first guests were due to arrive at the church. Daddy practically had a stroke, she thought. He screamed and yelled at Steve out on the back porch, but Steve stood there quietly waiting for Daddy to calm down. "I told you I'd be back in time," he said. "Well, here I am." Daddy was screaming about how much he'd spent on the wedding and how Steve had come close to wrecking everything through his selfish behavior. Steve got very quiet, like he always did when he was especially *indignant*. "Well, Mr. Robinson," Steve said, "neither Lisa nor I asked for this great big wedding. That was your idea. The money you're spending entertaining your friends today would have paid for our whole last year of school. This whole wedding-dress, bridesmaids, champagne-breakfast business is a very *selfish* gesture on your part. Lisa and I couldn't care less about it. You just want to impress your friends and business buddies by parading Lisa and me around like pretty little bride-and-groom dolls. You have your selfish moments and I have mine. Only I think that going down to Mississippi with my friends from CORE and helping some of our fellow citizens practice their constitutional rights is a lot more important than getting drunk with you and your pals at a bachelor dinner."

That's the way Steve was then and that's why she fell in love with him. But now . . . ever since they'd joined the Foreign Service, he had changed. He was still the same person, he looked the same . . . the lean, boyish good looks that always reminded her of Anthony Perkins in *On the Beach,* but he wasn't *daring* any more. He didn't take chances. He had begun to do things just like everybody else. Maybe he was just getting older, more mature. They weren't kids any more. He was the man and it was up to him to take the lead in their life together. That was fine, but she missed the old excitement. Now with Robert she had a chance to have it again, just for a little while at least.

She had consciously made her own decision to begin the affair, and she was pleased. Next year they would be in a new post and the credit-union loan would be repaid and she would stop taking her little pink pills and they would have a baby. It was all planned. In two years she would be a mother and a year later there would be another baby and her life would be over. She would be alive, of course, but she would no longer be Lisa as she had been, naked on the river. She would be a mother and a wife and this was good. She would go toward this future naturally, almost eagerly. But now she had this one chance to live as an independent adult woman, and she would enjoy it to the fullest. She walked slowly away from the mirror, humming to herself. The next week would be very exciting.

Steve had drawn back the drapes so that as he lay on the bed he could look out the glass doors, past the little balcony, five floors down to the long arc of cassia trees bordering the Boulevard du Trente Juin. As the sun lowered, the city lost its bleached-out shimmer and regained coloration, the canopy of tall hardwoods, oil palms, and flame trees again turning a rich mélange of greens. An occasional metal water tower or the red brick steeple of a mission church showed above the trees.

"That was Robert Henderson on the phone," Lisa said. "He's having some people over for drinks before he goes up to the Reeds' dinner and asked us to come too. I said we would. Is that O.K. with you?"

"Sure. I need more drinks like a hole in the head, but he always has such neat people around."

"He always has pretty girls around. That's why you like to go there, I bet."

"*You're* a very pretty girl."

"Maybe that's why he keeps inviting us."

"Maybe," Steve said. He was silent for a moment, staring off toward the green roof of the *cité*.

"You know what I was just thinking?" Steve asked, rolling over as Lisa lay back down beside him on the oversize bed.

"Hmmm?" She was tired from the picnic and their long lovemaking.

"I got to thinking about the tropics today at the pool. I suddenly realized that they're really *different* from the rest of the world, from where we come from . . . the north. All of a sudden I could see that we're really fooling ourselves when we come down here and try to change things one way or another."

"That sounds very interesting, baby," she said, rolling over to her side as she curled her arm under the pillow. A nap would be wonderful, she thought; just a little cat nap after the wine and the sun and making love.

"I guess I was mad at myself for blowing up the way I did at those guys who came to the door this morning and especially at those poor little kids in the parking lot." He sat up in bed, leaning back against the foam-rubber pillow. "I've been trying to figure out why I got so irritated, and it suddenly came to me. It's because I've been trying to lead a *northern* life here in the tropics. We all have. Do you see what I mean?"

"Not really," Lisa said sleepily.

"Well," he continued, "it's kind of hard to explain, but I think I might really have discovered something important. Listen . . . why was I in such a bad mood this morning? Because I was hung over and hot and the air conditioner was broken, right? O.K. What about all those thousands of Africans out there in the *cité?* They don't have air conditioners, do they? The thing is that they don't try to live in these big, stuffy concrete towers, either. Their houses have high roofs and plenty of ventilation. They don't stay up all night running from one air-conditioned apartment to another, drinking quarts of imported champagne and eating all those fancy hors d'oeuvres. They drink beer in outdoor bars and sweat it off dancing. Then they go home and are able to sleep through the heat of the day the way you're supposed to do down here in the tropics. The Europeans have tried to import the whole Northern Hemisphere down here along with their champagne. Like in one of those underwater habitats.

"In the north it's cold most of the year and the sun is a friend. Down here it's always hot and you have to protect yourself from the direct sun. So what do we do when we come down here? We build these big apartments the same as we would in Brussels or Chicago and have to stick an air conditioner in every window to make them livable. The housing's just a small part of it. Everything we do here is all screwed up and ass-backwards; we're still living in the north even though we're in the tropics. Do you follow me?"

Lisa sighed. Steve rose and paced the room.

"We all say that the Africans are lazy and shiftless, right? Well, that's another northern value judgment. Where we come from everybody's got to work hard to grow enough food or to make enough money to buy food, right? Well, here you've got to work hard to *stop* things from growing—weeds, fungus, mold. Everything makes sense if you start to think of it that way. Even the politics. We're always ridiculing the Congolese politicians for not being in their offices during the day. We laugh at them for staying up all night, sitting around drinking beer. Jesus, that's the Africans' system of politics. You get together at night for a palaver, all the chiefs together, and you drink beer and talk things out. There's no hurry, there's no pressure. The women stick some manioc roots in the ground and pick some bananas and the little kids tend some goats and your food problem's licked. These cabinet ministers and politicians may have chauffeured limousines, but they still think the way their fathers did and they still are Africans. We laugh at them, but, damn it, they're right, don't you see? *We're* the ones who are out of step with things."

The persistent whine of Steve's words grated in Lisa's ear. She could not sleep. Rolling over onto her back, she looked at him.

He continued pacing. "This trip is going to be good for me," he said. "All of this crazy northern superstructure is centered on the cities. It'll do me a lot of good to get out in the bush where the Africans still live the way they always have and haven't been corrupted yet. You were right, though, this morning. I am all worn out by the running around we've been doing. Maybe I should rest next week and do the trip after New Year's."

"Aren't they expecting you to go tomorrow?" Lisa said evenly.

"Sure, they're expecting me to go, but they wouldn't get mad if I delayed it for a week or so. They don't need my opinion on how things are going. They've got enough CIA people up there already. So you know nobody's going to read the report of a State Department *trainee.* I want to make the trip, all right, get a chance to see what Africa really looks like, but I could easily wait until after New Year to go."

"Whatever you think best, Steve."

He sat down on the bed and took a cigarette from the night table. "The thing is that I haven't done enough reading on the places I'm supposed to visit. I'd like to stay home here next week and read up on some Congolese history."

Lisa thought ahead to her week with Robert Henderson.

"Didn't the Embassy make flight arrangements for you to go tomorrow?"

"Yes, but I could always call and cancel out. There are plenty of military flights going up to Stanleyville."

"I think that if they expect you to go, then you should go, Steve. You can always take the books with you."

"I suppose you're right, Lisa. Maybe it'll be easier to think about things outside of Léopoldville. I joined this lash-up to see Africa, and I guess it's stupid not to go now that I've got the chance."

Lisa got up. "I'm going to take a shower and start getting dressed for tonight," she said. "Robert said to come around six so we'll have to hurry."

"Right," Steve murmured absently. He drummed his fingers on the glass door in rhythm with the air conditioner's chugging. "This trip's really going to be good for me."

CHAPTER 4

"Robert, is that man really a count?" Lisa asked.

"Which one?" Henderson said.

"The gray-haired man with the foulard talking to Steve." She nodded toward the end of the Reeds' terrace where Steve stood with a tall European casually dressed in a well-cut bush jacket.

"He's from Elizabethville," Henderson said. "Big wheel in the Union Minière. I suppose he's a bona fide count, all right. The Société Générale is fairly strict about fake aristocrats."

Robert was standing close to her in the blue dusk that hung about the terrace. He was taller than Steve, heavy through the trunk and arms. Tennis and water sports kept him a deep brown and more vigorously fit than most men in their late forties. He drank heavily but smoked very little. Since the war he had lived in Europe, Latin America, and the Far East. He had an almost insatiable appetite for rich foods, but his daily round of exercise kept his thick mid-section in reasonable profile with his barrel chest. Lisa allowed her bare arm to rub softly against his as he leaned forward across the bamboo cocktail bar.

"That's such a nice shirt, Robert. Where did you say it came from?"

"The Philippines. The only sensible men's dress for the tropics. It's ridiculous the way these Europeans and Congolese politicians insist on Italian silk and sharkskin in this climate."

"Were you in the Philippines very long?"

"A few years. Yes, I suppose that can be considered a long time to live someplace these days."

Lisa smiled to herself, casting an oblique glance toward the other guests on the terrace to see if she and Henderson were being watched. The other people stood in small groups along the stone terrace wall, taking in the sunset.

Far away, below the hills of the Djelo Binza suburbs, the Léopoldville *cité* was blurred by the smoke of evening cook fires. At sunset the Congo River was a gray sheet. Across the mile-wide pool of the river, the first lights of Brazzaville were twinkling on. The thunderheads hanging over the open hills flashed with orange lightning. The clouds towered up to terrific heights, standing shoulder to shoulder as the setting sun shafted up between them, gilding their edges. As Lisa and the others watched, the flattened orange ball of the sun dropped with visible motion beneath the base of the cloud line and fell behind the horizon. When the last limb of the sun had disappeared, the orange lightning show took on a new intensity. The storms were too distant for the thunder to carry.

"That's so pretty. I wonder if I'll ever get used to seeing it," Lisa said.

"I've been in the tropics on and off for over twenty years and I'm still not tired of it," Henderson said.

"That's such a long time to be away from America, Robert. Don't you ever miss it?"

"Oh, I get back regularly," he said, "for business."

Lisa edged nearer to him in the deepening gloom. "Do you know what the people at the Embassy say about you?"

"Not really. But I would suppose that it's something fairly

unimaginative, if you don't mind my berating your husband's colleagues."

"They think you're some kind of a James Bond character, a real SPECTRE agent or something equally exotic."

"As if they didn't have enough spies of their own right there on the second floor of the Embassy. That's one thing this town definitely does not need any more of. Léo's got its full complement of *espions.*"

"Well, that's what they think, the wives at least."

"Since when are the American Embassy wives actually thinking? I've certainly never known any of them to think. Talk, yes, talk your arm off on any subject. But not think."

She laughed loudly. Couples along the wall turned to stare at her.

"Lisa, I'd better circulate a bit, and you'd better rescue Steve from that Union Minière count. He's a well-known American-baiter. He's liable to put Steve into one of his real brown studies and then he won't take his trip and we won't have our little party next week."

"No!" she said, reaching out to touch his arm lightly. He stopped. "I was really serious. It's difficult to explain, Robert, but all of a sudden I realize that I'll be with you all next week and I really don't know anything about you. What I mean is"—she lowered her face and spoke in a whisper—"what if you really *are* some kind of an agent? I *am* an Embassy wife, you know. I'm not ashamed of anything we've done, but this is different. This is a whole week. Robert, why can't you just tell me what you *really* do? What your business really is. You know I won't tell anyone."

"Well, you never really asked. Let's say that I'm also a kind of diplomat. I don't represent a government exactly. I represent several big companies and certain financial groups which have large holdings in this country. I report to them on the true local situation and I sometimes carry out special business for them with the Congolese. None of it is really illegal—it's just that the financial picture here is so confused that it's better that my dealings and allegiances remain confidential."

"Is Michelle *really* your wife? That's what someone said, that she's not really your wife, just a partner or something."

"Michelle *really* is my wife. She just happens to like skiing in Austria better than sweating in Léo, that's all. We've been married a long time, you know."

"The Embassy wives can be very silly," she said.

He nodded and turned away from her. Lisa stood watching him from the shadows halfway down the terrace. She sipped at her gin and tonic, feeling the breeze touch her lightly on her bare shoulders, dry the damp beneath her arms. The people around her were beginning to move toward the buffet. She enjoyed standing unobserved in the shadows, watching Henderson. She knew that she should find Steve and be with him, but she preferred watching Robert. It was going to be a pleasant week.

The count took her hand, brushing his lips lightly across her fingers. "So this lovely girl is your wife," he said to Steve. "Not only do you speak such good French and expound such incredible theories, but you're married to the prettiest girl at the party." Turning back to Lisa, he added, "When I saw you in that white dress, I thought you must be one of Robert's conquests he had flown down from London to see him. That *is* one of the famous mini-skirts that all the English girls are wearing, isn't it?"

"It's not really a mini." Lisa smiled.

He was, she guessed, in his early fifties, lean and tanned, exuding a certain vigor not unlike what she felt in the presence of the taller and more muscular Henderson. A multicolored, rippling scar ran down the left side of his face, growing more vivid where it disappeared into the foulard around his neck. He opened a pounded-copper case and offered Steve a thin cigarillo.

"Tell me," he said to Lisa, "were you with your husband on this Children's Crusade among the Arabs—what do you call it? —the Brotherhood Battalion?"

"The Peace Corps," Steve said. She could not tell if the cold edge in his voice came from anger or embarrassment.

She nodded.

"So you were with your husband converting the heathen masses. Do you also share his theory about the nature of Tropical Man?"

"Yes, we were both Volunteers," she said, "but we didn't try to convert anybody. I'm not really very interested in theories either, I'm afraid."

"Extraordinary," the count said. "So you two are the new type of diplomats the Americans are sending abroad now. It used to be that one went to Harvard and then did the 'grand tour.' Now, it seems, one spends a few years living in a hut with the natives before being sent out. I suppose it's all for the better, what with all these new native republics you Americans are fostering all over the world." "Republics" was almost spat at them.

"Are you doing good works for the benighted Congolese ladies?" he continued, ignoring Steve as he faced Lisa more squarely. "Hugging their little brown babies and reminding them to wash?"

"Actually I haven't gotten out much," Lisa admitted. "We've only been here six months."

"Ah, *bon,*" the count said triumphantly, turning back to Steve. "You should be congratulated, Monsieur Sherman. I'm sure you have compiled your Universal Theory of the Nature of the Tropics in record time. I have only lived in this part of the world for thirty-one years, but my theory is nowhere near as well-developed. Undoubtedly it's that practical American education which prepares one to see right through to the kernel of the problem."

"If I've said anything that has insulted you," Steve said, speaking too quickly, so that his words slurred, "please excuse me. I meant nothing personal. I was just speaking off the top of my head, really."

"Ah," the count said. "I'm very pleased to hear that there was nothing personal in your negating the cumulative work of my adult life, canceling out, as it were, the entire efforts and sacrifices made by Belgium to civilize this country." The count's smile hardened. "I'm sure that if you'd go out to Léo II and expound your theory to the residents of the Pioneers' cemetery, you'd find an audience even more sympathetic than myself."

"You must have misunderstood me, monsieur," Steve said. "What I really wanted to say was that all of us, not just the Belgians, but the French and the British and the Americans, all of us, have deluded ourselves into thinking that we can turn the Africans into carbon copies of ourselves. Excuse the pun, it was unintentional." The count did not join them in their laughter.

"*We* did not make that mistake," the Belgian said. "We knew all along that the blacks were lazy animals, completely unsuited for civilization as we know it. It was not the Belgian colon who tried to stir them up for this nationalism and independence nonsense. It was the socialists, egged on by the scatterbrained racial theories of the Americans. It is the hypocritical Americans who have caused all this strife and bloodshed—sending your commissions over here to stir up the natives."

Steve tried to speak but was cut short by the Belgian. "No, monsieur, *we* did not make that mistake. We knew that the natives were no better than childish black monkeys. *We* did not assign them any ridiculously elevated position like your Tropical Man. We knew all the time that they were worthless savage animals. . . ."

Other guests turned to stare at them. The count turned his cold blue eyes on them and they quickly looked away.

"Well," Steve said, his voice heating up again, "this is exactly what I *meant*. At first you tried to make little Belgians out of them, working at it over a long time, but Independence caught you by surprise and your whole structure collapsed, so you rationalized your failure by calling them black monkeys. What I'm trying to say is that the Congolese are neither little black Europeans nor animals. They're people just like you and me who come from a different kind of world and who should not have been pushed into a European mold. It's like taking a man who's left-handed and making him do everything with his right hand. Of *course,* he'll make mistakes. Instead of continuing to force him to make mistakes with his right hand, we should show him that he's really left-handed."

"Just like your Red Indians," the count said.

"Pardon?" Steve said.

"I said, just like the way you recognized and helped your Red Indians. They're a good example of your left-handed man. I must say you certainly did help them to find their true destiny, didn't you? You simply slaughtered them. You wiped them out: men, women, and children. You exterminated them. You didn't bother terribly with your theoretical considerations then, did you?"

The count turned abruptly, and as he did, Steve realized that he had only limited articulation of his neck, thus necessitating the almost mechanical movements of his head.

He took Lisa's hand, bending to kiss it. "Madame," he said, *"bonne fête*. Monsieur." He nodded curtly to Steve and left.

"I should have warned you about Julien, Steve," Henderson said. "He's pulled that trick before—provoking arguments about the Congo with Americans. You really can't argue with the fellow. He's a bit unbalanced, I'm afraid."

"Really?" Steve said. Henderson had joined them at the end of the terrace.

"Yes," Henderson said. "He's pulled the same trick before. He'll get you into a conversation to sound you out about some aspect of the Congo or the Congolese, and then he'll pounce on you. He blames the Americans for all the trouble that's happened here. He's a real fanatic that way. Had a very hard time personally, though. I suppose you noticed his scar?"

"Yes," Lisa said. "It's awful."

"Happened in 1962, in E'ville when the UN troops were trying to push Tshombe's gendarmes out of the town. He and his wife got caught between the two sides during a fire fight. Their car was pretty badly shot up. It rolled over and the tank exploded. He was burned and his wife has been crippled ever since. Bullet wound in the spine."

"Jesus!" Steve said.

"He blames the American Government for the UN occupation and crushing the Katanga secession," Henderson continued. "Claims that the United Nations troops in the Congo prevented Katanga from achieving its rightful position at the head of the country, and that when the UN troops were pulled out they left a vacuum which the ANC couldn't fill . . . left the door wide open for the rebels. So, in his eyes at least, the Americans are directly responsible for the rebellion as well. That's the other thing he's blind to. His daughter and son-in-law were living on a lumber concession up in the Maniema when the rebels came through last year. They were taken prisoner and the husband was eventually beaten to death. His daughter was gang-raped so often by rebel *jeunesse* that she's been out of her head ever since. He lives down there in E'ville in an old Union Minière mansion with his crippled wife and crazy daughter. He's just taken them back to Europe for more medical treatment. He's staying at a company house up here in Binza. I guess that's why the Reeds invited him. They should have been warned. You can see he's a bit strange."

"You can say that again," Steve said. He turned toward Lisa. "What do you think about getting some of that turkey?"

C H A P T E R **5**

"Lisa Sherman, you come right back here and fill your plate up. Why you've hardly taken enough to keep a sparrow alive, dear!"

Maybe I don't want to turn into a hippopotamus like you, Lisa thought, turning to give her cocktail-party smile to Dorothy Reed, her hostess. Mrs. Reed was a thickset woman in her forties, fond of outlandish dresses and impossible hats. For her Christmas party she wore a scarlet chiffon frock, which, instead of ballooning as the designer had intended, clung damply to her like a sausage skin. She had spilled something on her green Christmas apron, soiling the cotton beard of the Santa Claus.

The long living room of the Reeds' villa had been cleared of furniture to accommodate the richly laden buffet and gigantic Christmas tree. "Well," Lisa said, "maybe I'll have a little more white meat. Everything looks so good."

As Lisa picked at the slices of turkey, she saw that Mrs. Reed was no longer paying any attention, having publicly fulfilled her indignant mother-hen role, chiding pretty, young Lisa Sherman into eating more of the food she had sweated over in the kitchen all day; she now turned her attentions to a young red-haired American. The Reeds were childless and had been with the Embassy's AID mission for three years, creating a tradition of hosting Thanksgiving and Christmas dinners for the young couples

and the single Embassy clerical personnel. This Christmas they
had outdone themselves. Lisa walked out through the high-ceilinged living room to the terrace that ran the length of the house
above the patio and small swimming pool. There were at least fifty
people at the dinner, she saw, not just the secretaries, but many of
the COMISH military mission families and most of the other
young couples in the Embassy. She walked gingerly across the
lawn, her heels sinking into the grass, to an empty place at one of
the red-and-green-decorated card tables.

Instinctively she had avoided Steve's table. It's only been six
months, she thought, but already they've got me trained into a perfect little Embassy wife. Rule number one: *never* sit with your
husband at a dinner party. *Mix,* circulate, make conversation, be
charming back to all those sophisticated, charming people. Out of
the corner of her eye she saw Robert talking with George White,
an athletic young officer from the CIA's Political Section II. She
felt a rush of satisfaction as she sat down. They might be forcing
her into a mold, but she still had her freedom. *Robert* was her de-
fiance against these mindless pushers trying to twist her into a
younger version of Dorothy Reed.

Robert Henderson stood on the terrace staring down absently at
the paper lanterns and the crowded tables. He had seen Lisa's attempt to catch his eye as she walked past him with her dinner
plate, but had glanced away to answer one of White's questions.
Lisa was becoming more brazen now that their affair was stabiliz-
ing itself. He would have to be careful with her. The girl had a
real wild streak.

"She's a good-looking young woman," White said softly in his
precise, headmasterish voice.

Henderson tossed him a fleeting, inquisitive glance and then
lowered his eyes to inspect the ash of his pre-dinner cigarillo.
Guests passed them on the terrace, threading their way carefully
with heavily laden plates between the few remaining drinkers.

"Been out water-skiing lately?" White continued in the same
dry tone.

You perfect ass, Henderson thought, turning to look George
White squarely in the face. About thirty, I guess, probably one of
the Agency's promising new African *specialists,* couple of tours

under his belt and thinks he can actually start thinking on his own, poor bastard. If I let him keep moving on this tack, he'll begin the recruitment feelers in a minute. What will it be . . . the old carrot-stick combination or a carrot-carrot-stick or maybe a stick-stick-carrot. Probably thinks he can blackmail me by threatening to expose Lisa and then perhaps dangle a sudden Sûreté deportation over my head and sweeten it by a couple thou a month on the side for a regular supply of microfilms of my clients' documents. That'd be the stick-stick-carrot. These people are so unimaginative —perfect bureaucrats.

"You used to play football at college, didn't you?" Henderson asked in a kindly tone.

"Yes, sure, at Dartmouth," White answered with a puzzled smile. "Why do you ask?"

"Ever play a varsity-freshman practice game where the junior coach had been given the best plays and whopped hell out of the varsity just to teach them not to be so cocky?"

"Yeah, I guess we did," White answered, his smile cooling.

"Tell your boss sometime that he would have made a crummy football coach."

"I'm afraid you lost me there."

"Like hell I have," Henderson said, breaking into his suntanned party smile. "The reason I'm important to the CIA, you pompous little bastard," he said softly between smiling teeth, "is precisely because I do *not* work for them. There are enough Agency people in the corporations and banks which I service with reports to get the information straight back to Langley, Virginia, the same day they read it. I'm sure they love getting it, too. If I went on your dole, I'd be trying to please you, telling you things you wanted to hear like all the rest of your salaried flunkies in this country. If your boss gave you the job of sounding me out, he's a bigger ass than I thought he was. If you're doing it on your own initiative to get some brownie points, then you're a bigger clod than everybody says. The trouble with people like you is that you think you invented the intelligence game and can make up your rules as you go along. I don't give a damn if you put a *color* television camera in my bedroom. You can make cinemascope movies of Lisa and me if you want. The people who pay *my* salary couldn't care less whom I sleep with. You put one ounce of pressure on Lisa Sherman, though, and that little lieutenant colonel who's the real head of ANC Pol/Mil intelligence up in the Ops Nord sector gets a full list of your ANC network in the Fourth Groupement. He's new, you see, came in since the coup, and I'm one of the few people who know him. He'd be pleased to get that list of your people. He hates to see somebody getting paid twice for the same job. Don't look so surprised. Your people up there are so obvious it's a wonder he doesn't have them pegged already."

George White stood silently, his lips taut white and his hands locked to his hips, creating an incongruous picture beside the affable, smiling Henderson.

"Mr. Henderson!" It was Dorothy Reed striding up to them, her face flushed. "George White! Why, you two are just standing out here drinking gin while all that lovely food is getting cold! It just makes me want to *cry* to see you."

White smiled apologetically, but Henderson looked at her coldly. "Would you mind terribly if I finished my cigar? I had a very late lunch."

Dorothy Reed took the loose end of one of the colored crepe-paper streamers and twisted it nervously between her short fingers. "Well," she said, "I know you mustn't be eating very well, poor man, with that lovely wife of yours way up in Europe. That's why Dwight and I were so anxious that you should come, so that you'd get a good Christmas dinner."

"Michelle," Henderson said, "has not cooked me a meal since we were married. If anything, I eat better when she's away on one of her trips. I have the cook all to myself then and can browbeat him into making all my favorites." The exchange left Mrs. Reed nonplused. She was a good, loyal AID wife who knew she had a duty to be nice to American "businessmen." Henderson was an American businessman. Why couldn't he be nice and compliment her on her lovely Christmas buffet by rushing in to fill his plate? "Oh," she said, "yes, of course, hmmm."

They watched her stride down the stairs to circulate among the diners, cajoling them to help themselves to seconds. She buttonholed Steve, who was sitting back contentedly with a cigarette.

Obediently he followed her back up the stairs to the terrace, his dinner plate and a red paper napkin in his hand.

"Horrendous woman," Henderson said.

White smiled, visibly clearing his features of the angry tension that had held him while Henderson spoke. "I'm afraid we have our fair share of boorish people in the Mission, especially in AID and COMISH," he said.

"Of course the anointed warriors of Poli II are all polished gentlemen, besides being perceptive and courageous," Henderson said. "There are times when you people really turn my stomach."

White tensed again, quickly scanning the terrace to be certain Henderson's softly spoken outburst was not drawing the attention of the diners. "I'm afraid there's been some kind of misunderstanding, Henderson. I think you misinterpreted something I've said. I . . ."

"You know damn well I haven't," Henderson interrupted. "I don't want to play games with you people. If you think I'm bluffing about that list of your ANC people in the northeast, I'll have a copy of it on your desk Monday morning. You still look surprised. You really shouldn't be, you know. Just because you *want* something to be confidential doesn't mean it will be. You people get all caught up in the whole electronic espionage gadget mystique and forget common sense. You needn't worry about me, though, as long as you don't stick your long noses into my personal life. That's what Lisa Sherman is. You can bug our bedrooms from now until next Christmas and you'll never hear me talking about my business with her. So unless your boys get their jollies that way, you're wasting your tape. I've hardly spoken two words to her husband, so don't imagine that I'm trying to recruit him the way you've just tried to recruit me. I've little interest in him. He seems a nice enough kid, but for obvious reasons I'm more interested in his wife. I don't get much leisure time down here, and when I do I like to enjoy myself. It's as simple as that. For her it's a nice change from this deadly Embassy existence of yours. For me it's a chance to forget about my business for a few hours each week. It's really as simple as that, so don't try to make it seem more important than it is."

"You're being amazingly frank tonight, Henderson. I bet some of your clients would appreciate such candor occasionally."

"What the hell's that supposed to mean? That you'll turn me in to my bosses for not being completely honest with them unless I work with you?"

White looked stricken. Henderson had spoken in an angry, rasping voice, causing several nearby diners to turn and stare at them. "This is hardly the place to talk about it," White said. "Why don't we get together next week and . . ."

"No," Henderson said flatly. "Just plain no. Period. And before you do anything stupid, talk to your boss. . . . You probably wouldn't be a bad guy, White . . . once you learned not to take all this crap so seriously. People tell me that you're a real gung-ho spook, though—God and Country and all that garbage. Is it true that you're a lay reader at the Protestant mission? Well, remember me in your prayers, White. If *you're* ever looking for a job, let me know."

The sweat stood in tiny droplets in White's bristly crew cut. He was about to speak when Henderson slapped him fondly on the shoulder. "Great to see you again, George," he bellowed. "As soon as Michelle gets back you really have to come out with us on the river for some skiing. You know how much Michelle enjoys your family. . . . Well, I guess we'd better eat some of that lovely buffet before it's all gone."

As Henderson strode past White on the terrace, he threw Lisa one of his warmest smiles. Lisa glowed back at him over the breeze-flared Christmas candle.

Steve stood beside a floppy banana tree next to the pool. The Reeds' garden sloped gently down to a forested bluff that dropped sharply away, exposing the panorama of the city's communes in a spider web of light. The breeze had risen, climbing silently up the bluff to set the paper lanterns in motion. He stood alone, smoking a cigarette and taking an occasional pull at a tall gin and tonic. There was a slight internal buzzing in his ears, signaling him that he had drunk more than he needed. Turning to the villa, he saw Dwight Reed, diminutive and natty in his crisp seersucker suit and bow tie, directing four sweating houseboys as they gingerly moved the lighted Christmas tree out onto the terrace.

The servants disappeared back into the crowd around the doorway and reappeared a moment later struggling with a squat electric organ. Dwight made a complicated show of connecting the instrument to an extension cord. Dorothy Reed was out among her guests on the patio, dragging them away from their second cups of after-dinner coffee to join the others grouped in a semicircle on the grass in front of the organ, which had been positioned five feet above them on the terrace, creating a churchlike tableau.

As Dwight pounded out the first rousing chords of "Jingle Bells," Steve saw what had provoked the complications with the electrical wires. The lights of the Christmas tree were blinking on and off to the beat of the music: red, green, yellow, blue, jingle bells, jingle bells, jingle all the way.

Instinctively Steve ducked out of sight behind the banana tree as Dorothy Reed strode to the edge of the pool and peered myopically out into the dark garden. When she had turned back Steve edged his way down the lawn to the wire fence separating the Reeds' plot from the scrub forest. The flood lamps on the aluminum foil display of the Three Wise Men cast a weak, reflected light to the edges of the garden. In the brush he heard a sudden snapping movement and caught a glimpse of two monkeys swinging away through the branches. Leaning against the fence, he could still see the city lights below twinkling up over the tops of the trees.

Suddenly he was aware of another person to his right, a white shirt bright against the shadows. He saw the orange trajectory of a cigarette thrown out into the trees as the figure came toward him.

"Hi," the man said. It was the young American with bright red hair he had seen at the buffet table.

"Hi," Steve said. "I don't think we've met. My name is Steve Sherman. I'm with the Embassy." He felt the young man's hand in the darkness, cool and surprisingly limp.

"My name is Hogan, Charlie Hogan. I'm with COMISH up in Stanleyville."

"Oh, really?" Steve said. "I'm going to Stan tomorrow."

"So am I. On that godawful six o'clock flight?"

"I'm afraid so. What do you do in Stanleyville?"

"Teach," Charlie said. "I'm supposed to teach the heroic soldiers of the Fourth Groupement how to run all those radios we give the ANC. Actually I only have a few hours a day with my class. They're a bunch of real geniuses. We've been going over and over the first week's lesson since I got there three months ago. The rest of the time I repair the damage the regular operators have done to the equipment. Aside from that I get drunk with the mercenaries and go fishing. Stan isn't quite the fleshpot that Léo is. What do *you* do at the Embassy?"

"Well," Steve said, prepared to give a vague description of his duties in the Political Section, alluding to "political-military" activities so that the young man would assume that he was with the CIA. He had done this before with other visiting Americans, especially when he'd been drinking. It gave him a perverted pleasure to deceive people in this manner while he was doing it, and a disproportionate, head-splitting guilt complex to accompany the next day's hangover. As Steve was about to speak, a car turned on the drive and illuminated the garden with its headlights. He saw Charlie Hogan's face, tired, bored, obviously disinterested in what Steve had to say. It was not the face he was expecting to see, a gullible young army sergeant he could impress with a lot of gobbledygook about his hush-hush work at the Embassy. It was the world-weary, tired face of a man who had lived longer than his years.

"It's funny," Steve said finally, "my job at the Embassy sounds about as exciting as yours. It would be nice to say that I'm involved in all sorts of top secret projects, but I'm not. I'm a trainee. I rotate between sections. They've got me in the Political Section now. That probably sounds exciting, but believe me, it isn't. All I do all day is type up little three-by-five cards for the Bio File. That's the list we keep of all the Congolese and Europeans who might be of interest to the Embassy. You know, politicians, labor leaders, businessmen, people like that. Since the Coup last month there've been a lot of them to be added and a lot to be deleted. The Political Section is supposed to be the central depository for all this information. If that were true I wouldn't mind doing the job so much, even though it is glorified clerical work.

The fact is, though, that the spooks down the hall have the *real* file. Whenever the Ambassador's office wants to know something about somebody they go ask the spooks, not us. Same for the military attachés—they've got their own file. So I sit there all day typing up these cards that I know nobody will ever read."

"Yeah, that's beautiful," Charlie said. "They've got you in the tobacco shed."

"In the what?"

Charlie laughed, a strange burst of laughter. "Sorry, sometimes I forget that everybody doesn't know my little names for things. The tobacco shed is what they do to you when you've got too much energy. It might be in the Army or, like with you, in the State Department, any big organization, I guess. They put you into some really boring job and just leave you there until all the juice and ideas have been dried out of you. It's just like drying tobacco. In the Army they're always talking about *maturing* young officers. That's the same word the tobacco men use, that's where the tobacco shed comes from. I'm alone a lot up in Stan and I spend a lot of time thinking about things like that. Probably sounds crazy, doesn't it?"

"Not at all, really. I do the same thing. My wife always tells me I spend too much time thinking up theories."

Dwight Reed was working himself up into a sentimental crescendo with "I'm Dreaming of a White Christmas." The voices of the singers had been loosened by the gin and dinner wine. They welled up into a ragged chorus. A fruit bat jerked by them, screeching in the hot darkness. The carol singers began "Silent Night."

Steve and Charlie Hogan stood watching the lights of the city below them.

"This is so weird," Charlie said. "It's just like the view down into L.A. from my parents' house in Brentwood. They've got this tri-level with a lawn like this and a little pool. We used to have our Christmas tree outside on the patio. We even had banana trees, just like this. I can remember singing 'White Christmas' when I was little and wondering what snow was like."

Steve watched him as he talked, his face just visible in the weak light. Although he did not have a drink in his hand, Charlie seemed to have already drunk a great deal. His voice did not slur, but he suffered lapses during which he stared out into the distance, suddenly breaking his silence with disjointed statements. As he spoke about his parents' home in California, his face took on a glowing childlike expression, reminding Steve of the Boys' Town poster—a freckle-faced, red-haired boy carrying his brother through the snow.

"Yeah, that's really strange, really strange," Charlie continued, apropos of nothing. He was silent for a while, then turned to Steve. "You know what else? The *same* thing happened last night as happened a year ago at Christmas. I was invited up to one of the COMISH captains' last night for this Christmas Eve thing and it broke up early so I got a ride downtown and went to that club they've got on the second floor of the Hotel Regina. I was hardly in the door of the place two minutes when I latch onto this chick, Alitalia stewardess. About three o'clock we're back in her room at the Memling really going at it when the door opens and the lights go on. Great big South African merc standing there with this little black bellhop and a Congolese whore. He's got his pistol belt and boots on, the whole works. Big son of a bitch. Sleeves rolled up over these huge muscles. And there I am with this little Italian dolly.

"The merc looks at us and, honest to God, he blushes. 'Beg your pardon,' he says in this Afrikaans accent. Then he kicks the bellhop in the ass, turns out the light, and closes the door. After they were gone we laughed about it all night."

Charlie hummed for a while with the organ music. "What was I going to say? What was I going to say? Oh, yeah. Last year. I was in Saigon, blowing a whole wad of money with a room at the Caravelle. Same thing. That was when there were still airline stewardesses in Saigon and not so many GIs. Me and this French chick from Air France are making it, and I was thinking how really great having money was, how you can really buy *pleasure* with money, when the goddamn door opens and the lights go on, just like last night. An Australian sailor and this bar girl. He was pretty bombed and came all the way into the room before he saw us on the bed. Same scene, exactly. Kicked the bellhop in the ass and apologized."

Charlie was laughing uncontrollably. Steve looked around the garden nervously. There was probably something wrong with this young sergeant, Steve thought. Perhaps a head wound he had received in Vietnam. Steve edged away from the fence, turning toward the crowd of singers. Charlie turned with him. "You've been to Stanleyville before then, I take it?" he said, his voice dry and precise, a complete reversal of his previous manner.

"No, this will be my first trip upcountry."

"You'll find it a lot different than Léopoldville," Charlie said in the same voice. "I think that the interior of any country is more interesting than the capital. It's just too bad that traveling isn't easier up there. The security situation is still too shaky to travel very far by land, though."

"Are there still rebels in the area?"

"Rebels? Yeah, still a few around Stan, I guess. The ANC thinks there are, at least. I wasn't thinking about the rebels being dangerous so much as I was the ANC. They tend to shoot first and ask questions later, and they're always screwing around with mines."

"Well, I'll enjoy the trip either way, I think. I've been cooped up here in Léo for six months. Sometimes you'd never know you were in Africa, living here. There's not a single Congolese here tonight besides the servants."

Charlie did not continue the conversation. He stared off into the darkness, watching the distant blinking red lights of a jet as it took off from N'djili Field below them. Dwight was winding up a rollicking version of "Rudolph the Red-nosed Reindeer."

"There sure are a lot of parties here, aren't there?" Charlie finally said.

"That's all we do is go to parties," Steve said. "Either official things, cocktails and receptions, or these kind of all-white deals. Not all white actually, all foreign. I guess they don't consider American Negroes as being black, because they're invited too."

"That's funny," Charlie said, his voice becoming cold. "That's really goddamn funny. The whole country's going to hell, kids are starving out in the bush and the Army's just shitting all over the poor little people up there and everybody's crooked and all you can think of doing is having parties down here, costume parties and swimming parties and play readings. I've seen it myself. I know. The whole fucking town's just one big party."

He walked away along the fence. Steve could hear him muttering to himself as he kicked at the grass. Suddenly he saw the red head thrust back sharply with a wild burst of the same uncontrollable laughter he'd heard earlier. Several of the guests on the terrace turned to stare angrily out into the garden. The teen-age daughter of one of the military attachés was singing a solo of "O Holy Night," her clear, piping little voice lost among Dwight Reed's organ chords in the hot night.

CHAPTER 6

"Where did you find anybody to watch your kids on Christmas night?" Lisa called across the beer-wet table to Emily McCarthy. Emily smiled and gestured to show she could not hear Lisa. The music was blasted out from the huge wooden speakers hanging at irregular intervals on the cinder-block walls of the café. Their table seated fourteen people from the Reeds' Christmas party— young couples and single people from the Embassy. Sid Jackson, a Negro code clerk, had insisted that they try his latest discovery in the *cité,* the Café Chicago, a large, open-air *buvette* covering half a block on a side street of Saint Jean Commune. The club was oddly shaped, even for the hodgepodge of post-Independence structures that had mushroomed up in the overcrowded commune. A lavender-painted cement wall ran the length of the café, separating it from an open drainage ditch. On the other three sides tall block walls, roughly mortared and unevenly laid, rose to a height of more than fifteen feet and were topped with an ugly fringe of broken glass. These walls enclosed a rectangular dance floor, partially roofed on the far side with split bamboo matting hung on a rusting pipe framework.

The seven-man band was playing on a bandstand beneath the roof. Opposite the band on the street side of the dance floor a long bar covered with printed oilcloth was almost hidden by the crush of customers. The dance floor itself was thick with rhythmically swaying Congolese, men and women in a wide variety of costumes.

There were several hundred persons jammed into the café, but a jovial atmosphere of comradely abandon prevailed. No one shoved. No one lost his temper. The band was made up of four electric guitarists in sweat-drenched gold blazers, a cocoa-brown boy playing the gourd rattles, and a baby-faced young man on an elaborate set of lighted drums which proclaimed the name of the group: In-Dé-Pen-Dance Jazz.

The music sounded off the walls, echoing far out into the night to blend with the noise of holiday celebration in other dancing bars in the flat commune. A constant rush-hour stream of men and women surged through the café, creating a laughing traffic jam, to the frustration of the waiters desperately maneuvering between the dancers and drinkers, carrying loads of two and even three wooden cases of cold Primus beer. The metal tables were awash with spilled beer and crowded to overflowing with empty brown bottles. In the hot light of the yellow bulbs the milling black crowd and waiters laden like farmer ants beneath their burdens took on a surrealistic aspect.

Lisa was fascinated. The heat and ripe odors of the beer and sweating Africans melted into the humid air about her. The music was too loud. Everyone was drunk. Everyone was laughing, black skins glistening. She drained the lukewarm beer in her glass, only to have Sid Jackson snatch it from her hand and refill it with icy Primus. She wished Henderson had joined the group. She would have liked to have been pressed against him out in that hot crush of dancers. Steve sat dully beside her, his face beet-red, his eyes glassy with too much alcohol. The song ended.

"I'm sorry," Emily said, almost shouting in the relative stillness. "What did you say, Lisa?"

"That you were lucky to have found somebody to watch the kids on Christmas night. The Congolese obviously think of it as a big night out."

"Oh, we've got a nanny now, a mission girl."

Randy McCarthy was tall and beefy, built very much like Rob-

ert Henderson but twenty years his junior. He had a smiling open-
ness and all-American-boy face, which helped him considerably in
his position as the assistant USIS press attaché. "Hey, Lisa," he
said, "dance with me." Randy ducked low on his chair as an over-
burdened waiter lurched past under a load of dripping beer cases.
"Christ!" he said. "Those guys are like the stokers in *The Hairy
Ape.*"

Lisa lost track of time while they danced. She knew that it was
well after midnight, but she had no idea whether it was one or
four o'clock. They were all dancing, all the people from the party.
Steve was doing the twist with a new secretary from USIS. The
band was playing Beatles songs now, the electric guitars resonat-
ing loudly on the cramped dance floor. The Randles, just back
from home leave, tried to show the others the proper method of
doing the frug. They looked absurd to Lisa, standing in one place,
waving their arms in the air and shaking their bottoms. She
danced a slow bop jitterbug with Randy, letting him take her
through a complicated variety of reverse turns and intricate foot-
work. No one watched them. The Randles stole the show with
their silly jerking. Most of the Congolese watched with amused interest, but did not attempt to imitate the frenetically shaking couple, preferring their slow, swivel-hipped shuffling step which fell
somewhere between a cha-cha and a highlife.

Someone bought a bottle of whisky, and reasonably clean
glasses were found. Toasts were exchanged. The owner of the
café, a rotund mulatto in an electric-blue suit, joined them in several toasts, delicately curling his beringed pinky as he drained the
whisky from his glass. Lisa's white dress was soaked with spilled
beer and sweat. She felt flushed and excited, a hot burning inside
her. Steve was trying to tell Don Randle some story about Morocco, but his words were thick and practically unintelligible. It
was obviously time to go.

They stumbled down the rough pavement of the lane toward the
Avenue. The McCarthys were giving them a lift downtown to pick
up their Volkswagen near Robert's apartment. Steve clung to her
arm as they swayed through the smoky darkness. The night was
noisy with music and insect sounds. The darkness held a rainbow

of *cité* odors. Somewhere nearby goat meat was being cooked on a smoky charcoal fire, a sewer had overflowed, manioc was being pounded and palm wine served from an open basin. They stood slouched against an American station wagon while Randy McCarthy struggled to turn his little Peugeot about in the narrow lane.

Lisa was aware of smells completely foreign to her. The stench of the open sewers and backed-up storm drains was forgotten. She flared her nostrils, sucking in the scent of the roasting meat, the overripe palm fruit, the sweetness of the mangoes and papayas rotting in the close night. The muddy ground around them was littered with trash, fallen palm fronds, and strips of decaying bark. The low houses exuded the smell of mildew under the white glare of the Avenue street lights. The trees crowded in on the makeshift buildings, pushing them deeper into the mud. Roots tore at the pavement. Vines and unbelievably vigorous weeds, their stalks thick and woody, pushed up through the gaping windows of abandoned vehicles. Overhead the stars were hidden by the dirty rose glow of the city.

There was nothing in the night about them that was permanent. Everything she saw, touched, or smelled was somewhere on a descending trajectory of decay. The metal was rusting in the humid air, the cement was being eaten by the mildew, the pavement and sewer pipes were being crumbled by roots. All wood, cloth, and paper were silently turning to dust as the termites moved eternally through the darkness, eyeless swarms undermining the deceptively solid walls. The fruit bats and rodents took the rest. Chickens scratched after the countless insects. Mosquitoes bred by the millions in the rusting sardine-can wilderness of the junk-strewn passageways between the older buildings, dating to the almost forgotten tranquillity before 1960 and the hopelessly crowded tin-roofed bamboo hovels that had grown up since Independence. There was no air to breathe. It was all mildew and corruption. This was where they were all traveling . . . death, corruption, decay. She had to live completely while she could, she saw with drunken insight. It would never come again.

Somewhere out in the commune a turntable blared a tinny recording of "Blowing in the Wind," sung in French with a strong echo-chamber effect, further distorting the scratched record.

"Remember *that,*" Steve said, his chin rising up off his chest as he sucked in a deep breath of septic night. "The goddamn Peace Corps national anthem. Remember that big show we all did at the end of training? When we all got up and sang 'Blowing in the Wind' and 'We Shall Overcome'? Remember how sentimental we were? Everybody was crying. The whole goddamn auditorium full of Volunteers, rocking back and forth, arm in arm, remember? . . . Deep in my heart, AHHH-EYE do believe that we shall AHH-over-COME so-o-meday." He rocked on his heels in front of the station wagon, waving his arms.

"Steve," Lisa said, "Steve, come on back here, honey. The car's coming. Randy's coming in the car. We're going home, baby."

"Goddamn," he cried. "Was that only two years ago? Jesus! Jesus, Joseph, and Mary, as the goddamn Irish say. Oops! Sorry, Emily. What I mean is, were any of us *ever* that young? Was it *ever* that simple? Man! It was all so fucking *perfect.* Do you remember, honey? How perfect it was? John Fitzgerald Kennedy was up there in the White House. How we had to sneak out of training to hitch down to D.C. for the March. Remember how hot it was and you threw up eating all that ice cream? Dylan and Joan Baez, and you just about creamed in your jeans when you saw Charlton Heston, remember? Goddamn March on Washington. We really showed them that time. And how we got back just in time to pack up to go to the airport. Peace Corps, boy! Charter flight all the way to Morocco. It was all so beautiful. It all clicked right into place. Remember how we were then? Remember the way Martin Luther King looked up there on the Lincoln Memorial? 'I have a dream . . . I have a dream.' "

But, Christ, we were right, Steve thought. Maybe it's stupid now, thinking back . . . CORE and the Freedom Rides and Peace Corps. Nothing's ever that simple. OK. But we did things that *had* to be done. People laughed at us, they thought we were crazy. How about that justice of the peace in Meridian who fined us all twenty-five bucks for *loitering?* He wasn't a red-neck. He was a real Southern gentleman, called all the guys "sir" and the girls, even the black girls, "ma'am," but he still fined us and then gave us that lecture on what . . . Jesus, I'm drunk again, can't remember things. What did he lecture us on in that little rinky-dink office of his . . .?

Propriety . . . that's what he said, right. He said we had no sense of propriety. . . . Well, maybe we didn't . . . charging down there in those buses, not knowing a damn thing about local traditions. He even said that things had to be changed but that there were ways of doing things that were proper and ways that weren't. Maybe he was right, maybe we were pushy, self-righteous little do-gooders with martyr complexes. Still . . . still what? Well, somebody had to go down there and shake things up, otherwise they'd still be the same today. Have they changed any? Can a black man *vote* down there or send his kids to a decent school or get a fair trial? Hell, no, he can drink out of the same water fountain as the whites if he's gutsy. He can wait in the same room in the Greyhound station. Big deal, big goddamn deal. We really showed them, all right. Yeah, boy . . . "We shall overcome, one day. . . ."

"Steve, baby," she called to him as he wandered off down the potholed road. "Steve, Randy's here. Come on, get in the car, Steve."

Randy drove slowly through the hot night, flashing his lights when he crossed the blind intersections. Every bar in the *cité* was jammed. The music echoed in the night: cha-cha, jazz, bush drums. The sidewalks were crowded with Africans. Everyone was happy. Everyone was drunk. "I have a dream," Steve screamed out of the window. "I have a dream that one day . . ." He paused, looking back into the car at Lisa. "How does it go from there, honey? You used to know the whole speech. We both did. Remember that time I did it in French for your class? How I had translated the whole thing, only they really didn't care, little Arab bastards. Didn't give a shit about their African brothers. Man! Nobody more goddamn prejudiced than an Arab. Were we ever stupid! Just a bunch of kids. What did that crazy *Belge* guy say? The count from E'ville? Children's Crusade, he said. He really hit the nail on the head."

As Steve rambled on, Emily sank out of sight in the front seat. Her husband drove with the exaggerated caution of a man who knows he has drunk too much and has a long, difficult drive ahead of him. He leaned his head out the window, clawing at his shirt buttons to catch the maximum effect of the cooling night air. Then they turned onto a brightly lit avenue and drove faster so that the breeze through the windows was actually chill. Steve had also sunk down in his seat, still mumbling.

Lights flashed behind them as a small Simca driven by a European pulled around them. "Boy!" Randy said. "That guy's really moving. Must have come from the Vis-à-Vis. I heard that a lot of Belgians were going dancing out there tonight."

The beer bars on either side of the avenue were packed with drinkers. Even little children wandered about. Lisa felt Steve's head heavy on her lap. A strange, drunken scheme was forming in her mind. If she let the McCarthys take Steve back to the Royal on the pretext that he was too drunk to drive, she could stay behind to drive their Volkswagen. Randy could see Steve up to the apartment where he would undoubtedly pass out. She would then be free to spend a few hours with Robert before returning. The prospect excited her. It held the same forbidden element of danger she had felt naked on the river. She ran her fingers up the damp flesh inside her thigh.

Suddenly Steve was stiffly upright next to her, his face paper-white. "Christ!" he whispered weakly. "I'm going to throw up. I've got the headspins."

"Breathe the air from the window," she said, gently guiding his shoulders and head toward the open window.

"Yeah," he said, "that's better. That's much better." The lights streamed by him. The music was whipped away in the hot wind, its pitch distorted like the whistle of a passing train. Smells of sudden nostalgic sharpness swept into the car: wood-smoke campfire smells that set him to thinking of summer nights in Wisconsin. He sat up even straighter. He would be all right. It was just the combination of drinks. He had mixed too many things. If he breathed the wind, he would not be sick.

The blurred smear of lights fell into focus and he could read the painted signs above the teeming cafés: Bar du Peuple, Café de la République. Strings of colored lights sailed slowly by in the night. There were women in their best wax prints gracefully swaying to the soprano chanting of the singers, their partners' white shirts ghostly in the flare of the gasoline lanterns. He drank in the greasy animal smoke from the lines of brochette stands. Smiling Africans hailed them from the curbs as he leaned precariously from the car to return their drunken greetings.

"Hey," he said, "let's stop and have one more drink. I'm going away tomorrow and it's Christmas. Come on, just one more drink in one of these cafés. They're such neat places. How come we never came down here before, honey? How come we always go to the Vis-à-Vis or the Afro-Mogambo? *These* are the places where things are really happening. Look at the way they're dancing over there. Come on, let's stop."

"It's pretty late, Steve," Randy said. "We've bot to get back up to the kids."

"What time is it?" he asked.

"Almost two," Lisa said dryly.

"Ah, well," Steve said. "I guess you're right. I've got to be out at the airport in four hours, anyway. Those sort of places sure do look like fun, though." He hiccuped loudly and they all laughed. Randy was just turning back to say something when Lisa screamed.

"Look out!"

Steve saw the whole thing happening but was powerless to speak. The Simca that had just passed them was driving fast up the center of the wide, one-way avenue. From a badly lit corner a group of drunken Congolese men and women carrying beer bottles staggered across the road. The Belgian braked sharply, laying down a screeching skid mark as he fishtailed into the group. No one was seriously hurt. A woman in yellow toreador pants and a gaudy smock fell to the pavement just before the bumper of the slowly moving car would have hit her. When she rose to her knees, her hands were bloody from the broken glass of the bottle she had been carrying. Her moaning scream blended with Randy's brakes as he slid to a halt behind the Simca. The road was quickly blocked by a wild-eyed mob of Africans, pushing at each other to see the spectacle of the bleeding woman who sat in the street, howling in the light of the yellow headlights.

The Belgian got out of his car to help the woman to her feet.

The mob was growing as drinkers poured out of nearby cafés. Grim, excited faces gaped into Randy's car as more Africans ran up the avenue to join the press around the Peugeot.

"We'd better get out of here," Randy said, jerking the car into reverse as he peered over his shoulder down the road behind them. "Boy! The whole street's filling up with 'em."

"Oh, God!" Lisa screamed.

A group of Congolese had pushed the Belgian up against his car. Suddenly one swung a piece of metal street sign, hitting the white man high on the forehead. He held his hands to his face as they pounded and kicked at him. The swollen mob closed in over him and he disappeared. Then, with a splintering crash, a rock struck the rear window of the Peugeot as they turned broadside to the mob, attempting to reverse their direction on the blocked avenue. Steve could see the European's Simca being smashed and rocked by the crowd. Angry Congolese were running toward their car, jabbing at the tires with pieces of wood and throwing pieces of broken pavement. "Close the windows!" Emily shouted, desperately working at her handle.

Just as they twisted out of the turn, Randy stalled the motor and the mob was on them. The rear door on Lisa's side had not been locked and was wrenched open; a clawing black arm ripped at her leg. Emily slashed at the African's flesh with a metal nail file, and blood spurted onto Lisa's white dress. Then the motor caught and they broke out of the wall of black faces. As they swung off, onto a side street, the first thumping rhythm of a flat tire began.

"Screw it!" Randy said. He gasped, "I'm driving on it. The hell with a flat tire."

The mob stopped their chase at the corner as the Peugeot bumped away on three tires like a crippled animal. Black men and women were running past them down the darkened side street toward the excitement on the avenue. As they turned onto another wide street leading toward the city's center, they heard the first notes of the pom-pom siren of the police jeep.

No one seemed to notice that Steve had vomited a thick, wet puddle on the floor of the car.

CHAPTER **7**

Steve took one of the cans of Campbell's consommé from the refrigerator, poured its contents into a picnic glass, added a huge
slug of vodka, some salt and pepper, and a shot of Tabasco. He
took a handful of ice cubes from the plastic bag in the freezer and
stirred them into his drink. Lisa came into the kitchen. In her
right hand she clutched the plastic codeine bottle, in the left her
cotton robe. Steve watched her as he sucked the cold beef jelly.
She leaned against the door frame, her eyes closed tightly against
the bright light. "Christ," she said, "I didn't even hear the alarm.
What time is it?"

"After five," Steve said. "I've got to go downstairs in a minute.
How do you feel?"

"Like death itself," she said. "What are you drinking?"

"Bullshot."

"Poor baby," she said. "I should have gotten up to make you
something to eat." She pressed against him, her full breast hot
against the tanned skin of his arm. "Do you really have to take
this trip?" she whispered.

"I was just thinking that myself," he said. "But I guess I do. I'll
be back for New Year's. It's only a week. What's wrong, baby?"

She was sobbing softly, her warm tears wetting his shirt.

"Hey, Lisa," he whispered, kissing her bare shoulder, "what is
it?"

"I love you, Steve," she said, looking up now with red eyes. "I
don't want you to go, that's all."

"I'll be back New Year's Eve," he said. He ran his hand down
her back to the cleft of her buttocks. Her flesh was firm, taut from
hours in the sun and water. "I'd like to finish what we started last
night."

"Do you have time?"

He shook his head. "Why do I always get so sexy when I have a
hangover?"

"Me too. Do you want to?"

The hall buzzer sounded three times in quick succession. The Embassy driver had arrived.

In the doorway of the apartment he kissed her very deeply, her mouth still tasting of alcohol, sleep, and tobacco. He drained the dregs of the bullshot and handed her the glass. "Give me a refill next week," he said, kissing her again.

She took the glass and stood silently, her lips tightly pursed. "What's wrong, Lisa? You look sort of scared."

"I don't know really. It's silly, I guess. I just suddenly had the feeling that this is the way things will always be . . . that we'll just keep moving from one embassy to another, and we'll always be drunk at night with all those awful people, and you'll always be chasing off on some trip, and then one day we'll be forty and it'll be too late to change. I know it seems stupid, but right now it all seems so inevitable."

Steve sighed, glancing furtively at his watch.

"Listen, honey," he said, "that's not stupid at all. I've been feeling the same thing. I've got a pretty good idea now that this job, that this whole life, isn't what we thought it would be. I really wanted to come down here to see Africa, not to get drunk on champagne with a bunch of bored Europeans. Like I said, this trip will be good for me. I'll have a chance to do some thinking. I'll be back next week and we can talk about it then. One thing I promise you, though, we're going to stop all this idiotic partying every night. Tomorrow morning before you take the car to the garage stop at the tennis club and sign us both up. Take in my racket for restringing, O.K.? Next week we'll start playing tennis in the evening after work instead of sitting around every night boozing with all the Americans. How does that sound for openers?"

She smiled out at him from the doorway of the darkened living room. Everything about her was right: splendid legs, narrow waist, just a hint of a stomach starting now, incredible breasts, her hair dangling down almost to the tight brown nipples. Steve looked at her, his foot holding open the door of the elevator. One day, he knew, she would grow heavy, her ripeness sagging. He saw the swell of her hips, the flesh on her shoulders. She would have to start watching her diet seriously now. It would be a shame to lose a body like that. She still had years, though. He had her now for these years of ripeness.

"That's what I really want, Steve. I just want to be with you. I don't care where we go or what you decide you want to do—as long as we're together I'll be happy."

"Jesus," he said softly. "I wish I had a few more minutes. I'd really like to take you back to bed."

From inside the apartment he heard the buzzer rasp again. "Got to run now, Lisa. I'll miss my flight. Take care, see you next week."

"Steve!" she said, stepping out into the hall to press her body hard against him. "Please be careful. Promise me you won't take any chances on this trip."

He kissed the tangled hair on her forehead. "Don't worry, Lisa. You know that I'm really a coward. I'll see you New Year's Eve."

As the elevator door closed, he still saw her standing naked in the hallway, smiling at him with the tears wet on her face.

An Embassy station wagon sat with its motor running in front of the Royal's C wing. André, the duty driver, was tall and heavy, his massive stomach and bull neck bulging out of his khaki chauffeur's uniform.

"*Bonjour,* André," Steve said, giving him the suitcase. André reeled a bit. Obviously he, too, had been celebrating the Savior's birth.

"*Bonjour, patron,*" André said. "*Bonne fête?*"

"Yeah," Steve said. "Too much to drink, though. Let's go."

"*C'est bon, ça,*" André laughed. He took a cloth from the seat to wipe the bugs off the windshield. Steve sat in the front seat, looking dully at the UNESCO and World Health posters along the arcade of the United Nations offices on the ground floor. "Hey, *patron.*" André pointed up.

Lisa was on the living-room balcony in her robe. She had something in her hand. "The codeine," she called down. "For your headache."

"Drop it," Steve yelled up to her. He saw the little green bottle disappear into the darkness. It fell next to the station wagon, the lid popping and a cloud of white tablets fountaining up as high as the top of the car. André laughed a throaty African laugh. He scooped the dozen-odd codeine tablets off the top of the car and the hood. *"Ça va,"* Steve said. "Enough." He swallowed three tablets, one at a time, salivating just enough to get each tablet down with a quick jerk of his head.

"That's a big mother of an airplane, isn't it?" Charlie said.

"You can say that again," Steve answered.

His headache was still there. He sat next to Charlie on an empty ammunition crate in the shade of the military hangar at the end of the N'djili Field runway. Directly before them on the tarmac an Air Force C-130 transport was being loaded for its trip into the interior. Steve looked at his watch. Only six-thirty, and already he needed his sunglasses to look into the pink glare above the eastern horizon. Overhead the wispy remnants of the overcast were dissolving with the rising sun.

Congolese workers, naked to the waist, swarmed about the fat belly of the aircraft, passing up crates of aerial rockets and machine-gun ammunition through the open maw of the tailgate. Dwarfed beside the big transport on the tarmac sat two shiny aluminum T-28 fighter bombers and an olive-green B-26. In the deep shade of the hangar Steve could see piles of crates and canvas-wrapped aircraft engines. Charlie took a long pull at his half-quart can of Budweiser.

"Sure you don't want some?" he asked. "Best thing in the world for a hangover."

"I guess I'd better," Steve said, taking the can of beer. "I don't think it could make me feel any *worse* than I do already." The beer was very cold, cutting into his sour stomach like a frozen knife. He shuddered. Charlie smiled.

"Go ahead and finish the can," he said. "I can always get some more off those WIGMO guys. They never go anyplace in the Congo without cold beer."

"This is the WIGMO hangar, isn't it?" Steve asked dully.

"WIGMO and COMISH," Charlie said.

"This probably sounds funny," Steve said, "me being in the Embassy and all, but I haven't got the foggiest idea what WIGMO really does or who they are. I know that we're not supposed to ask too many questions about them and that they work under the CIA Station Chief, but that's all I really know."

"WIGMO," Charlie said. "Yeah, funny outfit, all right. Ever hear of Air America out in Laos?"

Steve nodded.

"How about the Bay of Pigs?"

"Sure," Steve said.

"Same deal with WIGMO. Congo's got itself a little rebellion going on, right? The ANC and the mercenaries need air support against the Simbas, only the Congolese aren't cool enough to fly their own planes. Who do they turn to in their hour of need? Why, they turn to some clever private business cats who take old T-28s and B-26s and rebuild them to rent out to little governments in distress. They've got a company based in Liechtenstein. Really, no shit, in *Liechtenstein*. They've got a bona fide contract with the ANC to provide them airplanes and ground crews and what I think they call 'logistical and *other* support.' Of course these two guys just happen to be CIA officers and the planes are U.S. Air Force surplus, same as in Laos, Guatemala, and the Bay of Pigs. But *officially* at least the American Government has nothing to do with it. The guys who fly the planes are Cubans. You must have run into Chico and Raphael and all those other Cuban guys at parties."

Steve nodded again.

"Well, they get paid by the ANC. On the surface this is strictly a deal between the ANC and some private citizens. Christ knows that the *American Government* would never mess around in the internal affairs of an independent African country. God forbid. That's against the UN charter. . . . Didn't you read that thing in *The New York Times* last year about the Congo's 'Instant Air Force'?"

"No, I never saw it."

"Yeah, well, the reporter who wrote it really knew what he was talking about. He spelled the whole thing out, just how much we're doing for the Congolese on the military side. Ever since then the WIGMO and COMISH people have been pretty careful about who they talk to. The truth is we're up to our necks in this rebellion. See those two guys over there, inside the hangar there, talking with the loadmaster?"

Steve saw two Americans, one tall and gangly, dressed in faded but sharply pressed khakis bearing no insignia, and the other in a well-tailored Army fatigue uniform that bore the gaudy badges of a Special Forces major.

"That's Spencer, the tall one," Charlie said. "He runs the WIGMO air and boat group out of Albertville. He's a CIA type, ex-Air Force, officially head of the WIGMO ground crew, who are supposed to be doing *maintenance* for the Congolese Air Force. Actually he's got a regular fighter bomber squadron running up there. Boats too. They've got these fancy fiber-glass PT boats with radar and machine guns, the works. They're out every night on Lake Tanganyika shooting up the gunrunning boats the Chinese are sending across from Tanzania. Christ only knows what the Special Forces guy does here. I've seen him around up in Stan. Looks like he's going up to A'ville with Spencer now. Officially these guys don't exist. Really something, isn't it?"

"Yeah," Steve said sleepily. "I guess they know what they're doing, though."

"Right," Charlie answered with an ironic smile. *"They* know what they're doing all right. But nobody else does. This is supposed to be a *civil* war. We had Adlai Stevenson up there last year in the United Nations to raise all kinds of sanctimonious hell about the Russians and the Algerians shipping arms down here to help the rebels and all the time we're flying in loads of crap ourselves. Know what's on that one-thirty? Engines and radar and stuff for the boat group. Ammo, too, for the WIGMO planes. That plane's just come in from the States. It'll stay here a week, supposedly doing logistics for the ANC, but actually they'll spend all their time hauling stuff for WIGMO and the other CIA operations in the bush. Christ, if some Senators in the States knew about half the shit we do in countries like this they'd raise such a stink you could smell it all the way over here."

Charlie's voice had risen again in pitch as it had during his final outburst in the Reeds' garden the night before. Steve glanced apprehensively at the plane's crew and the other Americans in the hangar.

Charlie looked closely at Steve's face and then at the toes of his own unpolished boots. "Right," he said softly. "Yeah, that's cool, too. Sorry I forgot for a second that you're stuck there in the old tobacco shed. I should keep my mouth shut until I get out of this fucking Army. If I get my early release to go back to school it won't be very long."

Steve sensed the tension and frustration in Charlie's face. "Maybe you're right, Charlie," he said. "I haven't been as many places as you have. I'll have to make up my own mind about it all once I've seen things. One thing I'm sure of, though—if the Communists are helping the rebels as much as everybody says, then we're right to be helping the ANC. Even if it means using the CIA and mercenaries. This country's too important strategically to let the Russians or the Chinese have it. All you have to do is look at the map of Africa to see that."

Charlie got to his feet, sighing as he rose. "Yeah, beautiful," he said, his voice soft and bitter. "So we should bring all these planes over here and bomb the Commies before they get too far. Only thing is, how do you know they're Commies? Do you think those Simbas up there in the bush have read a hell of a lot of Marx and Lenin?"

"Well, they're being supplied by the Communists—"

"Right," Charlie interrupted with a wave of his hand, "and the ANC's being supplied by us—does that make *them* a bunch of New England Republicans? No, it's much easier than that. You seem like a nice guy, and even if I do shoot my mouth off, I don't really give a shit any more. I'll clue you in. I'll give you the real low-down. The rebels are a hundred per cent card-carrying Commies, all right. Know how you can tell?" Charlie's face was deeply flushed and his smile demonic. Steve stared at him nervously without speaking.

"It's just like the VC," he said, his voice even softer than before. "Just like the body counts. If you find some dead people after an air strike, then they're VC. Same thing works here. If you want to know where the Commie rebels are, just check where the WIGMO planes are bombing. That's a sure-fire test for Commies. A *Communist* is a person who gets bombed by the *Americans*. It's as simple as that." Charlie's raucous laughter echoed off the walls of the hangar as he strode away toward the C-130, kicking at the ground before him and muttering to himself as he had the previous night.

Charlie stopped abruptly and spun about to face Steve again. He lowered his voice so as not to be overheard in the hangar. "Hey," he said. "Listen, all of that doesn't really *matter*. Can't you see? That's what countries do. They fight each other. Remember how in high school there were always kids who had to run things their way, who were always so damn aggressive? How they'd even fight to get what they wanted, how they *liked* to fight? Well, that's the nationalism thing. It's all bullshit. Countries are just like those aggressive kids. That's not important. There's no question really of politics, you know. Free World and all that versus the Reds, or that struggling-young-nations crap. It's just guys getting their kicks that way, a lot of guys in governments. You know, a government isn't a *thing* like that airplane—it's people, like Lincoln said, of the people, by the people, and for the people. If the people are screwed up, then so is the government. Does that mean anything to you?"

Steve stood up, stifling a yawn with the back of his hand. "It sounds pretty complicated. I'm afraid I really don't catch what you're trying to say."

"Yeah, well, maybe I don't explain it the right way, but it's true, goddamn it! I know it's true. But even that's not important. What counts is what happens to *you* and *me,* to guys like us who have to work in this bullshit business. Just before you more or less said that the ends justify the means—you know, about the spooks and the mercs and WIGMO. You didn't really believe that. What you still believe—I can see it on your face—is the good-guy horseshit about America. It's easy to believe, it happened to me, too. Hell, we don't talk about Air America or WIGMO or the way we just went in and took over Santo Domingo. It'd be stupid to talk about that. What we brag about are things like AID food for the hungry and bringing those big jets over here to fly oil down to Zambia so that they won't suffer from the blockade against all those nasty Rhodesian racists. We're the good guys, right? We may be forced to play rough by the other side, but deep down we do good stuff for people. Well, that's just not *true*, Steve. We, the government, really don't give a living shit about people. It's all power and strategy and politics. Well, what I really would like you to see is that when you're involved in this stuff long enough you get to kind of like it. That's when they take you out of the tobacco shed, that's when you're *mature*. What the fuck does that mean?" His voice was rising again. "Means cynical, that's what. After a couple years of this you don't give a damn any more about people. You turn into a bullshit artist who's so good he doesn't even know he's bullshitting himself any more. Yeah, I know that it seems cool to be serving your country out here in Africa, helping these *emerging* nations and all. Well, that might have been cool with Kennedy up there, but times have changed. You were complaining last night about your job. Wait until you see some of the shit that's happening out in the bush. Try to imagine what you'll be like if you pull a Vietnam tour after the Congo—you know, out there as a deputy provincial rep under some really corrupt Saigon Mafia type. That'll make this place seem like kindergarten. You seem sort of hot to take this trip—well, keep your eyes open and watch what's happening to *you*, to you inside your head."

Charlie turned again and continued toward the airplane. His shoulders were slumped and his gait an exhausted shuffle. Steve stood for a moment staring after him. The outburst had confused Steve. He shook his head as a jangly collage of splintered emotions pulsed through him. He's crazy, Steve thought suddenly. I'd better stay away from him.

Under the lofty hangar roof the air had retained some of the coolness of the misty dawn. Steve walked slowly toward the other Americans, noting on his way the vaguely nostalgic odors of the piled equipment: sun-warmed canvas, the pitch pine of the ammunition crates, machine oil, sweat, and coffee. He closed his eyes, recalling in a sudden flash a long-forgotten church camp in Northern Michigan.

He took his place beside Spencer and the major on a pile of tightly rolled field tents.

"You going up to Stan with the one-thirty or out to A'ville with us?" Spencer asked with a friendly smile.

"Stan," Steve said and belched with a sickening shudder before he could say more.

"You look a little shaky, boy," the major said. "Too much Christmas cheer?"

"Way too much," Steve answered.

"Get yourself another beer from the office," Spencer said. "That'll fix you up in no time."

"Thanks," Steve said. "I will in a minute."

"What about your friend," Spencer said, "the COMISH sergeant? He looked like he could use another one, too."

"Oh," Steve said quickly, "he's not my friend. . . . I mean I just met him. I think he feels O.K."

"Looked a little strange to me," the major said in a soft Southern voice.

They were interrupted by the reverberating thunder of aircraft engines. A rakish-looking B-26 was taxiing smoothly down the access ramp toward the hangar.

" 'Bout goddamn time," Spencer said, looking disdainfully at his watch. He and the major picked up their canvas AWOL bags and walked out to the waiting aircraft. "Stop in and see us sometime in Albertville, boy," Spencer called back over his shoulder. "You can build yourself a *real* hangover out there."

"I'll do that," Steve called back.

He watched the two officers pull themselves athletically through the small side hatch of the fighter bomber. Very quickly the plane was out at the end of the long runway, revving its engines for take-off. Then it was airborne, a diminishing spot of solid in the bright liquid pinks of the morning sky. Steve yawned deeply and drained the last of the beer from the can. With the departure of the first WIGMO flight of the day the languid activity in the big hangar quickened. He saw the loadmaster of the C-130, big and hard-looking in his sweaty gray nylon flight suit, haranguing the Congolese workers to speed up the loading of the remaining ammunition cases. A jeep driven by a tired-looking WIGMO ground crewman skidded up to deposit the three flying officers and flight engineer of the transport.

"For Christ's sake, Peters," the flight engineer bellowed at the loadmaster, "haven't you got that shit on board yet? We ain't got all morning to spend here fucking the dog. Took us about an hour to file the flight plan with those frogs in the tower. Let's get a move on—we're late."

"You want to try it, Creighton?" the loadmaster yelled back. "If you can get those boggies to work any faster, you're a better man than me."

Without further comment the flight engineer disappeared up into the cargo bay. Steve heard the sarcastic edge of his Southern military accent echo down from inside the plane. Grumbling sleepily, the five GIs of the plane's armed guard stumbled down the loading ramp with their weapons and web equipment cradled in their arms. Slowly and with obvious annoyance at being awakened, they strolled to their positions beneath the wings and tail. Steve rose and walked to the nose of the plane. He pulled himself up through the front door of the plane below the flight deck. The whale belly cargo hold was filled with bulky canvas-wrapped crates. He wedged his bags between two of them.

As he watched, a Congolese soldier in plastic sandals and torn fatigue trousers got into an armored car parked in the hangar and, gunning its engine, drove it up the tailgate into the belly of the plane in one deft burst of speed that left the loadmaster shaking his head in wonder. The Congolese soldier got down from the car, glanced around the plane, and wandered away, whistling.

It was dim inside the plane. The bulkheads and roof of the cargo bay were a twisted maze of multicolored electrical lines, steel control cables, and hydraulic conduits. Steve stretched out on an empty section of canvas seat slightly forward of the high wings. He belched again loudly from the beer. Hard American voices filtered into the plane from the tail. Steve closed his eyes. The noises in the plane faded. The odor of the hot coffee sweetly churned his stomach. He was hungry. It wouldn't be such a bad hangover after all. Not if he was hungry. The real ones were when you couldn't eat. It certainly was a nice soft seat. Nice canvas. He was asleep.

"Hey!" the captain said, shaking him. "Sorry, sir. Hey, wake up. O.K.?"

Steve sat up. His head was splitting. The pilot was bending over him. They were still in the hangar. His mouth tasted awful. Outside the sun was bright. He looked at his watch: five after seven.

"Sorry," the captain said. "You speak French, don't you?" Steve nodded. "There's a Congolese soldier outside. I think he's an officer or something. I can't make out what he wants. You're going to have to translate 'cause Mr. Spencer's gone." Steve followed the captain out of the plane. The concrete of the tarmac was already hot.

Grouped in the shade of the hangar stood the four other crewmen of the plane and the GIs of the armed guard. In the center of the group was a slight Congolese Army lieutenant in starched fatigues and a tan beret. The tabs on the epaulettes of his short-sleeved fatigue shirt were infantry blue. He was thin, and his scrubby goatee and rimless glasses gave him a pathetic, schoolboy appearance. At his feet lay a scratched metal trunk and an Army duffel bag. One of the American soldiers, a young Negro PFC in tailored fatigues and gleaming jump boots, was trying to talk to the African.

"Find out what exactly this dude wants, would you?" the captain said to Steve.

Steve shook the lieutenant's hand, introducing himself. The lieutenant's eyes looked wild behind his glasses.

"These men have insulted me!" the lieutenant said nervously in French. "They have been ridiculing me for fifteen minutes. It's an insult to the Armée Nationale Congolaise."

"Lucky Pierre," one of the crewmen said. They all laughed.

"Again!" the lieutenant spat. The crew and the GIs smiled at the Congolese officer. The Negro PFC looked at the ground.

"Qu'est-ce que vous voulez, exactement, Lieutenant?" Steve asked softly.

"I have priority orders to proceed by military aircraft to the headquarters of *Opérations Sud* in Albertville. I was told that this plane is going there today. I have asked the pilot to take me, but he only laughed at me and pretended not to understand. These soldiers have taken my identity papers, and they too have insulted me. None of them speaks a word of French. I have priority orders. If the pilot will not take me, he must sign a paper to that effect. I can always take another flight. I must have a statement from this pilot, however, stating why he will not take me as a passenger."

It was a long speech. Spittle had collected at the corners of the lieutenant's mouth. Steve translated. "Lucky Pierre," the voice said again. It was the balding sergeant, the flight engineer. His long-billed flying cap was pushed back on his head. He looked contemptuously at the African.

"Enough of that, Creighton," the pilot said, trying to put some authority into his voice. He slipped into something approaching falsetto instead.

"Yes, sir," the sergeant said, turned and walked away.

"Oh, hell," the young pilot said. "I guess we'll take him if his orders are good. Can you read them? Nobody told us anything about ANC passengers, though."

Steve read the orders. They'd been signed at the Quartier Général. "They're good as gold," he said.

"Tell him he'll have to sign a liability release," the pilot said.

Steve tried to translate. The lieutenant looked puzzled.

"It is *they* and not me who must sign if they refuse my orders," he said.

"Oh, hell," Steve said in English, "just sign them if you want to go."

"Comment? Parlez français, monsieur."

"C'est simplement pour le billet," Steve said.

Steve filled in the lieutenant's name and service number on the three mimeographed copies of the "release of liability" form. Pierre-Marie Tshipama, Lieutenant de l'Infanterie, Armée Nationale Congolaise.

"You're a Muluba," Steve said, attempting to be friendly.

"Je suis Congolais!" the lieutenant said coldly. He signed the forms with a flourishing signature. "Is there no one to carry my baggage?" he asked.

"Yes," Steve said, walking back to the plane. "Lieutenant Pierre-Marie Tshipama."

CHAPTER **8**

The plane sat on the taxi ramp at the western end of the runway, awaiting take-off clearance. A high-pitched whistling came from the engines. Steve was strapped to the foam-rubber bench in the cabin directly in back of the pilot, co-pilot, and flight engineer. The sallow-skinned young navigator seated at his console to Steve's right looked no older than twenty. Tinted wrap-around windows in the cockpit gave him a splendid view as the crew went through their take-off check list.

Surprisingly, there was a lot of traffic. Directly ahead of them was a TWA Boeing 707, one of the two big American jets that had carried petroleum products around the clock to Elizabethville for transshipment to Zambia, cut off by the Rhodesian blockade two months earlier.

Another olive-drab and gray B-26 huddled close to the ground on its tricycle landing gear in front of the big jet. First in line, an Air Congo DC-4 was just starting its take-off run. Steve put on the pair of earphones. The Air Congo pilot was a Belgian and spoke French. The Cuban in the B-26 spoke English with a theatrical Spanish accent. The TWA captain sounded Southern. The fighter bomber made a very short run and whipped off to the left, its port wingtip tank almost skimming the high grass along the runway. He climbed out over the river and disappeared into the rapidly breaking overcast. "Where did he say he was going?" the captain asked into his microphone. "I could hardly understand him."

"Stanleyville," Steve said. "His name's José. He was in the Bay of Pigs."

They rolled out onto the end of the runway, the captain turning the plane neatly with the steerable nose wheel. To their left the white mist was rising slowly off Stanley Pool. Pale egrets flew above it. The scene looked very Chinese to Steve, like an old silk painting. The plane rocked like a rowboat in the blast of the

TWA jet as it plowed down the runway, disappearing into a tunnel of its own exhaust, to reappear out over the far end of the runway on its way to Elizabethville, a thousand miles away.

They finished their take-off check list and received clearance. The pilot cupped his gloved hand over the four engine throttles and slid them evenly back to the full position. The engines responded with a screaming whine that started a nagging, itching vibration inside Steve's nose. The brakes were off and they shot forward.

"What'd we figure? Two-forty or three-forty?" the pilot asked.

"Two hours, forty-seven minutes," the co-pilot answered. "Where you been, man?"

"I gotta get me some sack time tonight," the pilot said. "This trip's as bad as the fucking Dom. Rep."

"Ninety," the co-pilot called out. "One hundred, one-ten."

There was very little noise out in front of the engines. The runway raced by silently beneath the windows. They were up whistling into the sun.

"Gear," the pilot said. The landing gear came up with a bump.

"Gear up," said the flight engineer.

"Flaps."

"Flaps up."

They rose steeply into the breaking overcast and then through it. The wide expanse of Stanley Pool opened up below them to the left, through the breaks in the clouds. The mist had almost lifted now. Steve could see pirogues trailing spidery wakes on the calm surface of the water. The river islands were deep green. The whole scene was even more Chinese with the graceful dugouts. The rich sea of new green elephant grass spread out before them as the plane climbed to altitude. Pencil lines of gray smoke rose vertically from the scattered fishing villages along the river. The water glared like aluminum as the river arched off to the north and east.

"There goes that B-26," the co-pilot said. "Six o'clock low."

Steve opened his eyes. He could not see the little green plane below them. The country looked like a huge piece of camouflage cloth now. Islands of forest green scrub standing out against the rolling ocean of grass. Slowly the forest grew until the grassy spots became the islands and were quickly swallowed. The scrub, in turn, gave way to the unbroken roof of the hardwood forest. They continued to climb.

"What'd we say?" the pilot said, yawning. "Twenty-one or twenty-three?"

"Twenty-three," the flight engineer answered.

"You're in beautiful shape this morning," the co-pilot said.

"Yeah. Well, who the hell flew all the way from Ascension last night?" the pilot said, yawning again.

"The Honeywell Corporation," the co-pilot answered, patting the controls of the automatic pilot.

"My ass!" said the navigator, his voice very adolescent. "You guys were both asleep. Incidentally, I make it zero five three at twenty-three. You can go back to sleep now."

The pilot unstrapped from his seat and climbed into the bunk above Steve's seat. "Nighty-night," he said.

"Me too," Steve said, climbing down into the cargo bay. The loadmaster was stretched out on top of one of the crates, chewing a cigar, the long cord from his headset trailing behind him. The sleeping armed guard had taken the choicest positions on the canvas seats. The Congolese lieutenant, looking frightened and alone, was near the armored car in the tail. Steve found a stretch of seat near him and curled up on it. The cargo bay alternated from dazzling sunlight to near darkness as they cruised among the thunderheads already building up while they flew deeper into the Congo basin. Finally he slept.

The big plane bucked twice in quick succession as it sliced through the shoulder of a thunderhead. Steve opened his eyes to the welder's arc of sunlight flashing through the small porthole. Automatically he looked at his watch. They had been out almost an hour and a half—another ninety minutes to go. Still lying on the seat, he tentatively rolled his head on his shoulders, testing the state of his hangover. He felt better. After breathing deeply in the cool air of the cargo bay, he felt almost normal. Turning to rest his back, he snuggled into the nylon web backrest and stared down at the forest slowly unrolling below them.

The aircraft had just crossed over the curled gray edge of a squall line hiding the forest behind them. He leaned forward to peer ahead at the unbroken rain forest, a solid, pebbly-textured mixture of greens, like the nubby moss on flat granite. There were no villages, no paths or roads or other evidence of man's existence. As far as he could see, the solid canopy of trees spread toward the flat horizon.

They were over the heart of the central Congo basin, an area where hundred-and-fifty-foot hardwoods rose side by side, their branches intertwining for thousands of square miles. A brown river curved away in lazy meanderings to the north where it would join the Congo. Far down the river on a red mud shoal Steve saw what might be the primitive grid pattern of a small fishing village. From their altitude it was difficult to be certain.

He was glad now that he had come. It was good to have left the artificial gaiety and squalor of Léopoldville. Below him was the real Africa, the rivers and the untouched forest. He had wanted so desperately to see Africa, and now it was silently unfolding before him.

It would be good as well to be away from Lisa for a few days. He had a lot of things to think about; a lot of decisions to make. It would be easier for him while he was away from her. He had to decide what he really wanted. If he chose the solid, untaxing life of the Foreign Service, then he would content himself with it, relaxing to the plodding speed of his advancement, slowly learning the ropes, biding his time through several tours of duty, doing the bidding of uninspiring superiors, until one day he would have the necessary experience to be given real responsibility. He had to decide if this was what he really wanted to do with his life. If not, then he should stop tearing himself apart, trying to swim against the current, and get out of it. There were many things he could do with his life. There was the Peace Corps staff job he knew he could have. They could always go back to school. If they went back to the States, they could spend some time looking around. He had felt an uneasiness in the past few months, a feeling that things in the States were changing with surprising suddenness and that he was being bypassed. With their Peace Corps duty in Morocco and six months in the Congo, they had been overseas almost three years. A great deal had happened in America in that time. Perhaps they should go back and get involved in the new Great Society programs that were just beginning.

He had a lot of thinking to do and was glad for the isolation of the trip upcountry. But it was stupid to try to think about anything so important with the ragged remnants of the hangover and less than four hours' sleep. There would be plenty of time for that in the week ahead.

"How's the hangover now?"

Steve looked up from the porthole. Charlie Hogan stood swaying above the line of sling seats, supporting himself on the long static line cable that ran the length of the cargo bay. Steve shrugged his shoulders in a noncommittal manner and drew a neutral smile onto his face. Charlie bit his lower lip.

"Listen," he said quietly, "I was still pretty out of it this morning. If I said anything stupid, I'm sorry. I get kind of funny sometimes when I come down to Léo and get in with all those Americans. I was feeling sort of pissed off at the world this morning, you know, hardly got any sleep last night, and I was mixing things I shouldn't have at that party."

"Don't worry about it," Steve said. "We all drank too much last night."

A childish smile broke the tension on Charlie's face. He pointed out the porthole at the forest far below them. "It's really such a fantastic country, so big. Look at that—wow!—solid forest. How'd you like to have been hacking your way through that with Stanley?"

"Yeah," Steve said, shifting sideways in his seat to improve his view.

"Ever read *Heart of Darkness?*" Charlie asked.

Steve shook his head. "No, I'm ashamed to say. I was so busy in school that I only had time for the assigned reading. I was married and working to pay our way through. Then I got involved in civil rights work and just didn't get around to reading the things I always wanted to."

"How about *Through the Dark Continent?*"

"Same thing, I'm afraid," Steve said apologetically. "I can tell you all kinds of things about Morocco, though. I was there two years in the Peace Corps and did a lot of reading."

"Peace Corps," Charlie said in a neutral tone. "I was thinking about that once myself. Do you think the Peace Corps would have any use for a twenty-four-year-old retired sergeant?"

"Well . . ." Steve said, remembering Charlie's glazed expression and wild laughter of the night before. "Sure, why don't you apply? The test's not hard."

"I was only kidding. When I get out next spring I'm going to go back home and open a whorehouse—only civilized work these days for a gentleman."

"You're not career then," Steve said, not really curious, just making conversation.

"Me? A *lifer?*" Charlie said. "I may be crazy sometimes, but I'm not insane!"

They both laughed and then were silent, listening to the whistle of the turbine engines. Steve could see a thin veil of clouds below them again. They were crossing over the edge of another storm system.

"Yeah," Charlie said, breaking the silence. "That figures—civil rights, Peace Corps. Did you *ask* to come to the Congo?"

Steve looked up at him. There was no trace of mockery in his face. "Not specifically," Steve said. "I asked to be assigned to Francophone black Africa, and this is where they sent me."

"To sing Christmas carols and type up three-by-five cards."

Steve laughed. "You've got a good memory. I thought you were pretty drunk last night and wouldn't remember what I said."

"Unfortunately I wasn't drunk. That scene with the electric organ and the flashing Christmas tree got me going on a kind of crazy streak. It was just too much."

Wispy strings of cloud flew past the porthole as they approached the higher levels of the cumulo-nimbus cells. The plane began a gentle rocking motion that increased with the intensity of the head wind. Charlie took the seat next to Steve, digging beneath the sling for the twisted seat belts. "Well," he said, "it should be an interesting trip for you. If I hadn't already had my fill of tropical forests before I came here, I would have really gotten a kick out of coming up the first time. I've had some really nice times, though. The river can be beautiful, and some of the people out in the bush are great."

"They told me that the security situation is still not too good."

"That's what they tell everybody. The fact is the rebels are pretty well finished in this area. Like I said last night, the real menace is the ANC. They're a bunch of goddamn bandits."

"Well, they're the only ones we've got."

"Right," Charlie said, his voice rising again. "I suppose to Washington the ANC is better than no army at all. I just happen to have seen them doing their stuff to the local people a couple of times, and I think it would be better to have *no* goddamn army." He looked around the cargo bay. "I'd better keep my mouth shut. Sometimes I forget that I'm still in the Army and the ANC are our allies in the long struggle against the Marxist rebels."

Steve did not answer. Charlie was getting a strange flushed look on his face again. Steve turned away and watched the thickening clouds whip silently past the porthole. If he remained quiet, he thought, Charlie would calm down. They exchanged a glance, Steve quickly averting his eyes. Charlie giggled and loosened his seat belt. He swung away down the lurching deck of the cargo bay, steadying himself on the overhead cable.

"Boy!" the pilot said. "That's a beautiful radio beacon they got there. Wonder how far it carries . . . about a hundred yards?"

They were coming down through twenty thousand feet, the cockpit dark as night as they descended through the thunder cells. Steve was strapped in tightly on the padded bench at the rear of the flight deck. He could see the pale green finger of light rotating on the pilot's radar repeater. The crewmen were tensely watching the lighted instruments as the plane was buffeted and pitched by the storm around them.

"We should be sixty miles out," the navigator said as the nose of the plane rose crazily like a whale boat on a breaker.

"Jesus!" the pilot said, clinging to the control wheel with his left hand while he desperately adjusted the propeller pitch and throttles with his right. A solid wall of black rain and occasional meteorlike showers of hailstones beat against the windows. Steve raised weightlessly up and smashed back down on the bench with sickening regularity as if on a too-long roller-coaster ride.

With blinding suddenness they were out of the clouds and in a wide island of sunlit sky between the towering thunderheads.

"Those mothers right in front of us are really loaded, Bruce," the navigator said, peering intently into his radarscope.

"How about going below, then?" the pilot said, anxiety sounding clearly in his voice. The navigator readjusted the radar.

"The bases go all the way down to the trees," he said. "Take a look." The pilot throttled back slightly, spinning the stabilizer trim tab wheel to hold their altitude. They were coming up quickly on the wall of thunderheads.

"Look at those sons of bitches," he said, peering up out of the overhead window. "I thought they made them big out in Vietnam. Those bastards must be up around forty thousand feet, and it's not even afternoon." He rubbed his gloved hand across his face, puckering his lips into a grimly perplexed expression. "Shit," he whined, "what the hell do you guys think? Try to go around them or what?"

The heavy Southern voice of the flight engineer sounded in Steve's earphones. "You're the A.C., Captain," he said flatly. "It's your decision." He made no attempt to disguise the contempt in his voice.

"Stanleyville, Air Force, three nine four," the pilot said, switching to the VHF radio, "please repeat your weather."

"Three nine four, Stanleyville," the Belgian ground controller's voice came back, crackling through the static of the electrical storm in front of them. "Broken clouds at fifty-two hundred, visibility twenty miles, wind sixty degrees at four knots, temperature thirty-nine centigrade."

"Looks good as gold on the other side," the co-pilot said.

"Yeah," the pilot answered quickly. "On the other side of *that*." He pointed to the black wall of the storm.

"All we got to do is punch through one line of cells and we're there," the flight engineer said.

"I think we're turning around," the pilot said, banking the big plane off onto the starboard wing. "We had enough shit back there already, and then they stuck us with that fucking armored car. That's no load to carry through those cells up there."

"Ah, hell, Captain," the flight engineer said. "There's that Cuban guy down there someplace going through this shit in an old

B-26, no radar, no ceiling worth a damn, nothing. He ain't afraid of it."

"I'm not *afraid*, Creighton," the pilot said. "We've got too much junk back there. I don't like the way it feels in this turbulent stuff."

"We're only over here for eight days, Captain," Creighton said. "If we turn around every time we hit some weather, we ain't going to get half that stuff delivered they want us to, and if that happens we're in for a lot of static back at MacDill."

They were wheeling in a banking circle in the sunlight between the circular wall of storm clouds. "Besides," Creighton continued, "if that little B-26 makes it through and we turn around in this big-assed one-thirty, we're going to look worse than silly—we're going to look downright stupid."

There was a badly garbled burst of Spanish on the VHF. "What's that?" the pilot asked.

"The Cubans talking to each other," Steve said. "I heard another one back there before. WIGMO's got a C-46 on its way up to Stan today, too."

"How'd you like to be flying a C-46 in this stuff?" the co-pilot said.

As the plane orbited, the navigator scanned the wall of the storm before them. "Goes down a *long* way on either side," he said. "And there's another whole cell system starting up north of the river. Looks as bad or worse than this one."

The pilot sat hunched over the wheel, sucking greedily at a long filter-tip cigarette. In the bright sunlight his face looked young and very tired. Creighton sat in his fold-down seat just beyond the pilot's right elbow, glaring openly at the officer's head. The old sergeant drummed his thick fingers against his leg. "One line of cells is all we got to get ourselves through and we're in the good weather," Creighton said, making a show of looking at his aviator's watch on the underside of his left wrist.

"O.K., O.K.," the captain whined. "We're going through then. Give me the best heading through the thinner cells, Wally," he said to the navigator.

The navigator pressed his face close to the radarscope and bit his lower lip. "Bring it around to about one, one zero," he chirped in his schoolboy's voice. "That'll take us out of them due north of Stanleyville, and if we can't get it on the radar we can always double back on the river." He tapped the sheet map before him on his work table, but only Steve could see where he pointed.

Suddenly the pilot, co-pilot, and engineer were very busy, setting instruments and working on the engine controls. "You'd better go on back and strap down good in the troop bay, mister," the engineer said. "It's going to be kinda crowded up here."

When the roller-coaster ride began again, Steve was tightly strapped into the sling seat, his feet braced against the steel hull of the armored car. They bounced through the storm like a canoe in white-water rapids. Sunlight alternated with midnight black as they cut through the billowing cloud towers. Overhead he could see the control cables slashing across their pulleys as the crew fought to keep the plane on an even keel. The soldiers strapped in around Steve gripped their weapons and loose equipment.

More hail beat on the aluminum skin of the airplane. One moment the engines screamed into a crescendo; the next they seemed strangely muffled by the thick blackness of the cloud. Then they were in the very worst of it, the plane banging and creaking like a ferryboat in bad weather, the engine pitch changing with kaleidoscope bursts of white sun and darkness.

Steve was painfully shaken, banged against the tubular frame of the seat. With disbelief he watched the three-ton armored car rise several inches on its suspension system and float like a submarine before his eyes, then smash down onto its tires with a frightening crack. The process was repeated in quick succession. The chain shackles holding the vehicle creaked loudly above the other noises of the storm.

Steve felt the fear he had seen on the young pilot's face. This was no August thunderstorm in Wisconsin. The winds outside the delicate hull drew their sustenance from the equatorial sun, beating with primeval intensity on the wet forest basin extending for hundreds of miles in every direction. These clouds were thermal energy machines capable of shredding the wings and fuselage of the transport.

As the aircraft listed steeply, one of the soldiers' pistol belts went banging across the deck. Steve had a piercing flash of the metal being ripped apart, feeling the shocking wetness of the wind as they tumbled at great speed, lifted *upward* by the savage thermal currents inside the cloud. How high would they be blown before the earth's gravity reasserted its claim? How long would they remain conscious in the wind and hail? His mouth went dry and he itched all over. Why had he come on this trip? They were going to die. The plane would disappear. Their bodies, like the crates and the heavy armored car, would plummet unseen, puncturing the solid roof of the forest. They would rot unnoticed among the ferns and creepers.

For the first time in his life he recognized his own death, not as some esoteric abstract, but as an imminent certainty. There would be no pain. A hapless bacterium caught in the cosmic pressure of a cyclotron did not feel pain as it was hurled into the vacuum and smashed into its component elements. He would feel no pain when the honeycomb struts and braces of the aircraft were torn apart, spilling the cargo, human and inanimate, like milkweed chaff in a wind tunnel.

He envisioned an inconspicuous article on the bottom of page three of the Paris *Herald Tribune:* AIR FORCE PLANE MISSING IN CONGO. TWELVE FEARED LOST. Twelve. That was so few. Their deaths would hardly create a ripple. It was only the big ones, the mid-air collision, the massive funeral pyres of the take-off crash of a crowded jet, that made the headlines. Their hulking sixty-ton machine was going to be crushed like foil, and the world would see a tiny inch or two of type blandly announcing that an Air Force plane had disappeared on a routine supply flight in Africa. No one would wonder. No one would question it. These things happened. It could have been worse. There were only twelve killed, after all.

He smelled the stench of diesel fuel as the oil sloshed in the tanks of the armored car. There *would* be fire. There *would* be pain. Somebody screamed an unintelligible curse. A steel helmet, covered with a floppy camouflage net, came sailing back through the cargo bay to smash against the metal bulkhead near Steve. It had started. They were ripping apart. He tried to picture Lisa's face and could not.

The sunlight hit him through the porthole. They were *clear*. Below them the rolling green of the forest roof was much closer. They were out of it and they were still alive. The airplane had not been damaged.

The loadmaster in his baggy flying suit came back down into the belly of the plane, tugging at the tiedowns on the crates.

"You want to go back up front?" he asked. "The weather's good now. We'll be down in a little while."

C H A P T E R **9**

It was hot on the tarmac. Steve sat on an engine crate in the shade of the hangar, drinking a cold can of Coke from the refrigerator in the WIGMO office. A line of barefoot Congolese workers passed down the heavy crates of aerial rockets from the C-130. The major commanding the Stanleyville COMISH office had driven the plane's three officers into town to take pictures. When he returned with the jeep, Steve and Charlie would ride back in with him. There was no hurry, Steve thought. He wouldn't be able to see any officials today. A group of high-ranking ANC officers, including the Chief of Staff, had arrived earlier in the morning and a military parade was being staged downtown. The rest of the Sunday afternoon would be spent drinking by the provincial *fonction-naires*.

On the opposite side of the hangar a company of troops was lounging in the shade. They were the honor guard awaiting the return of the staff officers. Their captain, a fat little man in full-dress uniform complete with decorations and a long gilded sword, strutted in front of his troops, beating his white gloves against his leg. The back of the captain's uniform was black with sweat. MPs swaggered about in white helmets and red brassards. In the shade of the palm trees before the bullet-pocked old airport guest house, a platoon of scruffy-looking National Police were squatting on their heels, their helmets and Mauser rifles strewn on the ground.

Steve finished his Coke and walked slowly over to the WIGMO office to get another.

The office was crowded with radio gear, map boards, *Playboy* nudes, and weapons. A captured Chinese automatic rifle hung from a pair of antelope horns next to the door. Gordon, the WIGMO station chief, sat at the radio talking to José in the B-26. On the concrete hardstand next to the hangar three squat T-28s sat side by side baking in the sun. The radio squawked a burst of static which turned into a man's voice speaking Spanish. It was Lima Poppa Delta, the WIGMO C-46. Gordon answered in Spanish, telling the pilot to park his plane next to the fighters as the area in front of the hangar was already crowded with the C-130 and the Congolese Air Force C-47 waiting to transport the Chief of Staff and his party back to Léopoldville.

Two American four-by-four trucks roared up to the end of the terminal and slammed to a halt before the metal barricade. Brightly uniformed members of the military band spilled out of the trucks, shouting to each other as they threw their instruments down into the crowd of soldiers. They quickly assembled into four ranks in front of the C-47. The *om-pa-pa* of the tuba and the pounding of the drums were lost in the noise of engines as the WIGMO C-46 landed and taxied up to the hangar. When the pilot had shut down his engines, the tall Congolese bandmaster raised his baton again and the group burst into another military air. Again they were interrupted as the B-26 swooped in for a graceful landing and rolled toward them. The grinning Cuban pilot swung the plane neatly around on one engine and cut his power, the multiple barrels of his machine guns pointing directly at the band. The bandmaster looked around the sky and down the runway. He raised his baton in a third attempt to rehearse. The troops and the platoon of police strolled languidly out to take their places beside the band.

They had finished unloading the Stanleyville cargo from the C-130. The plane's guard kept their places in the shade of the wings, curiously watching the honor guard and band. Steve stood outside the WIGMO office in the slight breeze blowing down the shimmering runway from the river. Somebody was running on the other side of the C-47. The Congolese lieutenant who had ridden up with them that morning was being chased by two club-swinging ANC military policemen. He ran between the band and the honor guard. The fancy-dress captain joined the chase, waving his sword. The MPs caught the lieutenant at the barricade, pushing him to the ground. There was more shouting and confusion. The band kept playing; the bandmaster half-turned to watch the beating. The troops broke rank and swelled into a disorderly mob around the group at the fence. Motorcycle sirens swelled above the band.

The loadmaster, his flight suit sweated through, ran over to Steve. "What the hell is going on?" he said. "What is this—a nigger riot or something?"

"Damned if I know," Steve said. "I think we better stay out of it, whatever it is."

An ANC jeep, its siren howling, careened up to the barricade. The metal gate swung open and the vehicle drove out onto the tarmac, dispersing the mob of police and soldiers. In the back of the jeep another ANC officer in dress uniform was shouting wild commands in Lingala. The lieutenant was pulled into the hangar by the two MPs assisted by several excited soldiers. Helmets and weapons lay scattered on the tarmac. The officer from the jeep was in a frenzy, kicking at soldiers and police and waving his sword wildly. The band continued to play.

The sirens grew louder and the first motorcycle drove slowly out onto the tarmac, its red lights rotating. Somehow the officers managed to reform a semblance of order among the honor guard, pushing the helmetless soldiers to the rear ranks. Two olive-drab Chevrolet convertibles pulled through the gates behind the motorcycles. The Chief of Staff and his party of senior officers looked at the disorderly mob around them with disbelief. The officer in charge of the honor guard gave a sword salute, spun on his heel, and bellowed a command. The disorganized band of soldiers and police presented arms in a jerky maneuver. The band broke into a spirited march. The Chief of Staff glanced coldly at the troops, returned the officer's salute, and turned away to say something to the local garrison commander who had been a passenger in the leading car. The two officers exchanged salutes, and the Chief of Staff climbed aboard his plane with his party.

The Belgian pilot leaned out of the cockpit and shouted over the band that he would not start his engines until the jeep and motorcycles were moved. There was more sword-waving and then the engines started with backfirings and clouds of choking blue smoke. The honor guard and band marched sloppily out to their waiting trucks. As soon as the plane was on the runway, the two MPs began to shout and menace the little lieutenant with their clubs. The sword-waving officer screamed a command at them and they stopped shouting.

Suddenly the lieutenant made another dash for the open fence gate. He was halfway there when he was again seized by the MPs, who threw him down roughly to the pavement. Several wildly shouting soldiers from the honor guard joined the fracas, and when the lieutenant was pulled to his feet, there was blood pumping from his nose and mouth. The larger of the two MPs swung his club, hitting one of the soldiers a solid blow to the neck just as the soldier was about to bring his rifle butt up into the lieutenant's abdomen. For a moment the angry screaming and arm-swinging confusion reached an almost uncontrollable level, and then the sword-bearing officer again regained a semblance of control over his men. The excited soldiers were sent muttering back to their ranks, and the lieutenant was led back into the shade of the hangar.

The officer questioned him sharply, examined his crumpled orders, then waved to the loadmaster of the C-130, who stood with his hands on his hips in the shade of the wing.

"What's he want?" the sergeant called over to Steve. "I don't speak no French. Tell him to wait for the captain."

Steve joined the MPs and the two ANC officers under the wing. *"Qu'est-ce qu'il y a?"* he asked the major.

"This officer," the major said, pointing at the lieutenant, "says he cannot travel in the American plane because he has been insulted. He tried to hide himself on the aircraft of the Chief of Staff. These military police caught him. How do you explain this?" Steve translated the major's remarks for the sergeant. The lieutenant was wiping his bloody face with a sodden handkerchief.

"Hell," the loadmaster said, "we went over all that this morning at N'djili. He's got orders, and the captain says we take him to watcha-call-it, Albertville."

"There's no problem, Major," Steve said. "The plane will take him. There was some confusion this morning, but I wouldn't say the lieutenant was insulted. If he still wants to go, he can."

The lieutenant tried to speak. *"Taisez-vous,"* the major spat. "I think that this officer was trying to desert. However, he is assigned to Opérations Sud and not to this *groupement*. He will go to Albertville. We shall send a full report to his superiors at Ops Sud." He spoke rapidly to the lieutenant in Lingala. The lieutenant looked at the ground, holding the handkerchief to his face, then climbed shakily aboard the C-130.

"You see, monsieur," the major said, "there are still some bad elements in the Armée Nationale, even among the officers. Would the sergeant permit me to inspect the plane?"

"Be my guest," the sergeant said.

Gordon walked over to the plane, laughing, a flat Super-8 movie camera in his hand. "Nigger heaven," he said. "I got the whole thing down on film. They never believe the crap I have to put up with. Now I'll just show them the movie."

CHAPTER **10**

"How many people did the rebels execute here?" Steve asked. He and Charlie sat in the jeep in the shade of the coconut palms bordering the Place des Martyrs in the center of Stanleyville. It was three o'clock Tuesday, a hot afternoon and the last day of Steve's visit to the town. The streets were deserted.

Charlie looked across to the triangular park, weedy and overgrown, in the center of the square. Directly opposite them the fieldstone arcade that had once framed the Patrice Lumumba memorial lay crumbled in the sunlight like the toothless jawbone of a skull. The gaudy glass-and-stone monument that once had stood there had been used by the Simba rebels as an execution block during their occupation of the city a year earlier. After Stanleyville's recapture by the mercenary-led ANC the monument had been dynamited in a public effort to exorcise the ritualistic magic of the bloody spot. High weeds now grew in the rubble.

"It's really hard to say for sure," Charlie said. "Depends on whose side you want to take, whose story you want to believe. I know a United Nations doctor here who came back to Stan with the first civilians after the air drop. He told me that the blood and guts was caked a foot deep in front of the monument the day the ANC blew it up. You've got to kill a lot of people to get that much blood on the ground. The rebels claim they put a couple saboteurs in front of the firing squad after giving them fair trials. Like everything else in this goddamn country it's hard to tell what to believe. I think that most people agree, though, that the rebels butchered a hell of a lot of people here. You know, it wasn't very pretty either, so it got a lot of play in the papers—lots of *dawa* and magic involved, cannibalism, stuff like that. They'd eat some poor bastard's liver while the guy was still laying there watching them."

Steve sat staring at the weedy park. In his head he heard the screams of the victims and the flailing thuds of the pangas. He glanced around the square. Stanleyville's center was less modern than downtown Léopoldville. Most of the buildings were low and tin-roofed, blending with the tropical vegetation so that the occasional multistoried building seemed out of place. The vines and weeds had made inroads, combining with the battle damage to give the town a desolate, forsaken feeling.

During the two days he had driven and walked about the town, Steve had not seen a single building that did not have at least one bullet hole. Most of the cement façades were badly pockmarked by the machine guns of the rebels and mercenaries after five years of rebellion, secession, and reprisal. Looters from the rebels' People's Liberation Army and from the ranks of the ANC and the white mercenary commandos had gutted most of the former European and Asian stores that had thrived when Stanleyville was the commercial center of Orientale Province. The glassless, smoke-blackened stores now housed pitiful families of refugees. Even they were few in number.

Stanleyville's pre-Independence population of 80,000 had fallen to less than 35,000 in the five years of fighting. Most of the residents had either died or fled to the bush as crisis succeeded crisis and renegade troops replaced the savage tribesmen of the rebel army. After five years of independence the few remaining whites still carried weapons and the hard-eyed mercenaries drove about the decaying streets brandishing their guns. It was a sad, haunted city, slowly sinking back into the bush.

"It's really funny," Charlie said. "I was thinking about what you were saying last night. You know, the nature of the tropics— about how the whites can never understand the Africans and how we've got them turned ass-backwards to wanting what's good in the north. Look at all this—all these bullet holes and buildings falling into piles of weeds. You might have something there, boy. This is what happened to the cities. The villages—the African places—have hung together."

Steve smiled. He had shared the government apartment in the Immaquateur Building with Charlie for two days, and in that time he had come to like him, despite occasional periods of unsettling behavior.

"Well," he said, "it's just a theory, you know. I wouldn't put too much stock in it."

As Charlie drove around the empty square, a Congolese police-man dashed out of the shade and stood at the intersection, his arms spread apart, blocking their way. They waited blinking in the sun while he went through the motions he had been taught in traffic school, pivoting on his toes and twirling his white baton as he signaled them to pass. The two Americans and the solitary po-liceman were the only humans in the square.

"Poor bastard," Charlie said. "He's one of your Tropical Men, all right, really thinks that he has to do that to impress the whites. We're probably the first car he's stopped all day."

They were going down to the river to fish, the back of the jeep filled with fishing gear and a foam picnic cooler. They drove out a deserted avenue littered with the wheelless bodies of abandoned vehicles already stripped of windshields, seats, and all usable parts. Fallen palm fronds lay in rotting heaps beneath the trees. Unlike the houses in Léopoldville, the prewar brick villas built by the colonial civil servants had not been maintained and presented a shocking spectacle of decay. Liana vines ripped at the roofs. Most of the villas had been fought through in the street fighting and had served to billet troops at one time or another. Window and door frames had been ripped out for the cooking fires of the squatters now living in them—one family to a room. Black smoke stains competed with the cancerous mildew and mercenaries' obscene graffiti on the stucco walls. Potbellied children splashed in the mud of what had once been carefully tended gardens.

Steve reached back to open two bottles of Stanor beer. They were dripping cold. In the shade of the baobab trees along the airport highway the breeze felt cool, a relief from the malignant heat in the heart of the city. They passed the steel skeleton of the unfinished university buildings. A group of ragged children picked in the rubble of the abandoned construction site. Charlie took a long pull on his beer and began humming.

"That's fascinating stuff to think about," Charlie said. "Did you study much political science in school?"

"Mainly history," Steve said. "How about you?"

"Three and a half years of physics, and then I knocked this chick up—just some girl I met at a party at Berkeley, nurse, too, she should have known better—I had to quit to make some money. My parents would have kept helping me out if I'd married the girl, but I couldn't see marrying somebody I didn't even know. I was going to get drafted then, so I enlisted. She's gotten married since. Had a little girl, I understand. I guess I'll go back to school and study poli-sci when I get out next year. Although the idea of running a whorehouse certainly appeals to me. Actually I put in for an early release to start school again in February. I'm not counting on it, though—too much bullshit red tape in *this* army for something like that to come through so fast."

They laughed, bouncing over the potholed road in front of the sleeping complex of airport buildings. "Shit!" Charlie said, stopping at the barbed-wire barricade blocking the road opposite the guest house. The ANC had set up a barbed-wire and wooden-frame roadblock. It was guarded by a sand-bagged machine-gun emplacement on the baked mud beside the road. There were no soldiers at the barricade. Heavy metal slabs, studded with spikes, lay on either side of the wire.

"I'll pull that stuff out of the way," Steve said, getting down from the jeep.

"Wait a second," Charlie said. He pushed back his fatigue cap and scratched at a bite on his leg where his uniform trousers bloused over his boots. "They're around here someplace, probably up at the guest house drinking. They go down to the *cité* and drag girls up here in the afternoon to keep them company at night. They usually don't have the roadblock closed until dark, though. Don't mess with it. That's a good way to get shot."

Steve sat down again. They waited in the spotty shade watching for the soldiers. Off to their right on the airport tarmac a WIGMO mechanic was running up the engine of a T-28. The sun disappeared behind an afternoon thunderhead, causing Steve a sudden, unexpected chill as a breeze blew through the open front of his sweaty sports shirt.

"Come on, for Christ's sake," Charlie said. "I want to get some fishing in today." He sounded the horn. No one appeared at the glassless windows of the guest house. He honked again, beating out an insistent rhythm on the horn. As the sun came out again, he stopped. Twisting around, he reached in back, pushed the short-barreled M-16 aside, and jerked open the cooler. He pulled two long brown bottles of Stanor out of a bed of ice cubes. As he turned back, a tall black soldier appeared in the doorway, reeling there shirtless, an expression of drunken anger highlighting the tribal scars on his face.

"*Allez,*" he yelled. "*Va t'en. Pas moyen, c'est fermé.*"

"Horseshit it's *fermé,*" Charlie yelled back, standing next to the jeep with the beer bottles in his hand. Within ten seconds the drunken soldier was joined by another racing to pull aside the barricade. Charlie opened both bottles and handed the tall soldier one, indicating with a splitting motion that the two should share the bottle of beer. The smaller soldier wrinkled his brow and bent to pull the spike plate back into place. "O.K. Tonto, O.K.," Charlie said, handing over the second bottle.

As they drove through the roadblock, the two soldiers waved and grinned like children, calling, " '*Voir, patron, au 'voir.*" "The Noble Savage," Charlie said, glancing back over his shoulder. "That big son of a bitch killed a fisherman last week, right there at the roadblock. He was coming back on his bicycle from crocodile hunting, and the big bastard didn't like the way he looked or something. Cut him right down with his burp gun. The next day the fucking *groupement* sends a message to Léo that there had been an attempted rebel infiltration but that it had been repulsed by the vigilant troops at the airport roadblock."

They turned off the paved road onto a mud trail that wound through a stand of thick-trunked elaeis oil palms. Many of the older trees were beyond production and were smothered by parasitic vines. On others Steve noticed ripe clusters of copperish orange palm nuts. The lane was deserted. "Doesn't look like people have been cutting these palm nuts," he said.

"That's right," Charlie said, "The villagers are still hiding out in the bush. They're afraid to come out here and cut them because they'd have to go back through the ANC roadblocks. ANC won't come out because they're afraid of the rebels. In other words, we got a real happy little community here."

The jeep bounced along the double furrow of hardened mud tracks, occasionally striking a hidden soft patch which Charlie skillfully negotiated. The palms gave way to a mixed scrub forest of small hardwoods, mangoes, and a scattering of vine-covered pepper trees. They broke clear and drove along the low bank of the river, a screen of coconut palms between their path and the water. They coasted down a smooth incline, across a muddy stream bed, and shot up the steep ledge of the bank, the gears screaming in four-wheel drive.

In front of them was a flat tongue of grassy land and palms extending out into the current of the gray-green river. Beneath the trees a cluster of conical palm-frond huts lay silent and apparently deserted. An immense spotted nanny goat was tethered to a stake in the shade of one of the huts. Multicolored chickens pecked in the dust between the huts. Steve could smell cook fires and the sour odor of manioc. Charlie stopped the jeep in the shade and killed the motor.

"Nobody home," Steve said.

"They're here, all right," Charlie said. "They're just hiding in the bush. Heard the motor and figured it was the ANC looking for goats or the mercs looking for girls." He got down from the jeep and walked to the edge of the clearing. "Hey, Boniface. Come in.

It's all right. No danger. It's me, *Bwana* Charlie." The only sound from the forest was the chattering of monkeys, disguising their calls to sound like birds.

They unloaded their fishing equipment and went down to the water's edge. The river was narrower here, so they could clearly see individual trees on the opposite bank. A long, well-made pirogue was pulled up onto the grass of the riverbank. Its bottom was swept clean, and three handsomely carved paddles lay against it. They loaded their gear aboard and waited.

Charlie took off his uniform and boots and waded into the swirling water in swimming trunks. Steve joined him and splashed in the shallows as the softness of the current tried to pull them out into the main channel of the river. When they came out, they dried their faces and hands on their shirts and stood shivering in the slight but steady breeze off the water.

In the forest a dog snarled and barked twice before it howled in pain from an admonishing blow. An old man and three younger men, obviously relatives, came into the clearing. The old man wore a faded piece of wax cloth, saronglike about his waist, but the younger men had on dirty khaki shorts. *"Jambo sana, Boni- face,"* Charlie said, shaking the old man's hand. Steve joined him and they exchanged *jambos* and handshakes formally with the group. In broken Swahili Charlie explained his intention to fish, and the four Africans listened intently, nodding their heads and uttering guttural noises of interest as Charlie pointed to the pirogue and the fishing equipment piled in it. Charlie turned to Steve, smiling. "I go through the same deal every week," he said. "They really dig this palaver bit. They know they're going to get some beer and maybe two hundred francs, but they have to hear the whole proposition all over again each time and let the old man decide. It's great."

Boniface's pirogue was beamy and stable in the swift current spiraling off the riblike roots of the hardwood trees farther down the bank. The three younger men paddled as Boniface crouched in the rear of the boat, his cloth tucked up like a diaper. They tied the pirogue to a clump of roots so that it floated free in the shade and they were able to fish another wider patch of deep shade ten meters farther downstream. Charlie opened two bottles of beer, gave one to the old man and the other to the three paddlers to share. They baited their spinners with fat grubs the old man produced from a folded leaf. With regular strokes of the paddles the pirogue was kept broadside to the current so that Steve and Charlie could both fish the shady patch without tangling their lines. It was very pleasant with the water still wet on their backs and the steady breeze off the river. The forest was silent around them; the only noise in their entire world was the faint gurgle of the river on the blades of the paddles and the clicking of their reels.

A capitaine took Charlie's spinner with a wild jerk and tore off downriver, bowing the rod sharply. Steve drew in his bait. The three paddlers jumped to move the pirogue out into the current to give Charlie room to maneuver the fish away from the safety of tree roots along the shore. Charlie played the big fish, pulling it in and letting it out until it tired. A silver shadow appeared in the water next to the boat. It was huge. The old man crushed its skull with one stroke of a paddle handle, and it lay inert on the bottom of the boat.

"Wow," Charlie said. "That's the biggest damn fish I ever caught. Looks just like a muskie, doesn't it?" He turned to the old man. *"Makubwa,"* he said.

"Makubwa sana," Boniface chuckled. *"Makubwa sana, bwana."*

Later they swam again in the shade in front of the huts. The women and children had returned. They cleaned Charlie and Steve's catch and, following Charlie's directions, cut the fish into filets. Charlie selected several choice pieces but left most of it for the Africans. He and Steve sat in their wet trunks on low, carved wooden chairs that Boniface had placed at the river's edge. Downriver, thunderheads they had seen building up from the apartment had now risen to fantastic heights and were billowing out into classical mushroom formations. They split the last bottle of Stanor as they sat smoking in the shade. "Not a bad life, is it?" Steve said.

"Beats the hell out of working for a living," Charlie said. "Yeah, the major would be wild if he knew I was goofing off, but it's ridiculous to try and get anything done with the ANC in the afternoon. Everybody's either drunk or sleeping. The major's kind of a hard charger—you know. Makes me carry this M-16 whenever I go out of town. I guess he knows his business—it's just that this place isn't Vietnam."

The clouds of the thunderhead system to the south were reflected nicely in the wide river. Charlie belched loudly and smiled. "Such a pretty place here. Vietnam's pretty too, but nowhere near as wild-feeling as this. Sitting on the river like this, I can really feel the whole geography of Africa, know what I mean?

"It's *all* right there," Charlie continued, describing a slow arc across the forest horizon. "The Lualaba comes in down there to join the Congo—same river, really, like the Missouri and the Mississippi. Then it climbs up north to the equator in that big curve and takes in the Ubangi and the others and dips down south to drain the Kasai and all the smaller ones. The Congo basin—it's just like an artery system in a body. Can't you feel it? Sometimes sitting up there on the terrace of my apartment watching the river, I think about Léopoldville a thousand miles downstream like I was sitting in Minneapolis thinking about New Orleans, and the size of this goddamn country really hits me over the head.

"And then, back there . . ." He swiveled in his seat, pointing behind him to the northeast. "Over there you've got the whole Nile system beginning—little streams and rivers all flowing together to form tributaries and lakes and rivers, and then the Nile running off through the savannah to the desert all the way on up to the Mediterranean. I know the Nile itself is a long way from here, but sometimes I can just feel the whole pattern clicking into place and all of a sudden I'm right in the heart of Africa and I can really feel it stretching away in all directions."

They were silent for a long while, absorbed in the river surging by between forested banks. One of Boniface's sons went past them toward the palm trees on the point. Skillfully, using a braided fiber belt wrapped around the trunk, he climbed a tree with a series of graceful motions and appeared silhouetted against the sky beneath the green fronds. Swinging his panga in short strokes, he cut several coconuts, which plummeted to the ground with loud thuds. Behind him the lowering sun was beginning to gild the thunderheads and the gray river flowed by.

"Wow!" Charlie said softly. "How about *that* for Africa!"

The man slid back down the trunk, his toes gripping the smooth bark. Smiling, he hacked off the husk of a coconut and chipped away a hole in the end. They drank the cool milk. From the charcoal fire in front of the huts they could smell the fish cooking in a spicy palm oil sauce.

"Want to try some of Boniface's wine?" Charlie asked.

"Sure, I guess so," Steve said. "Is it any good?"

"It's fantastic."

They drank the milky palm wine from carved coconut shells. Boniface had placed a large calabash of wine next to their chairs so that as they sat watching the thunderheads and the river they could refill their cups. The day was still quite bright, and despite the low angle of the sun, deep metallic-blue patches stood out sharply among the dark clouds.

"This stuff is pretty good," Steve said. "I never would have guessed it."

"Haven't you ever had a real African meal? You know, a big crocodile mwamba with rice and manioc greens and pili-pili and plenty of palm wine?"

"I'm afraid we don't have very much contact with the Congolese down in Léo."

"That's a shame," Charlie said, refilling his cup. "In a way, though, it might be a good thing. Could you picture old Dwight and Dorothy Reed sitting here drinking palm wine?"

"You know," Steve said, "I think I'm getting a little drunk on this stuff. I feel kind of strange."

Charlie smiled. "It's sort of sneaky, this palm wine old Boniface makes. I think it keeps on fermenting in your stomach. I never had a bad hangover from it, though. But it can give you a pretty good case of the runs if you don't watch out."

Steve went to the jeep to fetch his shirt. With the shifting of the breeze he felt the evening chill falling on the river. Boniface and the other men sat on their heels near the largest hut, nursing the beer Charlie had given them, as they talked softly of the day's fishing, gesturing flamboyantly with their hands. Steve felt dizzy. The palm wine was working. Charlie was walking along the edge of the water, kicking little clods of earth into the current when Steve returned.

"Hey, listen," he said excitedly, "you want to try something really nice? I don't know how you feel about it or anything, but maybe you'd like to try it."

"Try what?"

"Smoking some of Boniface's stuff. It's really out of sight."

"You mean hemp?" Steve asked.

"Right. They call it hemp and that sounds pretty strong or evil or something, but it's really just grass, same plant as the stuff you get in the States only so much better. Best stuff I ever had, honest to God."

Steve was silent for a moment, avoiding Charlie's eye.

"Hell. You must have smoked in Morocco, didn't you? With all that good kif they've got there?"

"Actually, we never did. A lot of the other kids were doing it, but we just never did, for some reason. I think I was mainly worried about the side effects—of what it would do to you afterwards."

"You mean would you all of a sudden wake up with this irresistible urge to start shooting heroin or something, that you'd turn into a *dope fiend?*"

Steve laughed self-consciously. "I guess that's what I thought." He paused. "There was the whole legal thing too, you know. I was in the Peace Corps and I guess I was a pretty straight shooter. I didn't want to screw up my whole life by getting kicked out for smoking pot."

"Yeah," Charlie said, shaking his head, "they really can *control* you. They've got this law club to hold over your head. Well, listen, if you smoke some here *I'm* not about to blow the whistle on you."

"I know. It's just that I was thinking, what about the wine—would it be O.K. to smoke pot after drinking so much of that?"

"They're *beautiful* together. This grass of Boniface's is so strong that you almost need the wine like a clutch or something to slow down. It's a great experience, believe me. You won't find better grass than this anyplace. Congo Red, wow! It hits you stronger than most hash, but it doesn't last too long. What do you say?"

Out of nowhere Steve had a sudden vision of the shirt drawer in his bedroom dresser. Neatly stacked in it by the houseboy were his starched button-down-collar shirts, pastels and white, like the uniform display in a military locker. Each morning after breakfast, always running several minutes behind schedule, he would dash into the air-conditioned bedroom, dust quickly with talcum, and slide into a crisp shirt. Next followed the striped tie. As he flew from the cool bedroom, he would hook his thumb through the lapel loop of that day's wash-and-wear suit coat or jacket. That was his life—short sleeves in the morning and cuff links for the evening's reception. Every six months another Sears order would arrive with new wash-and-wear clothes to protect his body from the cold drafts and imitation leather of the Political Section. That was all there was.

"O.K.," Steve said, breaking sharply from his unexpected reverie. "Yeah, why the hell not. I really think I'd like to try a little of that Congo Red."

"You see how it's turned into an elephant's head? See, there's the trunk." Steve sat upright in his chair, pointing out across the sky at the big thunderhead on the horizon. A limb of the cloud was now distended to the right, becoming a trumpeting elephant outlined in incandescent peach by the hidden sun.

"Yeah," Charlie said, looking up. "That's really something, all right." He leaned back and finished refilling the conical stone bowl of Boniface's gourd pipe. The pipe was bulbous, filling the palm of his hand, the water inside it gurgling softly as he swayed and tilted the last of the leaf-ful of chopped hemp into the bowl and tamped it with his thumb. "That should just about do it, old buddy," he said. "That's four pipesful, or is it five?"

"God only knows." Steve giggled. "Hey! *Now* I see, O.K., you were *smoking* Christmas night up at the Reeds'. I thought you were drinking, but you weren't. You were *smoking*."

"Brilliant deduction, Sherman, you'll be an ambassador someday."

Steve took the lighted pipe. The smoke entered his lungs easily. There was practically no taste, no discomfort as the sloshing water in the gourd cooled and washed the smoke. Following Charlie's instructions, he pulled deeply, holding the lungful until his chest ached. He felt fantastic. His mind raced through a kaleidoscope of thoughts. He shivered with the unexpected softness of the late afternoon. He'd had no idea smoking would be like this. Charlie's laughter shattered out over the river. "Man, that old Boniface is a *genius*. This Congo Red is so *good*. He could make a million bucks off the kids in L.A. alone. *So* good, wow!"

Steve stood up and paced slowly toward the water. The earth beneath his feet felt strangely soft. Suddenly he could smell the decay of the forest all about him. Like the sluggish wash of the backed-up *cité* sewers, the mildewed wave of rotting vegetation washed over him and he almost retched. Even the soil under him was dead. Eyeless columns of ants and millipedes tunneled the ground he walked on. It could collapse at any moment.

On the horizon the sun hung dull as red lead paint. He did not want the sun to sink. The thunderhead elephant smeared into the skull of a crocodile, laughing at him for his ridiculous pride. Brushing his leg, he saw with horror that a mosquito was sucking his blood. How could there be such things, animals that lived on the *blood* of other beings?

Charlie was there next to him, smiling. "How you doin', Steve?"

"I . . ." Steve began, but his mouth was gummy from the sticky dried palm wine on his lips. "I feel kind of weird. I don't know how I feel."

"You're just stoned," Charlie said. "The first time is always strange. Don't worry. Nothing's going to happen to you. You're supposed to feel funny. It's normal."

A long time passed in Steve's head. He and Charlie were perfectly still beside the moving river. "Yeah," Steve finally said. Then there was another long silence. "Yeah, but I really feel weird. Everything looks very strange."

"You're stoned, Steve. Sometimes it's a little weird, like being paranoid."

As the sun fell, Steve was suddenly aware of the chattering bands of monkeys swinging through the high branches above Boniface's huts. He had a flash of the infant monkeys clinging precariously to their mothers' fur. If one fell from that height, its blue-veined skull would shatter like an egg. Closing his eyes, he waited in terror for the monkeys to pass safely by.

Charlie dragged Steve's chair to him across the beaten earth of the riverbank. "Is it always like this?" Steve asked, moving his lips and tongue with great effort. "With sounds and colors, I mean."

Charlie stared out at the water, humming. "Yeah," he whispered, "but with the two of them together, the pot and palm wine, it's always a little different each time. . . . I'm really zonked myself, but I've had so much of this shit that I know where I'm at. It must really be strange for you."

Another mosquito alighted on Steve's bare arm. This time he felt only curiosity. Holding his arm against the sunset, he watched the insect tilt itself and plunge its hollow beak into his flesh. He could see that the mosquito, silhouetted against the sky, was swelling. Satisfied, the mosquito disappeared into the sky. "What a freaky thing to do," Charlie said. "I couldn't do something like that stoned. I'd really flip out. Wow! Listen, how does your head feel now?"

"Weird," Steve said. "But if you say it's O.K., I won't worry. How long does it last, this weird part?"

"Not very long. After a while you learn to play with it. You get these really awful insights that seem so fucking terrible you can't stand them, and then when you're down they all seem so silly. As far as I can see, that's the only negative thing about grass, especially really strong stuff like this. You've got to be careful how you take it. You can't be in a freaky situation, otherwise you can get blown out of your skull. How do you feel now?"

"I feel beautiful now. That thundercloud down there is incredible. It's changing all the time. Do you see the crocodile's head now?"

"You don't feel aggressive, like getting in a fight or breaking anything up, do you?" Charlie got up again and paced along the riverbank very slowly. His voice changed. "That's why they're down on this stuff in the States. Booze makes you aggressive, but grass calms you down. That's why they don't like it. They're afraid of it. If we had been sitting around drinking whisky all day, we wouldn't even be able to see the river right, let alone the sunset. A little bit of grass opens up your mind and you can see things. Booze just shuts it down. . . . In California there's a whole lot of kids now who never drank booze, just smoked grass. . . . They can see stuff that's really beautiful, and then they see a lot of really ugly stuff too. So that's why the government and everybody's trying to bust them. They don't want people to see things. They want them to stay drunk all the time and not make any trouble. They don't give a shit how many hoods beat the crap out of people with chains or how many guys get all boozed up and aggressive and kill themselves and twenty other people on Interstate 90. That's O.K., but if kids smoke a little grass and go down to a park and want to take off their clothes and sing a couple songs in the sunshine, then they get their heads smashed open and their asses dragged off to jail."

As Charlie spoke, Steve's field of vision condensed down to a rectangular screen of grays, so that Charlie appeared to be speaking on a television screen, his voice becoming electronic in quality. Steve could still see the river and the polychrome sky, but they became less important than the rectangular window through which Charlie was speaking. Charlie had become THE SPEAKER—THE COMMENTATOR. Steve did not answer. One did not talk to a machine.

"Yeah," Charlie continued, "well, all that's going to change. We're not buying that shit any more. You know what they want us to do? They want us to poison ourselves. . . . Did you ever see those places in New York along, say, Forty-Second Street, or up and down Sixth and Seventh Avenues? Those great big booze bars that open up at seven o'clock in the morning? They've got absolutely no atmosphere. They aren't supposed to have any. They're just like a Phillips 66 gas station, only instead of gassing cars they pump out poison to keep the poor zombies of the cities moving. They've got these great big upside-down bottles of whisky and gin with little steel nipples on them to suck out instant shots. The counters are red fake marble plastic and there's a million red-hot fluorescent tubes burning your head like an H-bomb. There's usually about three TV sets going with some asshole quiz program, and then the jukebox pumps this sweet kindergarten melody shit at you, and you stand there and put down your money and suck down your poison. It's best to see them about seven, eight in the morning. They're all lined up there at the plastic bar, drinking their shots and beers, getting themselves ready for another day. The zombies—truckdrivers, cabdrivers, guys who work down in the goddamn subway like *moles* all day long, when they come out it's dark already, off-duty cops and a lot who aren't off duty. They're beautiful places, those no-nonsense poison bars in New York.

"But you know what? They're a hell of a lot more honest than the sweet armpit, two-fifty-a-drink cocktail bars. I mean, they're both poison joints, right? Only one looks like a poison joint, so that's honest. The other looks like some kind of a hospital, or like how a hospital should look, all comfortable and cozy with these sweet-talking young chicks to bring you your poison in little bowls of crushed ice. When a guy who's a bolt turner on an assembly line goes into one of the plastic hard-drink places, he knows that he's still a creep who drives screws all day into the same hunk of metal for three-eighty-three an hour, he knows what the hell he is and he doesn't like it, so he gets drunk and goes bowling and comes home and bitches at his ugly wife, right?"

Steve did not answer; he stared at Charlie's face on the screen.

"But," Charlie continued, holding up a finger like a school-teacher, "when some dopey young *management trainee* stumbles into one of these leather-upholstered, stereo places, he *forgets* who the hell he is and starts imagining he's some stud out of *Playboy*. And pretty soon the whole crummy cocktail lounge is full of these guys, drinking down their fucking Gibsons and putting each other on and hoping to squeeze the ass of the vacuum-headed bouffant hairpiece down the bar there who looks like she might do TV commercials but really runs a switchboard and tells all the dopey guys that she's at CBS. So that's the scene in America, baby. Poison. Only the people who won't buy this shit any more are finally getting together, and there's going to be a lot happening pretty soon."

Steve laughed and Charlie frowned. "What's funny?" he said.

"I see your face like it was on a TV screen. No color, all gray, a little box."

Charlie rummaged clumsily in his tackle box in the jeep for a cigar. The only light left in the sky clung to the pillar of crocodile cloud downriver. Now Charlie was laughing. At first he chuckled to himself and then he flopped onto his chair and rolled with laughter. "Oh, wow! You know what I was doing? I was *compensating!* Holy Christ! I got all boozed up last week with the mercs, and I must have been feeling guiltier than shit ever since, so I get a little stoned and start putting you on about booze. Wow!"

Steve broke into giggles and together they laughed until their throats constricted with painful gasps. Charlie tossed Steve a bottle of GI insect repellent, which floated through the air. "It's true though, what I was saying. I was just being pretty shitty about the way I said it. That's the great thing about grass—you can see yourself doing stuff like that."

One of the young men approached and stood just to the side of their chairs, shifting shyly from one foot to the other. He carried a low hardwood stool and an enamel basin of food. Charlie nodded his head with regal solemnity, and the boy placed the food before them on the stool.

They ate the steaming fish with their fingers, breaking off orange pieces of boiled plantains to soak up the rich palm-oil sauce. Steve felt carried away with the food. The sweet-potato texture of the plantains seemed to have been expertly contrived to aid in absorbing the sauce. Suddenly he thought that this was easily the best food he had ever eaten, that this was the *perfect* meal. With a meal like this he didn't have to think, he didn't have to worry, to ponder the alarming oracles which Charlie had delivered as THE COMMENTATOR. He wouldn't think about such things. He would concentrate on the food.

Steve stared at the last light on the river. In his mind he saw America, his country, disintegrating into a sea of repression. His mind went racing ahead of itself. Kids in Freedom Rider overalls were being herded down the streets by club-swinging hoodlums, whisky bottles in their hip pockets. Electronic slogans flashed across the skies of smoky, crowded cities: "Work Harder to Drink Harder." "Kill the Weaklings." Long-haired kids lay tortured on operating tables. His brothers became police informers. They were coming for him. They had already taken Lisa; the police sergeant arresting her confided to Steve, "Nothing really wrong with her that a little gang rape won't cure, right?" He winked obscenely at

Steve, and they dragged her out by the hair to the paddy wagon.
"Hey," he said weakly to Charlie. "What about this paranoia
you were talking about? Is it really strong sometimes?"

"When you smoke as much as we did, you get some freaky
thoughts," Charlie said, sounding to Steve like a medical professor
explaining the symptoms to his class. "Like I said, you learn after
a while not to let them worry you. To play with your brain and
see which way it'll go. You can see what's really bugging you
then. Look at it that way. The only thing to avoid is a really
freaky scene like a fight or anger or a war when you're stoned like
this. Then you can't handle scenes like that."

"Did you ever have one like that?" Steve asked, afraid of Charlie's answer, but driven by curiosity.

"Yeah, baby," Charlie said, "yeah, I sure did."

"In Vietnam?" Steve said, his voice almost cracking.

"Yeah, in old 'Vit-name' all right," he said, pronouncing the
word in GI hillbilly patois.

"What happened?"

"You really want to hear about it? It's not a very pleasant story.
You don't feel freaky now, do you?"

"Not really," Steve said too quickly. "I feel fine. I'd actually be
very curious to hear what happened to you." His voice rang in his
ears. *He* was a management trainee. Why had he spoken that way
to Charlie? Charlie would despise him for it. He would be pun-
ished for his insincerity.

But that was the way they *all* spoke, all the bright young men at
the Embassy. Sitting about the life-giving maw of the air-condi-
tioning duct in the Political Section over morning coffee and the
reading file, that's the way they spoke. "Good *morning,* William,"
they would say. "And how are *you* this morning? That certainly
was some party last night, wasn't it?" "You bet! Anything happening in the world today?" "Nothing that we have to get too excited about, just the usual riots and revolutions. They're rioting in
Africa, tra-la-la-la-la-la." "Ha, ha, ha, ah, heh, heh, heh." "Would
you and Ginny feel like a little bridge tonight after the do at the
Canadians' . . . you *are* going, aren't you?" "Well, *ac*tually, we
didn't receive an invitation, but I saw What's-his-name, their
DCM, Thornton, at the Mission Culturel concert last night and he

seemed to assume I'd been invited. I guess we'll go. It sounds like it might be a fun thing for a change. Ginny wants to go, I know, the hors-d'oeuvres at the Devinière are really too much of a temptation to pass up." Tra-la-la. Expensive, well-tailored wash-and-wear, crisp and witty. Princeton ties and Phi Beta Kappa keys. In the airlock of the Political Section, a staging post on their way upstairs. Steve sat in the corner, the junior, the new boy who showed promise but had a lot to learn about the serious business of drafting cables, airgrams, memoranda.

That was so good, *memoranda.* Twice in a single morning he had been gently corrected with just the proper amount of castigation. First he had said memoran*dums,* and Pete Joyce had quickly prevailed with "Yes, these *memoranda* of conversation *do* seem a bit long, don't they?" Worse still, he had dared to venture an unpopular opinion, compounding his error by saying, "I really think the fellows at USIS know best what media are effective. I've always thought that motion pictures were a very effective media." "Well, *we* feel that films as a *medium* might be a little too overworked." Little slashing slaps delivered with a smile. He was a trainee, after all, very good potential for a boy from a Big Ten school, but he had a long way to go before he could pull his own weight. Media? Memorandums? These things were not serious in themselves, but they were *indicators.* One really had to be careful with a new officer. One did this and one did that. Indicators pointed to cans of worms and the whole ball of wax needed clarification on a priority basis or interests might well be compromised to the detriment of wider policy considerations which would very possibly kick up dust on the Hill which would be unfortunate in view of the Area's desires to see this thing through to a mutually satisfactory conclusion. . . .

Is that the way he really talked? Was that what he was grooming himself to become? Somewhere under his gun in the old Co-op briefcase there was even a pipe. He had actually ordered a good Turkish meerschaum pipe. How long before the shell-rimmed glasses appeared?

Charlie sucked at the tip of his cigar. "Hey," he said, "you look like you seen a ghost or something. You O.K.?"

"I'm O.K.," Steve said, his voice more natural in his head.

"Yeah," Charlie continued, "so anyway, that was my last night in Vietnam, down there in Saigon processing out. Me and this other kid, Jerry, had been hanging out together. He got paranoid about carrying back this big stash of mellow grass from the Delta, so we smoked most of it in our room out at the NCO billet and got really superstoned. Then we went down and had a Chinese dinner and went over to Jerry's favorite whorehouse and smoked some more and Jesus we were stoned! There was a terrorist scare on and we couldn't get a pedicab, so we start stumbling back to the billet about one o'clock in the morning."

Steve watched Charlie's bobbing head as he walked along the riverbank. The television screen dissolved and Charlie grew in stature until he was talking down at Steve from a long extension ladder that was his body.

"So then," Charlie continued, his cadence accelerating compulsively, "We're walking down this long, busted-up street where they're putting in water mains or something, and it was really a bitch to cross over these piles of dirt and broken pavement and stuff, stoned like that in the dark. At the end of the ditches some MPs stopped us and checked our IDs and passes, brand-new spec fours fresh from Fort Gordon, all uptight about the VC. Jerry's been there for two tours in the Delta, and he starts putting these kids on, telling them war stories like how you can always tell a real VC by a little notch they cut in their ears or some stupid shit like that, and these kids are sitting in their jeep eating it up. They had their flak jackets on and everything, and they were sweating like pigs and Jerry's trying to act straight 'cause he still has one of those great big mother joints in his pocket. We were about twenty yards down the street from the billet and it was way the hell after midnight and there was nobody on the street.

"Then a scooter comes bouncing up from around the side of the billet with a guy in an ARVN Ranger tiger suit with a carbine on his back, and he goes past us smiling, and the MPs wave him through like they were traffic cops. Jerry's still putting them on, and I start to take a piss in back of the jeep when the whole fucking world blows up.

"The cat on the scooter had laid down a big *plastique* in the alley next to the billet, blew the front off the building, shit falling all over the place, big hunks of glass and plaster. There must have been something wrong with the fuse 'cause the VC guy on the scooter was right near us when the thing went off—he was trying to haul his Lambretta over the piles of dirt where they had dug up the road. Everything slowed way the hell down for me right then. These big pieces of bricks and windows were flying through the air, and the MPs and Jerry were on the ground, and I couldn't hear a fucking thing except my own heart, which I really couldn't hear so much as feel in my ears, pumping away.

"One of the MPs was trying to put a tourniquet or a dressing on Jerry's crotch, and his fatigues were all black and purple. He was just deader than shit. A big hunk of steel or something jagged had got him right in the balls. The other MP was hit too—one of his ears was hanging down the side of his head and he was screaming like a stuck pig, only I couldn't hear him, like a silent movie. I'd been leaning against one of those big dirty trees like a catalpa, in back of the jeep, so I'd been protected from the blast and flying stuff. Then a guy in shorts and shower clogs carrying an M-14 grabs me, pointing at the VC in the ARVN uniform who was also hit and had dumped his scooter and was trying to run away down a side street. I picked up my M-16 and followed this other guy, and we come to a long wall down an alley and he says like you go that way and I'll go this way and then he takes off. The streetlights were all off, except on the next street over there were lights, and you could just barely see what the hell was happening. And I was still completely stoned on my ass, only more so 'cause I couldn't hear anything." Charlie's words flowed out in a nervous blur, pinning Steve to his chair.

"So I sat down on the ground. Don't ask me why. And I was sitting there for a long time when I think I hear these shots like an M-14 on auto blasting away, and then in the dark I see this figure limping up the alley, and it's the VC, only he's taken off the top of his tiger suit and he's got a gook shirt on underneath that's covered with blood. He doesn't see me sitting there, so I raise my weapon. So as I start to pull back on the operating rod, I think, really slow, slower than I ever thought before, even when I'd been stoned, I think, do you really want to kill this cat? I mean I'd been up in Dalat a year teaching ARVN cadets and never even *seen* a VC, not even a prisoner. And he's coming limping up this alley and still doesn't see me, so I cock my rifle, and when he's about five feet away I just blow his head off with a long burst. Then—you'll never believe this—the *streetlights* all come on again, and about sixteen jeeploads of MPs show up with their headlights all pointing at this dead VC. His eyes and the top of his head are all gone and there's hot blood all over the ground. And I've just killed me a real VC. Wow!"

Charlie stopped bobbing his head and stood perfectly still, facing Steve. From his position in the chair Steve could see Charlie's red hair and eyebrows glowing faintly against the dim evening sky. The grin on his mottled, sun-red face was demoniacal. "Isn't that a beautiful story?" he said, his voice thin and metallic in Steve's ears.

"Did it really happen like that?" Steve whispered.

"Fucking straight it really happened," Charlie said. "I oughta know—I've been a little crazy ever since. That isn't the end of the story, though." He made a trumpet with his hands and did a tinny fanfare. "The moral," he said in an announcer's voice, "of this tragic episode will now be made clear to each and every one of you." He dissolved into laughter.

"Like I said," Charlie continued, "these twenty-five jeeps full of MPs show up with their spotlights and people are yelling stuff at me, only I can't hear so I sit down and give away my weapon and just start crying. Back at the billet there's a *thousand* MPs and about a hundred ambulances with real doctors, not just medics, and bottles of plasma and bloody shirts and jockey shorts all over piles of plaster and glass. Nobody in the billet was killed except the gook janitor, who, I heard later, was probably VC—the guy who was supposed to move the *plastique* into the billet so that it'd really do some damage. Anyway, he got blown into two pieces and they had the body sort of put together in a pile, hands and feet gone completely. They had him tucked under a poncho. Right next to him they had Jerry on a stretcher. He was under a poncho too, just his boots sticking out.

"All of a sudden about three cars, full of colonels, show up and everybody's busy sucking ass and saluting. Then the reporters and TV crews show up right in back of the colonels. Pretty soon they've got floodlights hotter than hell on everything, and this TV guy's standing there with a microphone talking into a movie camera. The colonels who'd just gotten there were busting their asses to get into the TV show, so the first thing I really hear again is this one really RA light-colonel with a moustache and a pearl-handled .45 in a shoulder holster talking about how the vigilance of the MPs prevented a real tragedy from occurring. He's an MP colonel, you see, so he can't miss a chance to put in a little commercial.

"It was all pretty weird because no matter how hard I tried I couldn't come down from the high—I was still so stoned that it all seemed like a big joke. Then they had me up in front of the camera with the guy in the underwear who got me to go with him to chase the VC. This light-colonel was running around crazy, trying to shove MPs into the scene too. The TV lights were really hot, and I could smell the blood-and-gut shit from Jerry and the two VC laying there at our feet, and I was stoned on my ass and I knew I was going to start laughing.

"But then I see this little group of gook civilians edging around the side of the crowd to get a look at the bodies. There were a couple men, husky guys like they were dock workers, and some old ladies and a bunch of little kids, still sleepier than hell, but also really scared by all the confusion. They were all looking at the two VC, the janitor blown in two pieces laying in a big shitty puddle and the guy I killed, his face all gone. They didn't even bother looking at Jerry's body. The little kids were especially impressed. They kept looking from the stiffs up at me and back at the stiffs. Then instead of laughing I started to cry, real tears like I hadn't cried since I was a little kid. They shined the camera lights in my face really hard then and a lot of flash bulbs went off and then they took me away."

Charlie went over and slouched down in his chair. From the darkness they could hear the low voices of Boniface's people preparing for bed. A small, smoky fire burned before the main hut.

"So," Charlie said. "The moral like I promised. Every good story's got to have a moral.

"They took me out to the Bien Hoa airport early in the ambulance with a couple other guys who were getting evacuated. Believe it or not, I was still a little stoned. It had only been about four hours since Jerry and I had smoked those last joints. I swore I wasn't going to start crying again, not with all those other guys around who were really wounded. So I wandered around for a while over to where they're unloading a bunch of C-130s. They were just finished taking crates of small-arms ammunition out of this one and fueling it up for the return trip at the same time. So, I sat there with my red evacuation tag pinned on my shirt watching them start to load the plane for the trip back to the States.

"The ground crew guys are looking nervous and the loadmaster from the crew that's taking the plane back is walking around chewing people out. They're waiting for something, I could see that. Then a big helo comes in, one of those big old flying bananas with the double rotors, a red cross painted on it. When they start to unload it, I see why everybody was a little nervous. They were carrying bodies, you know, dead guys, dead kids inside green rubber bags, no stretchers, just these stiff green rubber bags with the long zippers in them."

"Bags," Steve gasped, "green bags?"

Charlie nodded. "Yeah. All I could think of was the seed pods in *Invasion of the Body Snatchers,* and I thought I was going to start laughing. Except then I *knew* that Jerry was inside one of those bags, and I started to cry again, not loud like a little kid, just sort of weeping, soft so nobody would notice. Then do you know what? As they started to load them on the plane, the loadmaster checked the tag on each one to see how much it *weighed.* They had other cargo to carry, and he had to weigh these dead guys to make sure they weren't overweight. And then it all fell into place, what the whole thing was all about.

"It wasn't a question of politics or freedom or infiltration or allies or any of that stuff they tell you on TV. It's just a question of room in a *plane.* We were going to win—I could see that just as clear as anything. We had more planes. We had bigger planes and more guys to fly them. All we had to do was fill those one-thirties up with ammunition and fly 'em out and then fill them up with *Invasion of the Body Snatchers* bags for the trip back and we would win. It would probably be better to send small guys over because you could get more bodies in that way for the trip home. The perpetual motion machine—ammo out, body bags back, courtesy of the Military Air Transport Service, MATS at your service."

Charlie's weird laughter burst out loudly, startling night birds. He turned to Steve and continued. "So from *there* I was home in two days. Hell, it wasn't even a couple of days, more like thirty-five hours, direct from all that blood and shit to my old man's tri-level in Brentwood. What the hell could I talk to them about? They'd seen the whole plastique number the night before on TV, and they thought I was a real hero. My old man's in the fucking *insurance game,* see what I mean? He's a Legionnaire. First night back he brings around a bunch of his real estate and insurance buddies and expects me to give them the real lowdown on the war, right down there in the rec room smoking cigars and drinking Scotch with these old farts. Christ, I really thought I'd flip that night. But I kept it cool. How I did it I don't really know.

"I went down to Long Beach the next morning and bought a whole bag of grass that I smoked on the beach or driving around on the freeways. The rest of the time I just got stoned at home and watched TV.

"Everything was cool for about a week and then Watts happened. We were all out on the patio in back getting a barbecue ready. There were neighbors coming, and I had just smoked a joint in my room and was drinking pink ladies or some other shit when my sister comes running out of the house saying that we all should come in to the TV because the niggers are rioting and it looks like they'll burn down the whole town. So that night we brought out the little TV from the den and had our barbecue watching the niggers burn down Watts. I kept going to my room, getting more stoned, and slept pretty bad. The next day it was still going on, and that night it was really bad, and I kept smoking more shit, and that night I freaked out. You could actually *see* the glow in the sky from the fires. It was just like Saigon with the flare planes out on the paddies.

"Then on the TV they start showing all these bodies laying around bloody with the cops and state troopers and National Guard guys all sucking up to the camera the same way the MP colonel did and these pissed-off, scared black faces in the TV lights just like the gook civilians in front of the billet in Saigon, and all of a sudden it was too much. I could really *see* it. We go all the way across the world to kill people, and then that ain't good enough, so we start in on the poor spades in Watts. It was all just body bags. I got really stoned that night, and then I packed my suitcase and took my old lady's Mustang and spent the rest of my leave in Mexico."

Charlie swallowed and spat out a fleck of cigar. "Yeah," he said wearily, "I guess we better be going. The ANC at the roadblocks will be good and drunk by now and we'll probably have a hard time getting through. How do you feel anyway?"

Steve did not answer, but rose slowly and dragged his feet toward the jeep. Even the inevitable round of handshaking with the four Africans became a solemn ritual.

Driving back along the rutted track, Charlie began humming but soon stopped. As they dipped into the low hollows, Steve felt the wet coolness of the swamp air cloak him, clinging to his skin with a cloying shroudlike sensation. In the yellow blast of the jeep's headlights fruit bats and night birds displayed flashes of jewel eyes. Overhead the dusty banks of stars could be seen through gaps in the trees. It was a hot, lonely night.

As they jolted up off the trail onto the broken pavement of the road to Stanleyville, Charlie swore loudly and braked the jeep. Twenty yards ahead on the town side of the little intersection, a large open-bed truck sat facing them with one dim parking light glowing. Before the truck an ANC Land Rover sat broadside across the road. Black troops milled about in the darkness, shining flashlights. The truck was crowded with Congolese civilians. As Charlie rolled onto the road, they saw a sudden flurry of action take place between the Land Rover and the truck. Troops swung rifles and kicked wildly at two doubled-over civilians. Charlie drove to within ten yards of the Land Rover before he was waved to a halt by two drunken ANC with frantic Negro eyes, carrying automatic weapons. Charlie spoke quickly in a mixture of French and Swahili, shining his flashlight on his *laissez-passer* as he spoke. The two soldiers disappeared.

Before them the scene had become even more chaotic. The two crumpled figures lay inert on the road and the soldiers climbed up into the truck to pull down young girls, piles of bedding, and leaf-wrapped market baskets. There was a howling mélange of plaintive cries and the drunken laughter of the troops. Four soldiers surrounded a young girl on the pavement, stripped off her cotton mission dress, and held her down while a fifth soldier wearing the epaulettes of an adjutant pulled open his trousers and raped her. Once her initial flailing efforts to escape were extinguished, one soldier stood over her with a gun while the others dragged another girl from the truck. With diabolical efficiency the soldiers soon had three girls from the truck spread-eagled on the road. The adjutant quickly finished with the sobbing girl. He stood panting against the truck, laughing encouragement to his men. In the lights of the jeep his face was bloated from liquor.

"What the hell's happening?" Steve said.

Charlie stood up in the jeep. "Mission truck," he said. "They were probably coming back from a church service in Stan. They're on the way to that English Baptist mission past Yakusu. These bastards are from the brigade across on the left bank." They watched helplessly while the soldiers took turns and fell to quarreling loudly over the bundles of goods from the truck. The remainder of the men and boys in the back of the truck sat impassively in the glare of the headlights. A boy in his early teens suddenly flung himself onto the back of a soldier who was just about to mount one of the girls. In the blurred confusion Steve could see the boy being clubbed. Then Charlie flashed the headlights onto high beam and pounded savagely on the jeep's tinny horn.

"You cocksuckers!" he screamed in English. "Leave those people alone!" The soldiers glanced inquisitively up from their clubbing. "Stop it!" Charlie yelled in French. In the half darkness the clubbing continued. The boy no longer moaned or struggled.

Then Charlie was up on the hood of the jeep with his M-16. He cocked the weapon and let off a long jagged burst, flame erupting from the rifle's muzzle. He fired another, shorter burst just above the heads of the soldiers. The effect was magical. Like actors in a Max Sennett comedy the soldiers dropped their weapons and fled into the high grass alongside the road. Charlie reloaded the weapon. He was down on the pavement in a single bound. The people in the truck were crouched in terror. "Where's the driver?"

he said in French, then in Swahili. One of the older men they had seen being beaten struggled up to a verticle position and lay against the hood of the truck. His mouth was smashed and one eye was closed. Even with his injuries it was easy to recognize the courtly Old South dignity of an African preacher.

"I am the pastor," he said gravely in thickly accented English.

"Listen, Pastor," Charlie said. "Get your people down here to help me with this vehicle." Charlie had the Land Rover's hood open and deftly removed several thick wires from the motor. With the men from the truck he pushed the Land Rover into the steep, water-filled ditch on the river side of the road and threw the pieces of engine wire into the darkness.

"Now get this truck down to the ferry and stay there tonight. There are white soldiers there, so you'll be all right. Go!" The pastor leaned against the truck, blinking with his one eye, trying to speak. "Go!" Charlie said. The girls and the bundles were pulled onto the truck, and with Steve directing him, Charlie inched the big truck past the jeep. They stood watching the tail-lights wind away down the road.

On the pavement before them lay a scattering of market produce, abandoned weapons, print skirts, and beer bottles. Charlie dragged the weapons over to dump into the ditch water. "Mother fuckers!" he spat into the darkness. Then he seized one of the FALs and sent forth a pounding orange tracer burst into the elephant grass where the ANC had fled. "Cocksuckers!" he screamed. As they drove down the road, they heard a flare pop above the left bank and then saw a long cherry-colored stream of machine-gun tracers erupt across the river. A moment later they heard the popping rattle of the weapon. "Our *allies,*" Charlie said. "They'll probably be firing all night. In the morning it'll be another big rebel attack repulsed. Cocksuckers!"

Steve closed his eyes tightly against the insane swirl of images —Charlie's Saigon bodies and the muzzle flash of the weapon. The picture of the raped girls melded with a newsreel echo of the Watts riot. His mind was spinning out of control. He gripped his seat frame desperately against the mounting dizziness.

pierre

CHAPTER **11**

It was cold in the back of the big airplane. Pierre-Marie Tshipama lay on a canvas seat holding to his face the wet cloth the black American soldier had given him. In reality he was not badly hurt. One thing he had learned in the past five years was how to protect himself during a police beating. *Une des leçons de l'Indépendance,* he thought ironically, just like the politicians always said. He ran his tongue over the rough edge of his tooth broken by the soldier's fist. His back and legs were throbbing and his groin felt smashed, although he knew from past experience that it was not. He looked at his complicated watch that had been a present from Da Silva. Miraculously, the crystal was not broken. They had left Stanley-ville an hour before; in one more hour they would be in Albert-ville and he would have to face his punishment.

It simply was not fair. What incredibly bad luck. If the MPs had not been drunk, he probably could have bluffed them. But they were drunken Katangans who certainly were in no mood to be intimidated by a Muluba lieutenant. In retrospect, it was a stu-pid gamble to take, attempting to stow away on the general's air-plane. It was a gamble, of course, but it easily could have worked, and once back in Léopoldville he could have disappeared into the *cité* and they never would have caught him. Now he was trapped.

His assignment to a rifle company in the Opérations Sud sector was as good as a death sentence: of this he was certain.

What terrible luck. In the past three months everything had fallen apart. After five years of grasping struggle he finally had something worthwhile, only to have it snatched away. Now it did not really matter; he was a dead man. The black American brought him a paper cup of sweet coffee and a hot can of some meat and sauce. He spoke to Pierre, but he couldn't answer. He knew no English. The harsh consonants sounded vaguely like Flemish. *"Merci,"* he said, his lips swollen from the clubbing. He ate his food with a white plastic spoon and drank the coffee, his broken tooth twinging sharply.

The airplane whistled softly across the sky. After the violent weather of the morning the flight was unusually smooth. Below him in the sunlight the rain forest of the Lualaba valley rolled away toward the Maniema mountains. The country was savage and hostile. He did not want to go there. He did not want to fight in the forests and vine-choked ravines. He was not really a soldier. He had never wanted to be a soldier. He wasn't strong enough. He has been such a sick child; now they were sending him out into the forest in this barbarous region to fight the wild Bahembi tribesmen. It was a punishment, he knew, but it was unjust. It was another in a long series of injustices he had suffered for many years. How long, actually? He closed his battered eyelids and tried to remember.

His bad luck had begun five years before, during March and April 1960. It was his last year in the *deuxième* cycle at the Catholic Groupe Scolaire in Coquilhatville. If he passed his examinations—and everyone was certain that he would—he would go to Louvanium University in October. It was a very exciting time. Not only was he finishing secondary school, but the Congo was gaining its independence. Suddenly there was nothing else to talk about. Men who had previously been clerks and mechanics were now *délégués* and provincial ministers. There were election posters, sound trucks, and rallies. The Belgians drove about the sleepy equatorial river town with long, preoccupied faces. It had been hard for Pierre to study during these exciting months. He knew that he must force himself, however, and his father made him report daily on his progress. Pierre had a very careful schedule arranged. He was confident that he would pass the examinations, hopefully with honors, assuring him a place at Lovanium.

Then the examination dates were advanced to accommodate the panicky Belgian teachers who wished to leave the Congo before the proclamation of Independence on June 30. Worse still, Pierre fell sick with a violent attack of running boils which kept him agonized and in bed for almost five weeks. He could not study, but insisted on taking his examinations despite the illness. He failed them. His father was crushed.

Pierre's father had been a very good man. He was the senior medical assistant at the provincial hospital. He was the town's first registered *évolué*. When Pierre thought of his father, he saw a small, thickset man with a black, balding head, gold-rimmed glasses, and a very white shirt. Henri Tshipama was a sober, serious man. He was a Muluba from the Kasai and had spent three years in the senior seminary at Baudoinville in the Katanga before deciding that his vocation to the priesthood was not strong enough and transferring to the *école d'infirmiers*. He was a dedicated civil servant and a good Catholic. He had left his family and clan in the Kasai to work in the heat of the swamps and forests of Equateur Province. Henri was known as a diligent worker and an honest employee. An insatiable reader, he devoured everything his Belgian superiors could supply him on the complexity of tropical medicine. He even read Flemish textbooks, putting to use the Flemish he had absorbed from the White Fathers during his years in the seminary. After several years as an *agent sanitaire-adjoint,* his talents were recognized, and he was transferred to the central provincial medical center in Coquilhatville.

It was only then, after seven years of service and at the age of thirty-one, that he married. Marie, his wife, was also mission-trained, a Muluba. During his yearly leave in August 1939, he returned to Tshiputa, his native village, to complete the arrangements for his marriage to Marie. The wedding was an unparalleled social event in the village. The native son had returned covered with glory. Henri had a dazzling black serge suit complete with gray leather gloves, his only vanity.

Somewhere in a trunk Pierre had lost in Léopoldville, there was a photograph of his parents' wedding. It was a double cardboard folio on mat paper displaying his father, very grand in the black suit and gray gloves, kneeling with his mother in a lacy white dress on a kneeler in the studio of some native photographer in Luluabourg. They were both very black, his father's collar rimmed with sweat. The other side of the folio showed the couple with the old Belgian priest in front of the crumbling brick mission church, the priest's salt-and-pepper beard blending with the ragged cotton of his white cassock. Among the photographs his mother had left him Pierre also remembered a snapshot of the newly married couple on the deck of a wood-burning riverboat, his father still in the black suit, but no tie, his mother wearing a modest European cotton print dress and head scarf. A plume of black wood smoke curled out behind them on the hot river.

After the fall of Belgium in 1940, Pierre's father immediately answered the call to arms and enlisted in the Force Publique. His military service was short-lived, however. He spent six months assisting with the physical examinations of native troops and then was sent back to the hospital in Coquilhatville. During the resulting war boom on rubber, palm oil, and cacao Henri's status rose even further. Not only did he carry out his regular duties at the crowded hospital during the day, he volunteered to help train native medical auxiliaries in the evening. For the six years of the war he would not take his annual leave, preferring instead to travel to the rubber plantations and timber camps to supervise the new medical auxiliaries he had helped to train.

It was during one of Henri's trips out to the rubber camps, in September 1941, that Marie gave birth two months prematurely to their twin boys. It was a very difficult birth. Dr. van Horten was forced to perform a Caesarean section after Marie had been in labor for thirty hours. It was late on a Sunday night and both the doctor and the sisters assisting were very tired. Henri Tshipama's wife, however, received the best treatment available to either native or white in Equateur Province. The doctor was proud of Henri and saw in him one of the basic building blocks of a new, self-reliant, self-directing Congo. Henri was living proof of the wisdom and success of Belgium's Mission Civilisatrice. Henri's wife would not suffer through any negligence on his part.

The babies were tiny, impossibly weak. The Tshipamas were lucky, as Dr. van Horten had only the week before completed the installation in the maternity section of three crude but effective incubators which he himself had designed and constructed. So respected was Henri among the Belgians, both colons and *fonctionnaires,* that a special message was passed on the Lever plantation radio network calling him back to Coquilhatville to be with his wife.

He arrived late Monday afternoon. Marie was very weak and the babies were barely alive, but he was happy. His *patrons* had been good to them. Marie was no native woman who dropped her babies in a reed hut under the guidance of an ignorant midwife and a fetish-evoking *mufumu.* His sons' and his wife's lives had been saved by the white men's science, and he never forgot this. Even Père Luc came to the hospital to baptize the pitiful little twins in their metal-box incubators the very night Henri arrived back in Coq. During the week complications set in, and despite exhaustive efforts by Dr. van Horten, Jean-Claude, the smaller and weaker of the twins, died of pneumonia early Saturday morning. Again the old Belgian priest performed his offices and, saddened as they were, both Henri and Marie knew that one day they would see their baby again in heaven. Pierre-Marie continued to grow. Three weeks after his birth he was strong enough to be taken home.

In 1944 the family were the first natives in Coquilhatville to be given one of the new brick bungalows, complete with electricity and running water, which had just been constructed for the senior Congolese employees of the provincial administration. It was in this snug, almost European home that Pierre was raised. Among his first memories were the endless stories of his birth and of joining his mother and father to pray for the little soul of his dead brother, Jean-Claude. It was a happy childhood. There were no other children to compete for the affection of his parents. Henri was an *évolué.* His family were far away in the Kasai. There were no bands of uncles, aunts, and tribal relations to crowd them out of their comfortable brick house. Complications stemming from the Caesarean operation which had brought Pierre and his brother into the world prevented Marie from having more children.

It was a sad blow for Henri. He was far away from his tribe. His young, attractive wife was irrevocably barren and his only surviving son sickly. Henri Tshipama was a good Christian, however. Unlike most of his fellow *évolués,* he was not committed to the Bantu tenet of fathering as many children as possible in order to prove to the world his masculinity and guarantee the security of his old age. His pension would guarantee his old age, and he loved his wife. He did not find a pretext to send her back to her village and take another. Instead he devoted his life even more fully to his work and to the church.

Pierre remembered countless Saturday afternoons riding out to the mission station, clinging to his father's shirt on the back of the bicycle as they pedaled along the shady laterite road beneath the oil palms. At the mission the old priests in their long white robes always gave him a little piece of hard rock candy at the end of these visits. He remembered the arching vault of the red brick church on the bluff above the gray river, the smell of incense, and the voices of the choir at Easter as he sat in the heat between his father and mother and the Lingala voices rose through the smoke to the far wooden rafters.

Pierre's father was good to him. Henri had a long pirogue, complete with an American outboard motor with a shiny aluminum flywheel. Henri used the boat to visit the dispensaries along the river. Many Sunday afternoons after mass Pierre and his father would take the boat to motor up the green tunnel of the Ikelemba to fish for capitaine in the root-choked inlets of the river. Pierre loved these boat trips alone with his father. School was forgotten and Henri would often consent to tell him rambling tribal legends in the musical vowels of his native Tshiluba, a language almost never spoken to Pierre at home. Henri believed that there was no future for tribal vernaculars in the emerging Congo and that Pierre's education would be much better served if he and his wife spoke French to him as much as possible. Pierre, he hoped —he more than hoped, he somehow *knew*—would one day be a doctor, a black surgeon trained in the then inaccessible universities in Belgium. His French must therefore be pure and reflexive rather than the ungrammatical patois spoken by most Congolese. Pierre's body was weak, but he did have a good and an active mind.

To stimulate the boy's interest in science, Henri would sometimes beach the long dugout on the sand bars and he and Pierre would catch and dissect the flat litoke and small mponde fish swimming in the clear water of the river. Pierre would sit fascinated as his father explained the workings of the gills or the metamorphic cycle of the frogs, evolving from the slimy egg sacks clinging to mangrove roots into little swimming tadpoles and then into croaking green frogs. His father knew the birds also and would proudly declaim their complicated Latin names.

Pierre would always remember a particular Sunday on the river when he was twelve years old. They sat on a bar of fine sand in the shade, his father enjoying his second bottle of Primus beer, a luxury he permitted himself only after his duties at the hospital and at the church had been completed for another week.

They had caught a small capitaine and Henri had carefully traced the fish's alimentary canal, spreading the skein of gray, red, and blue guts out on the flat blade of the paddle. He traced an imaginary morsel of food from the fish's mouth through the processes of chewing, digestion, and excretion. Pierre was dumbfounded by the beautiful simplicity of the operation.

"You know so much, Papa," he said.

"Very little, really," his father said. "Everything I know, however, has been taught me by the Europeans. I would have liked to have been a real doctor, but that was impossible. We have come a long way, though. My father, your grandfather, could not read or write. He was a pagan and was never baptized. He was a good father, though, and worked hard for his children. He was a laborer, a simple *ouvrier* on the railroad. He was illiterate, but he recognized the value of the Europeans' education. All his children, your uncles and aunts, were baptized."

"Maybe one day I'll be a doctor," Pierre said. It embarrassed him to speak so before his father, who knew so much more than he did and yet was not himself a doctor.

"You will if you work hard, Pierre," his father said gravely, "and if you remember one thing above all. The Europeans are here to help us out of darkness and ignorance, to raise us to their standards. It is only through their help that we can advance. They have an incredibly difficult task, Pierre. I have traveled a good deal through the Congo. The people are still the captives of the *féticheurs* and all their pagan superstitions. The Protestants also have warped their minds, as have the anti-Christ sects like the Kimbanguists and the Kitawala. I only hope that by the time you are ready there will be enough boys like you to merit a real university."

"The European children have a school that prepares them for the university," Pierre said.

"Yes," his father answered, "but that is for the European children, who are much more advanced than you. What we need is a school that will one day train African boys like you for better things. The Groupe Scolaire is a beginning. I hope that the Brothers will continue adding classes. We are so ignorant compared to the whites. We must have schools."

"I'm sorry, Papa," Pierre said, twirling a branch in the water at the edge of the sand. "But if I am to go on to a European university to be trained as a doctor, why can't I go to a school with European children *now*? Will I be smarter later?"

"I hope you will have more humility later," Henri said sadly. Pierre was deeply embarrassed. "Listen, Pierre," his father continued in a softer tone, "all the African children here in Coq are not like you. Their parents do not spend time with them the way your mother and I do with you. They cannot even speak French correctly. Their fathers do not go to church. They have several wives and squander their money on palm wine, gambling, and women. You are special. If you were permitted to attend the European Athénée, the other parents would claim the same right for their children, don't you see?"

Pierre nodded. "Is it because we are Baluba that we are better?" Pierre asked quietly.

"We are not better, Pierre," Henri said. "The Baluba people in the Kasai are lucky because the Catholic fathers came to them early and they were able to profit from their teachings before the other tribes of the colony. That is the only difference. God does not see any difference between your soul and the souls of the Mongo or Ngombe."

While they spoke a turreted phalanx of thunderheads, billowing steel-gray and illuminated by lightning, advanced toward them over the ribbon of blue sky above the forest on either side of the river. The water rippled into real waves. Brightly plumed martins-pêcheurs and parrots flew wildly against the wind in a desperate effort to regain their nests before the storm. Radiant blue butterflies danced above the water in the still remaining patches of sun. Then they, too, were swept away by the rising wind. It grew cold. Henri watched the approaching storm calmly. He had spent many years in small boats on the Congo and its equatorial tributaries. Pierre was terrified. The lightning stroked white in the sky, followed instantly by stomach-slapping thunder. The wind howled across the water, blowing soaking spray onto their sandbar.

"Papa," Pierre said, "I'm afraid."

Henri smiled. "When God made Africa," he said, "He made a very strong and violent land. This is the way all the world was before the coming of Our Lord—a wild, storm-racked place. Watch the tops of the trees."

The gigantic gray-trunked bola trees so high above them swayed in unison, their leafy crowns slashing wildly in the wind. The lightning and thunder continued unabated. "I'm afraid, Papa," Pierre said. Without a word Henri rose from the sand and strode to the end of the bar where the sand widened into a decomposing heap of driftwood and fallen seed pods against the roots of the forest wall. He had his panga from the pirogue. Pierre huddled shivering against the side of the boat. The lightning came closer. When Henri returned he had an immense bundle of freshly cut bamboo and a coil of dripping vines. He carried the load high on his back like a peasant, supporting most of the weight with a vine strap to his forehead. Pierre was shocked. He had never seen his father work like this. Quickly in the face of the advancing storm Henri turned the heavy dugout on its side in the sand.

"Dig!" he shouted to Pierre. "Dig the sand like a dog does." Pierre scooped the fine river sand away from the open side of the pirogue, forming a shallow depression in the shape of a river mussel's shell. As he pawed at the sand, his father deftly split the long green columns of bamboo, lashing together a snug roof, anchoring the reversed interlocking sections securely with the springy liana vine. He dashed off again to the forest. Pierre cowered against the pirogue as the first heavy raindrops pelted against the sand and the wind peaked to a howl. His father was back again with a flopping armful of wide green leaves. He lashed them to the roof of their shelter with the vine and then dropped down beside his son, panting.

The storm swept over them in a startling wash of wind-borne rain and thunder. The river danced as the hail pelted with machinelike violence. Under the bamboo roof they were snug and warm. Lightning struck close by. They could smell a cooking fire stench in the wet air and the piercing chemical ozone. Pierre trembled against his father. "Don't worry, *petit*," Henri said, "the lightning always strikes the very tall trees. We are protected here up against the edge of the forest. The forest is really your friend if you understand it. Most of the Africans, however, know nothing of the real nature of a storm, or of the forest, either. They are still very superstitious." His father laughed. *"C'est bien ici, n'est-ce pas?"*

Henri opened his last bottle of Primus with his teeth to amuse his frightened son. "When I was a little boy like you, I often used to fish the forest rivers with your grandfather and your uncles. I was very sad to leave that life for the mission school. But now I am happy."

Henri dug another little pit in the sand just under the bamboo's edge next to the rain-sodden sand. With the tip of his panga he gouged away several handfuls of chips from the inner sides of the pirogue. From the split edges of their bamboo roof he expertly fashioned a basket-weave grill which he tossed out into the rain to soak.

Again using the tip of his panga, he cut out two slender, boneless filets from the fish they had caught. When the hardwood chips had burned to a mass of coals, puffing red in the wind, he wedged the grill above the coals, draped a wet leaf over it and covered the leaf with wet sand. From a tobacco tin in the boat he poured a mixture of red pili-pili and rock salt into a leaf. When the fish was cooked, he rolled the filets in the leaf and handed one to Pierre. The steaming fish was deliciously spicy. As they ate, the storm abated and soon the wind had died. Henri lit his pipe and belched contentedly from the beer. Then the sun broke through low in the sky to illuminate the vibrantly colored forest after the storm. The air had been washed clear. Multicolored birds flew above the water again and butterflies rose in columns over the brown islands of sun on the muddy river.

As they motored back down between the galleries of trees at sunset, the sky was a deeper blue than Pierre had ever seen it. Suddenly as he lay against his father's leg, it was night and the sky was dusty with stars. The darkness was soft; the insects had been driven back by the rain. Before them the channel opened and they were again on the wide expanse of the Congo. The *lukole* talking drums spoke in soft metallic tones in the wet tissue of the night.

The sky was unbelievably clear, as if the storm had peeled away a translucent skin that had always hung between the earth and the fields of stars. The Southern Cross hung on the open horizon of the black river, and along the banks of the forested islands orange fires of fishermen served as beacons to guide Henri. "Can you understand the drums, Papa?" Pierre asked.

"Not really very well," Henri answered. "They are speaking Limongo. Wait, be quiet. Let me listen." He cut the motor and they drifted silently with the current. The staccato music drifted to them across the water. Then there was silence and they were suspended alone on the black lens of the river. Suddenly, very near, another *lukole* drum answered. Henri used the carved paddle to swing the boat nearer to the bank. "A chief is dying up near Lulonga," he said softly. "He is not an old man, and the clan fears evil fetishes." Henri relit his pipe and, sighing audibly, started the motor again. "There is so much ignorance in this country," he said. "It is only through science that such fears can be ended."

CHAPTER **12**

The next years were very happy for Pierre. He entered the Groupe Scolaire and began the study of natural sciences. The Flemish Brothers who taught him were proud of their new student, the son of Henri Tshipama, the town's first *évolué,* a native trusted and respected, a man of religious devotion and a pride to the mission schools which had formed him. Henri Tshipama's only son, Pierre, seemed to be following in his father's path.

Every morning of the week Pierre rose before dawn, cleaned his tiny room, carefully folding his mosquito net and sweeping the floor. He would wrap his breakfast of bread and fruit in a clean cloth and pedal the new bicycle Henri had bought him to the red brick church by the river to serve as an altar boy. Pierre loved those misty dawns before the six o'clock mass. He would stand on the walk at the rear of the church with Jean-Baptiste, the other altar boy, watching the orange disk of the sun glide up above the arcade of palms near the governor's mansion. After communion and mass each morning he would take his bicycle down along the riverbanks to eat his breakfast in the shade of the coconut palms and watch the crews of the OTRACO barges shifting monstrous loads of crates and bales.

And then there was school, each class more interesting than the one preceding. He loved his teachers and the books and the prizes he always won in the *concours scolastiques.* There was no subject in which Pierre did not excel, but he had a special talent for science and mathematics. Like his father he had a hunger for books.

Pierre had few friends among the children of his age. His parents never forbade him to associate with the children in the *cité,* but it was difficult for him to join in the rowdy football matches after class in the afternoon, to come all the way through the communes and be back at his parents' bungalow before dark. He spoke Lingala fluently and had a good understanding of Limongo, but somehow his father's position with the Belgian doctors at the hospital, or the fact that Henri Tshipama was a Muluba from the Kasai and the town's first *évolué immatriculé,* turned the other boys away from Pierre. He had never been very strong, and the rough chasing and stone-throwing games of the other boys held no appeal for him. Also, he could never relax in the evening after class until he had completed his *devoirs* for the next day and carefully recopied them in his spotless notebook.

Pierre did have a few friends in the Scout troop at the church, but again, the rough games and the long hikes with knapsacks out to the mission station were too tiring for him. He liked the uniform, especially when he won award badges for his science and religion projects. As he grew older, the sense of self-imposed isolation grew into a smug feeling of superiority, especially as his classmates began to practice homosexuality blatantly and to go with bush girls from the fishing tribes, to drink palm wine and smoke the forbidden hemp. The priests had warned them all about these temptations, but it was only Pierre who truly resisted. Pierre did not need friends. He had his parents. They were alone and his father was not a young man, but still he set aside several hours every night to spend with Pierre and his studies.

Times were changing in the Congo. Henri repeated the wild political rumors to his son. There was talk of communal elections, and he said that educated men who should have spent more time at their work or with their families were organizing into political clubs and submitting petitions of grievances against the provincial administration. Henri, being a Muluba, a foreigner, was never asked to join these groups. He would not have done so in any case. He had traveled widely in the colony and had seen the sacrifices made by the Belgians to bring prosperity and enlightenment to the warring, backward tribes. He would sign no petition criticizing them. He found the Mongo intellectuals foolish. Certainly they were educated and capable of more responsibilities and better salaries. No one would deny this. But their claims for autonomy and emancipation for *all* Mongo people were blatantly ridiculous. The majority of the Mongo people were pagan savages. Henri knew this from his years of travel to the dispensaries of the province. If the intellectuals were superior, it was because they had been able to profit from the mission schools put there by the

Belgians against whom they were now organizing protests. If they wanted a better life and greater freedom, they should demonstrate that they merited these things and make formal application for the *carte du mérite civique* as Henri had done.

It was just as well that Pierre did not befriend his rowdy classmates, Henri thought. These were uncertain times and there were a lot of wild ideas floating around, especially among the young students who already fancied themselves intellectuals. It was also fortunate that they were considered foreigners and not expected to join in this agitation. Henri was happy right where he was. He had a respected position, a good wife, and his son would one day be a doctor. The squabbling and endless arguments about political theory disgusted him. These men were all hypocrites in any case. They were more than willing to kick away the ladder that had raised them to their present status, so that the ignorant masses they claimed to be protesting for would be left to drown in the sea of savagery and superstition from which the intellectuals themselves had only so recently emerged. They were immoral men as well, drinking palm wine at their political clubs and squandering the dues they collected so frequently on flashy clothes and unnecessary trips to the whores in Léopoldville. None of this interested Henri Tshipama. He had a respected position, his house, and his family.

During the last three years Pierre spent at the Groupe Scolaire, events began to move with an accelerated pace. African burgomasters were finally elected, taking up their offices with great flourish and ceremony.

Boys in Pierre's class talked knowledgeably about Congolese political parties like the Mouvement National Congolais. Names like Patrice Lumumba and Joseph Kasavubu were on everyone's lips. Soon, the students said, the Congolese would be able to share the Belgians' power, Congolese students would be sent to Belgium, not just to Louvanium University in Léopoldville. The Congolese, they assured Pierre, would be the complete masters of their own destiny by 1970. It was they, the young intellectuals, who would rule the new Congo after they had gained the necessary training and political experience that the Belgians soon would be forced to provide them. Pierre listened to their talk, but he was not impressed. These boys always talked wildly. One day they were going to become professional soccer players, the next they would be bishops. As Pierre's father had said, *"Ce ne sont pas de garçons sérieux."*

During this period Pierre's father listened closely to the radio at night and read the African newspapers with growing concern. There was something radically wrong with the colonial government, he felt. The Belgians actually seemed to be taken in by these fast-talking hoodlums. Then, in 1959, the riots began. For a number of years the cities had been swelling with waves of rural immigrants, belatedly trying to gain their share of the postwar economic boom that had long since reversed into a severe recession. There was no work for these people and no place in the crowded schools for their children. They should have remained in their villages, Henri thought; in the cities they were prey for the new politicians.

The rioting in Léopoldville was worsened by these rural immigrants from the villages of the Bakongo and the Bangala. When the Force Publique troops fired on them and a number were killed, Henri realized sadly that there would now be no turning back. Immediately following the riots, the Belgian Government announced that the Congo would be granted its independence without undue delay. The local politicians were ecstatic; suddenly they saw themselves as ministers; some even bantered nonsense about a Mongo kingdom and allowed how their particular clan had always been among the ruling aristocrats.

Henri was deeply disturbed by these events. The Church accepted the inevitability of independence and quickly proclaimed its neutrality in the struggle. Nothing, it seemed, would stop the irresistible slide toward what Henri was certain would be disastrous anarchy. It was widely accepted, however, that the Belgians would remain in their positions as advisers to the new Congolese government officials until the Africans gained the necessary experience to manage alone. Henri felt that this formula was doomed from its inception; he had worked too long with the Europeans to believe that they would suddenly consent to take orders from some semi-educated parvenu politicians.

Henri sought consolation with the priests who had always

guided him in the past. The old Fathers were dedicated missionaries who had spent their lives in the Congo. They knew the country and the people intimately. They were naïve, however, concerning all things political. The Fathers saw no good whatsoever resulting from the decision of the Belgian Government: a coalition government of socialists and liberals that had amply demonstrated its lack of sympathy with the Church and its clergy. But they were convinced that the promised independence would not in reality be more than a long-term training program during which the Belgian colonial administration would maintain the machinery of government while the politicians were lulled with titles and chauffeured cars so that a generation of able young Congolese leaders could be guided through the universities and technical institutes. The independence promised by the Belgians would be simply a sop to quiet the rabble-rousing nationalists and calm the masses of ignorant displaced peasants in the cities and on the plantations. "Your pension, Henri," old Père Louis said, "will be paid by the Banque du Congo *Belge."* Henri Tshipama was due to complete his thirty years of service to the colonial government in July 1964.

His anxieties were quieted by the priests. Certainly for most of 1959 the course of events seemed to bear them out: the elections being prepared for December were only the first round of a complicated and protracted electoral process which was designed eventually to create a prototype Congolese parliament. The ten-year grace period necessary to train the needed Congolese technocrats still seemed possible. Then in October two days of bloody rioting erupted in Stanleyville. Patrice Lumumba, the erratic nationalist politician, was jailed for inciting the riots. The rumors began to grow with increasing frenzy and primitive ignorance: Lumumba had been shot by the *Belges,* but the bullets would not kill him; Lumumba had been crucified and gone to heaven, he would soon return with *Indépendance* in his hands. Even King Baudouin had been attacked by mobs in Stanleyville on a surprise visit just before the December elections. He was the king of the Congolese just as he was the king of the Belgians, and insults to him could only bring further bad luck, Henri knew.

Suddenly the newspapers and radio were full of reports of a

great political *Table Ronde* in Brussels in January. All the important Congolese politicians were there: Kasavubu, Kalonji, Lumumba, and Tshombe. Henri was certain that some sane agreement could be reached between these wild-eyed nationalists and the Belgian parliament. This was not to be; the date for *Indépendence—Totale et Complète* was set for June 30, 1960, less than four months away. The previously frenzied activities of the politicians took on a new aura of madness. The Belgians, it was now certain, would be gone in July. The city erupted like a disturbed ant heap in an insane campaign for the May elections to fill the positions vacated by the departing whites and create the provincial government and parliament. The promises of the politicians became increasingly unreal as the Mouvement National Congolais–Lumumba vied for power with UNIMO and the confused hodgepodge of other new parties that seemed to have sprung up full-blown.

When Independence came, they said, there would be no more taxes, no more police, no more *tribunals*. There would be work for everyone, and wages would be triple their pre-Independence level. Peasants would all be issued new Russian tractors if they brought in their "Belgian" hoes and were able to produce a Mouvement National Congolais–Lumumba party card dated before May 1, 1960. All children would be sent to school, and any person wanting a university diploma could simply apply for and receive one. The Congolese would be given the Belgians' automobiles and houses. Congolese wishing to marry the Belgian women could make the necessary arrangements in a process similar to the application for a university diploma. Belgian trucks and automobiles could be obtained in the same manner. There was no need to work hard now or save money as everyone would be financially secure after *Indépendance*. With the onslaught of this insanity Henri sank into depressed isolation, worse than anything his family had seen in the past.

Pierre's inexplicable attack of boils and subsequent failure in his examinations drove Henri into even blacker despondency. Then, in early June, he received a letter from his mother, an urgent plea that he return to the Kasai to help her settle the family's affairs. The incessant strife between the Baluba and Lulua had finally caught up with the Tshipama family, even on the mission station where they had taken refuge six months earlier. Two of Henri's brothers were dead. The old woman needed Henri to come take her and the two youngest children, schoolboys like Pierre, back with him to Coquilhatville. Henri did not hesitate. He withdrew several years' savings from the bank and made the necessary arrangements to fly to Luluabourg. Dr. Le Grand, the new Belgian doctor at the hospital, cautioned him about the wisdom of traveling to the Kasai just before Independence, in the face of the anti-Baluba pogrom taking place there.

"I *must* go now, before Independence," Henri said. "Now I am still a *fonctionnaire* of the State. No one would dare attack me."

Henri's flight left at noon on a Sunday. After the early mass he and Pierre walked down to the river to remove the motor from the pirogue. It was a soft, breezy morning, the gray trunks of the coconut palms bent lightly against the blue river. The water was high, flooding the forested islands across the channel. "The boys at school say that the river is flooded by the Belgians who are angry because they have to give us back the Congo," Pierre said.

"The boys at school are unfortunate imbeciles," Henri said, struggling to lift the motor from the blunt stern of the dugout. "You will hear much more foolish talk now, Pierre. You must not believe it. When Independence comes, the only difference will be that we will not have the Europeans here to help us and we must work even harder than before."

"They say that there will be free university for everyone and we will all be given money," Pierre said.

"I'll be gone for perhaps as long as one month," Henri said. "You must stay home and study and take care of your mother. When Independence comes, stay at home. I don't think there will be any real trouble, because the Belgian officers will remain in command of the Force Publique. But there will be many people drinking too much and everyone will be very excited. It will not be a good time to be out in the *cité*."

Dr. Le Grand drove Pierre and Henri to the airport in the hospital pickup truck. Marie had stayed at home. They drank a bottle of Primus on the terrace bar of the terminal. Then Henri kissed his son and walked across the shimmering asphalt to the DC-3 that would carry him to Luluabourg. It was the last time Pierre ever saw his father.

C H A P T E R **13**

During the last weeks of June Pierre stayed close to home, leaving only to bicycle twice a week to the hospital for his penicillin shots, the last of the treatment for his boils. The OTRACO shipping company docks were hopelessly jammed with the crated effects of the departing Belgian officials. The results of the elections had been announced, and the new provincial *députés* and *sénateurs* were in great evidence in their European suits, driving about the central square in the new automobiles they had acquired. Mobs of young men roamed the streets, chanting "IN-DÉ-PEN-DANCE," throwing stones at the cars of the remaining Belgians, and making obscene gestures at the priests and nuns. Twice Pierre was dragged from his bicycle by rough young men who demanded to see his MNC/L card. Each time he was able to extricate himself, claiming to be a seminary student and therefore exempt from politics. Luckily he was able to sing parts of the liturgy in Latin and thus impress the drunken bands of party *jeunesse*.

Independence Day itself was quiet. There were ceremonies celebrating the transfer of power, and a reception was held at the newly elected governor's residence. Loudspeakers had been set up to broadcast the speechmaking in Léopoldville. The inflammatory anti-European speech of the new Prime Minister, Patrice Lumumba, in the presence of King Baudouin, was received with wild applause in the *cité* of Coquilhatville.

The four-day "Independence Holiday" continued with long drinking parties and wild dancing in the communes. Pierre and his mother stayed at home. The OTRACO boats stopped running, their crewmen and the dockside personnel striking for the immediate increase in wages promised by the politicians. On Monday morning Pierre was due for his last injection. As he rode his bicycle through the quiet streets toward the hospital, he realized that something was very wrong. Groups of rural tribesmen armed with spears and bows crowded the market, drinking calabashes of palm wine and openly smoking hemp. Their urban relatives were dressed in their best white shirts and Sunday trousers. They argued with the few soldiers who stood around looking confused and angry. By eleven o'clock crowds had formed and were surging out of the communes toward the European quarter and the offices of the new provincial government. A Land Rover full of soldiers trying to protect the residence of the governor was stoned by the mob. The people wanted their tractors and their promised fifteen-thousand-franc Independence bonuses. They wanted the European houses and automobiles and the new *contrats d'emploi* that would guarantee them an income triple and quadruple the old Belgian salaries.

The politicians had obviously taken most of *Indépendance* for themselves. The people wanted their share before all of it had been broken up and hidden by the politicians; it was widely believed that *Indépendance* was a very perishable substance and if not kept in the Belgian "frigos," it would rot. By early afternoon there were fires burning and the mob was in a frenzy. The soldiers were out and by three o'clock Pierre and his mother heard the first smack of rifles. Marie closed the windows of the house and pulled down the shades. It became hot in the small darkened salon where she and Pierre knelt saying the Rosary.

Outside there were screams and the sound of cars racing through the streets. Twice the soldiers fired their frighteningly loud rifles directly in front of their house. Later in the afternoon a loudspeaker car passed before the house, blasting out the proclamation of a general curfew. Anyone found on the streets would be shot. Pierre and his mother said another Rosary. It grew dark in the salon, but Marie would not light the overhead bulbs. Outside in the night they could hear more firing, and the drums were very loud in the *cité*.

That night Pierre felt the fever returning, the skin of his lower back and buttocks stretching, which marked the resurgence of the boils. For the next ten days he lay in a fever as the huge boils burst open again.

Pierre recalled very little of those first chaotic weeks after the riots and the mutiny of the soldiers. As it was impossible to secure the necessary drugs, the infection of boils spread even farther than the first attack. He was forced to lie in discomfort on his stomach while his mother regularly changed the boric-acid dressings, the only medication she had available. His mind floated on the fever; the reports broadcast sporadically on the radio spoke only of swelling disorder. Political diatribes increased against the intervention of Belgian troops after the mutiny of the new Armée Nationale. Marie welcomed the news of the restoration of order by the Belgian paratroops from Kamina Base. Her optimism was short-lived, however; it soon became clear that the Belgian soldiers were not at all interested in protecting the Congolese civilian population, but only the demoralized bands of shocked Belgians, clergy and colons alike, who streamed into Coquilhatville from all over the province with horrendous tales of rape, humiliations, and murder.

The relative order in the town was maintained when the intervening Belgian troops were relieved by a battalion of Indonesian paratroopers, members of the hastily assembled United Nations Force called to the Congo to prevent further anarchy. It was obvious that the newly elected provincial government was utterly incapable of managing the affairs of the province. Blatant theft, embezzlement, and all forms of graft and corruption became commonplace. The deposits at the new Banque Nationale du Congo disappeared almost at once. The payrolls and operating funds of the municipal utilities and provincial services were stolen during the first six weeks of Independence. The ANC garrison, which had been disarmed by the Belgian troops, was given back its weapons, and soon armed robbery and extortion of the African population found their place in the growing list of new hazards to be faced each day.

Twice during this period families of new Congolese provincial *fonctionnaires* descended on the Tshipama bungalow, waving forged requisition orders. Twice Marie was able to appeal successfully to the mission priest, who, in turn, somehow managed to bring about the intervention of the United Nations troops to prevent the seizure of the house. Pierre's fever had broken by this time, but he still stayed close to home, making a halfhearted effort to prepare for his make-up examinations scheduled for October. Then, on the evening of August 4, Père Louis and Abbé Armand arrived at the bungalow on the father's motorbike. Père Louis had just received a message through the mission radio network. Henri Tshipama had been seriously wounded in the latest outbreak of tribal warfare between the Baluba and Bena Lulua in the Kasai. He had been taken to one of the missions near Luluabourg where he had died of his wounds on July 24. A former classmate from the seminary had been with him and had been successful in passing the message.

Marie Tshipama and Pierre received the news in the stuffy salon. Père Louis, his white cassock discolored with pink laterite dust and sweat, sat between them on the plastic-covered armchair that Henri had always used. Marie was silent for a long time. The tears rolled steadily down her smooth-featured face, soaking the collar of her housedress. Pierre stared at the floor, unable to accept fully the reality of his father's death. "There could be some mistake, *mon Père*," he said. "There are many Tshipamas in the Kasai—Papa always told me this. There could easily be some confusion."

"No, Pierre," the father said, "your father is dead and we must accept it. The Lord saw fit to take him. Henri was a good Christian and a decent man. We shall, all of us, miss him. It is some small consolation that his death came at the mission where he had the sacraments and could be buried in hallowed ground."

The Congolese abbé turned to Marie. "We would like to offer a Te Deum for Henri on Sunday if you give your permission."

Marie was dumb. She stared at the wooden crucifix on the wall; the braided Easter palm fronds were dusty. Pierre was shocked to his core when his mother, who had knelt with him in prayer since his earliest memories, who had always spoken to him in softly accented French, and who with his father had continually stressed to him the value of his emancipation from tribal ignorance and superstition, stood up in the small room before her son and the two clergymen and ripped her dress from her shoulders, baring herself to the waist, her pendulous breasts exposed to them all. From deep in her throat a sound of animal anguish rose and was modulated into the ritual Tshiluba mourning wail of a widow. She walked past them to the kitchen at the rear of the house. When she returned, her forehead and breast were smeared with white ash.

"Marie!" the Congolese abbé said. "Stop this! Henri would not want to be mourned like a pagan."

She continued to chant, striking sympathetic cords inside Pierre's chest. Then he was beside her on the floor, moaning in unison with her. The words of the dirge were unknown to him, but their sobbing rhythm unleashed the hopeless pain inside him and it flooded out. The priest and the abbé left them alone.

They lost the house at the end of the month. The United Nations authorities were trying to reorganize the former provincial medical services, and their bungalow was needed to house the new personnel. Damien Itelé, a young man Henri himself had trained as a medical orderly, was now in charge of the province's medical services. He arrived unannounced one day with a tall, sunburned European. The doctor, he said, would be taking their house. They had one day to move.

One day, Marie said, was not adequate time to arrange new housing and to move their furniture. "The furniture stays here," Itelé said in Lingala. Marie protested and then addressed the European in French.

"You cannot take our furniture. This is all we have left."

"I don't know anything about it," the European said. He looked about the small bungalow, not attempting to hide his disgust with the tiny rooms and modest furnishings.

"But, monsieur," Marie said, "these things are ours. You cannot just keep them."

"Don't ask me about it," he said. "Ask Monsieur Itelé."

"*Monsieur* Itelé!" she spat. "He was barely competent to keep the village inoculation records and now he runs the Service. This is ridiculous."

"Shut your Muluba whore's mouth," Itelé said in Lingala. "The whites aren't here to protect you any more. You will be out of the house in one hour or I will give you and the boy to the police to play with. *Alors,* monsieur," he added, turning to the European, *"nous partons?"*

During the next ten days Marie and Pierre were given a place to eat and sleep at the mission, but it soon was obvious that this would not be a permanent solution. They had no relatives in Coquilhatville. Marie had a brother living in Léopoldville, and early in September she and Pierre boarded the weekly OTRACO boat for the capital. They had very little money. Two small suitcases and a cardboard carton contained all their possessions.

The boat was a typical Congo river courier, a small diesel riverboat pushing two flat steel barges and pulling another astern. Pierre and his mother traveled deck class and were allowed freedom of movement only on the lowest open deck and on the barges. Pierre was excited. Despite the sadness of their departure from Coquilhatville and of their financial straits, he was eager to see Léopoldville. Marie sat forlornly on their small pile of baggage remembering her first trip on a riverboat with Henri after their wedding. Then they had had a fine cabin with running water, a cabin normally reserved for Congolese priests. They had been served hot meals and cold beer. Now, on the crowded deck of the barge, she was almost choked by the stench of manioc and dried fish. Sitting on the battered suitcase, staring out at the passing forest, she sang an old Tshiluba hymn.

CHAPTER **14**

Marie Tshipama's younger brother, Paul, lived in the Kintambo Commune of Léopoldville with his wife, four children, his wife's unemployed brother Philippe, who also had a wife and three children, and Philippe's mother who was almost sixty years old and blind. With the arrival of Marie and Pierre, Paul had thirteen persons to support on his salary as a part-time welder at the Chanic shipyards. But Paul had not worked since Independence. Each day he would walk to the yards in hope of a day's work, only to be turned away. He was a good man and had not squandered his meager savings in anticipation of Independence. By September the extended family was reduced to living on the remainder of a large sack of manioc flour and a smaller sack of rice that Paul purchased with his modest Independence bonus.

Pierre's first reaction to his uncle's house in Kintambo was one of disbelief. For as long as he could remember he had slept in his own room and eaten carefully planned meals which almost always included meat, fish, or chicken. Now he was sleeping on the ground beneath an improvised grass lean-to and expected to choke down his meager share of gummy manioc and boiled rice once a day. His constant hunger was not his only or greatest discomfort. It was the dirt: the two-room concrete-block house had no running water and no screened latrine. Two hundred meters down the sandy street there was a public water spigot that served more than a hundred households as big as their own. His little cousins wandered about naked in the scant shade of the beaten-earth compound, their heads covered with sores and their bellies distended with worms. His only suit, his school shirts, his mother's dresses and few bits of jewelry were taken at once to be bartered for food.

One morning, a month after their arrival in Léopoldville, Pierre was awakened at dawn, as usual, by the biting flies crawling on his face. His uncle's brother-in-law, Philippe, was squatting next to him, rummaging through the oilcloth bundle of schoolbooks Pierre kept with him on his pallet in the lean-to. Philippe had selected the three largest books: mathematics, physics, and religion. He looked evenly at Pierre as he stood up holding the books against his chest. "They're starting the schools again," Philippe said. "I can sell these books for food."

"No," Pierre said, "I need those books for my examinations."

"Your examinations," Philippe said scornfully, "are in Equateur. This is Léopoldville."

Pierre, wearing only his ragged underpants, dashed after Philippe, who walked down the sandy road toward the Avenue. Philippe spun around, striking Pierre a vicious blow full in the face. "Get back to your mama, you little turd!"

Pierre was suddenly down on the sand watching Philippe walk away with his books, his last link to the examinations, the university, and his future as a doctor. Late that afternoon Philippe returned without the books. He was very drunk and began to beat his screaming children. He did not bring back any food.

For the next week Pierre lay around the fly-tormented compound. He rarely spoke to his uncle or his mother. It was finished. He knew that he would never go on to the university. Marie tried to comfort him, but she herself was despondent, suffering from recurrent diarrhea and malaria. Paul had found some work with the United Nations troops, repairing damaged river barges for the shipment of supplies into the interior. The job paid very little, and when the word that he was working again got around in the commune, he was visited by three policemen who broke his nose and ripped an ear, persuading him to pay them half his salary as protection money.

It became clear that Paul would not be able to support Pierre and his mother indefinitely. Pierre lay on his smelly pallet at night listening to his uncle and mother arguing in Tshiluba. His head spun and his stomach knotted tightly.

One morning he rose even earlier than usual and walked from the commune to the nearby Catholic mission *collège*. He arrived at the school in time for the six o'clock mass and took a place in a pew near the altar. After the service he waited by the side of the church for the Belgian priest. In the pocket of his shirt he carried his school records from the Groupe Scolaire. The priest was a kind young man who listened carefully to Pierre's story and thoughtfully read Pierre's *livret scolaire*. "So you want to be a doctor, do you?" he said.

"Oui, mon Père," Pierre answered.

He took Pierre into his office adjoining the low block of classrooms. The priest sat for a long moment before a small portable typewriter on a simple wooden table. Pierre stood at his side, silent and nervous. The priest stared off into space, then inserted a piece of mission stationery and a carbon and began typing. He quickly typed two letters.

"Voilà, Pierre," he said. "This is a letter to the office of admissions at Louvanium, and this a letter to the director of the Groupe Scolaire in Coquilhatville."

Pierre sat down and read the letters. "I really don't think you'll have trouble being admitted," the priest said. "They are making all kinds of allowances these days. Your school records are excellent, and I'm sure your former teachers will give you a strong recommendation, but you'll have to be patient. Everything is very confused these days in Léo. There probably will not be room for you at Louvanium until January or February. I hear that they are going to start a special orientation program then." The young priest stood up, smiling, and looked at his watch. "I'm off to breakfast now, Pierre. Good luck."

Pierre shook the priest's hand and found himself out on the asphalt road walking back to the commune in the early-morning heat, the two precious envelopes carefully folded away inside the pocket of his one remaining shirt.

"Fermé! Fermé!" the drunken gendarmes screamed, blustering down off the porch of the Sûreté office. Before the mildewed brick building a swarm of disheartened, tired Congolese slowly began to disperse. It was five-thirty on a heavy Wednesday afternoon in December. Pierre had waited in the jumbled clot of supplicants since dawn. Throughout the day he had inched closer to the building and a chance of admittance. Now the working day had ended and he must begin the wait again in the morning. He was dizzy and sick with diarrhea. All day he had waited in the sun, jammed against the others—flashy boys from the *cité* and simple Bas Congo peasants from the bush villages. Now he must try again in the morning with little hope of ever reaching the porch.

He had come, as had the others around him, to the offices of the Sûreté Nationale to obtain a mysterious document entitled the *Extrait du Casier Judiciaire.* This precious official paper was the last remaining document needed for his scholarship submission to Louvanium University. All the other necessary papers—the medical certificate, the photostats of his school records—had been painfully and expensively procured from the hopelessly inept new Congolese administration. Now only the *Extrait* remained as an obstacle between him and his career as a medical student.

The deadline for the scholarship submission was three days away. Pierre looked tiredly at the swarm of people around him. That morning he had *run* all the way through the dawn streets, from the hut in the communes to this old red brick colonial office on the Avenue Lippens. The *cité* curfew ended at sunrise. Even if he could borrow a bicycle or even get a free truck ride in the morning, he couldn't get there before the mob.

He had only three days. He felt the sadness of his defeat welling inside his throat. Instinctively he shied away from the advancing, club-swinging gendarmes to join the sun-dazed crowd on the sidewalk. The deep shade of the Avenue's tung-oil trees felt almost cold.

Suddenly the answer to his problem came to him. He cut through the crowd and dog-trotted across the shady Avenue. Then he slowed to a walk and turned into the weed-strewn lot behind a four-story European apartment building facing the Sûreté office. Lethargic Congolese were streaming slowly back toward the *cité* along the shadowy streets. No one was watching him. He squatted in the weeds to defecate. Then, when he was sure no one could see him, he rose and with a heart-stopping burst of daring and athletic dexterity totally unfamiliar to himself he was over the glass-studded cement wall guarding the apartment compound and was hidden in the shade of the rusting sheet-metal shed littered with the apartments' garbage cans. The cans were covered with drowsy flies which erupted in collective spasms of green noise as Pierre wedged himself deeper into the smelly corner. The roving curfew patrols of the United Nations and the Congolese police would never find him here. He was hungry and his intestines ached, but he was happy. In the morning he would be first in the line before the Sûreté porch. By noon he would have the precious *Extrait*.

By dawn he had his place near the door and by ten o'clock when the first *fonctionnaires* arrived he was actually inside the building. The narrow, filthy corridors were jammed with Congolese who had gotten there before him. Club-wielding gendarmes periodically rushed down the hallways, screaming, and punched some hapless person into submission. By noon he had completed his application form for the *Extrait,* had been fingerprinted by two comically incompetent but deadly serious policemen, and was finally shown into the office of a young Sûreté *inspecteur.*

"*Tu parle français, toi?*" the man asked without looking up.

"*Oui, monsieur,*" Pierre said.

The inspector examined Pierre's application form and smeared fingerprint sheet. He took an impressive-looking yellow paste-board card from a pile before him on his desk and stamped it in various places with three rubber stamps. Asking Pierre's full name, place and date of birth, mother's name, father's name, he slowly completed the document. When he had finished, he looked up, holding the stamped and signed *Extrait*. *"Voilà,"* he said, "this is your *Extrait*. Now you will pay me one thousand francs."

Pierre stood before the smiling Sûreté officer in disbelief. The struggle to procure the papers had been so long and difficult. Several times he had wanted to abandon the effort and forget his dream of the University. But he had worked persistently and this was the last document. One thousand francs! The inspector might just as well have said ten million francs! "But, monsieur," Pierre said, "we were not told that there would be a fee for the *Extrait*."

"But there *is* a fee," the inspector said. "It is one thousand francs. Next week it will be two thousand francs." The inspector wrote something illegible on a scrap of paper. He handed it to Pierre. "When you have the one thousand francs," he said, "come back and give this paper to one of the guards. Do not give him the money, even though he asks you for it. Give the money only to me and you will get your *Extrait*. You have until next week." Pierre stood silently before the desk, clutching the paper. "It's for the University, isn't it?" asked the inspector. Pierre nodded. "Surely the University is worth one thousand francs." The inspector smiled.

Pierre leaned against a wide-crowned shade tree on the Avenue Lippens. The mobs of waiting Congolese surged toward the red brick offices of the Sûreté. There was very little civilian traffic on the street. A United Nations military convoy crossed the brightly sunlit intersection. On the shady sidewalks, where the hungry roots of the trees had cracked and twisted huge blocks of the asphalt pavement, small groups of Congolese wandered aimlessly.

For the past month the capital had been gripped in a state of complete confusion as President Kasavubu first dismissed Prime Minister Lumumba and was in turn dismissed by Lumumba. These events were followed quickly by the "neutralization" of the politicians by Colonel Mobutu.

Lacking a radio and enough money to buy a newspaper, Pierre

had been forced to content himself with the myriad rumors floating about the *cité*. Many, especially the young unemployed like
himself, spoke hopefully of the imminent Russian take-over when
all the politicians would be shot and *Indépendance* would be given
to the people. Others predicted that it would be not the Russians
but the Americans who would take charge of the Congo and bring
about the millennium promised before Independence. Several
nights before, while waiting in line for relief supplies of American flour and powdered milk, Pierre had heard that Kwame Nkru-
mah of Ghana was about to be named king of all Africa and
would rule the Congo as well. The only reassuring thing he had to
cling to in the prevailing uncertainty was his chance of admission
to Louvanium University. Now he knew that even this hope had
been shattered. The one thousand francs demanded by the *fonctionnaire* would be impossible to obtain.

A boy his own age came toward him from out of the mob of
waiting people. He had seen the boy before, at Louvanium and during the long wait for the medical certificate at the hospital. Like
Pierre, the boy was dressed in a threadbare but reasonably clean
white shirt and a pair of faded cotton trousers. He joined Pierre at
the curb and addressed him in Kikongo. "I was raised in Coquilhatville. I speak Lingala and French," Pierre said. "I'm sorry, but
I don't speak Kikongo. Do you speak French?"

"My name is Honoré," the boy said in French. "Did you get
your *Extrait?*"

Pierre explained the necessary bribe, holding out the scrap of
paper. *"Ça, alors,"* Honoré said. "They are worse than the *Belges,*
these new *fonctionnaires."*

"Where I lived," Pierre said, "the *Belges* were not at all bad, I
don't know how they were elsewhere."

"You're probably right. Some were good and some were bad.
These new ones are all bad."

Without speaking further, they walked slowly along the tree-
lined avenue toward the center of the city. Neither had eaten that
day and neither had a single franc with which to buy food. They
were hungry but were not anxious to return to their overcrowded
huts. "Well," Honoré said as they walked, "at least you managed
to get into the building and see the inspector. How did you do it?"

Pierre explained how he had defied the curfew and hidden in the apartment building garage shed in order to be first in line. "What a good idea," Honoré said. "You must be very smart. It's a waste for someone like you not to go to the University. What do you want to study?"

"Medicine," Pierre said proudly.

"Me, I want to become a lawyer, *un avocat*. I'm no good in science and mathematics."

They walked on in silence and soon were in the hot sun of the ivory market square. A few United Nations soldiers were bartering with the venders who had braved the midday sun to spread out their collections of carved ivory trinkets. They moved over to the shade of the spreading tree near the bus stop on the Boulevard du Trente Juin and watched the soldiers, who, Honoré said, were Canadian. A white soldier paid far too much for the badly made ivory work. The vender, a tall, white-robed Moslem, took the soldier's dollars and added them to a heavy roll of currency which he carefully thrust back under his robes.

"Look at the money that the foreign soldiers have to throw away on that useless ivory," Pierre said. "And for the lack of one thousand francs you and I cannot go to the University."

Honoré was quiet for a while, watching the clot of soldiers in khaki shorts stroll across the square. "How badly do you want the thousand francs, Pierre?" he asked.

"Very badly, why?"

"Because I've just thought of a way to get that much and probably a lot more."

Pierre felt his hope returning. "How?"

Honoré explained that near his uncle's house in Dendale Commune there was a large service station that had been commandeered for the maintenance of the UN military vehicles. Each night there were almost twenty jeeps and Land Rovers parked inside the barbed-wire fence surrounding the garage. He knew a man in the commune who would pay one thousand francs for each spare tire and battery they could supply him. "What about guards?" Pierre asked.

"I think that there are only two at night. Your idea of hiding in the apartment garage gave me an idea. We can go into the station and ask for work and then hide among the cars in the back. Late at night we each take as much as we can and go out the back way under the fence."

"Won't the guards see us going out?"

"That's why we need one other boy, to make a noise to attract the guards to the front so we can go out under the fence."

"It sounds difficult," Pierre said worriedly. "It sounds very dangerous too."

"Well, if you don't want to try, I'll find somebody else. *I* really want to go to the University."

"I'll try it," Pierre said quickly. "It's just that I think it is very difficult."

"Come on. We'll walk down and I'll show you the station. It's really easy. I should have thought of it before."

The garage was a Standard station just off the Avenue du Président Kasavubu in the tin-roofed monotony of Dendale Commune. Pierre and Honoré walked past the entrance several times that afternoon. The United Nations troops had ringed the station with a shoulder-high barbed-wire fence. In back of the station's asphalt parking area the ground was grassy, dropping down to the swampy land around the Funa creek. They walked back to Honoré's uncle's house where his aunt begrudgingly gave them a meal of cold manioc and pili-pili. Honoré's cousin, a young man named Luc, joined them. Luc spoke little French. Honoré talked with him in Kikongo while Pierre sat nervously beside them on a woven reed mat in the shade. Luc had come to the capital looking for work and had found none. He was willing to join them. Together they returned to the station to complete their reconnaissance. Luc, they decided, would hide in the tall grass across the road until late at night when the guards would be sleepy. He would cross the road and with a small bottle of kerosene light a fire in the grass just in front of the station entrance. He would yell to attract the guards, and he would stamp at the fire until they arrived. Then he would melt away to join Honoré and Pierre at the rear of the station and help carry off the loot. They decided to make the raid in two days' time.

The first big thunderstorm of the rainy season struck the after-

noon that Pierre and Honoré walked down the broad Avenue Kasavubu toward the garage. Pierre felt that he was being watched
by hidden observers. He trembled visibly. "Don't talk," Honoré
said. "I'll explain everything."

At the entrance of the garage a barbed-wire barricade blocked
the drive. A Malian soldier of the United Nations contingent
stood behind the barricade, a rifle slung over his shoulder, watching the black wall of the storm approach. Honoré strode brazenly
up to the barricade. "Do you speak French?" he asked.

"*Oui,*" the soldier said. "*Pourquoi?*"

Honoré waved a folded copy of the *Courrier d'Afrique* at the
man. "It's about these jobs they've advertised for mechanics," he
said. "My friend and I are mechanics and we need the work. What
can you tell us?"

"*Sais pas,*" the soldier shrugged. "You'll have to talk to the
chef." He pulled back the barricade and Pierre and Honoré went
inside. It was almost five-thirty and the Congolese mechanics were
drifting away from their work to the makeshift locker room at the
rear of the double garage.

"Follow me," Honoré said. They walked over and stood against
the row of blue-and-white Land Rovers parked near the fence at
the rear of the parking lot. Pierre was very nervous. He almost
wet himself as an angry-looking Congolese in mechanic's coveralls
strode toward them.

"What do you want here?" the man asked.

"We're the new assistant mechanics," Honoré said calmly. "The
chef told us to wait here until he finished with what he's doing. I
guess he wants to talk to us." The man looked at them suspiciously, but just then the first slapping drops of the approaching
storm smacked the hot concrete. In the running confusion during
the initial onslaught of the storm it was easy for Honoré and
Pierre to hide themselves in the rear of one of the Land Rovers in
the parking lot.

It grew dark and the airless canvas cubicle in the back of the
vehicle was stifling. Pierre wanted to break and flee over the
fence, but Honoré restrained him. "Wait," he said. "It's almost
time. Think about the money."

From a toolbox under the seat Honoré produced two pliers and an adjustable wrench. "With these we'll take out the batteries. We'll take six. Then we can each carry two when Luc joins us outside. We'll carry them with this rope, over our shoulders like the men carry baskets of dirt to repair roads." With the pliers he cut a piece of rope he had found into two-meter lengths. As they waited in the dark, more vehicles were parked in the lot, blocking their view of the garage building and the two patrolling soldiers. Despite his fear Pierre dozed fitfully in the hot black box.

Honoré awakened him. "Now, Pierre. Follow me very quietly. Take off your white shirt." Outside the car the pavement of the parking lot was still warm. It was a dark, close night, with a mustard-colored overcast low in the sky reflecting the lights of the city.

Honoré knew exactly what to do. They worked as a team on the line of vehicles parked at the rear of the lot. Some of the batteries were under the hood, others beneath the rear seat. After a long time they had six greasy batteries roped together in yokes of two each. They crouched in the shadow of a small truck five meters from the fence and the safety of the high grass. The gap was perfectly open and well lighted. It was impossible to cross the distance without being seen. "Now," Honoré said, "we wait for Luc."

The mosquitoes were bad after the rain. Pierre sweated, wishing desperately that he were someplace else, that this were all a nightmare brought on by the boils, that he would awake to find his father and mother in their little house in Coquilhatville, that he were still a student at the Groupe Scolaire serving mass for Père Louis each morning. But that would never be again.

He heard the soldiers yelling before he saw the fire. There were three instead of two. They called wildly to each other from different parts of the compound, speaking in some strange African language. "Now!" Honoré said. Pierre could not move. "Now!" Honoré repeated, grabbing him roughly by the wrist and dragging him out onto the exposed piece of pavement. "Take your batteries." They crossed quickly to the fence, dragging the heavy batteries behind them with a loud scraping sound. Honoré was through the wire first. Pierre handed him the arm-wrenching batteries one at a time. Over his shoulder he could see smoke and orange flames in the grass along the Avenue. The soldiers were running with a hose. He crouched lower and handed the second yoke of batteries through to Honoré. They were going to make it.

A change struck Honoré's straining face. He seemed to be looking through Pierre at something beyond. Silently he was gone in the high grass. Pierre did not have time to turn before the rifle butt caught him in the back of the neck.

C H A P T E R **15**

Pierre was never fully unconscious. The blow of the rifle butt dulled his senses sufficiently to blunt the pain of the kicking he received from the three African soldiers. He lay on the greasy floor of the garage, trying to protect himself while the soldiers kicked and cursed him. They raised him to his feet and he collapsed again onto the floor. The rest of the night was impossible for him to recall in detail. At some time a grim European in a military tunic slapped his face with a leather stick, hissing at him in bad French that the batteries were worth more than twenty black street hoodlums.

His first memory of the next day was of waking with a throbbing headache on the floor of the cell in the *commissariat central*. With some surprise he realized that his limbs had not been broken by the kicks and blows. In reality his greatest discomfort on his first morning in jail was the swollen bites from the countless vermin which infested the cell. In the dim light of an overhead bulb he could see that the two long benches on either side of the cell were completely filled with bruised prisoners, their faces swollen from beatings and lice, their eyes downcast. With a sense of revulsion that shook him as deeply as had his mother's act of ritual mourning, he rose from a puddle of urine in which he had been lying.

There was no empty place on the benches so he painfully walked the length of the cell and leaned against the barred cage of the door. In the distance, down the dark corridor outside the cell, he could hear someone screaming. Pierre spent nine days in the reception cell at the *commissariat*. He was lucky. His crime had been committed against the United Nations so he was tried by a mixed tribunal of United Nations and Congolese authorities. Some of the prisoners in the crowded cell had been there since their arrests during the first post-Independence riots, four months earlier.

Pierre was given no defense. He admitted that he had taken the batteries, adding that he needed the money to pay a bribe to obtain the necessary documents for admission to the University. The white chief mechanic from the United Nations garage testified against him as did the three Malian soldiers. Pierre was convicted of theft and attempted arson. For theft he was given three months. For arson he was sentenced to four years in prison. The two terms were to run concurrently.

His first few months in Makala prison were almost as bad as his days in the cell at the *commissariat central*. What little food there was, mostly wormy rice and manioc, was taken by the strongest prisoners. Just before Christmas the United Nations police and civilian authorities took over the administration of the prison and conditions improved. He was put in a four-man cell with seven other young first-offenders and finally had enough food to fill his stomach. The Congolese guards were still brutal, but now there was a semblance of medical care and the prisoners were allowed to exercise in the yard mornings and evenings. For the next several months he amused himself by teaching his cellmates French and writing them lessons with a piece of charcoal on the boards of their bunks.

In April the prisoners were herded in shifts to the prison dispensary where they were inoculated against smallpox and yellow fever. A recently promoted Congolese medical assistant was the acting prison doctor. As Pierre waited in the line of silent prisoners before the dispensary door, he could see the "doctor" tiredly going through the motions of the inoculation procedures he had been taught by the Belgians. When Pierre's turn came, he looked at the medical assistant and said, *"Monsieur le Docteur,* you have too much work. I can help you. My papa was an assistant medical. I myself was a medical student. You need an assistant. Why not try me?"

The man looked up from his tray of syringes. "Do you know how to sterilize? Can you measure vaccine?"

"Oui, monsieur."

After he became the doctor's assistant, Pierre's life in the prison became more than tolerable. Once he had gained the trust of the older man, Pierre was given increasing responsibility. The crudely equipped dispensary was his to clean and organize. When the "doctor" went to the women's prison or to the jails in the city, Pierre went with him, wearing a white coat over his blue prison shorts. At Pierre's suggestion the doctor was able to increase the meager collection of medical texts in the dispensary with loans from the World Health Organization doctors who visited the prison weekly.

Pierre's life in prison improved slowly as his position in the dispensary became regular. He was moved to a comfortable two-man cell which he shared with a political offender, a young Lumumba politician named François who was able to pay for better food and occasional books and magazines. François even had a transistor radio, which brought them the news of the outside world and music to enliven their nights. When François was released in 1963, he left Pierre the radio. By this time Pierre had learned that small thefts of drugs could easily be bartered with the guards for precious commodities like radio batteries, cigarettes, and dried fish. His life had taken on a kind of stability. He was no longer abused by the guards or the other prisoners. He had his work and he had his cell and his books. It was more of a home to him than the fly-tormented lean-to in his uncle's house in Kintambo Commune had been.

The years went by slowly but not without a certain comfortable security which Pierre associated with the distant memories of his early family life in Coquilhatville. By 1964 he had established a profitable medicine smuggling business, depending on his duplicate key to the dispensary's pharmacy and the compliance of two Baluba prison guards. Just before his release in July 1964, Pierre was able to arrange the theft of a large supply of World Health Organization penicillin originally destined for the syphilitic inmates of the women's prison.

On his frequent trips with the doctor outside the prison, Pierre had seen the face of Léopoldville change during the four years of his sentence. Now, in July 1964, the capital was very different. The streets were patroled by Congolese Army troops brandishing machine guns. There was talk everywhere in the *cité* of the Muléliste rebellion in the East and wild rumors about Lumumba's resurrection. The United Nations troops were gone.

With the help of the prison guard, Pierre sold the case of penicillin tablets to a Portuguese merchant named Da Silva. He owned a small wholesale warehouse just off the Avenue Charles de Gaulle. It was a drab stucco building of two stories, its plate-glass windows patched with plywood and the interior smelling of mildew. A rusting sheet-iron gate opened onto a small courtyard where Da Silva parked his battered Peugeot truck. At the rear of the courtyard Da Silva's mulatto wife kept chickens and tried unsuccessfully to regain control over the four small children who crawled in the chicken droppings and played under the greasy chassis of the truck.

Da Silva's bulky metal desk was placed directly in front of a large American air conditioner. The high-ceilinged room was walled with floor-to-ceiling metal shelves containing a variety of merchandise: wax print cloth, straw hats, work shirts. He maintained a string of mulatto and Bakongo assistants who rode the village truck-buses peddling goods between Léopoldville and Thysville.

Pierre had heard that Da Silva was a rich and powerful man, but on his first visit to Da Silva's storeroom-office it was hard to picture the sallow-cheeked, unshaven little man in a frayed, once-white shirt seated across from him as either rich or powerful. Da Silva had three gold teeth and an ivory toothpick. While he discussed the price of the penicillin with Pierre, he worked constantly with the toothpick, alternating between his mouth and his fingernails.

Pierre was unaccustomed to the staggering inflation rate, the result of four years of post-Independence anarchy. In prison he had traded his stolen medicines for concrete goods such as books and food. The thirty-five thousand francs Da Silva was offering him for the drugs sounded extravagant.

Da Silva smiled when he saw Pierre's perplexity. "You've been away a long time?"

"I've been in prison since December 1960," Pierre said evenly. He felt it was right to tell a European of the injustice he had suffered at the hands of his own people.

"Political?" Da Silva asked.

"No, I was trying to steal some small car parts from a United Nations garage and they caught me. They charged me with arson as well and I got four years. It was an injustice. The only reason I stole was to get money to pay a bribe to get into the University. If there hadn't been any bribe I wouldn't have tried to steal."

"But you stole the penicillin."

"That's different. In prison you learn that if you don't steal somebody else will, so why not do it yourself?"

"*Exactement,*" Da Silva said, smiling. "You'll see now that Léopoldville has become much the same as prison in that regard. The United Nations soldiers are gone and Tshombe is now prime minister. People are all terrified of the rebels so they're stealing as much as they possibly can before the rebels come."

"People do seem very excited," Pierre said. "It's almost as bad as it was just after Independence."

"What are you going to do now, Pierre? How long have you been out of jail?"

"One day. I don't know what I am going to do. My mother and uncle have disappeared from the house in the commune. No one knows where they've gone. I don't know anybody here in Léo except the people in the prison. I don't know what I'm going to do."

Da Silva opened his metal cashbox and took out a pile of dirty bank notes. He counted out forty thousand francs and handed it across to Pierre. "Whatever you do you'll need money."

"But this is five thousand too much," Pierre said.

"Keep it. You'll need some clothes, too. Here, try some of these." He rose and selected several cellophane-wrapped white shirts and a pair of blue Japanese slacks from the piles of merchandise on the floor. "Take them. They're free. Do you have a place to stay?"

Pierre took the pile of clothes in his arms. Da Silva added several packages of locally made cotton singlets and shorts. "Why are you giving me these things?"

"I like you. You're smart, not like most of these cheap young crooks I have to deal with and the greedy oafs in the police and Sûreté I have to bribe to stay in business. I asked if you have a place to stay."

"No. I guess I'll get a room someplace in the *cité.*"

"Stay out of the *cité.* You're just out of prison and you've got a lot of money and no papers. They'll have you in five minutes. I've got a room here where my drivers stay sometimes. It's not much, but it's clean and safer than the *cité* these days."

"What do you want from me in return?" Pierre asked suspiciously.

"Nothing," Da Silva said, smiling again. "If I liked boys I wouldn't have to bribe one with all this to get him. I like the way you look at things, and I think I might have a business proposition for you in a few days. But first you'll need papers, *carte d'identité* and all the rest." He wrote a short note on a piece of office stationery. "Take this around the corner to the Hindu who has the picture-taking machine and get twelve photographs of yourself right away. Put on one of those shirts first and wear this necktie." He handed Pierre the note and a cheap snap-on tie from the top of the littered desk.

For the next two days Pierre stayed in the shady room on the side of Da Silva's compound, enjoying the luxury of sheets, hot food, and a real shower whenever he wanted one. Da Silva had cautioned him to stay out of the shop until his new papers could be procured. From the courtyard Pierre could see a continuous stream of Congolese policemen, army officers, and flashy young men from the *cité* come and go. Whatever Da Silva's business really was, Pierre realized, wholesale textiles were only a part of it.

After two days Da Silva called Pierre into his office and presented him with a new identity card and a certificate of residence in Kinshasa Commune. "Now," Da Silva said, "you're free to go any place you want. You may want to stay here, though. That business I was talking about seems to be possible now. Do you want to hear about it?"

Pierre sat down in front of Da Silva's desk. "Go ahead."

Da Silva sat back in his swivel chair, working his ivory toothpick around in his mouth. "I need an intelligent young Congolese who is not involved in politics and who is not well known either in Léo or in the Kasai. He must speak French and Lingala and preferably Tshiluba as well. It's absolutely necessary that he be able to keep his wits about him and not panic under pressure. There's really very little risk involved. The job pays enough to make the young man financially independent within six months."

Pierre watched Da Silva's unshaven cheeks sucking at the toothpick. "What is the job?" Pierre asked after a long silence.

"Diamonds. Carrying diamonds from Bakwanga and Luluabourg to Léo, once or twice a week. You—" Da Silva smiled, correcting his error. "The *young man* would be given the papers of a military courier, an officer, probably an adjutant or lieutenant. He would have orders to travel aboard military airplanes with his courier's valise. At his destination he would be met and the valise exchanged and he would return. He would be met at the airport and bring the valise to me. It's very simple. I have all the necessary contacts inside the ANC headquarters. They only specify that the courier used have no political coloration, as they say, and that he be someone from outside the ANC."

"What's the pay?"

"Fifty thousand francs a week plus a house near one of the military camps. Other things as bonuses if everything goes well."

"I know nothing about the army."

"You don't have to. As a courier you won't have to answer questions. You'll have all the necessary documents. It's really very simple. Once or twice a week you sit in an airplane for a few hours and you get fifty thousand francs. As a courier you are not required to know the contents of your valise. You can't be touched. What do you say?"

"I'll have to think about it."

"Don't think too long," Da Silva said. "Tell me tomorrow morning what you've decided."

The job was, as Da Silva had predicted, ridiculously easy. Equally easy was Pierre's sudden transformation from a rootless young ex-convict to Lieutenant Pierre-Marie Tshipama, *Armée Nationale Congolaise*. Late one night in Pierre's first week out of the prison, a small bespectacled ANC adjutant came to Da Silva's shop with Pierre's new uniforms and a brown envelope containing a forged service and pay record. The next afternoon another Congolese soldier returned with Pierre's ANC identification card and other confusing military documents. He instructed Pierre in the proper manner of wearing his uniform, how to salute and how to address enlisted men and superior officers. Early the next morning Pierre was awakened by Da Silva and the ANC adjutant who delivered the uniforms.

"Put on your green battle dress and the web belt," the adjutant said. "I've got your orders and you must come with me to report at the Quartier Général."

Over steaming bowls of coffee in Da Silva's office the adjutant explained the stenciled orders to Pierre. The type was blurred and difficult to read and the military language unfamiliar, but with a marked feeling of unreality Pierre read that Tshipama, Pierre-Marie, Lieutenant de l'Infanterie, was being transferred from a staff position at the Kitona training base to be attached to the État-Major, ANC Léopoldville, for duty as a military courier. Travel was to be performed by military aircraft; quarters and rations allowance would be provided on arrival in Léopoldville.

As Pierre got into the adjutant's car, Da Silva put his hand on his shoulder. "I'll see you tonight at your new 'quarters.' You take your first trip tomorrow." Pierre tried to smile. "You still have time to say no." Pierre remained silent, sitting in the car, the door open. "What do you say, Pierre?"

"I want to do it," he answered.

Driving through the hot morning traffic, Pierre saw many vehicles filled with black soldiers and white mercenaries. This was a serious thing. This was not like stealing car batteries and penicillin. The country was in the middle of a savage rebellion, actually a civil war, and here he was blatantly impersonating an Army officer to help a foreigner smuggle stolen diamonds. For this they could shoot him.

Climbing the narrow road toward the ANC headquarters on Mount Stanley, they passed a school bus jammed with students from the National School of Law and Administration. They glanced curiously at the young ANC lieutenant, and Pierre looked long and hard at them. Then they were beyond the bus and he saw the massive concrete block of the Quartier Général atop the naked hill overlooking the rapids of the Congo River.

The next morning he made his first trip. It was in an old rattling Force Aérienne Congolaise C-47 flown by a scruffy-looking Belgian crew. The plane carried some truck engines and tires, a few crates, and several huge sacks of manioc flour. The only other passenger was a Congolese sergeant with his right arm in a plaster cast. Pierre sat uneasily on the metal bench as the aluminum panels of the floor and fuselage vibrated into a tympany while the pilot ran up the engines. Pierre had never flown before, and with the sudden shocking burst of power as the plane rolled down the runway for the take-off, he was afraid that he would be sick. All the rich meat and spices he had gorged himself on during these first days out of prison seemed to rise in his throat. Suddenly they were in the air, banking sharply off on one wing with the elephant grass and wide river tilted crazily and the pale early-morning sky twisted beneath them. He closed his eyes and clutched the leather dispatch case between his knees.

When he opened his eyes, the engine had changed to a quieter pitch and they were flying level, high above the rolling hills of scrub brush. The sun was rosy on the metal skin of the wing. An unshaven Belgian crewman in khaki shorts and an undershirt wandered back to check the cargo straps. He saw the stricken look on Pierre's face and laughed. "*Ça va,*" he said, "*ça va,* we're not going to crash yet." He walked back up to the cockpit, laughing.

The small airport terminal at Bakwanga was swarming with soldiers and angry-looking police. It took all the courage Pierre could muster to leave the airplane and face this reception. Two tall Police Militaires carrying black submachine guns saluted him and requested his orders. To his own amazement he was able to return their salute, calmly handing over his courier orders. Without stuttering or panic he requested directions to the office of the airport commandant where he was to exchange his pouch.

The office was filthy: beer bottles crowded the commandant's desk and lay broken on the floor, ripped bits of paper and cigarette ends everywhere, most of the windowpanes either cracked or broken. The only person in the office was a heavy man with glasses who was also dressed in the uniform of an ANC lieutenant. After carefully verifying Pierre's identification and orders, he said in Tshiluba, "Do our brothers fare well in the capital?"

Pierre answered as he had been instructed, "Our brothers are hungry there."

The man then took Pierre's dispatch case and signed the receipt. From inside the cluttered desk he produced two leather dispatch cases identical to the one Pierre had carried from Léopoldville. They were secured with heavy combination locks. "This one," he said, touching one of the cases, "is marked for Commandant Mulago. The other is simply for the Quartier Général." Pierre examined the two bags and nodded. Commandant Mulago was Da Silva's designation. Pierre signed the two receipts and picked up the dispatch cases. Da Silva's bag felt heavy. Pierre walked out to the tarmac with the lieutenant to await the unloading of the C-47. The man put his hand on Pierre's arm. *"C'est facile, n'est-ce pas?"* he said.

"Yes," Pierre replied, "it's very easy."

In the terminal building a crowd of Congolese passengers awaiting the arrival of an Air Congo flight was being pushed about by the police and soldiers. The passengers' trunks and bundles were torn open and pawed over, and each passenger was led into a curtained cubicle to be stripped and searched. "What are they looking for?" Pierre asked.

"Diamonds," the other lieutenant said with a full-throated laugh.

CHAPTER **16**

It was an easy life for Pierre. Once or twice a week he flew to either Bakwanga or Luluabourg, delivered a dispatch case and picked up two more, one destined for ANC headquarters, the other for Da Silva. Each week he was paid in cash. He had no other duties. The "quarters" Da Silva provided him with were very agreeable, a small cinder-block house in Ngiri-Ngiri Commune. The bamboo gate and entrance were covered with hibiscus

and purple bougainvillaea. The house reminded him of his family's government bungalow in Coquilhatville. Da Silva even arranged the installation of an indoor toilet. The house had once
been owned by a Congolese accountant; its furniture was solid and
almost new, the garden carefully tended and the street quiet and
well-shaded. Pierre was pleased. His only sadness was that his
mother had been swallowed in the chaos of 1960 and was now
probably dead.

The work became increasingly simple. As Da Silva had explained, he could not be caught. He had a real identification card
and service record. He worked under his own name. He had *become* a lieutenant in the ANC—a military courier. He delivered
the dispatches, but he was not responsible for their contents. It
was a strange life for him, but it was not unpleasant. In many
ways it was similar to his life in prison. He was detached, living
alone in his neat little house on the quiet street with his books and
his radio. One or two days a week he would fly away in an airplane and return to his home at night. He felt completely separate
from the convulsions shaking the Congo. The Muléiste rebels, or
Simbas, had captured Stanleyville, and more than half the country
was under their control. Desperate battles were being fought,
with foreign mercenaries giving backbone to the dispirited ANC
troops. For all that these events affected Pierre, they could have
taken place in India.

Two months after he began the courier run, Da Silva gave him
a Lambretta motor scooter. "Take it," Da Silva said. "It will give
you a chance to get around a bit. You don't seem to ever go out.
What are you afraid of? That the house won't be there when you
come back?"

Pierre laughed. Da Silva was right, of course. It was silly for
him to be making all this money and not to spend it on anything.
Somehow he could no longer become excited about things the way
he had before prison. The University now meant little to him. He
experimented with whores, but, aside from the quick physical release, they were repugnant to him. He enjoyed a bottle of beer occasionally but never got drunk. He told himself that when he had
made enough money he would quit the courier job and go to Brussels to study. He did not know what he would study, perhaps some

form of natural science, botany or biology, birds and fishes as his father had taught him. When he had enough money, he would travel.

In the interim he had plenty of books and with the scooter he could drive freely around the city and the surrounding hills. He could fish with the fishermen in the river villages above N'djili Field and hunt monkeys with the villagers in the steep hills of scrub jungle on either side of the Matadi road. In his army uniform he could go where he pleased; no one questioned him.

Late one afternoon, coming back on his scooter, he saw Da Silva's truck in front of his house. The Portuguese was sitting on the front steps with a bottle of beer. He smiled broadly as Pierre pulled up. Pierre smelled the delicious aroma of *mwamba* coming from the house, the sweet palm oil and pili-pili pungent in the warm air.

"Where have you been, Pierre?" Da Silva said. "You almost missed your supper." Da Silva was smiling strangely, as if he had another surprise. He had smiled in the same way the day he had given Pierre the Lambretta.

In the kitchen Pierre found the girl. She was dressed in a bright new piece of wax cloth wound loosely around her waist, and a clean white blouse. She did not see him enter the small kitchen as she knelt to fan the charcoal brazier beneath the large pot of *mwamba*. She was very young, perhaps sixteen or seventeen, small and slender. Her neck was gracefully long, her face sweet and childlike. She rose with a start when Pierre spoke to her. "Who are you?" he said in Lingala. She stood against the wall, not frightened, but a bit wary of Pierre. She looked into his face and at his uniform, then answered in Tshiluba.

"I am Christianne. The white man said that I will live here now with you and cook and wash your clothes and be your woman."

The next year was the happiest Pierre had ever known. Christianne was young, but she knew how to cook and manage his house, and especially how to please him at night in bed. He bought her dresses and swimming suits and took her on long picnics to Lac Vert and Zongo Falls on the Lambretta. At night they would go to the cinema, not just the outdoor Congolese cinemas in the *cité,* but to the European films at the Petit Pont or the Albertum. Some afternoons they would go to different communes to dance in the breezy shade of the outdoor cafés. She was a very good girl. She would dance only with Pierre and refused to return the glances of the leering hangers-on who lay about the cafés drinking Primus.

Christianne loved their house and was talented in her efforts to decorate the rooms. She spent hours with the Belgian picture magazines, showing Pierre the type of chair or curtains or mirror she wanted him to buy. He was making so much that the money he spent on the house barely affected his savings. It was an easy, pleasant life. He was a soldier; the police left him alone. Christianne knew little of the Congo outside her native village in the Kasai and what she had seen in Léopoldville. She was not troubled by the radio reports of the rebellion, and so Pierre lost the little remaining interest he had retained in the country's affairs.

They lived completely absorbed in each other. Pierre became used to his new life. He enjoyed wearing his neatly pressed uniform and taking the salutes of MPs and drivers. With Christianne and the money it was much better than being a doctor. His father had worked hard his entire life only to leave a hungry widow and orphan. In reality, Pierre felt, he had been fortunate not to have gone on to the University. The rest of the country might be tearing itself to pieces, but he was getting rich. He had no complaints.

One night in May as they lay under the electric fan on their big European bed, Christianne took Pierre's hand and put it on the velvety skin of her naked stomach. "Pierre," she whispered, "there is a little baby in there." He felt the thrill of the secret run up his fingers into his own body. That night he lay awake long after the girl had fallen asleep. The commune was dead-still; only an occasional rooster crowing at the moon interrupted the silence outside the windows. He had fathered a baby. Inside the girl there was another living person who would be his child. He smiled in the hot darkness. This was much better than being a medical student. Now they were a real family: mother, father, child, and house. He was a respected officer. With all the money they would never have to worry. It was a warm, snug feeling that filled him as he drifted asleep, a good feeling that he had often felt at home on the nights before examinations for which he had studied hard and which he knew he would pass.

The baby, a boy whom they named Henri after Pierre's father, was born in September 1965, during a grave political crisis in which Moise Tshombe, the former Katanga rebel, was dismissed as Prime Minister by President Kasavubu, a move which was clearly contrary to the wishes of the majority of the voters who had given Tshombe's government massive support in the April elections. Once again there were wild rumors, one predicting a take-over by Tshombe and his white mercenaries, and another an alliance between Tshombe and the leaders of the Simba rebels he had only recently defeated.

For the first time since leaving prison, Pierre took an active daily interest in the events that were shaking the country. During the *matatá* following Independence and his father's death and during the long years in Makala prison he had become, he thought, irredeemably fatalistic. He had tried as hard as anyone could to lead a proper Christian life, to work for an education and help his mother, but events had been too powerful for him. The harder he struggled to better himself, the worse were the misfortunes that overtook him. At some moment in prison he had decided to struggle no longer, to let himself float on the currents that flowed around him. He had learned the futility of planning a future in a country that was bent on destroying itself.

So he had moved through the days like a piece of uprooted vegetation in the river, traveling wherever the water took it. Up to that moment the current had carried him very well. In prison he had been lucky enough to get his position in the dispensary and to build a comfortable life. Da Silva had picked him up at once, and he had, for the moment, a job that provided him with all he required to be happy. But now he was no longer alone. Now they had the baby and they were a real family. Now he could no longer trust to blind luck; he must once again try to take an active role in shaping his own future. He owed that to Christianne and the baby.

With the political uncertainty following Tshombe's dismissal, his regular runs to Bakwanga and Luluabourg increased, almost as if Da Silva were anticipating some new development that might menace or even prohibit the continuation of the smoothly run smuggling operation. If this was so, Pierre thought, he would be left out in the cold. He would lose the house. He would have the money he had saved, but that wouldn't last forever. He had no skills, no profession. When the money was gone, he would be thrown back into his old status of friendless orphan. This time, however, he had Christianne and his son to provide for. He needed security. He needed to acquire so much money that even when he lost his job or when the smuggling operation was discontinued, as he knew it must be, he would be able to live in security.

These thoughts gnawed at him for several days, and then one afternoon as he sat on the front steps, the girl next to him nursing the baby, he decided to seek her advice.

"Christianne," he said, "you know what I do when I go away each week in my uniform?" The girl nodded without speaking. "This job cannot last forever. You realize this, don't you?" She nodded again. "When the job stops, the money stops. Now that we have the baby we must plan what we are going to do when the money stops."

"I don't know anything about these things," the girl said. "Besides, we have plenty of money."

"Yes. *Now* we have plenty of money, but how long will it last if I lose the job?" He thought about his uncle's struggle to support the unwanted hoard of relatives. "I must have some way of getting a lot of money now so that when I no longer have the job we can still live as we do now." The girl nodded, shifting the baby to her other breast. "Well?" Pierre said. "Can you suggest anything?"

She shrugged her shoulder and a painful expression wrinkled her forehead. "These things are not my affair. If you need advice, you should talk to either a priest or to a *féticheur*. The future is their concern."

Pierre laughed. "You're a good girl, Christianne," he said, squeezing her waist. "I'm afraid I'll have to find my way without the help of either a priest or *féticheur*."

As he flew back from Luluabourg the next day with his two dispatch cases, the solution suddenly came to him. It was so simple! For more than a year he had carried Da Silva's diamonds for him. For this service he had been paid very well. But, he knew, Da Silva had made a fortune on the smuggled diamonds. The fifty thousand francs he paid Pierre each week was just a fraction of the actual value of the stones Pierre delivered. And yet it was Pierre who had taken all the risks. This was plainly an unbalanced equation. He decided that it was up to him to balance it. That night he made his proposition to Da Silva.

As in the past Pierre had first delivered his real dispatch case to the duty officer at the message center in ANC headquarters. The driver had then driven him to a corner on the Avenue Charles de Gaulle where Pierre got out of the car and walked the rest of the way to Da Silva's compound, carrying the second dispatch case hidden inside a cheap travel bag.

Da Silva shifted back the dirty curtain from the glass door, verifying, as he always did, that Pierre was alone. Pierre stood by while Da Silva completed the remainder of the ritual, laying the leather case on the desk and slowly working the dial of the combination lock. From the case he removed two book-sized packages wrapped in oilcloth. He closed the dispatch case and began to open the squat steel safe behind his desk.

"Wait," Pierre said as Da Silva was about to place the two packets in the safe. "Can I see what's inside them just once? I never have *seen* a diamond, you know."

Da Silva looked up at him with a blank expression in his dark eyes. "Why do you want to see them unpolished? They don't look like anything, you know. Just like dirty pieces of broken glass."

"I know," Pierre said, "it's just that I'm curious, that's all. I've been carrying them for over a year and I've never seen one." Da Silva opened the corner of one of the packages and shook out several stones onto the stained surface of his desk. They glittered very faintly in the light of the fluorescent tube on the ceiling. The diamonds looked like small, slightly blue-tinted quartz pebbles Pierre had often seen on the sandbanks of the streams and rivers near Coquilhatville. "May I touch one?" Pierre asked.

Da Silva looked impatiently at his watch. "All right," he said sharply, "but make it quick because I'm in a hurry tonight."

"Ah, *oui?*" Pierre said as he fingered the stones. "I had hoped to have a talk with you tonight."

Da Silva was openly suspicious now. He took back the diamonds, resealed the oilcloth, and put the two packets into the safe, slamming shut the door and spinning the combination. "What kind of talk is it you want to have?"

"About diamonds and about money," Pierre said.

"Eh bien," Da Silva said. *"What* about diamonds and *what* about money?"

Pierre could not return the icy stare on Da Silva's face. Instead he looked past the Portuguese at an old SEDEC Motors calendar with a white lady in a long blue dress. "I have heard that two sacks of diamonds like that from the mines at Bakwanga are worth many million francs, and I began thinking. If I carry, say, four or five sacks of diamonds like these each week for you, then you are making many millions of francs and doing very little for it and I am making fifty thousand francs and taking all the risks."

"You think I make that much money each week?" Da Silva asked in a soft, cold voice.

"I don't know. I'm sure you make more than fifty thousand francs, though."

"Do you think that my contacts in the Kasai *give* me the diamonds? Don't you realize how much it costs me in bribes just to stay in business?"

Pierre said nothing. He felt Da Silva's old persuasiveness working to change his mind. He shook his head stubbornly. "I don't know how much you make for certain, but I know that the fifty thousand you pay me is far too little for the risks I take."

"What risks? I was careful to use your real name on all your army records. With the ANC as confused as it is these days, you face no risk at all. You *are* a lieutenant in the ANC. Your courier assignment is perfectly valid. As I once told you, a courier is not going to be held responsible for the contents of the dispatches he carries."

Again Pierre fought to dispel Da Silva's logic. "I want half of what you get. We are going to become partners. Half for you and half for me."

Da Silva laughed out loud. He replaced his ivory toothpick with a half-smoked Kivu cigar. "And what happens, Pierre, if I decide to throw you out in the street and find some other young *macaque* jailbird to play the army officer? What are you going to do? Go to the police and say that your friend the diamond smuggler will not give you more money for impersonating an officer and fraudulently using army channels to traffic in contraband? You must like jail."

Pierre had already thought this out. *"Non, patron.* I'm a jailbird and a *macaque,* but I'm not that stupid. On my flights to the Kasai I've had the chance to meet several high-ranking officers. I feel quite sure that they would be happy to continue your little business, using me as their courier and just forgetting about the *petit commerçant portugais* altogether." Pierre had never spoken to a white man like that before. He felt triumphantly flushed as Da Silva bit hard on his cigar and stared at him across the desk.

After a long pause Da Silva stood up, wiping the sweat from his face into his coarse black hair. "I'll have to think about it. I'm not alone in this affair, you know."

"Don't think too long. I'll wait until tomorrow morning."

Pierre left Da Silva standing slack-jawed in the dingy storeroom and walked out into the early evening darkness. It was a splendid night. Thunderheads were rumbling with green lightning. He strolled through the crowded streets past the Memling Hotel and turned onto the Boulevard.

He was going to be a rich man. Shabby groups of street boys were making their rounds among the tables of the European cafés, peddling black-market cigarettes, razor blades, and poorly made wood carvings. Only that morning Pierre had known the sick fear that, when his savings were exhausted, he too would end up like them, on the street again with an empty stomach and a future devoid of hope. Now he would be a rich man, a partner in a profitable business. The brilliant lines of streetlights came on along the Boulevard. Shiny cars of diplomats and politicians sped past him. He would buy a big new car so that he and Christianne and the baby could drive out into the country. It was going to be a very good life.

He wandered slowly up the Boulevard, pausing to look into shop windows displaying meager supplies of shirts and dresses. These cheap store clothes wouldn't do. He would hire a Senegalese tailor in the *cité* to make him silk suits the way the politicians did. Christianne would wear lace from Brussels flown all the way on Sabena airplanes. He crossed the Boulevard, walking casually among the foreigners who bartered for the paintings and carved work in the ivory market. He heard their voices speaking French, Flemish, and English as they knelt to examine the crude bracelets and jewelry boxes. When he was rich he would have a regular European house in Djelo Binza, not just a native bungalow in a commune. He would give dinner parties; there would be European girls like that woman kneeling there in the short yellow dress examining a necklace. He turned abruptly away from the Belgian girl and walked out of the market square.

He had to be careful. He was not rich yet. But he *was* going to be rich. He knew this positively. Da Silva could not refuse. The years of *matatá* and hunger were all behind him. He had to celebrate. He would take a taxi back to the commune. He had plenty of money in his pocket. What would he do in the house, though? Listen to the radio. He wanted something more, something befitting his new status.

As he passed the entrance of a European cocktail bar, a suntanned couple opened the door and a cold draft of the air-conditioned interior wafted about his ankles. He saw the expressions of longing and envy on the faces of the street boys who stood aimlessly on the sidewalk in front of the bar, waiting for a possible white customer to buy their shoddy goods. Without hesitating, Pierre entered the bar. On the door there was a painted treble clef and the name of the cocktail bar: The Blue Note.

Inside, the chill air flowed under the sleeves and collar of his shirt. It was very dim. The room was crowded with whites, seated at small tables and in booths in the cigarette haze. He smelled the piercing perfume odor of the men's deodorant and women's powders, blended with alcohol, tobacco and the sweat of the white-jacketed Congolese waiter. The room had a carpeted floor. The booths lining the walls were deep and well-padded. This was the way the whites lived. This was no pounded-dirt terrace with sloppy beer-wet tables in the *cité*. This was a real nightclub, just as he had seen in the films.

He sat at the padded leather bar, his back turned to the inquisitive stares of the white clientele. Behind the bar a young Belgian in a red polo shirt and tinted eyeglasses was adjusting a spool of tape on a dazzling chrome machine. The music began, encompassing the room from hidden speakers. Pierre sat nervously on the bar stool waiting for the man to take his order. He fought not to shiver in the cold air. The Belgian looked at him with a vaguely sarcastic smile. *"Bon soir, Major,"* the young man said. There was a choked laugh from the rear of the room.

"Bon soir," Pierre said. "I would like a drink."

"Well, you've certainly come to the right place." This time the laughter was plainly audible. Pierre spun on the swivel bar stool to see who was mocking him. As he turned, his heel lost its purchase on the rail and he lurched sharply against the bar.

Several couples hidden in the shadows of the booths joined in the laughter. A harsh Flemish voice made a short, unintelligible comment and the laughter became general. *"Oui, Major,"* the young man said. "We've got all types of drinks here: beer, whisky, gin, Martini. I'm afraid we don't have any palm wine, though." Pierre felt the hot anger mixing in his chest with a childlike fear and shame. He wanted to bolt from the room, but something held him to his stool.

"I imagine," he said coldly to the bartender, "that you don't have any cold champagne."

"Cold champagne?" the man said. "Yes, we have several kinds: Mumm, Cordon Rouge . . ."

"What is the best?" Pierre interrupted.

The man squatted to open the metal door of the refrigerator beneath the bar. He hummed faintly to himself with the music as he slowly examined the bottles in the refrigerator. "I would recommend," he said in mock seriousness, "the Piper-Heidsieck, 1959. Nineteen fifty-nine was a good year, you know."

"I'll take it," Pierre said. He reached into his trouser pocket for his plastic folder of money. The young Belgian's quizzical expression deepened.

"Do you want to drink it here or are you going to take it with you?"

"Here, of course. Why?"

"Oh, nothing," the man said, wiping off the bottle. "It's just that our guests normally take off their hats when they're going to stay awhile." Pierre's face burned again at the laughter. He removed his beret and set it before him on the bar.

The popping of the champagne cork was met with muffled cheers from the whites. Pierre turned his back on them and took his glass. The wine was slightly sour. He had expected a sweet, candylike taste. It was very cold, however, and filled with countless tiny bubbles. He drank down each glass quickly and waited for the Belgian to refill his glass. Customers came and went. He sat quietly at the bar, beginning to feel the effect of the wine.

This was the good life. Perhaps the whites had laughed because they weren't used to seeing a Congolese drinking champagne. Well, they were going to have to get used to it because from now on he was going to drink only champagne. Soon the bottle was empty and he called for another.

"A whole one or a half?" the bartender asked.

"A whole one," Pierre said. He belched loudly with unexpected violence. The bartender smiled as he opened the second bottle.

"It's very good champagne, *mon Colonel?*"

Once, with Christianne, out dancing in the *cité,* they had each drunk three bottles of Primus and they'd been drunk. That had been his only previous experience with intoxication. Now he knew, sitting dizzily on the tall bar stool, that he was drunk and that he was going to be sick. Slowly, with carefully controlled movements, he paid for the second bottle, pocketed his change, and walked toward the distant door. He felt the white people watching him, but he seemed to walk correctly. Just as his hand touched the metal handle of the door, the bartender shouted out at him over the subdued music.

"*Eh, Général, votre chapeau.*" He sailed Pierre's beret at him through the dim air. Pierre made a drunken stab at it and fell over a low table. The entire room rocked with laughter. Someone handed Pierre his beret and he was out the door in the heavy night air, reeling with the sound of the Europeans' mocking laughter.

In the broken rear seat of an old Chevrolet taxi he vomited up the acid wine in thick, heaving bursts. The young Mukongo taxi-driver swore loudly at him in Lingala, swerving the car hard to stop beside the broken curbstone on some street in the *cité.* Pierre leaned against the side of the car, vomiting choking mouthfuls of champagne. Finally, when the liquid was exhausted, he retched up evil-tasting bile, gasping for breath between each burst of nausea, his eyes filled with tears, his nose blocked. Around him in the wet darkness he dimly perceived noise and movement in the *cité*. Packs of ragged children were running between the pools of light thrown down by the occasional street lamps, their voices shrill and disembodied to his distorted sense of hearing. Chickens were clucking. Somewhere very near a loud record player in one of the ubiquitous *buvettes* was bellowing Lingala dance music. The sour smell of clogged and broken sewers mingled in his head with the charcoal smoke and sour milk stench of spoiling manioc. He braced himself against the body of the car, resting his head on the roof, and tried to stare at a distant star that showed weakly through the haze of the city lights.

After a long while he was ready to continue the trip. The taxi-driver was still complaining; his nagging, singsong voice drove into Pierre's head. He fumbled in his pocket and thrust a thousand-franc note over the seat into the man's lap. "Take this and be quiet," he said weakly. The man was quiet. Pierre cradled his head on his arm and let the hot air play against his forehead and cheeks. Whatever the white man had put into the bottle of champagne, he thought, it was certainly evil.

It was impossible that the wine had been unadulterated. It was either already spoiled or the Belgian had deliberately altered it to make him sick. It was an unkind trick to have played on him. The whites, it seemed, were no longer the same as those whom he had known and who had always helped him as a child. The Congo had suffered an irrevocable transformation; the Africans were lazy criminals and the whites were all bent on seeking vengeance for the loss of their colony. He had only himself now to rely upon. He thought with a sudden drunken insight that he could no longer trust anyone, either white or black.

Late that night he lay naked in bed after Christianne had helped him out of his vomit-fouled uniform, washing his face and chest with cool water from the kitchen faucet. For a long time he had tossed on the hot sheets, but finally he had been able to sink into a shallow sleep. Then he was awake, his head held immobile in a vise of pain. Lying very still in the darkened room with the girl beside him, he silently endured the sick headache. The baby rolled in his sleep in the little crib beneath the ghostly canopy of the mosquito net. Pierre listened to his son's little sighs and whimpering. He was going to be all right. He had simply drunk too much of the foreign champagne. It had been a foolish thing to do, to go into that frigid European bar and attempt with a great show of sophistication and squandering of money to force himself upon the Belgians. He had spent more than ten thousand francs for the two bottles of champagne and yet they had mocked him with their laughter. He would never again act so stupidly.

He had curled himself into a tight ball, pressed his face into the pillow, and was thinking that he might sleep again when the jolting noise of a vehicle stopping before his house brought him upright in bed. He had just pulled himself shakily to his feet when the front door was splintered open. He was blinded by several flashlights and received the sickening weight of a kick to his unprotected groin. There were more blows. The girl was screaming as they dragged him from the house.

In the faint light of the streetlamp on the corner he saw that there were four huge military police. They grunted to each other in Lingala monosyllables, threw him into the back of the Land Rover, and manacled him naked to a steel ring on the floor of the car. The center of his body burned from the kicking. Through the cloud of pain he could hear the girl screaming and then pleading in a lower voice, and then she was silent; only the grunting of the MPs was audible.

After a long time they returned, carrying small things from the house. One had his transistor radio, another an armload of his civilian shirts and Christianne's dresses. They laughed and jostled each other as they buttoned up their trousers. He was grabbed savagely by the hair and his own uniform, crumpled in a ball, was thrust hard into his face. "Hey, Muluba boy," one of the guards said, "that smell good? That's your little Kasai bitch on there. We all wipe our peckers on that shirt." They laughed again and the car lurched off into the night. As they sped down the silent road, Pierre thought that he could hear little Henri howling.

Once again Pierre was in a cell, but the prisoners' barracks at the paracommando camp on Mount Stanley was more comfortable than the cell he had known in Makala prison. It had a grilled window from which he could see the burly commandos in their sharply pressed camouflage uniforms and red berets. His slop bucket had a cover and it was emptied by another prisoner regularly each morning. The food was passable, including hot coffee in the morning and a small piece of meat or fish several times a week. The spring bunk was free of vermin. For the first three days Pierre was in a state of shock similar to that during his first taste of prison four years before. He lay on his bunk watching the green and yellow geckos crawl across the ceiling in search of flies. From down the echoing concrete corridor of the barracks he could hear orders being bellowed and groups of military prisoners being formed up into ranks.

They had caught him. Da Silva obviously had much better connections in the ANC headquarters than Pierre had guessed. Now they had him in jail again and the white man was still free, no doubt still receiving his weekly dispatches from the Kasai, carried by some new courier.

For more than a year he had served Da Silva with absolute fidelity, and this was how the white repaid him. Pierre knew that they were now in the process of preparing some trumped-up charges to be heard at a sham trial, after which he would be executed. That was the normal method of dealing with defectors like him. He knew too much, so it would be easier and safer for the others if he disappeared. The prison block at the paracommando camp was notorious for that kind of thing. The victims were almost always political prisoners who could not bribe their way out. The stories he had heard at Makala had it that once the prisoner was marked for death the guards no longer bothered to beat or torment him; he was given decent food and allowed to fall into a state of false security. Then one night they would come and take him down to the river, and the crocodiles would dispose of the body.

As he lay on his bunk watching the lizards, he was sure that this was the fate they had chosen for him. He was afraid. He did not want to die. He did not deserve to die. For the first time in almost five years Pierre began to say his prayers again. They were his companion in the long airless nights as he lay in his cell with the fear of death so huge that he was almost crushed against the wall by it.

For the first several weeks he kept track of the days with little marks scratched on the cement wall beside the bunk. But then one morning he stopped. There was no use. They could do with him what they wished. There was no way to resist them. What was the sense of keeping track of time in a world that had gone insane, a world he was about to abandon in any case? He found much more solace in his prayers. Using a long piece of cotton thread from his prisoner's shorts, he patiently fashioned a kind of primitive rosary, working from memory and tying triple knots to use as beads. It gave him infinite satisfaction to run the knots through his fingers and chant the old prayers in a whisper. If they were going to come for him, he would be ready when they came. He lost himself completely in prayer. He prayed for the repose of his father's soul and that his mother was still alive and well. He prayed a bit for the girl, but mostly for his baby son. He prayed that the baby would have a happier life than he had known.

One morning shortly after coffee two guards came for him. He sat up stiffly on his bunk when he heard the key in the lock. They were going to take him now, he thought. They walked him down the corridor to a small windowless room lighted by a fluorescent tube and closed on the corridor side by a metal mesh door. He sat trembling on a wooden stool for an hour, and then two different guards and an ANC officer came for him. He was given a pair of plastic sandals and a sleeveless, buttonless shirt made of the same blue cotton as his shorts. They walked him out into the sun, down along the raked gravel paths of the camp to another barracks.

The courtroom was at the end of the barracks and was open and breezy with high windows on three sides. A large overhead fan moved the still-cool morning air. At the far end of the room two ANC officers and a Belgian in military uniform sat at a long table with trays of papers before them. Pierre was seated on a plain wooden chair directly in front of the table. The two guards stood on either side of him.

The officer who had come for him with the guards took his place with the others. "I am Major Bokanda," he said. "This is

Lieutenant Kayembe, who is on the staff of the Adjutant General; this is Captain Mwenda from the État-Major, and finally Commandant Grisson who is a military judge from Belgian technical assistance. Commandant Grisson," he added, "is only an adviser here. Do you understand?"

"Oui, monsieur," Pierre answered.

"Proceed," the major said to the young lieutenant seated next to him. The lieutenant rose and began reading in a squeaking accent.

"Tshipama, Pierre-Marie, Lieutenant de l'Infanterie, service number 62 / 569734 . . ." he read very painfully, making frequent mistakes and doubling back to correct himself. It took a long time to complete the reading of Pierre's forged service record, which included the dates of fictitious transfers from the garrison at Kikwit and from the training base at Kitona to the courier assignment on the État-Major.

"Is this your service record?" the major asked. "There's no use denying it because your fingerprints are on file. This is just a formality. Answer the question."

Pierre stared across at the court-martial panel for a moment. "I'm sure that there is no use denying it," he said softly so as not to alarm by an angry tone the two MPs poised above him. "I would like to state, however, that even though that service record has all the necessary stamps and signatures, including fingerprints which are undoubtedly mine, it is a forgery. I was never a real Army officer. I was hired by a Portuguese named—"

"That's enough!" the major said, slamming his fist down on the table as he glanced sideways at the Belgian. The guards jerked to nervous attention. "You will answer the questions put to you, not make speeches. Carry on," he said to the captain.

The captain stood and began to read from another paper. "On September 26, 1965, the counterintelligence unit of the Sûreté Nationale reported to my office in a confidential report numbered SN / L 443 / 99 / 25 / 65 that one of the members of the communications section of the État-Major, namely the courier Lieutenant Tshipama, Pierre-Marie, was trafficking in illegal political propaganda while ostensibly carrying out his regular duties. An investigation was made and these charges were validated. Lieutenant Tshipama was arrested at his house in Ngiri-Ngiri Commune,

Léopoldville. Large quantities of political propaganda of a pro-rebel nature were discovered. Samples of this material are displayed at this hearing." He indicated a small pile of roughly printed leaflets and two or three folded posters which lay on the table. The major whispered to the Belgian commandant, then addressed Pierre. "Do you deny or admit to the charges?"

Pierre was silent. Finally he said, "May I ask a technical question?" The major nodded. "If I admit to the charges, that means that I agree that all the evidence, including my service record, is correct, *n'est-ce pas?*"

The major had another whispered conference with the Belgian. "That is correct," the major said. "Why do you ask?"

"Because the service record states that I was in Kikwit and Kitona in 1963 and 1964 when I was actually in Makala prison here in Léopoldville. It would be a very easy thing to verify."

"We're not here to verify the lies of traitors and rebels," the major spat, then added in Lingala to the guards, "Get him out of here!" Pierre was jerked to his feet and pushed into the corridor. A few minutes passed and the guards bullied him back into the courtroom. This time there was no chair for him to sit on. The major stood and read the sentence. Seven years at hard labor. He would be transferred to the military prison in the Bas Congo and begin serving his sentence on January 3. Due to the national emergency and the irrefutable evidence against him, he was not eligible for appeal. Pierre was returned to his cell.

For several days he lay despondent in his cell, his rosary forgotten. They were not going to kill him outright, it seemed. They preferred to have him die in the sweltering prison camp in the Bas Congo. He would have chosen a painless bullet in the back of the head. It was odd that they had bothered to stage the trial at all. Obviously there were high-level officers in the ANC involved with Da Silva, and after General Mobutu's November coup d'état these officers were eager to have him out of the way, but they were not secure enough in their own positions simply to have him murdered. Proof of such a murder could later be used against them. Mobutu had the reputation of being an honest man, so, Pierre guessed, the smuggling operation was probably being closed down for the moment until the nature of the General's new government became known. All the loose ends of the operation were being disposed of and he was obviously a loose end. He had absolutely no defense.

CHAPTER **17**

Just before Christmas a guard came to his cell to tell him that there would be a priest saying confessions and that the prisoners interested should sign a paper. Pierre signed the paper. Then he turned to the guard and said, "Do you know Major Bokanda, the officer who came to get me the morning of my trial?"

"*Oui*," the guard grunted. "Why?"

"Tell the major that I want to talk about one million francs."

All the next day no one came to his cell except the prisoners for the slop bucket and the food detail. The next day was Christmas, and although he had signed the sheet for confession and mass he decided not to go when the guards came for the faithful. The day passed very slowly. He could hear the sound of church singing far away in the camp's chapel. Later there was a wild blasting of car horns, some disjointed drunken laughter and rowdiness. The troops were celebrating Christmas in the manner in which they celebrated every other holiday: by getting as drunk as they could and making noise.

At eight o'clock that night the guards were relieved. The new watch had evidently been drinking throughout the day. They could be heard screaming obscenities at each other, singing drunken marching songs, and stumbling about. It was a close, still night. The rain clouds that had been building up all afternoon had passed over Mount Stanley and broken in a violent storm on the Brazzaville side of the river. In a week they would come for him to herd him into a boxcar with a levy of prisoners for the swampy labor camp downriver. It was the end of everything.

The singing and laughter down the corridor stopped suddenly. There were heavy footsteps on the echoing concrete. His cell door was opened and the overhead bulb turned on. Major Bokanda en-

tered the cell and closed the door behind him. Pierre sat up on the
bunk, rubbing his eyes. The major stood by the grilled window
catching the slight breeze. "What's this story about one million
francs?" he said.

"You know all about me and Da Silva and the diamonds, don't
you?" Pierre asked. The major was silent, staring out the window.
He reeled slightly, his elbows resting on the window ledge. Pierre
could smell that he had been drinking. "I have one million francs,
perhaps a bit more, hidden here in Léo," Pierre said. He spoke
slowly, carefully choosing his words. "If you can get me out of
this prison sentence, I'll split it with you."

The major turned from the window to face him. "I'll have all of
it and I'll have it tonight. Where is it?"

"What happens to me?" Pierre asked.

The major sat down next to Pierre on the bunk and took out a
folded sheaf of papers from a small imitation leather folder. "I've
drawn up orders to have you assigned elsewhere. That would be
the best for all of us. The rest of . . . the people involved with Da
Silva don't want you here in Léo. It would be a lot simpler to
have you shot while trying to escape. These are strange times,
though, politically. You no longer know who you can rely on. The
soldiers are acting suspiciously. In any event, I get the money
now, and tomorrow"—he tapped his finger on the papers—"you
will be sent to Opérations Sud in Albertville as a replacement officer. I'm sure that with your talents you'll soon have half the
troops organized as smugglers."

Pierre was not happy. He wanted his freedom, not to continue
the sham as an Army officer. "Isn't there any other way?" he said.
"Can't I just be released here as a civilian and sent away?"

"It's either our way or the labor camp," the major said. "Make
your decision. Incidentally, we'll get the money either way. All I
have to do is call down the hall to those guards. They'll put you
on that table in the room next to the dispensary and you'll be talking your head off in ten minutes."

"It's hard to explain how to find it," Pierre said. "It would be
better if I could show you."

"*Allez,*" the major said. "Let's go, then."

The major guided him down the darkened corridor to the

guardroom. The guards were subdued in the presence of an officer. They were glassy-eyed drunk. The major took him through
the room to a darkened vestibule. Switching on a light, he pointed
to Pierre's old metal trunk and his army duffle bag. "These are
your uniforms from your house. Put one on."

The uniforms were still starched and carefully folded just the
way Christianne had done them. After a month in prison shorts it
felt strange to wear long trousers and underwear again. They
drove out of the camp in the major's Land Rover, Pierre and the
major in the back and two silent, grim-faced paracommandos in
the front seat.

As they rolled through the hot night in the *cité,* a raucous mélange of music and shouting laughter swelled out of the bars. The
streets were crowded with weaving men in white shirts and laughing, drunken women dressed in their best wax prints for the holiday. The tiny beer cafés were brightly lighted with flaring gasoline
lamps, casting long shadows up into the overhanging roof of
branches. The soldiers in the front seat eyed the scene eagerly, lin-
gering on the swaying hips of the dancing women.

Pierre's former street was quiet in comparison with the rest of
the *cité.* Most of the houses were dark behind their creeper-cov-
ered bamboo fences. He sat in the car with the driver while the
major and the other soldier went into the house. Pierre thought a
moment about Christianne and the baby. They seemed like people he had known many years ago. They were gone now and it
was no use worrying about them. The major returned with a mid-
dle-aged, big-bellied Congolese, his wife and four small children.
The papa was buttoning up the fly of his military trousers. One of
the children cried loudly. The mother, holding the two smallest
children, stared around her blankly and fussed with the loose
piece of cloth she had hastily wrapped about herself.

"You wait here by the car," the major said to the papa. "We
won't be very long." He nodded to Pierre and they entered the
house.

The rooms stank of cooking smoke and garbage. The walls were
stained as high as the children could reach. The furniture was
chipped, the cushions punctured. They walked straight through the
house out through the cluttered, roach-infested kitchen to the rear

yard. "The house was not built with a flush toilet," Pierre explained to the major. "I had that installed. The old latrine is back here. That is where the money is."

The soldier switched on a flashlight, leading the way to the sagging wooden outhouse. The screen door had been ripped away and the stench was overpowering. Working quickly, Pierre ripped off the wooden bench seat and took a grip on a thin metal cable attached to it by a steel eyebolt. He walked backward out of the doorway, pulling so that his hands would not have to touch the fouled lower stretch of cable. He had walked a little more than four meters when he gave a hard jerk and a large metal object, encrusted with slime and filth, flopped over the edge of the wooden seat frame and fell to the floor like a grotesque fish. The soldier played the light on it. The object was a large military jerry can with a wide-mouthed lid secured by a snap spring. Pierre dragged the can across the yard by the end of the cable to a faucet on the outside wall of the house. When the can was thoroughly washed, they removed the cable and lugged the can into the living room. The major opened the lid and took out a twine-wrapped bundle of thousand-franc notes. He tentatively held the money to his nose and smiled.

The major was left at the paracommando camp. He carried the heavy jerry can himself from the car to the stairs of the shabby villa. He walked back to the Land Rover and handed Pierre three one-thousand-franc bills. "You'll need a little money until you get paid. There are several military flights this morning," he said. "Your orders are priority so you won't have any problem getting to Albertville. I've sent them a message that you're coming. Don't try to come back to Léo. If you're found here, you'll be shot as an escaped prisoner. *Alors, bonne fête.*"

They drove Pierre through the dawn directly to the military hangar at N'djili Field where the confused episode with the American airmen took place. For a brief moment he had been hopeful that he could trick the pilot into not taking him and somehow persuade the two waiting paracommandos to release him with the promise of more hidden money. But then the young civilian American had intervened and he was trapped on the airplane. Somehow he knew that the message the major had sent ahead to

Albertville was really a death warrant. They did not want to dispose of him in Léopoldville, but Albertville was 1500 kilometers away. There he could easily become another casualty of the still smoldering mountain fighting against the rebels.

He lay in the canvas sling seat far back in the tail of the huge American airplane. He could hear the engine noises changing and feel the familiar blocking pressure in his ears which told him that the airplane was descending. They were coming into Albertville. He watched the clouds whip by outside the round window, and then as the plane sliced out of the overcast, Lake Tanganyika was flat green-gray as it lapped along the thin sand beaches of the coastline beneath them. The country looked similar to the open rolling hills of elephant grass he had seen so often on his flights to the Kasai. As the plane tilted into a banking turn, he caught a glimpse of the dull green mountains to the north rising into a forbidding layer of clouds. A crewman in a gray flight suit and earphones motioned to him. He sat up and fumbled with the straps on the seat. They were about to land.

PART III **lisa**

CHAPTER **18**

Lisa Sherman stood naked in the big stainless-steel-and-tile kitchen of their apartment. Her hair hung dripping from the shower as she brushed it before the open door of the refrigerator. She knew that she should eat something, but nothing she saw appealed to her. It was a little past eleven, and outside the air was stifling. In the bedroom and the living room the drapes were tightly drawn against the glare; the heavy air conditioners surged mechanically against the heat. She moved slowly from the refrigerator to the cupboards above the kitchen counter. Cans and packages, bright in American labels, offered her Vienna sausage, spaghetti, and Whip 'n Chill, chocolate, butterscotch, and vanilla.

She had slept longer than Steve, but still the sour stomach, dizzy headache of the Christmas night drinking grew steadily inside of her. She found a package of orange-flavored Constant Comment tea which had arrived in the last order from the Copenhagen wholesale grocers. As the teakettle heated, she padded down the long corridor to the bathroom where she removed one pink Enovid tablet from the plastic membrane of the calendar package beside her toothbrush glass. Clutching the pill and her hairbrush, she walked slowly back toward the kitchen.

The codeine—she knew that she had handled the bottle earlier that morning, but in her hangover daze she could not recall where she had left it. She leaned against the open door of the kitchen, closing her eyes against the headache, trying to remember. Then she saw the little green bottle falling into the hot darkness and bursting like a snowstorm. She giggled self-consciously to herself. Better try some aspirin.

There was a huge bottle of Rexall aspirin next to the stove where the houseboy could take it for his malaria and rheumatism and flat feet and God-knows-what-else he had, the poor old man. He was an excellent cook, though, and he enjoyed working for a childless couple. He did everything: washing and ironing, most of the marketing, always waxing floors and polishing furniture. A clean, sweet old man, and even though they probably overpaid him he really didn't cost anything. It was almost like having a slave to whom you occasionally gave pocket money.

The teakettle boiled with a piercing shrill. The aromatic steam rising from the teapot caused her stomach to flip weakly with vestigial hunger. She sat with her hairbrush and her pill and her cup of steaming tea before the mouth of the living room air conditioner. She needed something cold to drink, and she had forgotten the aspirin. Once again in front of the supermarket-hypnotic refrigerator: ice. She needed something iced. The bright green and red cans of diet cola were an insult. Why had she ordered them, anyway? Her long fingers ran down her belly and the hardness of her legs. She wasn't getting fat. She had a nice body; Steve had always said so. Robert loved her body. He kissed her everywhere. He delighted in her youth, her ripeness. Why had she wasted their money on that ridiculous case of diet cola, almost six dollars? Everything was so expensive from Denmark. It all looked so cheap in the catalogue, but then there were the shipping charges and the insurance and the pilferage. It had been stupid to order the diet cola. She shouldn't have wasted their money.

Their money. Was it wasting *their* money to have bought the see-through black panties and bra that she kept in the night table next to the bed in Robert's apartment? Was she wasting their life with the things that she and Robert did? She had thought through the whole affair before. She must not think like this. What she and

Robert did had nothing to do with her and Steve. It was *her* life, her youth that was being spent, *wasted* on Embassy wives' teas and coffees and bridge parties and hypocritical charity committees. She had never had a real life as a woman. She had been a college girl when they married and now she was only catching up, snatching at the chance to have a brief life all her own. They would leave the Congo soon. Then they would settle down in a new post and have a baby and she would become a model wife and mother. Just this once she had the chance to be with an older, more sophisticated man and that was all she wanted: just this one chance. She had needed to discover how it really felt to be an independent person, not just Steve's pretty young wife, or Mrs. Sherman, or the new wife in the Political Section, but herself. It was an experiment. It was her life. She had the right to try it.

As she stood thinking, the refrigerator motor buzzed, protesting the intrusion of the heavy kitchen air. Quickly she removed the frosty plastic box of ice cubes from the freezer. She poured herself a long gin and tonic, tearing back the crinkly cellophane on a new forty-ounce bottle of Beefeater. Back in the living room, she took her aspirins and her baby pill. Next year they would have a baby and she would be a good wife again and an excellent mother. With delightful alternation she sipped the icy drink and her cup of spicy tea.

The telephone rang. She dashed across the tiled floor and then paused before the ringing phone. She mustn't seem too eager. It had to be Robert. She felt her heart pumping hard. They would have a whole week together. Steve would be gone five nights.

The phone rang again. "Hello, Robert darling," she said in a firm clear voice.

"My," he said, "aren't we being adventurous this morning!"

"That sounds nice," she said, "adventure. I can think of some delightful little adventures we could be having."

"I'll be over in half an hour. I've got a surprise for you."

Lisa finished her tea and sat staring absently at the sunlight patterns on the drapes. Somewhere under the long expanse of cloth there was a fly trapped. It buzzed incessantly as it collided with the windows. It would have been nice to sleep a few more hours. Perhaps when Robert came they could just go to bed and then take a nap. She lay back in her chair, and her long suntanned fingers played up her thighs. She would wear the new white bikini Robert had given her. How was she going to explain the bikini to Steve? They were almost overdrawn on the checking account. The bikini was obviously very expensive. She had all week to think of a story. Oh, well, she wouldn't worry now. Why spoil their week? She peeked around the corner of the drapes. The magnesium-white sun blinded her. Better have another aspirin. In the kitchen she also refilled her plastic glass, letting the colorless gin gurgle down over the column of ice cubes. Such a nice drink on a hot day.

In the bedroom she quickly made the bed, then stood unsteadily debating whether or not to change the sheets. She and Robert might be making love there in ten minutes, on the same sheets she and her husband had sweated on for so long only eight hours before. She twisted the yellow percale between her fingers. There were no spots. Then with sudden recognition she saw that these were their honeymoon sheets. They had been a wedding present from Steve's Aunt Rita, monogrammed percale sheets and bath towels. These same sheets had clothed their first marriage bed in that little efficiency apartment above the pizzeria on State Street in Madison. Had that been so long ago? She had better change them. But first she would dress.

On the shelf above the bathroom sink she saw her package of Enovid. Had she taken her pill? She tried to remember but could not. It was so hard when Steve was not around to remind her. "Baby pill, baby," he always said. As she washed down the second pink pill with the gin and tonic, she heard the buzzer from the basement garage sound twice. Robert would be up in a minute.

Quickly she pulled on the abbreviated white bottom of her bikini and stepped into a fresh blue sundress. Into a string bag she dropped the bikini top with its two white cups large and provocative. She added her little knit mad-money sack with her keys and lipstick and the clear blue silk scarf that Steve had bought her at the Catholic mission vocational school. She was sitting with her drink and a copy of *Elle* in the cool darkness of the living room when the front doorbell rang.

He stood there filling the doorway with his bulk, his fishnet polo shirt very white against his tan. The hair on his legs beneath the knit swim trunks was sun-bleached. Without entering, he said softly, "He got away, I take it?" Lisa did not answer, but drew him to her, reaching up to his shoulders. She molded herself to him, smelling the man's smell of deodorized sweat, expensive shaving cologne, and a trace of Sunday morning gin.

The string bag and the sundress and the bikini bottom lay tangled with his fishnet shirt and sandals on the living-room floor. Lisa lay naked on her stomach on the sofa, Henderson's head propped against her thigh as he sat on the floor smoking a short cigarillo. She let her fingers intertwine among his chest hair. His legs were stretched out into a V before him.

"Was it all right for you?" he asked, his voice surprisingly high-pitched and youthful as it always was after they had made love.

"Lovely," she said.

He laughed an artificial, self-conscious laugh. "I guess I'm not a kid any more. After all this Christmas socializing and boozing it's just easier for me to come that way. Was it nice before, with my mouth?"

"It was beautiful," she said. "All of it. You don't always have to be hard as a rock for it to be nice."

He turned to rest his face, warmly nuzzling, against her rib cage. "You're a good girl, Lisa."

"I'm hardly that."

"No, really. A lot of young girls wouldn't understand how it can be sometimes for an older man."

"Do you know a lot of young girls?" she teased.

"It's not that. I mean you always do everything to please me. Most women only want their own pleasure. You're not like that."

"When it's nice for you, it's nice for me."

Henderson stood up with athletic grace and scooped up his gold bracelet watch from the floor. "Christ, almost one. We'd better go if we're going to."

"You haven't told me my surprise."

"I'll tell you on the way," he said. "Let's hurry now."

Henderson drove fast out along the empty, sun-blasted

Boulevard. Instead of doubling back in the direction of the yacht club, he squealed his tires into a sharp right turn and they were racing out past the factorylike Danish hospital toward the ghetto of foreign villas in Kalina on the riverfront. They drove smoothly in the small Mercedes through the mottled shade of wide-leafed tung-oil trees and feathery jacarandas. Henderson looked across at Lisa as she absently stroked the leather seat. Her light hair billowed out in the wind beneath the blue silk scarf.

They came out on the curving asphalt drive along the riverfront. Lisa shrank back imperceptibly as the car flew past the shaded compound of the American Ambassador's residence. Henderson flicked a quick glance at her, and she was back upright in her seat, smiling. Neither of them spoke again.

Some Congolese schoolboys in long Sunday trousers wandered along the road, staring up at the secluded fenced-in villas of the diplomats and white businessmen. Henderson down-shifted and they glided to a stop at the turnabout at the end of the drive. The wide bay at the downriver tip of Stanley Pool spread out before them, calm and lifeless, and above it on the chartreuse slopes of Mount Stanley the ANC headquarters hung in the sun like a sugar cube. The cranes and derricks of the Chanic shipyard across the bay were still. Fishermen were languidly poling their pirogues among the shallows close to the Léopoldville side of the bank; the tree-lined bank of Brazzaville across the channel showed no life. They got out of the car and stood in the shade of a flamboyant tree, enjoying the soft breeze off the river and the quiet.

A black Citroën station wagon, its windows closed tightly on its air-conditioned interior, pulled into the turnabout. The car carried Congolese plates and an Italian medallion. It sank on its hydraulic cushions as the Congolese chauffeur killed the engine and jumped out to open the rear door. Introductions were made in the blinding sunshine. Signor Pontecelli from Milan was with the Italian oil consortium prospecting in the Bas Congo. Gloria, a long-legged, suntanned girl wearing white model's lipstick, huge round sunglasses, and a sailor dress, was introduced as Pontecelli's secretary. She spoke neither English nor French.

Signor Pontecelli appeared small and sickly beside Henderson.

The Italian's skin was gray and his stomach bulged in an ugly paunch over the cloth belt of his picnic shorts. Once out of the car, he quickly covered his balding head with a straw sun hat. Only his eyes were youthful, slashing past Lisa and Henderson to dwell upon the cloudscape reflected in the pastel-blue surface of the river. He spoke quietly, using his dead-white fingers to accentuate his conversation. The chauffeur unpacked a large picnic hamper and a nylon beach tent tightly rolled around its aluminum poles. Henderson produced a pigskin picnic bar chest and poured a round of Bloody Marys.

He and Pontecelli laughed, speaking in Italian. Gloria studied her fingernails, and then through gestures asked for and received Lisa's blue scarf, which she examined closely. After a few minutes they moved to the shade of a fromagier tree and stood with their drinks, watching the pirogues on the river. Henderson and Pontecelli spoke with quiet seriousness just out of hearing of the two women. Lisa and Gloria smiled weakly at each other and made charade gestures on the beauty of the river. They all looked up as if on cue as the helicopter came sailing toward them above the rapids.

"A *heli*copter!" Lisa said. "Where are we going?"

"I thought it might be nice to go down to Zongo Falls," Henderson said. "It's too hot a day for the drive on that impossible road, though, so Signor Pontecelli suggested the helicopter. They normally use it down around Kitona for prospecting."

The pilot was a short young Italian named Carlo. He wore an RAF moustache and was raffishly dressed in a modified airline pilot's uniform, an open-necked shirt, tennis-style shorts, white knee socks, and desert boots. As Lisa stooped to take his extended hand helping her up into the side door of the helicopter, he stared with unabashed pleasure at her breasts clearly visible as the scoop neck of her sundress fell away. She met his stare as he bent to tighten her seat belt. His bronze-colored sunglasses were pushed up high on his pile of curly hair.

Henderson sat next to her, the canvas seat sagging with his weight. Across the small cabin Pontecelli sat smiling at them. Gloria had taken the co-pilot's seat in the plexiglass cockpit in front of them. Lisa could see Carlo openly fondling her bare thigh as he pulled in her seat belt. One of those kind of Italians, she thought. He's certainly attractive, though. The breeze had stopped, and it was sticky inside the cabin, the sun hot on her legs. She was sleepy from the drink. She could see Carlo's fingers moving about the blur of switches and instruments before him as the cabin filled with the scream of the turbine blades and the engine caught.

They took off smoothly, the cabin suddenly cool with the river air. Carlo tilted the helicopter steeply as they cleared the bank. Léopoldville was behind them, lost in green trees. Below them the fishermen in the pirogues waved. They were past Mount Stanley. The brown-and-gray rapids rolled quickly by, and then the narrowing gorge of the river fell away and they were flying at a thousand feet above alternating forest and savannah country. Henderson took Lisa's hand as they watched the landscape. They passed several villages, tin roofs winking in the sun and thin columns of gray smoke rising. Then Carlo had them steeply tilted again and they were racing along just above the flowery green tops of the forest. They shot across a red dirt road, and Lisa caught a splintered glimpse of a herd of goats leaping in panic into the high grass. Henderson and Pontecelli called back and forth to each other in Italian over the engine noise.

Her Bloody Mary was refilled. This was a pleasant way to travel. The sunlight felt good on her skin as Carlo climbed back up to the relative coolness fifteen hundred feet over the river. She could see him looking at his large-dialed watch as he spoke into the radio microphone. They swung off onto a course away from the river. Her drink felt icy and good in her hand. The hangover was going away. Soon she would be really hungry. Henderson was talking to her, but the wind blew his voice away. He pressed his face against her scarf and spoke into her ear. "Do you like it?" he asked. She nodded her head vigorously. Below them the forest was unbroken for several minutes, then they were above open grassland and she saw Carlo pointing out in front of them and to the left.

The Zongo River stretched away to the south, carrying its own sheath of high forest with it along its banks. A white plume of mist hung above the falls. "Look at that!" Henderson shouted. Directly below the helicopter they could see a jam of cars and motor scooters parked at the end of the dirt track leading to the forested bluff above the falls.

Henderson unbuckled his seat belt and gingerly raised himself to stand clinging to a cargo strap on the overhead. He thrust his head into the cockpit and by gestures directed Carlo farther up the river past the falls. The rocks and pools directly below them were covered with Europeans in swimming suits. The aircraft bucked wildly as they cut through the spray cloud above the falls and flew down the river's channel between the forest on the banks.

"There!" Henderson shouted, pointing to a wide sand island that stood at the bend in the river half shaded by the wall of trees.

Carlo hovered, carefully measuring with his eye the distance from the flat point of the sand island and the nearest rotor-snapping trees. They descended slowly into a storm of flying sand and river spray. As Carlo switched off, the turbine began a high-pitched wheezing as it free-wheeled to a stop.

Hardwood trees rose in a solid corridor on the riverbanks. The sand island formed a smooth eddy behind it. The river rushed past them in a narrow channel between the tip of the island and the opposite bank. Just beyond the bend they could see the piled brown granite boulders of a small rapids. As the flexible rotor spun slowly to a halt and the turbine whistling died, bird and insect noises could be heard in the forest. Lisa walked to the edge of the trees, turned her back on the group, and dropped the top of her sundress and bent forward to cup herself into her bikini top. She stepped out of her dress and folded it away neatly in the string bag. When she turned back, she saw Carlo watching her from a few feet away.

In the shade of the trees they ate their cold chicken paprika, endive salad, and freshly baked rolls, opening iced bottles of Portuguese rosé with great ceremony and casting the corked empty bottles away down the river toward the falls. There was a steady breeze off the channel of fast water. During the meal the spoken conversation was almost entirely in Italian. Carlo, sitting opposite Lisa on the orange sheet of Congo print cloth, carried out another, wordless, and more direct, conversation with her. Henderson did not seem to notice. After they had finished the little cups of chocolate mousse, he and Pontecelli paced slowly to the tip of the island with their cigars. They stood knee-deep in the rippling shallows, talking once again in subdued tones, their faces set with the seriousness of their discussion. Lisa and Gloria cleared the picnic things back into the hamper and went wading in the cool water of the eddy. Gloria called over to Pontecelli and they all laughed, Pontecelli making a broad gesture of consent with his hands. With a quick motion she unsnapped the top of her bikini and stepped out of the bottom, throwing the two pieces behind her onto the picnic blanket. She dove into the water, swimming beneath the surface, and came up smiling into the sunlight ten yards from the island. Lisa stood watching her in surprise. Carlo was very close to her on the sand. Then he, too, was naked, the white swatch of his untanned buttocks flashing as he dove into the water.

Henderson and Pontecelli were seated now in the shade on a water-polished snag at the end of the island. They smoked their cigars, taking little notice of the swimmers.

Lisa swam with strong underwater strokes to the center of the little bay. Gloria was floating on her back several yards away. She smiled and said something Lisa could not understand. Carlo dove in the shallow water, bringing up smooth river mussel shells. As Lisa watched, Henderson entered the helicopter and emerged a moment later with a cardboard file of papers. He and Pontecelli squatted in the sand with fresh cigars and another bottle of wine as they examined the documents, submerged in quiet conversation. Lisa could see Henderson making pencil notes in a leather diary. Absently, she wondered what it was that could have drawn them away from the beauty of the forest and the coolness of the river. She swam several lengths of the lozenge-shaped bay, pulling with a powerful crawl stroke that left her panting at the far end of the pool. She saw Gloria lie down sleepily on the blanket on her stomach. She didn't put her bikini back on.

Carlo swam across the smooth surface of the water toward her. He did a surface dive and pulled along the sandy bottom, rising beside her. Henderson and Pontecelli had moved slightly into the deeper shade of the helicopter. Their backs were toward Lisa and Carlo. He smiled at her with an open expression, his dripping moustache giving him a comic but not unattractive pirate's face. In the shallow green water she could easily see his nakedness. The excitement that had been aroused but unsatisfied by Henderson earlier was rising in her again. Without a word Carlo reached over, took her hand, and placed it on his body. For a long moment her fingers moved across his flesh, the cool water of the river playing over them. Then she realized what they were doing and panicked.

"No!" she said and pushed herself out into the bay, diving to the bottom and swimming in the submarine green light until her breath was completely expended. On the surface she sucked in the cool air and swam to the shore where the two older men sat. She crawled playfully onto the sand, supporting herself on her elbows like a child.

"Robert," she said, "how can you waste an afternoon like this? Come on in the water."

Henderson and Pontecelli looked up sharply, Pontecelli's expression quickly changing to a transparent smile. Henderson spoke to him briefly, and he nodded and turned back to his papers. Then Henderson joined her at the water's edge. He knelt next to her, twirling the long coils of wet hair on her shoulders.

"Come in," she said. "It's beautiful."

"I know," he said softly. "Lisa, I'm sorry, but I just can't. Signor Pontecelli has decided to go back to Europe tonight on the eight o'clock Paris flight. I thought he was leaving tomorrow instead. This Christmas holiday has slowed us up. We've got at least another hour here before we'll be finished. If I'd known it would be like this, I wouldn't have made you come."

"It's all right. I understand. It's just that I've got a little problem with Carlo."

Henderson looked across the pool to Carlo, then down at Lisa. He smiled an odd, boyish smile. "Is it really a problem?"

"What do you mean?"

Henderson laughed softly. "I was just thinking, Carlo's a good-looking young man and you're a beautiful young woman. You'll never see these people again—they don't know you. Carlo, I understand, goes back to Italy next week. I mean, what could be more—well, natural."

Lisa sat up next to him, speaking very softly so that Pontecelli could not hear. "But what about us? Wouldn't you be jealous?"

He laughed again, still speaking just above a whisper as he twisted a twig gently in the fine white sand. "When you and I first began, you told me that you were curious about a lot of things that you felt you would never otherwise have a chance to experience. Well, a casual flirtation like this with a handsome stranger is probably one of those things, so why should I, of all people, want to prevent you from trying it?"

Lisa did not answer. She bit her lip and looked back toward Carlo.

"Go on," Henderson said. "It's fun. I won't mind, Lisa. Really." He cupped her shoulders gently in his hands and slid her, feet first, back into the water. As she rolled into a side stroke, she could see him standing in the spotted shade smiling down at her.

"Besides it being fun," Henderson said aloud, but almost inaudibly, so that neither Lisa nor Pontecelli could hear, "Carlo and his helicopter have been very good to me. I guess I owe him a favor or two."

Lisa swam the length of the pool, smiled at Carlo where he sat in the water beneath the forest bank, and then climbed warily over the pile of driftwood jammed between the boulders that separated their bay from a smaller but deeper pool. She slid back into the water, undoing her bikini top and wriggling out of the bottom. She clipped the two pieces together with the snap of the halter and was standing waist-deep in the pool, her suit hung like a white flag on an overhanging branch, when Carlo stepped naked over the boulders to join her.

It was so strange; neither of them spoke. He swam close to her smiling as he circled like a bird seeking a perch. Then he was next to her, and she reached out to touch his water-smooth skin, and his hot tongue was in her mouth. Before she fully realized what they were doing, her back was pressed hard against the sun-warmed concave of a large boulder in the shallow water. He sucked greedily at her nipples as he fumbled beneath the surface to enter her. She lay back and then with a gasp of pleasure thrust her head onto his tanned shoulder beneath the mop of dripping hair.

She thought quickly of her first time with Robert, also in the water, but so different. Almost at once they fell into a timeless rhythm, her face hard against the warm flesh of his shoulder, her hands tight around his hips. Her back slid against the polished surface of the boulder. She rose slightly, lifting her feet off the sandy bottom, and wrapped her legs around him. He had her held very tightly. She opened her eyes and the water drops on her lashes broke the world of sunlight and shade into jewel-like prisms. His skin heated. Then, with a hot pounding, it was over.

Still neither spoke. Carlo smiled at her, making a smoking gesture as he crossed back over the boulders. A few minutes later he returned with a bottle of wine and cigarettes held high above the water. Soot-black swallows were flying high above the trees. Far away to the south there was thunder.

C H A P T E R **19**

Lisa could hear music from where she stood on the long terrace of Henderson's apartment. On one of the floors below there was a party. Loud American voices sang out into the night. She looked down the side of the building and saw the red sparks of cigarettes spiraling out from the terrace below. It must be on the seventh floor, she thought, Judy Pringle's apartment. The night was spicy cool after the full heat of the day. It was just after nine o'clock. All along the northern horizon thunderheads flickered silently green and orange. She stood on the balcony slowly drying her body with one of Robert's plush towels. The shower had been delicious after the nap in the deep air conditioning of Henderson's bedroom. He should be back by now, she thought. The Paris flight took off at nine.

On returning from the river he had driven her to the Cinquantenaire Apartments and left her there alone, explaining the necessity of seeing off Pontecelli at the airport. For Lisa the leave-taking at Kalina had been one of the strangest experiences of her life. They had all shaken hands on the flat grassy bank above the river where Carlo had landed the helicopter. It was insane. They had just smiled the standard, conventional smiles and shaken hands.

She and Carlo, Carlo and Henderson, Pontecelli, the girl Gloria. *"Arrivederci, mille grazie."* What did it all mean? Had it really happened or was her mind slipping? Was this how it was to be insane, to feel the undeniable insanity of a situation that everyone else found perfectly normal? She and Carlo had made love twice in the little pool, yet Henderson and the others had acted as if nothing had happened. Driving back from Kalina, she had sat stiffly, face straight ahead, avoiding Henderson's eyes. He, on the other hand, had talked smoothly of the beauty of the afternoon, the excitement of the helicopter ride above the river and forest. Had he thought that she and Carlo were just kissing there in the water? Was that what he meant by a "casual flirtation"? Of course not. He knew, and the others knew, exactly what had happened, yet they were so unruffled by it all. Was this how people like that really lived? People like what, she thought. She herself was now a person like *that*. She had joined into the mood of the afternoon with perfect ease. Now, as she stood on the terrace of Robert's apartment on the day after Christmas, she remembered that this was exactly where she had stood only twenty-four hours earlier with her husband. In the space of those twenty-four hours she had opened her body to her husband, to Robert, and to Carlo, an absolute stranger with whom she had barely exchanged three words of conversation.

Was this the freedom she had wanted when she first gave in to Henderson's skillful seduction? Where was Steve in all of this? In a moment of animal panic she realized that she could no longer remember his face. Lisa braced herself against the concrete railing of the terrace, desperately trying to recall the exact color of her husband's eyes. She could not.

If Steve were here, I could talk to him. I wish Steve were here with me. I could explain why I did it. Why? I don't know why. It was stupid and I won't do it again. I'm going to do it again tonight with Robert. But that's different. I *know* Robert. Carlo was a perfect stranger. I wish Steve and I were still in the Peace Corps. That was such a nice uncomplicated life. We were *healthy* then, we didn't drink every night, we didn't have to talk to all these silly people at cocktail parties. We had time to read. Maybe we didn't have a car and air conditioners and glass-doored showers, but we were happy. We had time to read and we talked to each other. Steve was so happy. He was doing something good with his life.

I wish we'd stayed in the States and gone out West to work with the Indians. Then we'd still be healthy. We'd have a jeep for trips to the mountains and there wouldn't be this awful rebellion and all those dreadful, boring parties and we could read at night and talk and make love just like we used to. Steve would be happy and I'd be close to him and I wouldn't need anyone else at all. Now it's different, now it's changed. I don't think it can ever be the same again.

Lisa felt an odd warmth on her tongue and realized with a shock that she had bitten her lip until it bled.

She relaxed after a long moment. It was just the day, the liquor and wine, the sun and the forbidden novelty of the love-making. She needed to put it all into proper perspective. She had to start thinking as a mature adult, not a simpering college girl. She was a natural mature woman, and she had the same appetites and curiosities as anyone else. She had simply had the opportunity and the courage to see them through. That was all there was to it. This was better. This was closer to the real truth. No one had forced her to go with Carlo. She had wanted to do it and she had done it. It had been marvelous sex. She could not recall how long it had been since she had enjoyed anything more. What was so evil about that? Had she hurt anyone? Had she been cruel or aggressive? No, she thought with smug comfort, this *was* exactly what she had wanted to experience when she began with Henderson, and she was glad it had happened.

Trailing the towel, she went to the kitchen and made herself a thirst-quenching gin and tonic in a Pilsner glass filled with ice cubes. Back on the terrace, she watched the little groups of Congolese and Europeans strolling about the palm-lined streets, directionless on a hot Sunday night. The lightning show across the river was slowly dying. As she stood there naked, with the drink beading in the night air, the first of the flying termites began falling in from the humid darkness, senselessly banging against the lighted windows behind her. Below her in the building the party was getting louder.

Robert would be back soon and then they would go out for dinner, probably to the Bruxelles, where very few Embassy people could afford to go. *That's* a catty thought, she commented to herself, smiling. It's true, though, so why deny it? Robert was goodlooking and had a lot of money and was charming and smart, and once again this afternoon he had been right. She *had* wanted to be with Carlo, and he had known it and helped her.

But she shivered as the full impact of what she had done that afternoon grew inside her. It was one thing to have a warm love affair with an attractive older man completely different from your husband. It was quite another to just *screw* with every desirable stranger who came along. It *had* been very nice, though, and she *had* undeniably wanted to try it. She laughed nervously into the night.

The telephone rang in the living room. Her stomach constricted sharply. Let it ring, she thought. Robert will be back soon. The steady rasping disturbed her. Whoever it was would not give up. She lifted the receiver, holding it lightly to her ear without speaking.

"Lisa," Robert said. "Lisa, is that you?"

"Oh, you scared me," she said. "I didn't know whether to answer or not."

"I'm still at the airport. Took me almost half an hour to find a phone that works in this damn place. Look, Lisa, I'm terribly sorry. Pontecelli's flight has been delayed in Johannesburg. He won't be taking off from here until midnight at the earliest, possibly later. I'm going to have to stay. We may be here all night. I got the loan of an office from those clowns in the Sûreté, so at least we can work out here while we're waiting. Why don't you call it a night? I'll telephone you in the morning and we can have lunch together."

"Whatever you say, Robert," she said. "I know you're terribly busy and it's important. Please call me in the morning, though."

"Good night Lisa," he said. "It was a lovely day."

"Yes, it was. Good night."

Clinking the ice cubes in the tall glass, she wandered about the empty living room, fingering the tastefully arranged collection of Kasai masks and Bakuba kings laid out along the African teakwood room divider. She sat naked on the plum-colored sofa, looking languidly through old copies of *Life* and *Paris Match*. Outside she could hear the termites striking the glass doors with small clicks. She took a cigarette from the carved hardwood box on the coffee table. Her fingers were trembling, but the drink tasted good; the cigarette was fresh and mentholated, the breeze from the humming air conditioner delightful.

She began to cry, very softly, almost inaudibly at first, but then she was on her stomach sobbing uncontrollably into the smooth fabric of the sofa. She was so alone, so terribly lonely.

After a long while she rose and went again to the kitchen to get a handful of paper towels. She wiped her face and blotted up the dark tear stains on the sofa. Robert's Zenith radio buzzed and crackled with the nearby electrical storm. She had never really understood the tuning mechanism of these expensive shortwave transistors. Turning the knob, she heard a succession of African stations. She clicked the bandspread dial, and the living room was filled with the nasal voice of an American announcer speaking about the Communist refusal to respond to President Johnson's temporary suspension of the bombing of North Vietnam. The longer she listened to the announcer the less sense he seemed to make. She twirled the dial. A babble of Slavic, Portuguese, and Afrikaans voices followed her across the wave band, interspersed with jolting rock-'n'-roll and sugary modern choral music.

Then a strong, static-free station broke through, bringing the comforting stability of a large church congregation singing a hymn. The voices were peaceful and reassuring. She turned off the light next to her and stretched out on the sofa. She did not want to go home alone to that antiseptic, ghost-haunted apartment. She would stay here at Robert's for a while with this comforting music for company. The organ rose to a crescendo and the congregation sang "Amen." She could hear the shuffling sound as they seated themselves in their pews. A man cleared his throat and began to speak in an English clergyman's voice.

"During this blessed and joyous Christmastide," he said, "it is well for us to take stock of the bounty we have received from Almighty God."

Lisa sucked at her drink, letting the paternal voice comfort her. The pastor droned on, and although she no longer heard his words, the steady cadence of his sermon squelched her swelling loneliness. Sitting up to finish her drink, she listened more closely.

"We at Saint Mary's have therefore asked our Senior Girls to address themselves to the task of composing a special Christmas prayer which calls for God's blessing for the poor and the hungry of the earth. Miss Mary Ann Ryan will now lead us in that prayer, which will be followed by the singing of hymn number one hundred and eleven, 'The Lord Doth Reign.' "

Lisa turned her face to the back of the sofa. The sound of the hymn had comforted her and the deep voice of the minister had given her a warm Christmas nostalgia she had forgotten in the tropical heat. But the squeaking Ulster accent of this young girl, painfully and self-consciously leading the unseen congregation in prayer, disturbed her. She refilled her drink in the kitchen. Back in the living room, the girl's voice still grated on. The insects smacked irritatingly against the windows. Below, she could hear glass breaking and wild laughter from the party. I'd better just go home and get some sleep, she thought. As she stooped to turn off the radio, the girl's voice grew more piercing.

"And so, dear Lord," she said, "in these times of trouble, in these times of strife and torment, confusion and despair, we ask for Thy blessing, not only for ourselves and families living already with the blessings of freedom and plenty, but especially for all those uncounted millions in the world who are hungry, sick, and discouraged, especially for the lonely and unloved. Amen."

The hymn began, but Lisa did not hear it. All she could hear were the words "these times of trouble," "lonely and unloved." They revolved in her head with increasing speed. These were, indeed, times of trouble, confusion, and despair. Because of what she had done with Robert and Carlo she had become one of the lonely and unloved. As the words of the prayer echoed in her mind, the weight of her loneliness came crashing down.

Quickly she washed her face in the kitchen sink and applied fresh lipstick, using the shiny stainless-steel cabinet door as a mirror. She dreaded entering the deserted silence of Robert's bedroom where she must go to get her dress.

Riding down in the stuffy elevator, she realized that she had worn no underwear, only her short-skirted sundress. It didn't matter; she would be home in a few minutes. She rarely dressed that way, braless, in a low-cut dress, only when she was picnicking with Steve or Robert. They both liked it. It excited them. The gray paint of the elevator shaft drifted by, punctuated by the narrow frosted glass doors of the landings. It must be almost ten o'clock, she thought. I'd better not try to take a cab this late. I'll just walk around the corner to the Embassy and get the duty driver to take me home. It definitely would not do to drive Robert's Mercedes into the Royal. That would certainly start the tongues wagging.

As the elevator dropped past the seventh floor, she heard the party, louder even than before. It's a good thing they're all Americans on these floors, she thought. The elevator jerked to a stop at the ground-floor lobby. The door opened before she could push it. Judy Pringle stood there, tall and plain-looking. Her hair was three colors from unsuccessful attempts to dye it, her lipstick was smeared, and, despite the heat, she wore heavy makeup. She looks exactly like what she is, Lisa thought: a lonely forty-year-old American secretary in the tropics. A crew-cut young American stood next to Judy, holding a foam ice chest. He was embarrassed, trying to look away, but the temptation to stare at Lisa overcame him.

"Hi," Judy said. "We just went for some more ice. You're not going home yet, are you?"

Lisa smiled, stepping between them. "Actually, I wasn't at the party. I was having dinner with a Belgian family we know. They had invited us, but then Steve had to go on this trip to Stan. I'm just on my way home."

Judy looked drunk and confused. "Well, that's *terrible*. I mean, you can't just go home when I'm giving a party for all these nice Pan Am men."

"TWA," the man said, still staring at Lisa.

"Oh, of course," Judy said. "I mean all the people from the oil lift. They're all here and it's a *great* party, only there aren't enough girls."

"Really?" Lisa said. "I'm tired so I don't think I'd be too much fun at a party."

"We insist," the young man said. "Just come up and have one drink."

Lisa hesitated in the doorway of the elevator. The man took her firmly by the arm and then they were all inside and Judy punched the seventh-floor button. They rode up in hot silence, the TWA man hardly trying to disguise his attempt to look down Lisa's dress.

The party was even wilder than it had sounded from the fourteenth floor, and it had progressed to the point where most of the lights were off and spilled drinks and trampled cigarette butts had made a sticky patina on the floor. There were more than forty people sweating to the beat of the music in the long living room and on the darkened terrace. As Lisa entered the apartment, she saw from the foolish, flushed expressions of the men and women that normal restraints had evaporated and all the pent-up frustrations of the single American women and the holiday loneliness of the Pan American and TWA pilots were coming to a sexual head.

A forty-five record spun on the turntable. The center of the living room served as a dance floor where the swaying couples could catch the slight river breeze through the open terrace windows. The Beatles sang "I Wanna Hold Your Hand." Lisa found herself pulled through the wet mass of dance-floor hangers-on to the middle of the living room where the young man from the elevator danced opposite her in a painfully stilted twist. Lisa was a good dancer, and as she snaked her long legs with the beat, she noticed with pleasure that all these athletic, uninteresting young pilots' eyes were on her body, free and unencumbered beneath her light dress. She looked around the room for familiar Embassy faces. Aside from a few girls from the communication section and some secretaries, she saw no one she knew. The men were a plain-looking group of short-haired, serious-faced aviators dressed in similar madras print Bermuda shorts and sports shirts. Some had been drinking heavily and gazed at her with ill-disguised sensuality, which on their smooth-shaven, homogeneous faces became a parody of adolescent lust. As she spun on the sticky floor she could hear snatches of their voices above the noise of the music, either boyishly high-pitched or deep with pseudo-radio-announcer bass. The record ended and she accepted a drink and a cigarette from her partner, who told her his name was really Gary and not Jerry as Judy had introduced him. He knit his brows as he stooped to light Lisa's cigarette. You look ridiculous, Lisa thought. You probably think that looks sexy.

He walked her through the press of bodies to the edge of the terrace where she leaned out to look up at the top of the building silhouetted against the pink city glow of the sky. The living room air conditioners spewed out the tobacco smoke. Gary said something, but before she could answer she was pulled back on the dance floor by another anonymous pilot. This one really made an effort, attempting to hold her close despite the jerking urgency of the music. "We gotta get outta this place," the record screamed, "if it's the last thing we ev-ver do."

The two gins in Robert's apartment had mellowed her, and as this faceless pilot clawed at her in the smoky darkness she thought that even this drunken party was better than the loneliness of her own empty apartment.

Back on the terrace, her little group of admirers swelled. It was cruel, she realized, for over in the far corner of the terrace two of the homelier AID secretaries stood stolidly against the balcony, alone and unnoticed, quietly sipping their drinks, periodically casting mournful glances in her direction. It wasn't fair, she thought. Why should these girls who had suffered months of sexless frustration be deprived of this reward of homogenized American flesh while she, who had already that day experienced so much pleasure, was surrounded by these bland giants? For the single girls of the American Embassy the oil lift was the deluge at the end of a long drought. Even the least attractive of the girls were constantly invited to the rounds of cocktails and buffets organized by the intrepid Embassy hostesses. Lisa and Steve had been able to avoid most of the parties organized as "mixers" to bring the unattached and supposedly unmarried air crews together with the twenty-five young and not-so-young ladies who kept the paper mill of the American diplomatic mission running around the clock.

Now, as Lisa stood with her back to the river, letting the soft air play over her damp neck and shoulders, she drew a guilty pleasure watching her circle of admirers wax larger. She had seen these faces so often before. This was a Greek Street fraternity beer supper with the assembly line young men carefully scrubbed and clipped, dressed to casual uniform perfection, lined up in their ranks, earnestly going through the task of ritualized mating. These square-cut, boyish faces were, some of them, ten and even fifteen years removed from the fraternity, but they had never really left it. They were indelibly branded with the air cadet graduation ball and the years of vapid officer club existence. Lisa politely accepted their cigarettes and allowed her drink to be refilled at decent intervals.

They split roughly into three categories: the third officers in their mid-twenties who stared but didn't touch; the boozy, hard-eyed thirty-year-old co-pilots who had been around and apparently had concluded that the perfect seduction was initiated by crooning hot whisky breath into the victim's ear simultaneously accompanied by the supposedly tender caress of a horny tobacco-stained thumb under the edge of her bare-shouldered dress; the third and, she thought, potentially most dangerous were the older captains, men, like Henderson, old enough to be her father, who had known hundreds of women in their careers and could instinctively recognize in Lisa something very different, and who, like the gray-haired old pipe smoker in *long* trousers, chatting quietly in a secluded corner of the living room, could see at a glance that the clumsy seduction attempts of their juniors were doomed to failure. Lisa saw all this in one slow brown-eyed glance at the wall of faces now surrounding her.

To her amusement, she also discovered after several dances that a ridiculous element of competition had entered into the drama. She had been escorted into the party by the tall boy from TWA. A Pan Am co-pilot had danced with her next. And so it went. Incredible. Very probably, she thought, they were exchanging odds and stupid ten-to-one bets on who and which *airline* would win her favors. What I should do, she thought, is just leave them standing here. The situation amused her, however, and although she did not admit it to herself, it was only within the past several months, since the beginning of her affair with Robert, that she had not been disappointed by and ashamed of her own voluptuous body. She had always envied the flat-chested, narrow-hipped models in

Vogue and *Elle*. But now she enjoyed the excitement her body provoked.

Also, she could not admit that the ghostly words of the Irish schoolgirl's prayer still were swirling within her. She could *not* go back to her empty apartment. She knew that the long day of drinking was working on her and that her barely submerged sensuality invariably surfaced when she drank, just as it had that afternoon with Carlo on the river. It was an exciting game she was playing, and as she was mashed about the dance floor, some stranger's fingers on her hot skin as he drunkenly attempted a hard pelvis lock, it was easy to forget these "times of trouble" and that she knew herself to be one of the "lonely and unloved."

Back on the terrace, she realized that part of the undercurrent of sexual tension running among the pilots was due to the fact that eight of them, all drinking Coke or grape punch, would have to leave the party at midnight to fly the two Boeing jets to Elizabethville to keep up the oil lift's round-the-clock schedule. What were these men so desperate about, she wondered. Did they seriously expect to have a chance to simply take her aside and fuck her someplace before they left? Or were they worrying that some other, luckier colleague would get the chance and that they would be unable to observe the scene?

It will be interesting to see who wins, she thought, dancing with one particularly aggressive Pan Am pilot in his late thirties, who, judging by the cocoa-brown whisky sodas he was drinking, was not flying any airplanes that night. The one remaining light in the apartment had been extinguished and as they spun slowly in a tiny circle to Frank Sinatra's voice, she suddenly realized that she wanted another man. It was a strange feeling, coming so soon after the dizzying shame she had felt for her behavior that afternoon. But this had been a day of honesty with herself, and in that spirit she was forced to admit that she did not want to sleep alone that night. The thickset pilot named Greg had succeeded in inserting four fingers through the half-opened zipper of her dress and was senselessly grinding against her. He thinks he'll be the lucky man. No, dear, she thought with a wild giggle, you're just the exercise boy. The real jockey will be somebody quite different.

Abruptly she broke away from him and strode angrily toward the terrace. "Hey, Lisa," he called as he stumbled drunkenly behind her, "what's the matter? C'mon, let's finish the dance."

Lisa ignored him. She snatched up her newly refilled glass and shouldered her way through the drinkers to the far end of the terrace. It was not crowded there and the river breeze was actually cooling. In the flickering light of an insect candle Lisa recognized Judy Pringle talking to the gray-haired captain. Thrusting her elbows up onto the balcony rail, Lisa turned outward to face the river. She took a small swallow of her drink and smiled. In the yellow candlelight she had seen the captain's eyes on her body. She stood there silently, knowing that she had aroused him. She could hear their voices clearly. It wasn't really eavesdropping. If they don't want me to listen, they can lower their voices. I know that he wants to talk to me, she thought, smiling. I wonder how he'll break away from Judy.

Judy had obviously been hard at work on her hair and makeup. In the soft light she looked almost attractive. She shouldn't wear silk in this climate, though, Lisa thought; the back of her dress is wringing wet. I'll just stay here and wait to see how long it takes before he comes to me.

"This feels wonderful," the captain said. "I got snowed in at Frankfurt last week, and the weather in New York's been miserable. It's nice to be able to stand around outside without getting frostbite."

"Maybe we could get together for tennis one day next week," Judy said. "In the evening after work. The courts are lighted. We could have a dip at the club pool afterwards and then come up here and I could cook you some teriyaki steak. I've got a little grill that works just great on the terrace. It's never too hot here with the breeze off the river in the evening."

"Tennis and teriyaki steak," he said, smiling. "Sounds like fun —takes me back to my misspent youth on that Honolulu, Wake Island, Bangkok run in the old strato-cruisers after the war."

"Were you in Bangkok in 1949?" Judy asked.

"Every Tuesday morning. We had crew rest there before starting down for Sydney."

"Bangkok was my first post," Judy said. "I was right out of college. I used to date a Pan Am pilot. Oh, isn't this terrible, I can't even remember his name . . . he was a big, tall boy, from Georgia."

"Beats me," the captain said. "I've been flying so many different runs since then that it's hard to keep track of names. Been on the North Atlantic and South American circuits since we went over to jets."

"Well, that's just wonderful," Judy said quickly. "I mean that you know Bangkok, too. Let's plan on the tennis and dinner next week then."

"I'd love to," he said, "but I'm headed back to New York tomorrow, I'm afraid. They just send old shellbacks like me down to troubleshoot. The front office wanted to see how the oil lift was shaking down after the first month of operations. They were toying with the idea of changing the 707 for a DC-8 and wanted the advice of a senior captain. I'm getting a little long in the tooth, you know, and I guess they're grooming me for a desk before retirement."

"Tomorrow?" Judy said softly. "Oh, I was hoping you'd be here for at least a week."

"I'm afraid not. Thanks just the same. It sounds like it would have been fun."

"Yes," Judy said. "Yes, it would have been lovely."

There were laughter and loud voices in the living room. Suddenly a bright ceiling light was switched on and Lisa could see a crowd of young pilots and secretaries stooping to search for an earring one of the women had lost. Lisa was illuminated in the rectangle of light flooding through the wide terrace window. She could see the captain staring at her as she stood motionless on the balcony. In the reflected glare of the light Judy's face had lost the illusionary girlishness created by the fresh makeup and the candlelight. She gulped down her drink in two long swallows. Her eyes glittered with a strange brittleness.

"Bangkok and Seoul and Singapore and Caracas and then those four years in the Department and half a tour in Lagos and now here. Doesn't that seem funny? It's all gone so quickly. I was only going to spend a couple years overseas, and then I was going to find some nice young guy and settle down and have some kids.

Now my *sister's* little girls are having kids. I got a Christmas card from my niece, Anne—she's got two little boys of her own now. It hardly seems possible, does it? Little Annie living there in Ohio with her husband and babies. She was *born* right before I left for overseas that first time, and now she has children of her own. . . ." Judy reached out absently and took a half-empty glass. "All those years in so many places. Christmases with pool parties and palm trees and everybody so far from home. It's been fun, though." Her voice rose as she looked up from her glass. "Oh, I wish they'd turn that goddamn light off. Don't those girls know anything about atmosphere?"

As Judy went past Lisa toward the open glass door to the living room, Lisa could see the tears smearing the makeup on Judy's cheeks. At that moment the light was extinguished and the music began again. Judy paused momentarily on the edge of the terrace. "It would have been lovely," she called softly to the captain. "I'm a good cook, I really am. . . . A person gets so lonely in these hot countries, especially at Christmastime. . . . Everybody else has their families with them, but people like us, we have to be our own families, don't we? We have to help each other when it gets so lonely." Judy turned abruptly and was lost in the press of dancers.

The captain whistled softly and shook his head. "Boy," he said in Lisa's direction, "looks like I really goofed. Was she *crying* or was I seeing things?"

"She was crying," Lisa said flatly.

"Jesus," the captain said, shaking his head again. "I suppose I'll live to be a hundred and ten without ever even beginning to understand women. Did *I* say anything to get her so shook up?"

"It's what you *didn't* say."

He joined Lisa in the shadowy half-light at the balcony. "I'm afraid I'm not very good at riddles this time of night."

Lisa stared out at the lights of Brazzaville across the river. In her mind she still saw the tear-wet makeup peeling like decaying flesh on Judy's cheeks. "It's simple," she said quietly. "She wants a man. It's really that simple. She's forty-some years old and she's lonely and she wants a man. . . . She started tonight with the young kids . . . making them drinks and sandwiches and trying to dance those fast dances with them . . . but that was no good, so she started working her way up the chain of command. She even tried that nasty Greg, but all he wanted to do was take her in the bedroom for a quickie, and then *I* came and Greg lost interest. And there you were, a nice, handsome older man, someone she could talk to. . . . Oh, she wanted to sleep with you, too. She'd probably be a very good lover. But it was more than just sex. She had this beautiful picture worked out in her head. It would have been just like Bangkok when she was young. That's all she wanted. That isn't so hard to understand, is it? You really can't hate her for wanting that, can you?"

The captain had composed his face into an expression of amused curiosity and was about to speak when he sensed the undercurrent of anguish in Lisa's voice. "Yeah," he said after a long silence, "yeah, I guess you're right. It's kind of sad, isn't it?"

"It's the saddest thing I can think of," Lisa whispered. "It's funny, too, strange more than funny. Less than an hour ago I was feeling very sorry for myself. I've got nothing to cry about. . . ." Lisa yawned suddenly. "Excuse me," she said. "That was very rude. I've had a long day and I've had too much to drink again. You seem like a nice man. What's your name?"

"Paul Rogers. You're Lisa Sherman, aren't you?"

"Paul," Lisa said. "That's very biblical, very fatherly and reassuring. It would have been nice to talk to you some more, but I'm very tired tonight. I'm going to go home and take a cold shower and open a can of soup and sleep a little. I have a friend who has to work late out at the airport. I'm going to set the alarm for twelve-thirty and then I'll call him and he can come over. Any other night I would have been glad to talk to you. You're a nice, handsome man."

Lisa walked blindly through the dancers to the door of the apartment. She could see Judy in the kitchen working on a tray of open-faced sandwiches with a barefoot houseboy. "I'm sorry, Judy," she said to herself. "I'm sorry that's the way your life has turned out. I can't help you, though. All I can do is live my own life. Don't worry, though. I won't take your Captain Rogers. He's a nice man, but I've got Steve and Robert and you don't have anyone. I won't take the handsome captain away from you."

Lisa stood just inside the dimly lit lobby of the Cinquantenaire Apartments building. The Embassy duty driver would be there in a minute. It was nice of the Embassy to send a car. I guess they really have to, though, she thought; a white woman alone can't take one of those awful taxis this time of night, especially with those police roadblocks all up and down the Boulevard. Those police and soldiers are drunk even during the day. I should have taken a key to Robert's apartment. It would have been much easier to wait for him there.

Two cars turned off the boulevard and crossed the Ivory Market Square toward the entrance turnabout in front of the building. The first car was the black Embassy station wagon. The driver wheeled it sharply into the narrow drive, and Lisa stepped forward to the dirty glass door of the lobby. Then she felt a flush of childish excitement as she saw Robert's little Mercedes pull smoothly past the station wagon and turn onto the steep concrete ramp to the building's basement parking garage. She laughed as she pushed at the heavy glass door. She stopped. The weight of the door slid her back into the lobby. She was cold inside, but her face was flushed red. In the glare of the station wagon's headlights she saw Gloria, still wearing her big round sunglasses. She was laughing and her bare arm was curled up around Robert's shoulder, her fingers playing with the curly hair on his neck. Robert's mouth was open in a greedy smile. The car hung there nakedly in the lights and then dipped down the ramp and out of sight.

"*C'est vous,* Madame Sherman?" the driver asked, squinting at his clipboard in the shadows of the lobby. He was a tall, very black man with tribal scars.

"I'm sorry," Lisa said, her voice breaking. "I've changed my mind. I won't need your car. You can go back to the Embassy."

"*Oui, madame,*" the driver said shrugging. "*Merci, madame.*"

Fewer couples were dancing as Lisa walked slowly back into Judy Pringle's living room. People sat in the darkness eating sandwiches and drinking coffee from paper cups. Several pilots with whom she had danced earlier looked up from their chairs and smiled at Lisa as she picked her way between them toward the terrace. Judy Pringle was making the rounds of her guests. She wore an apron and carried a large copper coffeepot with a quilted hot pad around its handle.

Captain Rogers had not left the far end of the terrace. He stood eating sandwiches with a young pilot. Lisa walked straight to him and stopped only inches away to stare up into his face.

"Would you get Mrs. Sherman a gin and tonic, Tony?" Paul Rogers said to his co-pilot. His eyes never left her face. "Unless you'd care for a sandwich, that is."

"A drink would be fine," she said.

The young man disappeared.

"What time do you leave in the morning?" Lisa asked.

"I've got an eight o'clock take-off, I'm afraid."

"Do you have a car?"

Captain Rogers nodded.

Lisa reached out and pulled herself against him, raking his chest with her breasts. "Let's go now then," she whispered, "so we can have a long time together."

CHAPTER **20**

Lisa awoke slowly. The chill of the air conditioner had dried the long night's sweat on her body. To her delight she was not hung over as she had been the morning before. Paul lay next to her asleep, the sheet tangled around his legs. What a fantastic twenty-four hours, she thought. She tried desperately to recall the details of the previous morning, the river and the party and finally the long night in bed with Paul. It was too much. There were too many faces, too many sharp moments of sensual intensity. Her first sleepy desire was to run to tell Steve, her best friend.

He had a right to share her secret. Then, with an internal sagging, the full reality of what she had done grew inside her. No, Steve would never be told. A woman didn't tell her husband things like that. How many women, she wondered, had ever had such an experience to hide? In twenty-four hours, the time it took the planet to rotate once on its axis so that the sky above the communes out beyond the glass doors was turning again from dull rose to candy pink, she had received into her body her husband and three other men. With two of these men she had enjoyed orgasms far more intense than anything she had ever known with Steve. They had been strangers, yet they had shared the most intimate of experiences. They had kissed her and licked her and she had played about their bodies as a child indulges itself with a new toy, with oblivious abandon, and then, once the secrets of the toy are revealed and its possibilities for pleasure exhausted, the toy is rejected.

In her mind she saw Carlo again in the river, falling away from her, his dark eyes dull, his mouth sagging. And then Paul was there in the darkness on the firm surface of the bed, arched above her, the groan rising from his throat. She would not forget that strange day. As she raised herself quietly and sat on the edge of the bed, Steve's face suddenly flashed up at her from the small frame on her night table. It was her favorite picture of him, taken in Morocco in the snow of the cedar forest above Azrou. His neck and shoulders were wrapped in the soft wool of a checkered Berber djellaba. They had been camping with another Peace Corps couple. Steve had not shaved for several days; the dark stubble on his chin tempered the fragile boyish cast of his face. He looked like a man in the picture, but his pale blue eyes retained their youth. That was her husband.

But then with a sickening rush of vertigo she saw that he could never be her husband again. Their marriage had been broken, shattered like the delicate gears of a clock. Why hadn't she seen it before? At the party it had been so easy to deceive herself about the import of her actions. Those men had not been fantasies. They were real, living people, and she had "fucked" them all. Say it, she thought, don't just try to hide it with fancy names. I *fucked* them. That's all it was. Don't try to call it making love. You can't love someone you don't even know. I fucked them. That's what a whore does. A man comes along and he wants her and she takes off her clothes and he fucks her. But she gets paid for it. What did *I* get? Why did *I* do it?

I drank too much and I was feeling lonely, I was feeling sexy; I couldn't help it. I've never been so brazen before, not even with Robert on the river. I was just feeling strange, and I drank too much. I could have controlled it, but the way I was feeling I probably would have broken down and masturbated because I was alone. That has a lot to do with it, chemistry, at least for a woman. Look at the way I was feeling Christmas morning. I came so well right after Steve began. It was supposed to be a treat for him, but then I came so quickly, just like with Carlo. A lot of it is chemistry. I couldn't help myself. I'm always a little like this just after my period, but this time it was so much stronger. Admit it, I would have done it with my hand when I felt that way if a man hadn't been there. What's the difference?

I don't know them; I just used them. But they fucked me. Robert on the living-room floor, and Carlo in the water, and all night with Paul right in this bed. It doesn't matter whether I was feeling sexy or not—this is very serious. You just don't go to bed with three different men besides your husband in twenty-four hours because you're feeling sexy after your period. This is adultery. This is crazy. But I was so sexy, this whole town is so *raunchy,* everybody's doing it. Look at all those parties, look at the way people carry on. The Belgians and the French and Robert's friends are doing it all the time. Steve knows that. What did he expect, going away and leaving me here? All the whites here are doing it. Look at the things that have happened right in front of Steve, the dancing at the pool parties in Parc Hembise and up in Binza. The women in their little bikinis and the men grinding up against them. What about that time after the German concert up at the Randles' when we all went swimming at four o'clock in the morning in our underwear? That was pure sex, playing water polo in bras and panties with all those guys slipping their hands all over the girls. Steve did it too. I saw him.

It's all right to go naked and dance that way and exchange all those supposedly innocent little party kisses, but you can't do the real thing. That's adultery. What about that time in October when Robert took us to the French banker's villa and that silly Belgian girl took off her bikini top dancing next to the pool and then everyone was singing "topless, topless" and we all took off our tops. Nobody said anything about that. That wasn't adultery. God, that Englishman I was dancing with could hardly stand up, he was so excited. And Steve—I saw him with that tall redhead from the

U.N. Everybody was kissing and laughing, and the women were almost naked. That was all right. That wasn't adultery. This place is too hot, too juicy, the dancing and all the party kissing and the bikinis. The ones the men wear are worse than the women's. Just a little triangle of cloth over that bulge. What do they want me to do? I couldn't help myself. I could only take so much.

It's not fair. It really isn't fair. It's so silly. You can do all that, kissing and dancing and everybody half-naked, drunk in a pool at four o'clock in the morning, but you can't do the real thing. Well, the hell with *them*. I wanted the real thing. I wanted to do it and I did. What's so different about putting a man inside? Why should what I've done hurt our marriage? What's so special about fucking? Why is it so different from all the other things people do here?

A man can put his tongue in my mouth three feet away from where Steve is dancing with some red-haired girl and he's doing the same with her. I can feel somebody's hand right down inside my panties in the pool when we're supposed to be playing a game. All those women, wives most of them, good, honest, *unadulterous* married women, can take off their bikini tops and rub their breasts right against some man they hardly know. *That's* fine; that's just fun and games. What I did is called adultery.

Adultery. She slipped her legs over the edge of the bed and rose quietly to a sitting position. Beneath the two paperback Nabokov novels and the pile of magazines on the shelf of the night table, she found Steve's dog-earred college dictionary. She thumbed through the first few pages of the book until she found the page she sought. "Adultery," she read silently, "sexual intercourse between a married man and a woman not his wife, or between a married woman and a man not her husband."

Lisa snapped the book shut with a dry pop that echoed above the deadening whir of the air conditioner. She glanced anxiously over her shoulder at Paul. The noise had not disturbed his sleep. The man who was not her husband slept deeply. Opening the dictionary again to the same page she read, "Adulteress. A woman guilty of adultery." . . . A woman guilty . . . "Adulterer. A man guilty of adultery." At least the dictionary's fair about it. That's as far as the fairness goes, though, isn't it? A man can *play around* or be a *ladies' man* or *fool around* with girls or even be a *playboy*, and it's considered a minor character weakness and that's all. What about a woman? Women don't *play around*. I never heard of a *playgirl*. Women *put out*. Women *get laid*. Women are loose or sluts or *whores*. That's just not right. . . . "Sexual intercourse . . . between a married woman and a man not her husband."

Lisa flipped toward the center of the dictionary, thumbing slowly back from the "M" section until she found the notation she wanted. "Intercourse. 1. Communication or dealings between or among people, countries, etc; interchange of products, services, ideas, feelings, etc. 2. The sexual joining of two individuals; coitus, copulation, usually *sexual intercourse.*" . . . Between two *individuals*. Goddamn them, the hypocritical bastards . . . two individuals. They don't believe that, they never have. I'm not supposed to be an individual. I'm supposed to be a *wife*. "My husband is with the American Embassy. *He's* a diplomat. . . ." ". . . My wife is . . . what?" "She's my wife. She doesn't *do* anything, you know, she's just my wife. I *have* a wife. I *am* a diplomat. I *am* a pilot. I *have* a wife. . . . My wife died last week." "Too bad, I'm very sorry." "Oh, that's all right. I *am* a successful international investment consultant. I can always *get* another wife. . . ." "It's a pity Lisa died. She made a very nice *wife* for young Sherman." "Don't worry, a bright young man like him can always find another. . . ."

Lying back tiredly on the bed, she closed her eyes. Images swirled in red flashes behind her eyes. She saw the week ahead of her peopled by a gang of faceless men . . . pilots and pimply Embassy code clerks and Marine guards sat about the living room playing poker; beer cans and cigar-choked ashtrays at their elbows as they bided their time, waiting their turn with Lisa in the bedroom. She saw the Ambassador throwing Steve down the front stairs of the Embassy. "Get that *whore* out of this mission," he screamed. Dressed in an ugly ankle-length woolen dress, she was led across the hot tarmac to a waiting airplane while the newsreel cameras whirred and throngs of their friends howled down obscene catcalls from the terrace of the airport restaurant.

"No!" she said, jerking upright in the bed. This is stupid. I drank too much and my nerves are shot. I can't let it affect me this way. I'll just go have a shower and make some tea, and then Paul will have to go and I'll wait until nine o'clock and I'll call Robert and I'll tell him it's all over. I'll stay home all week and read. I'll only go out during the day to the pool to swim and I'll drink my diet cola and lose three pounds just like I said I would so I can wear that new gold dress on New Year's for Steve. Oh, I hope that dress comes with the pouch this week . . . I'll have to lose at least three pounds, though. It will look beautiful and Steve will wear his dinner jacket, and. . . . No one knows about Robert and Carlo and Paul. Carlo and Paul are going away and I'm through with Robert so it really doesn't matter. Steve doesn't have to know. I did it for myself. It didn't affect Steve. I only wanted to see what it felt like and now I know. It's not my fault and it's not Steve's fault and we're going to live differently now—Steve said so. It will be so nice to live that way . . . healthy again.

Lisa rose and went to her dressing table to brush the tangles from her long hair. She was happy with her newly found resolve and the promise of the week ahead of her.

"You look fantastic there," Paul said. "It takes a very beautiful woman to look good at *this* time of the morning." Lisa turned her head and smiled at him, a fleeting, almost furtive smile. She resumed humming as she brushed her hair with long, even strokes. She saw him in the mirror as he walked toward her. His hands were suntanned, his fingers long and tapered as they touched the flesh of her shoulders and stole down to her breasts.

"You're wasting your time with that hairbrush," he whispered, bending to kiss her neck. "Your hair's going to be all tangled again in a minute."

"Paul," she said, "why don't we just have breakfast? You'll be late for your plane."

"Oh," he said, twisting her to pull her up against him, "I guess they'll wait a few minutes."

The excitement was suddenly there again, despite the dull soreness in her legs and pelvis. "It doesn't really matter," she whispered as he led her back to the bed. "You're going away today so once more doesn't really count."

Outside the bedroom windows the sun was changing from neon pink to the carbide white of full morning.

PART IV **matatá**

CHAPTER **21**

The waiting room stank of urine. Steve sat on a broken wooden chair in the outer office of the Congolese *chef de Sûreté* in Goma. It was three o'clock in the afternoon on Thursday, December 30. Outside it was raining hard. Thunder sounded heavily from the line of volcanoes lost in the clouds north of the town.

He yawned, stretched his legs, and looked again at his watch. His WIGMO flight from Stanleyville had landed at eleven-thirty and, after a quick sandwich and a beer at the town's one functioning hotel, he had been driven through the downpour and deposited in the muddy driveway at the *Territoire*. The drunken Gendarme officer at the airport had been adamant. Despite Steve's diplomatic passport and *laissez-passer* signed at ANC headquarters in Léopoldville, the officer had insisted that Steve gain the permission of the Territory's security chief before he would be allowed *"circulation libre."*

He got up and began pacing the room, noting as he walked the chipped plaster and mildewed paint. At a crumbling cork bulletin board he paused to read again a faded notice from the colonial health authorities that had been posted five and a half years before, during the last months before Independence.

He glanced up sharply as the chief's secretary, a balding dwarf-

like man in the dusty office smock of a colonial postal clerk, tiptoed back into the waiting room, carefully closing the door to the
inner office behind him. *"Très occupé,"* the African said gravely.
"Monsieur le Chef is very busy. It's a budgetary question, you see,
Monsieur le Consul. Being an *haut fonctionnaire* yourself, you can
appreciate his position."

"I'm not a consul," Steve said impatiently. "I'm just on a trip
from Léopoldville. I've been waiting for over two hours to see
him. This is ridiculous. I was told that my *laissez-passer* was valid
for every province in the Congo. I'm returning to Léo tomorrow.
What will my Embassy think if I have to tell them that all I saw
of the North Kivu was the inside of this office?"

The little man looked unhappily at Steve. "You must understand, Monsieur le Consul. If you had made an appointment earlier, Monsieur le Chef would have been happy to receive your
visit. Now, however, we have a schedule which is very filled." He
ran his hand over the impossible jumble of papers on his battered
metal desk. *"Chargé,"* he muttered, clucking his tongue. *"Oui, très
chargé."*

"Yeah," Steve muttered. "Is there a toilet that works in this
building?"

Steve heard laughter and Lingala songs on a radio as he walked
toward the toilet at the end of the porch of the decaying pre-Independence building. The offices of the territorial health and labor
services were deserted. The door to the toilet hung swinging from
one hinge. The commode and wash basin had been ripped out of
their fittings and the tile floor of the room was thick with excre-
ment. Gagging, he stepped back onto the porch. The rain pounded
on the tin roof above him. The town was almost completely hidden in the sizzling gray downpour. He rounded the end of the
building and, after looking back up the side porches, he stood and
urinated out into the rain.

A miserable-looking African child, dressed in a makeshift bur-
lap rain cape, drove a herd of goats through the muddy government compound. The laughter and music grew louder from the offices on the far side of the building. Steve walked slowly up the
opposite porch in the direction of the noise. He paused before a
door on which hung a crudely painted sign: TRIBUNAL TERRI-

TORIAL. Through the rusty screening of the window he could see people moving inside the courtroom. There was another outburst of laughter, and he heard glass breaking. He stood closer to the window and pressed his face against the screen.

There were eleven men and women in the long, rectangular courtroom. Beer bottles and jugs of milky palm wine crowded the heavy wooden table that served as the judge's bench. Looking closer, he recognized the portly figure of the Gendarmerie officer who had driven him from the airport. The man had removed the blouse of his uniform and held a bottle in each hand as he danced between two young girls who wore their hair in kinky tribal braids. A tall Congolese in the white jacket of a public health official lay sleeping on the floor. One of the girls made a laughing attempt to flee from the embrace of an official in a gaudy beer-stained uniform. She stumbled against the table and more bottles crashed to the floor. The laughter grew louder.

"Is *he* in there?" Steve shouted at the little secretary. Steve slammed the door to the porch and stood inside the waiting room, his hands on his hips.

"Monsieur?" the secretary knit his brows in a frown.

"If your *chef de Sûreté* is in there with that bunch of clowns in the courtroom drinking away the afternoon and he's kept me waiting all this time for nothing, then he's sure as hell going to hear about it when I get back to Léopoldville. I'm an American diplomat. My *laissez-passer* was signed at ANC headquarters. This is nothing but unnecessary harassment. . . ." Steve wanted to say more, but he saw that his polysyllabic French tirade was lost on the secretary.

"*Oui, Monsieur le Consul,*" the little man said nervously. "*Merci, monsieur. C'est la vérité, c'est très vrai. . . .*"

"Is there a car to take me back to the hotel?"

"A car . . . ?"

"Forget it," Steve spat. "I'll walk."

He snatched up his heavy briefcase and slammed the door behind him as he left the office. Outside on the porch the rain beat down with renewed intensity. The widening puddles on the muddy compound were ankle-deep. Steve stood shivering with anger and the sudden chill of the afternoon. Away to the south he could see the silhouettes of the concrete coffee warehouses that stood at the northern tip of Lake Kivu. The rest of the town was hidden beneath the rich mantle of tropical highland vegetation. Thunder sounded nearby with a sudden gut-slapping thud.

"Shit!" he said. "I don't even know the way back to the hotel. These goddamn people are hopeless."

A spattered Land Rover crawled through the mud toward the main gate of the compound. It jolted past the porch where Steve stood, then stopped and jerked backward in reverse. The driver was a stocky European with a creased and weather-browned face and vibrant blue eyes. He wore a dusty camouflage battle jacket. A Belga cigarette hung from his lips.

"Are you with the United Nations?" the man asked suspiciously in French.

"No," Steve answered, "I'm American, from the Embassy in Léo. Can you give me a ride back to the hotel?"

"Why do you want to go to the hotel?" the man asked, his voice becoming more friendly.

"I've got a room there—not in the hotel itself, they're booked up there. They put me in what they call the annex. I'm on a trip from Léopoldville doing a political and economic survey of the areas hit by the rebellion."

"And what have you discovered?" the man asked, openly smiling now.

"Not much," Steve said, smiling back. "This clown of a security chief has kept me waiting to see him all afternoon. I leave for Léo tomorrow afternoon. I just got in this morning from Stan."

"I know that you Americans work fast," the man said, "but did you really expect to learn much about the situation in Kivu Province in just twenty-four hours? Who have you talked to so far?"

Steve blushed. "Nobody really. I should explain. This is just a training exercise for me. To get me familiar with the bush, with the interior of the country."

"Well, monsieur," the man said. "I was born in the Kivu and I can assure you that you won't learn much about economics and politics or 'the bush,' as you call it, down at the hotel. My name is Dubois, Claude Dubois. I'm an adjutant in the CODOKI. I'm going back to my plantation up in the mountains. It's about a two-hour drive from here, just off the Bukavu road. Why don't you come along with me and spend the night there? You might learn a few things."

Steve stood hesitating on the porch. "What about the hotel?" he asked. "I already paid for the room and I left my bag there."

"Forget the hotel," Dubois said. "The only thing you would learn in that annex is how hungry the local bedbugs are. Come on, monsieur, get in. We have a long drive before dark."

Steve dashed through the rain around the back of the car and leaped into the front seat. The inside of the Land Rover smelled of tobacco and wet canvas. The roof leaked. Dubois's handshake was like a leathery vise. "My name is Sherman," Steve said.

"*C'est bien, ça,*" Dubois said as he drove out of the compound. "You have a famous general by that name, *n'est-ce pas?*"

"It feels strange to be cold again," Steve said.

Adjutant Dubois smiled. "That's one of the beauties of the Kivu," he said. "Hot sun in the day and a fire to warm your toes at night." They sat before a fire of eucalyptus logs in the salon of Dubois's plantation house. Outside it was dark and the mountain wind was beginning to moan in the stone fireplace chimney. Steve yawned. It had been a long, tiring day. Before them on a battered hardwood coffee table lay the debris of their supper: canned ham and tuna fish, biscuits, cheeses, and a plastic bowl of mixed Belgian mustard pickles.

Dubois refilled Steve's glass with whisky and soda water. "It's a pity, Monsieur Sherman," he said, "that you never saw this house before all the *matatá,* before the rebels took it and ruined everything with their *macaquerie.* My papa built this house with his own hands in 1920. It used to be a beautiful place."

Steve glanced around the bullet-pocked plaster-and-fieldstone walls of the room, noting in the shifting firelight the missing panes in the glass doors and the anonymous yet foreboding stains on the hardwood floor planks.

"Well," Steve said, "you've got your house and your farm back again. That's the important thing. The furniture and the equipment can always be replaced."

Dubois frowned across at Steve; setting his drink gingerly on the unsteady table, he thoughtfully bit at the cuticle of his little finger. Steve noticed again Dubois's fingers, the nails bitten back so severely that the exposed quicks were ripply with scar tissue.

"True," Dubois said, "the *things* which were once in this house can be replaced eventually. This farm will never really be the same again, though. You can have no idea how it was here in the Kivu before Independence. We were *building* something. We were, all of us, workers, striving toward a common goal. There was work for the blacks, and doctors and hospitals and schools. Prices were good and we were clearing new land, diversifying our crops. It was a good life, monsieur. A very good life. Hard work and long hours in the fields, but it meant something. Now—" Dubois swept his hand slowly to take in the damaged plantation house. "Now we may again have a chance, but it will never be the same as it was."

"Nothing ever is, is it?" Steve said quietly.

Dubois looked up at him sharply. He lit a fresh Belga cigarette from the smoldering butt in his fingers. As he bent forward to throw the cigarette stub into the fireplace, Steve saw that Dubois had retained the wiry muscles of a man much younger than his mid-forties. Dubois stiffened again, sitting upright on the sofa. "Five years ago, before all this Independence *matatá,* this was the best tea and quinine country in the Congo," Dubois said. "I had twice as many hectares than what I showed you this afternoon. I was spreading out, diversifying, going into market vegetables. We had it all planned, my cousin and I. We were going to quick-freeze any number of vegetables, fly them down to E'ville and Léo: cauliflower, artichoke hearts. . . . We had it all arranged with some Greeks down in Usumbura. They were going to put up the capital for an airplane. And then . . ." He paused, spitting out a shred of tobacco. "Then this immense jar of Independence *merde* was opened and we were finished." He flicked away his cigarette in a gesture of frustrated disgust, only to snatch impatiently at another.

"We lost everything," Dubois continued. "All of us did, all the planters in this region. It didn't hurt the big monopolies too much. But we small people, the ones whose papas had cut these plantations out of the bush, who had spent their entire lives building something good and permanent where there had been only forest and native *shambas* ruining the topsoil, we were the ones who lost it all. First," he said, sweeping his hand vaguely to the north, "that pack of Lumumba's MNC apes came pouring down from Stanleyville in stolen trucks with their witch doctors' *dawa* scaring the local blacks to death, burning the fields. Then the so-called National Army swept through, looting and raping. And then the filthy rabble from the Nations Unis. My God, they were almost as bad as the blacks themselves. And finally, after God knows how many evacuations and lies and rumors, we all came back in to pick up the pieces and the whole eastern half of the country exploded with this *Muléliste* rebellion. For most of them, my neighbors, it was too much. But there were some of us"—he slapped his chest—"some of us who could see that this time it was different. Tshombe was Prime Minister, there were *white men* running the Army again. The Americans were on *our* side this time, not mucking about with those Hindu Communists from the United Nations. That's when we formed the CODOKI, the Commando du Kivu. It made sense, men defending their homes. By God, we got results, too. If the Americans had helped us to do this in 1960, there never would have been any rebellion."

Dubois smiled, slapping Steve's leg in a gesture that made his flesh crawl as he glanced down sharply at the gnawed fingertips. "So this is why we keep the CODOKI organized. I know they call us cowboys, farmers playing soldier, but . . . it has worked. We have our plantations back and running. You see, Monsieur Sherman—and please tell this to your Ambassador when you make your report in Léo—there's something we all know, we old colons: that is that the black can comprehend only one thing, *power.* If you show him weakness, you are lost; if you are firm and fair, but especially *strong,* this is what he can understand. This is the way it was in the Congo for a thousand years before the first white ever came here, and this was the Belgian way, firmness and fairness, but especially strength. This is what they are used to and this is what they want. Now perhaps, with the help of the Americans, we can start building something again."

"I'll tell them what you said," Steve said.

"No!" Dubois protested. "Don't just tell them what I said. Tell them what you have seen—the plantations starting up again, the dispensaries for the blacks which we've rebuilt. Explain to them that we're not just a pack of cowboys, that we know these people and that we're getting results. It's hopeless to try to convince the Belgian Government; they're a bunch of socialist women. Perhaps in the Americans we will have an ally."

"Perhaps," Steve muttered.

"There should be no question of perhaps," Dubois said. "You cannot imagine how it was for us last year when the Simbas had all this." He pointed to the north again. "All the way from the Sudan border down into the Katanga, all the way over into Equateur Province, into the Kasai. We were huddling down there in Bukavu with our women across the border in Rwanda and we *knew* that this time it was lost, that this time they had won, that mob of savage *macaques*. That they were out there raping and killing and *destroying* everything it had taken the Belgians almost seventy years to build in this country. And then"—he turned, smiling, to Steve, opening his hand and waving flamboyantly at the ceiling—"then the Americans came with their airplanes, their big silver C-130s, and weapons, their B-26s to clear the roads and strafe rebels at the river crossings, their radios and advisers and, by God, we *held*. For the first time the ANC actually stood and fought and we beat the Simbas. We drove them back. Bukavu held out and the mercenaries began pushing them back in the Katanga and up through Maniema, and we knew then we would win and that we owed our victory to the Americans. And now, as you say, 'perhaps' we can start to build something real again, a country where the white man is still respected and can still lead the blacks, where a man can work and earn a decent living, where the natives in the government can have an example to follow. This is what you must tell them in Léopoldville—that we *are* succeeding, but that we still need their help."

"I'll try," Steve said softly.

"Déo!" Dubois called gruffly toward the darkened kitchen. Déogratias, a wizened old houseboy, trotted into the room, wiping his hands on a soiled apron. Dubois muttered something to him in Swahili, and the old man began clearing the dinner dishes.

"I wish my wife were here to cook you a real meal," Dubois

said softly. Then he rose impatiently to his feet and strode to the terrace doors. He took his camouflaged battle jacket from an antelope-horn coat rack on the wall and walked out onto the moonlit terrace. Steve refilled his whisky glass and joined Dubois outside.

"It's been ten—no, almost eleven months—since I've seen my wife and children," Dubois said. He stood against the terrace wall staring out into the soft moon shadows in front of the plantation house. "It's not natural for a man to be away from his family so long. This is *their* home too, you know. Mireille writes that Luc, my oldest boy, is having a terrible time adjusting to the school in Belgium. He's like me. He was born right here in this house. He's always had the freedom and the sun. He's *dying* inside up there in the fog and crowds and all that yé-yé nonsense that the European boys and girls seem to take so seriously. I hope they can come back soon."

"I hope so, too," Steve said.

The wind blowing down from the unseen volcanoes to the north was refreshingly chill. Dubois yawned. "If we're going to get an early start in the morning, we'd better call it a night," he said. "I'll have to be up before dawn to get the boys started on some transplanting, and I'll want to be on the way back down to Goma by eight o'clock at the latest. I've got some CODOKI business down there again. Another wild-goose chase, I'm afraid. We've been waiting for six months for the delivery of some armored Land Rovers, and there's a rumor that they may come tomorrow. Who knows? Nothing is certain when you're dealing with the ANC."

"Yes," Steve said. "I'm ready for bed myself. It's been a long day. I'm glad I had the chance to come up here, though. I had no idea how beautiful the Kivu was."

Dubois smiled, showing his twisted, tobacco-stained teeth. "Well," he said, "let's have one more for a nightcap. Déo," he yelled, *"lete mbili whisky-soda-mai!"*

As they sipped their last drink, smoking Dubois's Belgas, they heard the approach of a vehicle backfiring down the long incline from the ridge crest above the plantation. Dubois looked at the luminous dial of his watch. *"C'est la fille peut-être,"* he said quietly. "She was due back this evening." He smiled again, a tired, mischievous grin. "She said she might bring her sister back with her." Steve remained silent, taking a long pull at his drink.

Dubois cleared his throat. The noisy car drew closer. "That's Henri driving, all right. Sound's like he's been drinking. I sent him up yesterday. The girl wanted to fetch her sister from the village where she's been staying. They're Tutsis, refugees from Rwanda. Are you familiar with the Watutsi?"

Steve shook his head. Again Dubois grinned. "The sister's just eighteen. A very pretty girl, I've been told. I've never seen her. . . . Are you feeling at all lonely tonight, monsieur?"

Dubois used the French word *solitaire*. Solitary, Steve thought, isolated. He was feeling indeed very solitary and isolated up in the cold mountain darkness. He had slept little since the terrifying, drug-warped night with Charlie on the river at Stanleyville, his sleep being increasingly punctuated by nightmares of Saigon bodies and the shambles of the ANC raid on the hapless mission truck. The next day he would fly from Goma to Albertville and on to Léopoldville. The next night was New Year's Eve and he would be back home with Lisa, dancing beside some torch-lit swimming pool and drinking champagne. He would be with Lisa and their friends, far away from the ruins of Stanleyville and the haunted plantations of the Kivu. He shook himself from his thoughts to answer Dubois.

"I'm married, Monsieur Dubois," he said.

"I'm married too!" Dubois muttered. "That doesn't mean I can't enjoy a girl occasionally. I'm not a plaster saint, you know. The girl has been a comfort to me these past months. A man gets very lonely up here at night."

The car, a battered old Ford pickup truck covered with dried mud, skidded into the graveled drive before the house. In the flaring light of a gasoline lantern from the red brick servants' quarters, Steve could see the two women walking slowly from the vehicle with a stiff-legged gait provoked by the long ride over the rough Kivu roads. They were tall and, despite their stiffness, maintained the gracefully elegant carriage of the Watutsi. Dubois called across to them, speaking Kinyarwanda, a strangely tonal language that sounded vaguely Oriental to Steve. The girls answered shyly and disappeared into a darkened room at the end of the servants' wing.

"You sure you won't change your mind?" Dubois asked.

Steve had caught sight of the young sister's slightly flaring hips beneath the loose flow of the pastel robe she wore. He had noted the line of her neck gliding upward to meld into her egg-shaped coiffure, giving her head and upper torso a stateliness reminiscent of Egyptian tomb paintings.

"No, really," he said hoarsely, "I'll just go to bed. Thanks anyway. I'll see you in the morning."

"She's a very pretty girl, monsieur," Dubois said. "You sure you won't reconsider?"

Steve drained his glass and put it on the stone terrace wall. "Another time perhaps," he said. "Good night."

Steve lay beneath the mosquito net on the narrow metal-frame bed listening to the sounds of the night birds outside the open window. The room had been recently whitewashed, and the chemical lime odor was irritating. He had dozed briefly, but now he was awake again, aware that he had successfully caught himself on the dangerous edge of yet another nightmare. He sleepily debated smoking a cigarette, but the clotted tobacco and whisky staleness of his mouth dissuaded him. It was stupid to feel so edgy. I've just had a hard week traveling and seen a few unpleasant things. That's no reason to get so spooky, he thought. I'll be home with Lisa tomorrow and this whole stupid trip will be forgotten. I wanted to see some of Africa, and now I have. Just go back to sleep and don't brood on things.

He closed his eyes again, cupping his head in the crook of his elbow. It felt good to be cool without the grinding noise of an air conditioner. Then he was suddenly upright, naked on the sheet as he groped beneath the mosquito net for his flashlight. There was somebody standing in the open doorway to the graveled drive. It was the Tutsi girl. She wore her light blue sari-like robe as she stood silently in the moonlit doorway staring at him. Steve snatched on his khaki trousers and struggled out from under the net to face her.

She smiled, a very white, submissive smile. Shyly she held

something out to him in the darkness—a clean, folded bath towel. *"Serviette,"* she said softly.

"Comment?" Steve asked. *"Comprend pas."*

"Serviette," she repeated. *"Pour bain."*

Her voice was surprisingly low-pitched, uncharacteristic of her slender height. The girl stepped into the room and moved soundlessly on bare feet to the cracked enamel sink at the far wall. She carefully hung the towel on a peg next to the sink and then turned to face Steve with a new smile on her lips.

"Couché?" she whispered, gracefully pointing a tapered finger first at Steve and then at herself.

Jesus, Steve thought, she wants to go to bed with me. Dubois, that's what it is—he sent her in here with that towel.

"Viens," the girl said, slipping out of her robe and bending to pleat the folds of the mosquito net.

"Attend," Steve said; then, lapsing into English, he added: "Wait. You don't understand. I'm married. I was just having a nightmare. I'll be O.K. . . . Wait."

The girl giggled as she lay supine on the sheet. In the moonlight her skin was coppery-brown, her thin lips and narrow nose exotically attractive. Steve stood above her, and then her hands were on the waistband of his trousers and quickly he was down on top of her. *"Comment vous appelez-vous?"* Steve whispered. The girl giggled again, lying very still beneath him. "What's your name?" Steve repeated. He realized now that she knew little French. This is ridiculous, he thought. What am I doing here?

But then he knew. She took him gently with her two long hands, kneading his flesh until he responded. Still lying passively, her head on the pillow at a strange angle so as not to ruffle her elaborately done hair, she stared up into his face with her childishly shy smile as he groaned and thrust his body in long, accelerating spasms. It was over quickly.

Steve stood up, recognizing fully for the first time the strange, giddy dizziness that had plagued him since his night on the river with Charlie. He drank greedily from the bottle of boiled drinking water above the sink. Reacting to a flash of panic, he turned the chugging water tap fully on and scrubbed his groin.

"Non," the girl protested. *"Moi, pas sale, pas sale."* Steve

looked up from the sink. The girl had a troubled expression on her dark aristocratic face. Steve dried himself carefully with the towel, studying the girl's eyes.

"Viens," she whispered. *"Couché encore. Toi couche encore. Pas sale, moi."*

"Here," Steve said after a long silence. He dug his wallet out of his briefcase and handed the startled girl a crisp thousand-franc bill. *"Cadeau,"* he said, emulating the girl's pidgin French. *"Moi donne cadeau. Maintenant toi, tu pars, moi je dors."*

"Non," the girl whispered. *"Moi couche ici."*

"No!" Steve said sharply, his own angry tone surprising him. He had her off the bed and pushed her gently to the still open doorway, clutching her blue robe and the banknote.

"Demain?" she asked timidly.

"Yes," Steve lied. "Tomorrow night. *C'est pas bon ce soir, je suis un peu malade."*

"Bonne nuit, patron," the girl said and disappeared into the shadows. Steve stood swaying slightly in the doorway, and then, giving way once again to the weird, inexplicable panic he felt welling up inside him, he retreated back to the sink and repeated his violent ablutions.

CHAPTER **22**

They skidded around a washboard turn, dropping down rapidly on the switchback so that the red dust raised above would not engulf them. Steve clung to the windshield frame of the Land Rover, his feet wedged tightly beneath his seat, his free hand gripping the barrel of the shotgun between his knees. Dubois squinted under the edge of his dusty sunglasses. He drove the mud-spattered Land Rover with studied recklessness, allowing the front end to float to the very edge of the precipitous hairpin turns before slashing the wheel savagely back and ramming the floorshift into a lower gear.

They turned sharply at the corner of a terraced banana grove, the purple tree stalks and chartreuse leaves looking unreal in the mountain sunshine. Ahead of them to the north the view of the lake widened and Steve gasped. The mass of the Virunga volcanoes stood stark and clear, the mantle of morning clouds dissipated. The scene was primeval, suggestive of a painted backdrop in a museum display of Pleistocene fauna.

"You're very lucky, monsieur," Dubois said, stopping the car. "Normally they are only out of the clouds like this at sunset and at dawn. That's Nyiragongo, the big flat-topped one there on the left. The two pointed ones are Karisimbi and Mikeno. Off to the right there are Visoke, Sabineo, and Muhavura—they form the Rwanda-Uganda frontier. Quite a sight, isn't it, monsieur?"

"You can say that again," Steve answered.

"The summer I was sixteen, my cousin and I climbed them all, camping and hunting with the Batwa, the Pygmy hunters. It is something I'll never forget."

"Does your cousin still live here in the Kivu?" Steve asked.

"No," Dubois said flatly, gnawing at the cuticle of his thumb. "He was killed in a rebel ambush on the Uvira road last January." Steve started to speak, but Dubois cut him off.

"Mon Dieu, look at that!" He pointed below them into an open reddish-brown field, freshly hoed and planted. Before Steve saw what it was, Dubois had snatched up the shotgun and was bounding down the slope. Steve experienced a flash of hot panic as the image of a rebel ambush shot through his mind. He picked up Dubois's heavy automatic rifle and, feeling naked against the open mud slope, he stumbled down after the jerking figure of Dubois. Dubois's camouflage jacket disappeared into the banana patch, and Steve froze as five blasts of the shotgun echoed across the valley. He was dizzy from the run. A fly buzzed noisily about his face.

Finally Dubois reappeared, the shotgun cradled in his arm. A ragged African boy tagged behind him, clutching an armload of brightly plumed guinea fowl. One of the birds flopped squawking from the boy's grip and dragged itself along the ground. Dubois spoke sharply to the child and quickly smashed the bird's head with the butt of the gun. "It was easy," Dubois said, smiling. "They were all on the ground after the fresh bean seeds. They're such a stupid bird it's almost a shame to kill them. It's a pity you're leaving today. That Tutsi cook at the hotel in Goma makes a *coq au vin* with guineas that is unbelievable."

They trudged back up the hill, Steve feeling absurd with the FAL held awkwardly over his shoulder. The African boy panted several paces behind them, coughing from a respiratory illness. Just as they mounted the mud bank of the road, the boy jumped and broke into a shrill burst of Swahili. *"Isha, Bwan,"* he said. *"Ikko isha, moya makubwa, kulé! kulé!"*

"Wapi?" Dubois whispered. "Where?"

The boy pointed diagonally down past the corner of the banana grove. There, silhouetted against the dirt bank of a footpath, a small reddish antelope stood broadside to them, its nose quivering as it tested the wind.

"Take him," Dubois said to Steve. "The rifle's all ready, just release the safety. Aim a little high on the shoulder."

Steve raised the weapon and sighted on the animal's shoulder. Then raising the sight minutely, he began to squeeze the trigger. He heard a raven croaking in the sky. A cloud passed over the sun, and he felt the chill of the breeze as it ruffled the tangle of sweaty hair on his forehead. It was just a small antelope. What was wrong?

"Don't wait too long," Dubois whispered. "He sees us."

The shock of the rifle and the heavy thud against his shoulder stunned him. He saw the gout of red clay kick up behind the animal and the flash of auburn fur as it bounded into the bananas. *"Merde!"* he swore. "I shot over it." Inside his chest he felt a sudden happy release at having missed.

"Kufa!" the little boy exclaimed, jumping up and down and clapping his hands as he ran down the slope.

"Nice shot," Dubois said, taking the weapon.

"But I missed him," Steve protested. "I shot over."

"It was a solid," Dubois said. "Went right through the neck and into the bank. He was dead the second he was hit. They can always run a bit though, even when they're dead, just like the Simbas when they've drunk *dawa* water before an attack. I've seen antelope run a hundred meters with their hearts blown into jelly from a ten-seventy-five soft point."

The African child returned, dragging the animal by its spiky horns. The neck swiveled loosely, and Steve saw the bright trail of fresh blood on the muddy clods of the field.

He turned away discreetly while Dubois gutted the antelope with his skinning knife. Already the flies were clotting on the carcass as it lay in a wet pile next to the Land Rover. Dubois dumped the tripe and the sodden heart and liver into the banana leaf the smiling child held out. He wiped the blade on the animal's red fur and together he and Steve swung the spaniel-sized body into the back of the car. "Forest duiker," Dubois said. "Not a bad one either. They often come down from the mountains during the planting time. You want the head?"

Steve shook his head, *"Non, merci."* His fingers were trembling as he lit one of Dubois's Belgas. The strange, tight feeling had returned to his chest. As the car jolted off down the track, he suddenly remembered Charlie Hogan's description of the wet, leaking bodies on the Saigon sidewalk.

"We'll stop at Kando Mission," Dubois said. "We can give the *isha* and a couple of the birds to old Père André. God knows they can use the meat."

The summits of Mikeno and Karisimbi disappeared into the slowly mounting nimbus clouds as Steve and Dubois drove under the arcade of eucalyptus trees leading into the Kando Mission. The red brick church and school buildings stood in a ring of jacaranda trees at the end of a flat, thumblike ridge. They had dropped down almost a thousand feet from Dubois's plantation, but the air was still fresh and sparkling. Cattle grazed the already short-cropped grass on either side of the road.

"Jambo, jambo!" Dubois yelled to the ragged pack of children who had left their cattle and were whistling and rabbit-hopping beside the slowly moving car.

The mission buildings formed a *U* in the ring of shade, the odd, vaguely Gothic brick church dominating the lake side of the clearing. The school complex was made of the same laterite brick, but appeared to have been more recently constructed, as its corrugated sheet metal roof still glared brightly in the sun. A group of African women squatted about the smoldering remains of breakfast cook fires. Their leaf-wrapped baskets and shoddy blankets were drawn closely to them. There were no children with them. As the car passed them, they glanced fitfully with wide-eyed distrust at Dubois's uniform and weapons. Then, like a flock of birds wheeling on some telepathic command, they all turned away to busy themselves with imaginary tasks. Dubois called to them cheerfully in the dialect of the Bashi. None of the women returned his greeting. He stopped the car and spoke more slowly, enunciating a formal salutation in Kinyarwanda. Still, the women stared nervously at the ground as they poked about their pitiful heaps of rags and blankets.

"*Merde!*" Dubois said. "Looks like we've got some more *matatá.*"

The young cowherds hung back shyly, slipping from tree to tree and calling to each other in muffled whispers. On the covered porch of the school a tall Mututsi mission worker appeared dressed in a white hospital coat tinted a dull pink from the dust. "*Messieurs, bonjour,*" he said sullenly, then added in an officious tone, "*Vous cherchez quelque-chose?*"

Dubois answered him sharply in Kinyarwanda, jerking his thumb toward the pile of game in the back of the vehicle. The Tutsi smirked and made a pose of studying his tapered fingers. "I'll call one of the kitchen boys to take the meat," he said slowly in perfect French. "Père André is down in the shed working on the truck."

"How do you say it in English?" Dubois asked as they walked toward the workshed at the far end of the compound. "One of your officers in Bukavu told me the expression. I wish I could remember it. Yes, 'Their shit will not stink.' No, it's, 'They think that their shit don't stink,' that's it. Well, that's the Watutsi for you. They're all like that, no matter how good they can be, they are all arrogant like that one. They think that they are not black like the rest of the *indigènes.*"

"They're not really Bantu at all," Steve said quietly, remembering the curve of the African girl's neck on the pillow. "They're what is called Nilotic."

Dubois glanced over at him with an impatient expression on his face. "That may well be," he said quickly, "but they're still black, and that means they still have a bit of the old *macaque* in them, *n'est-ce pas?*"

Steve did not answer, looking away to take in the sparse collection of mission buildings. "When you've been out here a little longer, Monsieur Sherman," Dubois continued, "you'll see that I am right."

"That's what they keep telling me," Steve said in English.

Père André appeared out of the deep shade of the garage shed to greet them. They shook his hairy wrist which he extended, keeping his grease-smeared hand doubled back. "*Eh bien, mon Père,*" Dubois said, "it smells a bit like *matatá* about."

"*Matatá?*" the old priest asked. "Not really, the *matatá* is finished, and now we have the pieces to pick up."

As he scrubbed his hands in an open tin of gasoline, he explained. "Those are Bahavu women from up over the crest," he said. Like Dubois he gestured freely with his dripping hands while he spoke, spattering greasy droplets of gasoline on his cassock. "They've been coming in for the past month, while you and the others were still down in Bukavu being decorated for your glorious military exploits." Dubois laughed warmly at the priest, but interrupted his rejoinder when he saw the change in Père André's expression. "They've been coming in now at the rate of four, five a day," Père André went on. "Somehow they've heard about the milk." Turning to Steve, he spoke very slowly in a heavy Flemish accent. "Normally they get at least two bean and pea crops a year. This is their diet. They keep a few goats and chickens for a rainy day, almost like a postal savings account, you know. But it's the beans and peas that keep them alive. They have fewer cattle than the Bashi and none compared to the Banurwanda. The men do some trapping and snaring, but the game is quite small up in the forest. They're afraid of the elephant and don't know how to kill as the Batwa do. So you see, monsieur," he continued, taking the relatively clean rag Dubois handed him from the workbench, "the rebellion, all the *matatá,* as Adjutant Dubois calls it, has had a very serious effect on their daily lives. Not just the shooting and the fighting. That was over relatively quickly. It's the fear and the hiding, the burning and theft of the half-ripe crops. Most of them fled to the forest when the Simbas came and again later when the CODOKI and the ANC came through. They've had no regular crops for more than a year. It's not really a famine as they have in India or China. No one ever really starves in Africa, you know."

He had finished wiping his hands and folded the rag neatly into a pleated bundle which he thrust absentmindedly into the pocket of his cassock. They walked slowly back up the slight slope of the compound toward the spartan brick building housing the rectory. "No, no one starves in Africa," he said softly. "There are always roots and berries and *leaves*—something to put in your belly." He patted the hard bulge beneath his crucifix. "It wasn't starvation exactly, but there were just too many of them, you see. This is rich soil, very volcanic, especially up above where the forest has only recently been cleared and the sun hasn't bleached it out yet. Because of this there has been an overpopulation of the area. Tribes have moved in since Independence to escape the fighting and to be near the missions and big plantations with their dispensaries and their schools.

"And then, as I said, the rebellion came along and they all went to live like animals in the forest. They didn't starve, but they got practically no protein. The men and women and the older children could support it, even the babies who were still nursing— you know how these Bantu women will nurse a child until he's two or three? Well, most of them suffered badly, but they survived. It was only the children three to six or seven years old who really suffered. They became sick with what the natives call *bwaki,* the medical term is kwashiorkor; it's a protein deficiency. It works very slowly at first, but it's deadly. Once it has gone so far, there is no remedy. Unfortunately, most of the mothers only bring their sick children in to us when the disease is already well advanced. They're still afraid of the white man's *dawa."*

On the steps of the schoolhouse Steve watched a pair of hunting hawks wheeling in the sky. He could smell a sweet, mildewed odor seeping out from the open windows of the buildings. The squatting women cast nervous glances, hopefully at the priest, apprehensively at the uniformed Dubois and the massive canvas pistol holster on his belt.

"Do you want to see them?" the priest asked.

The tight dizziness Steve had felt peering at the antelope down the sights of the rifle suddenly returned to him. He nodded his head after a pause.

"Don't worry," Père André said. "There won't be any odor; we keep them very clean. You'd hardly know that there were more than a hundred little Bantu in that building, would you?"

The building was divided into one small and two large classrooms, connected by open doorways. Roughly made wooden blackboards hung on the whitewashed brick walls. In the large classroom they entered, rows of battered metal-frame army cots had been placed on either side of the room beneath the open windows. The silent children lay crosswise, two and three to a cot. The dizziness swelled abruptly as Steve stood with the priest in the center aisle between the cots. As Père André had said, there was not much odor. An old mission worker was bent over from the waist, wiping up the cement floor from a bucket of disinfectant solution. Père André spoke to him in Swahili. The old man nodded and padded out of the room on his splay feet, the bucket of dirty water sloshing. Then there was silence.

Steve felt that he was reeling in a slowly expanding spiral, that he would surely lose his balance and fall on the next revolution. The priest whispered to him. "I've sent Simone for the milk," he said, gesturing toward the cots. "These children get a quarter liter of powdered milk three times a day. We mix it with warm water, almost half and half. It's the only source of protein we have that their stomachs can accept. I tried meat broth at first, but they only died quicker, with diarrhea and terrible cramps. And then Dr. Tribain, the Haitian from the United Nations in Goma, brought us the American milk and we've been using it ever since. He comes up twice a week to look at them. Unfortunately there's not much that can be done besides the milk."

Steve felt Père André's bony hand on the small of his back gently edging him forward toward the row of cots. There were three little boys on the end bed. It was impossible for Steve to estimate their ages; he had never been good at judging an African's age, and the children had been so grotesquely transformed by the disease that the faces staring up at him might have belonged to another species.

It was the hair. Like the other children in the ward, the three boys on the cot wore tan cotton hospital smocks, covering them from their necks to just below their skeletal knees. A gray institutional blanket covered the webbing of steel bedsprings. Their exposed arms and legs were tinted gray contrasting with their hair, which had been discolored a rusty yellow, retaining in random patches only the black springiness normal to Bantu children. The three lay on their sides. Their bulbous heads covered with the sickly yellow fluff appeared bloated, out of proportion to the rest of their bodies. Their limbs looked almost transparent, like sharply angled pieces of glass laboratory tubing, dirtied by the black-gray residue of a chemical experiment, overheated, then too rapidly cooled, so that the crystal structure had been destroyed and the very slightest touch would shatter them. Two were awake, watching his movements, but the third slept. At the far end of the room Simone and a short woman with tribal braids were filling clean tin cans with milk from a plastic tub. The three little boys on the blanket had somnolent, glazed expressions that struck a sharp chord of memory in Steve's mind. Somewhere he had seen it before. He remembered with a sickening rush of *déjà vu* the concentration camp newsreels of his childhood: Buchenwald and Dachau, the tangle of living dead, stretched out on wooden pallets in zebra pajamas, skulls bloated, eyes lazy liquid, worn, exhausted by the tedium of their deaths, too weary for an active manifestation of impatience, yet still too alive to surrender to death.

The pressure of the pulse in his head was easing, giving way to a giddy sensation akin to the *déjà vu*. He saw the newsreels again, but in negative. The clean cotton of the children's smocks replaced the filthy death-camp pajamas, the skulls were not shaved but covered with unreal polychrome fuzz, the skin was not the transparent, cadaverous white, but a translucent gray-black. Only the eyes were the same.

A cooing whimper began at the end of the room and slowly drifted toward them as Simone and his assistant made their way up the row of cots, propping up each child long enough for it to suck down the warm milk. At the faint murmur of the patients the Bahavu mothers squatting in the courtyard rose in unison and moved eagerly to the steps of the building. The Mututsi was there to turn them back. He held a polished shovel handle loosely in his hands, waving it regally at the women like a scepter.

"I'm afraid that we have to keep the mothers away from their children," Père André said wearily. "They were all right in the beginning when we only had a few children here, but then"—he paused, looking at Steve in a strange way, a frustrated pucker to his lips as he gestured—"it was the constant arguments and fighting about the milk. It upset the children and caused many problems when the women got back to their villages. None of them could understand why some children got more than the others."

"More?" Steve said.

"Yes," the priest answered. They had walked up the row of cots and entered the second large classroom. There were little girls on the cots in this ward. "The mothers were very quick to see that the children here in the two large rooms were given one little can three times a day while those in the small room got a much bigger can five times at regular intervals during the night and day. They knew that the children from the big rooms were dying and the others were being taken home well. We had a terrible battle one day —some of the fathers came down from the villages with their pangas. They accused me of favoring the baptized Christians. That's ridiculous, of course. Just as many baptized children die as pagans. It was only that they could not comprehend the difference in the milk rations. It's all very sad, monsieur. Most people do not realize it, but African parents love their children just as much as we whites do."

"But why is there the difference?" Steve asked.

"It's in the diagnosis," the priest said. "When Dr. Tribain comes, he examines the new patients. For those in whom the disease has already gone too far there is really no hope, no matter how much protein they now are given. Their bodies have already been destroyed. There can be no recovery. We give them a little milk like the others because it keeps them comfortable. We don't have enough, however, to give all of them the massive doses. We reserve most of it for the few who can still be saved. Generally speaking, once the hair and skin discoloration has gotten to this point, it is already too late. They will live like this on the beds for perhaps one week, ten days at the most. But, in reality, they are already dead."

As Steve crossed into the smaller room, a muffled sobbing arose from the last of the cots in the girls' ward. He turned to see Père André kneel beside a bed. Of the three small bodies on the cot, one had slipped sideways and was hanging, head down, partially wedged against the wall. The two others on the bed had begun sobbing, a very faint, surprisingly guttural sound. Soon the others in the room had taken it up. Père André softly called down to Simone, who had just dragged the milk tub through the far doorway. He disappeared but was back a few moments later with a clean piece of cotton, already cut into a one-meter square. The priest dug into the pocket of his cassock, first absentmindedly pulling out the folded rag with which he had cleaned the grease from his hands, and then from the other pocket he removed the blue-and-white embroidered silk stole which he tiredly hung around his neck. Simone stood behind him while Père André said a mumbled benediction. Then, as soon as the priest had risen, the old African scooped up the child's body and carried it from the room, tucking the cotton about the flopping limbs as he walked.

"That's the third this morning," the priest said. "Usually we come through at dawn and take them from the beds before the others are awake. They almost never die like that during the day, for some strange reason. It's odd, isn't it? The poets are always writing about it—how death comes in the last hour before dawn. *Eh bien,* that's certainly been the rule with these children. But today, for some reason, three have gone since mass this morning."

The woman was feeding the children at the other end of the room, and the sobbing had stopped at the sight of the milk cans.

"Do you mean that they're all going to die," Steve whispered, *"all* the ones in these two rooms?"

"I'm afraid they will," Père André said. "Look at their hair."

Suddenly Steve was on the floor. The spinning wheel had flung him down. He saw the splay feet of the two mission workers and heard the thuds of Dubois's heavy boots through the cool cement. They had him sitting up, and then, propped between Dubois and the priest, he was being walked out into the sunshine toward the rectory.

"Is it malaria?" Dubois asked.

Steve shook his head. "I'm O.K. now," he said in English. His lips tasted dry. "I'm O.K. Let me walk alone."

"You mustn't let it affect you that way," Père André said, whispering so that Dubois could not hear. "It's a very sad thing to die so young, for so many to die this way, but we mustn't let it affect us too much. We must realize that we are all doomed, that none of us is immortal, that there is another life after this one for which we must prepare ourselves."

Steve pulled away from the priest's grasp. "What the hell are you talking about?" he spat. "Those people—they're dying like animals there. They're . . ." But he saw that Père André did not understand his English, that there was no use trying to explain. He felt very tired. He could see the lake sparkling blue through the green of the banana groves. Again he saw the flash of the antelope's red fur as it bounded into the floppy green. He heard Dubois's words, "They can always run a bit, even when they're dead." From behind the school building the mourning shrieks of the mother went up. She was instantly joined by her tribal sisters. Steve ran toward the car, but Dubois took him by the shoulder. "Come, monsieur, you're upset. Come into the rectory. We'll eat here and you can rest a bit."

Père André opened three sweating cold bottles of Primus beer. "This," he said, "is the adjutant's great contribution to the spiritual well-being of us priests at Kando Mission. He came several months ago and rebuilt our kerosene refrigerator which the rebels had torn apart during the occupation. I had tried to fix it, as did Père Julien." He nodded at the other priest, a very old man with steel-framed spectacles and a curly iron-gray beard. "Neither of us made any progress, however. We old Flammands don't understand technology." They all laughed, and Père Julien made an unintelligible comment. His French was severely limited and he took little part in the conversation. He sipped his beer with great satisfaction and listened to the others.

They sat on the breezy veranda of the rectory looking out over the hills and the lake below. Steve had washed his face and taken two of the ten-milligram phenobarbital tablets the Peace Corps doctor in Morocco had given him for gastritis two years earlier. He still felt the odd tightness in his head, but, sitting down, the dizziness had evaporated and he felt the magical chemical erosion of the tension inside of him. He knew that they were watching him, that they were just being polite; they thought there was something wrong with him. There was nothing he could do, however. He had to sit there and talk with them and not think about the children or the antelope or green rubber bags. The pills were helping. He had to be patient.

It was Friday, New Year's Eve. He would be in Albertville, hundreds of miles to the south, in a few hours. And then by eight o'clock tonight he would be home in bed with Lisa. He sat back, taking a long swallow of beer, letting his mind move warmly ahead to the night before him . . . Lisa dancing with her face tightly against the shoulder of his dinner jacket. He was leaving the dead children behind. He was leaving the roadblocks and the drunken black soldiers and the ripped mission skirts abandoned on the dark road. He was going home. And then, then he *would* take a few days off. They'd just stay home and he would be able to sleep late with her, and slowly he could tell her about Charlie's rubber bags and the antelope and the yellow fuzz on the children's heads, and it would be all right.

Steve swallowed. He closed his eyes and saw again the Tutsi girl's egg-shaped coiffure. He heard her voice, *"Pas sale, moi, pas sale."* Somehow he would find a way to tell Lisa about the girl as well. It had been an accident, that's all, just a stupid accident. He was all alone there in the cold. He'd been scared by the nightmare. Dubois was right. He had been *solitaire*. He hadn't hurt anyone. He'd paid the girl. Lisa couldn't blame him for that. She *had* to understand. He had to find a way to explain it all to her.

Dubois was speaking to him. "I'm sure that it's malaria, Monsieur Sherman," he said. "You must be certain to have a blood smear made in Léo. I've seen it happen often when someone comes up here from Léopoldville. Somehow the altitude and the cooler weather bring it on. A person doesn't always get the chills and fever immediately. Very often you feel . . . well, nervous

. . . little things can upset you unnecessarily. You feel strange, dizzy, and people—*unpleasant* people and situations—disturb you. I think that is what's happening to you, Monsieur Sherman. I'm sure of it. It's happened to me just the same way too often in the past for me to confuse the symptoms."

The three Belgians nodded agreement. Steve knew that he should say something, that he should register some sign of interest, return their kindness by joining in the conversation. He smiled; his lips felt rubbery, stretched back like the petals of an artificial flower as his tongue glided lightly over his teeth. They tasted of beer and tobacco and the dusty road. His lips had become green rubber like the body bags. His mouth snapped shut. Dubois watched him in silence.

"Yes," Steve said, able to speak after a long while. "I can't remember if I took my malaria pills this week or not. It's so easy to forget when you're traveling." They all agreed. Père Julien said something in Flemish to the other priest, who smiled and slowly shook his head. Steve felt the internal flutter again, but was able to suppress it with a quick swallow of beer. Dubois refilled his glass and pointed toward the line of volcanoes. He spoke to Steve in an earnest, beer-mellowed tone. "You must promise to come up here with your wife sometime soon, before the dry season when it's too hazy to enjoy the view. It would be easy for you with all the military flights. My own wife will be back with the children in January. We could take a trip up into the volcanoes. I know some incredible places to camp. I will arrange the whole trip: porters, Batwa guides. It's like another world up there. The vegetation is unearthly, and if we have luck, we can see large numbers of gorillas."

"Gorillas or guerillas?" Père André asked, smiling.

They laughed, Père André whispering in Flemish to explain the pun to his old colleague.

"Once you are above two thousand meters," Dubois continued, "it is really Africa; it's unchanged. There are none of your *macaque* politicians up there to ruin things."

"Only the real *macaques,*" Père Julien said, proud that he had followed the turn of the conversation.

As if on cue, the tall Mututsi appeared around the corner of the veranda and stood apart, disdainful of their laughter. *"Oui, François?"* Père André said.

"They are ready. If we do the burial service now, I can take the three mothers and the others from yesterday up in the truck past those soldiers' roadblock at the junction and they can be in their own villages before dark."

Père André pulled a battered silver watch from his cassock. "Have all three decided on burial here at the mission?"

"Two have," François said gravely, "The third is from a village just below the crest. She will take the child with her in the truck. I think it's better; with the dead child the soldiers will leave us alone. It's a *fête* today and they'll have been drinking."

Père André got tiredly to his feet. "Very well," he said. "I'll be along in a moment."

François stood above them. He hesitated and then said, "They ask permission to cut some of the palm fronds to cover the body, from the young trees next to the church. The mother also wants to have a small piece of plastic from the sheet the milk sacks come wrapped in. She wants to make a bag to put the child in."

"Very well," Père André said. "See to it, will you please, and tell Marcel to hold lunch for a few minutes and to bring these gentlemen some more cold beer."

The Tutsi nodded curtly and turned away.

"Plastic!" Dubois exclaimed when Père André had left, suppressing a laugh. "Sounds like a bit of *dawa* to me."

"Dawa?" Steve asked, again hearing his own voice as a ghostly echo.

"Yes," Dubois said. "I suppose they think putting palm fronds on it and wrapping it up in *wazungu* plastic will keep the child's soul from escaping until their village *féticheur* can go to work on it and discover the *real* cause of its death. You know that they simply cannot accept the idea of disease the way we understand it. They feel that there's always some kind of *dawa* to blame for these misfortunes. Undoubtedly, the village *mufumu* will decide that the whites at the mission are to blame, or maybe the patron of the plantation where the child's father worked. That always gives them a good excuse for some *matatá*. In the old days we could simply thrash some sense into the *féticheur* if he tried these kinds of tricks. Now it is not so easy. Plastic! *Merde!*"

Steve rose clumsily to his feet and walked toward the end of the veranda. His head felt soft and feathery-light. Perhaps it was malaria, after all. "You know," he said, turning back toward Dubois, "it's not such a bad idea to transport a body in a leakproof sack, especially in the tropics. It's not just the Africans who do so. Maybe the woman was just using common sense."

"Probably she wants to use the plastic for a tablecloth afterwards. She may be the wife, or I should say, one of the wives of a provincial *fonctionnaire* and wants to spread a nice table on the floor of her hut, make use of some of the looted china and silver they've stolen from the plantations."

Père Julien began a painfully slow anecdote concerning a piece of Belgian crystal he had once seen hanging as a fetish on the corncrib of a native shamba. The farmer had guaranteed him that it would keep rats and civet cats away as the crystal had once stood on the sideboard in a plantation house and the ex-houseboy who had sold the crystal to the farmer had carefully explained that, while the crystal had stood on the sideboard, none of the houseboys had been able to pick the lock of the liquor cabinet below.

They laughed again, Steve's laugh too loud, echoing in his ears. The pills had definitely been a good idea. As long as he kept smiling and took part in the conversation he would be all right. Marcel, the cook, stole up on his bare feet and refilled Steve's beer glass. He stood at the end of the veranda staring down at the lake. Dubois's proposal of a volcano-climbing expedition began to appeal to him. Maybe that would be the thing to do, not to stay in Léopoldville brooding on things, but to get on a WIGMO flight and come right back up here with Lisa. God knows, she could use a change of scene, he thought. He pictured her in the new bush jacket he had ordered from Nairobi, climbing gracefully up through the black volcanic turf of the game trails in the highland forest. Fires at night and the native porters chanting. That was the way Africa was supposed to be—not those absurdly drunken pool parties in the sealed compounds of Parc Hembise, not the frigid discotheques and the lewd innuendos of the pampered Léopoldville whites, but the mountains and the rain forest and the animals. Yes, that was what he would do.

From where he sat on the concrete railing of the veranda he could see behind the rectory the end of the school building. In the banana tree grove behind the school were the figures of the burial party, the mothers, swaying and keening, now in a faint dirge, Père André with his bright vestments, and the Tutsi with the Holy Water. The red soil of the fresh graves was piled in irregular mounds as far as he could see between the tree stalks. He began counting graves, but lost interest after forty-one. He watched, occasionally sipping his beer, while the two mothers made a ritualized attempt to throw themselves into the tiny open graves, only to be gently restrained by the other women. Then two mission boys shoveled in the red dirt and the group moved toward the courtyard, their voices blending into a Swahili Christian hymn, punctuated by archaic Bantu funeral chants. He found that if he braced himself securely against the railing, the dizziness could be contained.

The vegetable soup was excellent, made of leeks and carrots from the mission garden. They sat silently at the table waiting for old Marcel to bring in the meat course. Steve knew that he was drinking too much beer, but Père Julien insisted on refilling his glass each time he compulsively drained it.

Père André nodded and looked up as the cook entered the room with the platters of meat and fried potatoes. "We can thank you for this excellent meal, monsieur," he said, nodding at the antelope filets on the plate.

"Is this the *isha?*" Steve asked.

Dubois nodded. "We really should have let them keep it in the frigo a few days to age," he said, "but I wanted you to have a chance to taste it before you went back to Léo."

Steve's stomach began the spasmatic contraction he had experienced stumbling down the bean field with the FAL in his hands. The heavy wooden table seemed to roll as if on a ship at sea. Then he caught himself and was stable again. Very quickly, he cut the meat, accepted the gravy bowl. Stuffing the chunks of pinkish meat into his mouth, he found that he was able to clear his mind by returning to the mathematical tables he had been taught as an irrigation surveyor in the Peace Corps. The others talked softly, smiling at his obvious good appetite. Then there was silence; they were all looking at him.

"I'm sorry," he said. "Were you speaking to me?"

"Yes," Dubois said. "Père André was wondering how you liked the isha."

"It's great!" Steve said loudly. "Much better than North American venison."

"Do you hunt much yourself in the United States?" Père André asked.

"All the time," Steve lied. "I never miss a season."

"What types of game do you have in your part of America?" Dubois asked.

"Oh, all types," Steve said quickly, "Deer, pheasants, bears, all the smaller animals."

"Which do you prefer to hunt?" Dubois continued, studying Steve's face.

There was a stream of chilled sweat dripping beneath his arms, wetting the dusty cotton shirt. "I think that bear are the most interesting to hunt, but deer provide better meat."

"Do you also have wolves?"

"Not very many," Steve said. The older priest passed the meat platter again. Steve saw his hand go out to take the biggest slice. "Although," he added, "I've heard reports of wolves very near my father's farm." Father's farm, he thought wildly. Steady, ease off, you're moving too fast.

"I read that the wolves were extinct in the United States," Dubois said flatly.

"We're very near to Canada."

"Ah, Canada," Dubois said. "Canada is known for its wolves."

Finally the meal ended. Steve had forced down wads of the gummy mission bread, soaking it with more beer. His stomach was leaden, the wet clot of beer and bread successfully tempering the bleeding meat of the antelope.

As they passed through the doorway of the dining room to the veranda to have their coffee, Steve noticed a colorful poster on the wall of the rectory office. With his coffee cup in his hand he wandered back indoors to study the poster. It was a large, rectangular Swahili wall newspaper, a product of the U.S. Information Service. The border was in bright yellow, the ten photographs sharply printed. Moving his lips to pronounce the unfamiliar words, he scanned the poster. At first the pictures appeared to be a random collection of news photographs. Then he was able to see a pattern emerging. There were two main themes developed with text and pictures: American aid to the Congo and other countries and the efforts of the Congolese Central Government to alleviate the suffering caused by the rebellion. He began to laugh. One picture showed a group of three smiling young American Negro paratroopers ladling out cans of dried beans to lines of grim-faced children before a bullet-pocked wall. The soldiers wore sharply pressed fatigues and bulging ammunition pouches. Steve recognized the words Santo Domingo in the text, but was unable to read more.

"This is beautiful!" he exclaimed in English, laughing loudly again.

On the lower left-hand side of the poster were three pictures depicting the humanitarian efforts of the Congolese National Army. One portrayed a squad of ANC troops, also in clean, sharply pressed uniforms with Red Cross arm bands, operating an open-air dispensary in the street of a Congolese village. The soldiers were smiling. The ragged children lined up before the white-draped medical table stared at the camera with fearful expressions. Another series of pictures showed American wheat and rice being unloaded in various ports. Steve read the captions: Saigon, Stanleyville, again Santo Domingo. Beneath the port pictures, a smaller photograph showed a Negro United States Navy medical corpsman inoculating children in a Vietnamese village. From the palm thatching and mud wattle walls of the huts it appeared that the Congolese and Vietnamese villages might have been the different sections of the same specially constructed stage set. A red-bordered box in the center of the poster marked "World News" contained two photo stories with longer captions. One showed a map of the Indochina peninsula. The map was covered with lines and symbols in red and black ink. After careful examination Steve discerned that it was drawn to illustrate the infiltration routes from

North Vietnam to South Vietnam. His eye shot to the upper left-hand corner of the poster where another map was printed. This one showed the Congo and the neighboring countries to the east. Red lines similar to the infiltration lines on the center map illustrated the previous year's flow of Soviet and Chinese weapons from Burundi and the Sudan into the rebel-held areas of the Eastern Congo.

He was still laughing. He caught himself swaying and began reading Swahili aloud, slowly at first, then more quickly as the nonsensical words became more familiar. He launched into a loud reading of the text of the central story: the orbital rendezvous of Gemini 6 and Gemini 7. Automatically his voice fell into the singsong lilt of the language. He had no clear idea of the words' meaning, but the sound of his voice rippling over the polysyllabic Bantu phrases was strangely comforting.

Dubois and Père André stood now in the doorway of the office. Steve smiled at them, unaware that most of his coffee had spilled on the floor.

"This is really pretty great stuff," he said in English.

They stared at him. "Oh, sorry," he said and began in French, "I was just trying to read the Swahili. This is a very good idea, this wall newspaper. I suppose you find them very useful—here at the mission, I mean."

"I've only received a few," Père André said. "From your consulate in Bukavu. With the roads so bad now, we don't get down there as much as we used to. It ruins the truck to take it so far."

"Could you use more? For the other churches in the parish, for when you get the schools opened again?"

"We can always use more of everything," Père André said, sweeping his hand slowly in front of him. "The missions aren't as well-endowed as they used to be. In theory we must depend on the Congolese now for our school supplies. You know how that works out."

"Yes," Steve said. "I'm sure I can get you more of these, more recent editions as well. We also have books and films. Would you like films? I know that the Embassy has made some very good ones recently on the reconstruction efforts of the ANC." He heard his voice jolting through the French and knew he should speak more slowly, but he could not. The priest and Dubois exchanged a quick glance.

"By all means," Père André said, "if it is possible we would be very grateful for any assistance."

Dubois stepped close, squinting in the shadowy room to read the photo captions. "This is all right," he said finally in a flat, unenthusiastic tone. "I don't agree with the stories about the ANC, but perhaps they have been better in other parts of the Congo. Here in the Kivu they have not been involved in projects such as these." He slapped the picture of the Congolese village. "The part about the Communist weapons, however, is very good. It's high time the blacks realized the danger of flirting with the Russians and Chinese. I'm afraid that most of the natives I've seen don't have the slightest idea where Vietnam or South America are, though. For them, any place that is not in the Congo is in Brussels. They have no idea about yellow Asians." He tapped the photo of the Vietnamese village.

"I realize that," Steve said hoarsely, "but we've got loads of books and films down at the Embassy in Léopoldville that can help them understand all this. It's senseless for them to be moldering in the warehouses down there when they are needed so badly out in the provinces." He walked quickly to the veranda and got a notebook from his briefcase. He felt his pants leg wet with coffee.

"I'll make a note of these things," he said. "First the wall newspapers. How many copies could you use each month?"

Père André shrugged, again glancing at Dubois. "I don't know," the priest said. "Ten perhaps."

"Oh, no!" Steve said. "Take more. Take fifty. How about the books? We have a very good title on American aid to the developing world. And we have books that explain the American civil rights struggle and labor unions. They're in very simple French, written especially for Africa. And films, too, excellent films on the rebellion and how America and Belgium helped the central government, and on the Army, how we're helping to build a new and better ANC. I've seen this film. It's excellent, they call it 'Le Soldat de Demain.' It's all about how the ANC beat the rebels and is now being trained to help in the reconstruction. It's a beautiful film, very easy to understand. There's a whole series we've made

here in the Congo. You should have them. You can't imagine—
we have an entire film-making group in the Embassy's information
section. They're professional and they really know their business."

He heard his voice bouncing off the whitewashed bricks of the
rectory office. He stopped and they were all silent for a moment,
staring at him. Finally Père André broke the silence.

"I've seen one or two of these films at your consulate in Bukavu," Père André said. "Please do not misunderstand me, but"
—he shrugged, again waving his hand as he searched for words
—"I don't think that the people up here really understand what a
film is. They get very excited when they see images on a screen,
especially when they see soldiers and fighting. They cannot understand that it is only a film. When they see these things, some of
them think that the rebels have come back or that the soldiers are
shooting in their village. It can be very unpleasant. As Monsieur
Dubois has said, most of them have no idea where America or
Vietnam or Latin America really are. They think that these places
are in the Congo and they become afraid. I do not think that it
helps them to be shown the *matatá* in the rest of the world. They
only know their own villages."

Steve paused. He knew that he was doing a stupid thing, but he
had to keep talking or the dizziness would catch up again. "I'll see
that you get the new films," he said, "and arrange the loan of a
projector and portable generator. You can control who sees them.
I think that you'll agree there are some that have a very great potential. The books, too—you can give the books only to the most
intelligent people in the parish. At the Embassy we call them
opinion molders. If they can understand the problems, they can
help the others to understand. I'll make notes of these things.
You'll be hearing from me very soon, I promise. I won't let you
down. You can count on me."

Dubois took him gently by the arm again. "You're very tired
from the fever, Monsieur Sherman," he said. "We really should be
on our way if you're going to meet your plane in Goma."

"It's odd," Steve said as they walked across the beaten earth of
the mission courtyard. "I'll be back down in Léo tonight celebrating the New Year in all the heat." He looked away from the windows of the school building.

"I have a small present for you," Père André said, catching up with them. In his hand he held a package wrapped in paper.

Steve peeled back the wrapping. Inside there was a smooth sheet of plastic, covering the severed rear quarter of the antelope.

"You can cook it for New Year's Day tomorrow with your wife in Léopoldville," the priest said. "I've had Marcel wrap it in plastic so that it won't drip in the airplane."

Steve stared down at the web of blue veins set against the white fatty sheet on the flat of the animal's thigh. His laughter came back to him off the tall walls of the church. The group of waiting Bahavu mothers stirred in discomfort from their vigil around the cook fires. Père André was about to speak when the old, splay-footed mission worker came trotting out of the school toward him. *"Icko mbili zaidi,"* the old man said. "There are two more."

CHAPTER **23**

Abruptly, the rutted laterite road became smooth pulverized lava. On either side of them the grotesque volcanic flows stretched away, softened occasionally by green tangles of creepers and scrub brush. They were out of the mountains now, almost on the level of the lake. Steve relaxed his grip on the windshield frame. The muscles in his shoulders and neck were painfully knotted from the long effort of protecting himself from the jolting ride. Ahead the white buildings of Goma curved along the northernmost tip of Lake Kivu where the moonscape gave way to rolling hills clothed with vibrantly green banana groves. The volcanoes rose behind the town and disappeared into the early afternoon cloud cover.

He felt drained after his unsettling outburst at the mission. Dubois had left him alone, preferring to whistle and pick at his fingers between cigarettes. The WIGMO flight was due in at two-thirty. They were going to be early. Trying to think of nothing, he slouched against the dusty cushion, letting his mind run away with the dazzling light and cloud shadow patterns on the lake. He fought to maintain the peaceful numbness that had been pounded into his body on the potholed road. He would be home with Lisa in a few hours and it all would be behind him. He was now tired from the pills and the beer. Perhaps there would be a quiet, shady place at the airport where he could sleep while waiting for his flight. He would sleep and then he would be home.

They drove past the concrete coffee warehouses on the edge of town, bounced off the paved street, and continued toward the airport on another black lava road. The mud and thatch huts of the Goma *cité* were crude compared to the gaudy façades of the Léopoldville communes. Beer cafés lining the road were loud with recorded music. Africans stared out at Dubois's uniform with open contempt. Only the small children waved. Behind, the black dust hung in the air like smoke.

A kilometer from the airport Dubois passed a convoy of six ANC trucks, an old Mercedes confiscated from colons, and two new American-donated four-by-fours. The truckdrivers were drunk and would not give way until Dubois had used his horn repeatedly and shaken his fist at them. Finally he swung up onto the far shoulder and raced past the careening trucks with a burst of speed. The soldiers in the open trucks laughed at them, waving bottles. As they shot past in a gritty dust cloud, Steve saw groups of prisoners in shoddy blue-and-yellow-striped jerseys squatting at the soldiers' feet on the trucks. The prisoners did not wave.

"We're not too early, after all," Dubois said as they turned into the airport. "Look, there's your plane."

"Where?" Steve asked. He could not see it at first, but then, squinting against the hazy sunlight, he saw a flash of a metal wing and recognized the high-tailed silhouette of a C-130 against the shadow of a volcano. The plane turned out over the lake and he saw the landing gear drop down.

"That's not my plane," Steve said. "I'm supposed to go on a WIGMO C-46. That's an Air Force plane."

"Ah, *bon*," Dubois said. "Maybe they're finally bringing us our 'tanks.' That would be very nice if it was so."

A smiling Congolese policeman pulled aside the gate of the barbed-wire fence, giving them a stiff military salute as they drove onto the tarmac. They sat in silence, smoking Dubois's Belgas as they watched the big plane settle at the end of the runway.

With a raucous outburst of truck horns and shouting, the ANC convoy arrived. The policeman tried to make a show of authority, demanding to see written permission for the convoy to drive onto the tarmac. The thickset ANC captain in charge of the soldiers jumped from the lead truck and kicked the policeman aside. His soldiers cheered loudly, beating on the roofs of the truck cabs and brandishing their weapons.

Dubois said, "God help us if they decide to stay in town for the *fête* tonight. They're the worst unit in the whole ANC."

The C-130 had turned off the runway and taxied slowly toward them. It stopped halfway down the access ramp to sit like a beached whale, its engines turning over with a high-pitched whine. A tall Congolese wearing a white shirt and tie came out of the delapidated terminal building and, carefully skirting the truckloads of soldiers, trotted out onto the tarmac, gesturing to the C-130 pilot to advance.

A small window opened on the pilot's side of the cockpit, and Steve saw a gloved hand point at their Land Rover and beckon them forward. Dubois drove up to within ten feet of the slashing propellers.

Steve saw the strained young face of the pilot and remembered the storm on the Stanleyville flight. The pilot was yelling something, but his voice was lost in the noise of the engines. They were motioned around to the rear of the plane, where they were pulled up into the open hatch by one of the GIs of the armed guard. With the soldier as a guide they were led up through the cargo bay to the flight deck, past three green, armor-plated Land Rovers.

"They've finally come!" Dubois shouted. "Our 'tanks.' They're beautiful, aren't they?"

"What the fuck is all that?" the pilot asked, pointing out the cockpit windows at the trucks and the gang of bottle-waving soldiers. "Looks like a mutiny or something."

"Tell him they're from a bad battalion and I do not know what their business is here. That we ourselves have just arrived."

Steve translated. The pilot sat smoking, staring nervously out at the ANC troops. "They warned us about that in Kamina," he said. Both the co-pilot and the flight engineer nodded agreement.

"They said we weren't supposed to turn over these vehicles to no ANC. That they were for the Belgians in the CODOKI, whatever the hell that is."

"Adjutant Dubois is a CODOKI officer," Steve said.

"Can he sign for them then?" the pilot asked. "There was supposed to be a Commandant Grisson here. Only trouble is we're a day early. Kamina said they'd send up a radio message letting them know about it, but it looks like another fuck-up."

Steve consulted with Dubois. "He'll take the responsibility for them," he said. Strangely, the slippery dizziness in his head was gone. The sight of the big plane and the necessity of involving himself in the straightforward military transaction had driven away the ghosts. It felt good to be speaking English again.

"O.K.," the pilot said. "But what about that bunch of drunken monkeys out here on the hardstand? I don't like the way they're waving those goddamn burp guns around. Who are those other ones, anyway—the ones in the blue outfits?"

"Prisoners," Steve said. "They must be getting ready to ship them someplace."

"Don't look good, Captain," the flight engineer said. "I told you about that riot the niggers had up at Stan when you all were in town. Came damn close to wrecking something on the aircraft, the way they were chasing around."

The pilot bit his lip just as Steve had seen him doing during the storm. "What do you think we ought to do about it?" he asked Steve.

"Maybe Adjutant Dubois could get them to move back to the other side of the fence."

They watched while Dubois drove up to the ANC captain and exchanged salutes. There was a good deal of angry gesturing by both men, but finally the trucks and soldiers were removed to the other side of the barbed wire. The pilot spoke into his interphone. "I want those guards out there standing tall," he said. "Nobody comes near this aircraft unless I say so, understood? O.K. Get to it." He inched the throttles forward and slowly released the brakes. "I hope those dudes don't try to pull anything," he muttered.

Steve could smell the bitter, unwashed odor of the soldiers as he sat with his back to the barbed wire in Dubois's vehicle. The troops had crowded up against the fence, scuffling over bottles and waving excitedly as the three armored Land Rovers were backed down the ramp out of the belly of the plane. They were all Lingala speakers, and many bore intricate tribal scars which he could not recognize.

There was a loud burst of Lingala behind him, and he turned to see the African soldiers pointing at the Negro PFC who had taken his post beneath the right wing of the plane, his short black M-16 held at high port. Like the other members of the armed guard, he wore his steel helmet, web gear, and armored vest. The photographs of the wall newspaper spun through Steve's head, the images shattering into a hot, shameful recollection of his behavior at the mission. He felt himself swaying again, but quickly suppressed it. Dubois was talking seriously with the ANC captain, and Steve walked over to join them.

"We have trouble maybe," Dubois said in his broken English, but continued in French. "Captain Lokosé wants to send those rebel prisoners back to Kamina on this plane. They heard the radio message that the plane was coming and want to transport the prisoners on it. You'll have to translate for us with the pilot. I think it's just an excuse for them to come into Goma for the New Year *fête*."

As they walked toward the plane, Dubois whispered, "He wanted to take the new vehicles as well, but I was able to dissuade him. I wish Grisson would come. He's a higher rank and the captain is afraid of him. He hates me because I'm an old colon. Grisson is a businessman and Lokosé needs him for truck parts, but he has no use for planters. Be very careful how you translate—this captain is a very unpredictable man. You can see that he's been drinking." Then, turning to the captain, Dubois said, "A very beautiful airplane the Americans have, isn't it?"

Captain Lokosé only grunted.

The pilot and the co-pilot were seated on the grass in the edge of the shade cast by the towering tail, eating C-ration spaghetti and meatballs. The young co-pilot got slowly to his feet as they approached. The pilot sat back, draining the last of the juice from his can.

"Captain Lokosé here wants to talk to you," Steve said.

"Let him talk," the pilot answered.

"I have ninety-seven Simba prisoners. They are for the prison at Kamina. I have six hundred kilos of broken ordnance—machine guns, rifles, tripods, things of this kind, all in wooden cases. They are for the repair shops at Kamina as well. Some of my soldiers will fly with the prisoners as guards. I have the papers here for you to sign."

As Steve translated, Creighton, the flight engineer, approached them. "The vehicles are off and we're ready when you are, Captain," Creighton said, staring contemptuously at Captain Lokosé.

"Yeah," Creighton continued, "and why don't we take a couple of those nigger whorehouses, one of them volcanoes, and half the lake with us, too? What does he think we are, anyway—a tramp steamer or something?"

The Congolese captain looked angrily at Dubois and demanded a translation. Dubois only shrugged his shoulders. The pilot sat up and yawned, scratching at an itch through the open zipper of his flight suit. "What did he say—twelve hundred pounds of stuff and *ninety*-seven prisoners?"

"Plus a squad of ANC to guard them," Steve said.

"Yeah," Creighton said. "And who the hell will guard *them?*"

Ignoring the proximity of the airplane, the pilot lit a cigarette and got slowly to his feet. He turned to Creighton and the co-pilot. "We can take the ordnance stuff, I guess, but they can damn well use one of their own planes to haul those prisoners. I swore off the livestock-moving business when I left Pleiku. Remember that time we had that whole shit house of slope refugees, women and kids and roosters, everybody pissing and crapping on the deck?" He turned back to Steve. "Tell him no thanks, not unless he's got signed Strike Command orders, which I know he don't have."

"They are forbidden to take passengers," Steve said slowly to Captain Lokosé. "They will carry your cargo to Kamina, but they don't have permission to take the prisoners."

"I received authorization for the transfer of these prisoners this morning by radio from Kamina base," the captain said with a guttural slur.

"Pardon," Steve said, "I didn't understand."

"Don't play jokes on *me!*" the captain spat. "This is an operational zone. *I* am in command here. I will not tolerate mockery. Here are the orders—read them."

Steve read the smeared handwriting on the ANC message form, translating the text for the pilot. "Tell him that those orders don't apply to us," the pilot said.

"This is an ANC message, Captain," Steve said. "This airplane is under the command of the Americans at a base in the State of Florida. They are over here temporarily to carry out flights as directed by the American military assistance mission. If they had to move supplies and men for every local ANC unit in the country, they'd never accomplish their mission. You must understand this. This is an American plane, not part of the ANC."

Captain Lokosé was shuddering with anger, pointing at the prisoners. "Those animals *are* an American affair. Look at this." He pulled a crumpled piece of paper from the pocket of his uniform and handed it triumphantly to Steve. It was a printed surrender pass, one of a series that American psychological warfare specialists in Léopoldville had prepared for the ANC. The leaflet bore a photograph of a shattered Congolese village littered with the rotting, mutilated bodies of civilians. "Enough Violence!" was printed in bold characters above the photograph. Below it the text explained that the bearer of the pass would be given safe conduct to his home village if he surrendered himself and his weapons to the ANC. The validity of the pass was pledged and signed by the commander-in-chief, General Mobutu. Steve handed the pass to Dubois.

"It was the Americans who started this *histoire* of safe conduct," Captain Lokosé said. "Now they must take the prisoners away. We have no place for them. I don't have enough men to guard them. They must be taken to Kamina today. I need the trucks to transport supplies back to my camp."

Steve translated the captain's statement while the pilot and Creighton examined the surrender pass.

"It don't say anything on there about the U.S. Air Force flying prisoners, does it?" the pilot asked, waving the pass.

Steve shook his head. "No, but he's right about the Americans starting the whole thing. We're trying to get the ex-Simbas back in from the bush and start the economy going again. It's part of the pacification campaign."

"Yeah," Creighton said. "Well, we know all about pacification and all that happy horseshit, don't we, Captain?"

The pilot laughed. "Listen," he said to Steve, "just tell him we're sorry, but we don't have enough fuel to carry that many people. We'll carry his goddamn weapons down to Kamina for him 'cause we're going there, anyway, but he'll have to get some ANC planes up here to take the prisoners. I'm sorry as hell and all that, but we got orders just like he does. Tell him to get some of his people to start loading the crates and to get a move on 'cause we got some weather between here and there." To Creighton he said, "Let's take another look at those circuits in the nose gear. It still made that buzzing noise coming up."

Steve translated as the crew members walked toward the nose of the plane.

"Is that the final decision?" Lokosé asked.

Steve nodded.

"Tell your young pilot," Lokosé said, "that he has not heard the last of this." He crumpled the leaflet into a ball and ground it into the tarmac. "It's sabotage by arrogant whites like him and interference by your foreign embassies that have caused all these problems since Independence. But now with General Mobutu the Army is in command. Things will be different now." He strode away from them, staggering slightly. Turning back, he shouted to Dubois, "Adjutant, come here!"

"He's very angry," Dubois said. "He may look all right to you, but I've seen him like this before. There's going to be serious trouble. Did you get a good look at his eyes? He's like a wild pig when he's been drinking."

Steve walked slowly around the far side of the plane, whistling, his hands deep in his pockets. Strangely, despite the argument and the bitter anger of Lokosé, he felt very good. The pressure in his head was gone. What had it all been about, anyway? Why had he given in to it? Dubois was right; it probably was just malaria. He should not have let things get to him. There was a war on. It was so easy to forget about it back in Léopoldville, but it did exist.

Wars were not pleasant, especially civil wars. People died. Children died. There were pain and suffering and anger, but he must learn not to take it all so *personally*. Look at Dubois—the suffering he had experienced, the danger and the losses he had known. He could still smile. Look at the pilot. He's not much older than me, maybe even younger. Look at the pressure *he* is under. He's got an airplane to fly and decisions to make all the time. He's been to Vietnam. He has to act like a man. You wouldn't find him crying over a bunch of sick African kids. A person has to harden himself, to put up a little wall against such things; otherwise he gets caught in the middle and comes apart.

He had to learn not to get so involved in things as he had with Charlie's Saigon story. Those things happen. They were happening all over the world every day. He had to learn to look at them and not get sucked in.

He laughed, a natural laugh, devoid of the jangly edge he had heard echoing back at him from the mission walls. That Captain Lokosé was really a character. There were so many like him, the poor bastards. Always ready to make a speech, to run together a string of senseless political crap. "The Army is in command." Beautiful, just like that little pimp of a Congolese lieutenant at N'djili, full of speeches and threats. He'd been taken in by it all at first. It was good to be back among some Americans again. He had to get a hold of things, not just go to pieces like a girl. This was the real world, not a Peace Corps utopia with Host Country Nationals instead of natives and Grassroots Infrastructure instead of backward tribal anarchy. He laughed again. The trip had definitely been a good idea. He had had his chance to see Africa, all right. Wow!

"You look pretty happy," the pilot said. He was standing by the black radar dome of the nose, drinking a can of Seven-Up.

"Yeah," Steve said, "this trip's almost over. I'll be back in Léo in time for New Year's."

"Beaucoup parties, huh?"

"Oh, I suppose there'll be one or two. You guys going back to Léo today?"

"Negative. Got to get down to Kamina and get some electrical stuff repaired, then we'll head on back to MacDill. Take off for

Ascension Island tonight after we get some sleep. Better flying down here at night, storm activity's not so severe. I got some leave stashed, though, so I'll still have time to catch some of the Christmas vacation action at Fort Lauderdale. Ever been there?"

"No. I was one of those real bright guys who got married in school."

"Where'd you go to school?"

"Wisconsin," Steve said, "at Madison."

"No kidding? I went to Michigan State. Used to go over to Madison for pistol matches. Quite a place, all those bars full of dollies. Hell of a place to be married at."

"You haven't seen my wife," Steve said. A warm, longing impatience ripped through his midsection and he looked away.

"Here comes Hopalong Cassidy again," the pilot said as Dubois walked quickly up to them. "They getting those crates on O.K.?" he asked Dubois.

Adjutant Dubois looked pale. "This is very serious, monsieur," he said. "Please translate for me." He pointed back toward the Congolese soldiers. "Lokosé is drunk and very angry. He says that if the Americans do not want the prisoners, then he must take them. He says he will need more vehicles to carry both the prisoners and the supplies, so he will make use of the armored Land Rovers. I heard him speaking Swahili to his sergeant. They are going to take the CODOKI vehicles and then kill the prisoners. There is a small volcanic lake just north of here, very deep. They will take the prisoners there and shoot them all. He's serious about it, I can tell."

After Steve had translated Dubois's warning, the pilot stood for a long moment looking back at the groups of prisoners who squatted under guard next to the trucks. "He won't really shoot them," the pilot said. "He's just bluffing to get us to carry them. Every place we've been in this country some jigaboo second lieutenant who thinks he's a general has tried to bluff us. I ain't going to lose any sleep over it."

"That's not true," Dubois said. "Tell him I'm sure that Lokosé means what he says. He said it to one of his men, not to me. He didn't even know that I heard. If he shoots them after they've come in under the surrender passes, it will damage American prestige in the Congo. These stories have a way of getting back to the natives very quickly."

"He won't just shoot them," Steve said to Dubois. "That's impossible."

"This is the Congo," Dubois answered. "Anything is possible. I know that the Americans who made the passes don't want prisoners shot, I know General Mobutu and the Groupement Commander don't want them shot, either. That is not the point. The American Embassy and General Mobutu are in Léopoldville. The Groupement Headquarters is in Stanleyville. They are all far away. Here it is only Captain Lokosé who has power. He's killed prisoners before, in cold blood—I've seen him. His men are like wild animals. Look at them. He means what he says, monsieur."

"I don't think he's bluffing," Steve said to the pilot.

"Well, even if I could take some of them, I couldn't take all ninety-seven," the pilot said. "Have they got any baggage—duffel bags or anything? It's always those goddamn duffel bags full of lead that kill you."

Creighton and the co-pilot climbed down from the forward door to join them. "What's the story now?" Creighton asked.

"That ANC captain says he'll shoot 'em if we don't take them down to Kamina. Says he'll steal old Frenchy-here's jeeps, too. What do you guys think?"

"Well," Creighton said slowly, "the weight's not really too much sweat. It don't look like there's a hell of a lot of weight on them. But we got other problems. Lot of weather between here and Kamina, Captain. By the time we get out of here, those big babies we saw building up past Kindu will really be popping. What I wonder is, what happens if we got a planeload of rebels and we really hit some weather, like that squall line going into Stan last week? Then what? People flying all over the plane. You know as well as I do that there'd be trouble."

"He's right," the co-pilot said.

"Yes," Dubois said. "But this is an emergency, don't they understand? Lokosé will *kill* those prisoners if they are not taken to Kamina. His troops are drunk already. They're not going back to Rumanagabo tonight. They'll stay on and drink in the *cité* and have women. It may not be in the regulations to take that many passengers, but they will die unless they leave on this airplane."

Watching the pilot's face as he translated what Dubois had said, Steve was suddenly aware of the dizziness again. It had come back silently, like a recurring nightmare.

"Wouldn't you know it?" the pilot said. "Our last day in this goddamn country, our last trip, and we get stuck in the middle of a bind like this. What do you think?"

Steve stood silently for a moment. For the first time he saw the faces of the Simba prisoners. Most of them were very young, squatting with the terrified look of villagers in the big city. The swaggering ANC guards ignored them and concentrated instead on drinking and boisterous explanations of the workings of the airplane. There were several self-styled aviation experts among them who argued loudly as they pointed at the C-130 making whirling propeller motions with their arms and whooshing engine noises. The prisoners stayed close to the ground, rubbing rope sores on their wrists and ankles, except for a group of twelve who had been mustered to carry the heavy crates of broken weapons from the trucks into the plane.

"Well," Steve said, "Dubois is right that the word would get out all over if they do kill them. It *would* look sort of strange with this big American plane here flying away empty. None of the Congolese understand anything about your technical problems, of course. They'd all think that the Americans were in on the deal to have them shot. I don't know what to tell you really. Can't you get Léo on the radio and get their opinion down there?"

"Come on," the pilot said. "We'll give it a try, anyway."

After a long delay the pilot made contact with the COMISH office at N'djili Field. The COMISH radio operator explained that it was lunch hour in Léopoldville and all the officers were gone. He suggested the plane call back in an hour.

"If we wait an hour," Creighton said, "it'll really be late before they're all loaded and we get out of here. That'll put us right down in that weather at the worst time."

Steve stood on the stairs leading up to the flight deck, watching the Simba prisoners straining under the weight of the crates as they trotted up the tailgate of the plane to deposit their burdens in the cargo bay. He heard a muffled scream and saw one of the pris-

oners lying on the loading ramp. The heavy crate he was struggling with had slipped from his grasp, the jagged edge of a steel
band slashing the inside of his leg. The arterial blood was vivid
red in the sunlight.

The man lay on his side, vainly trying to stanch the flow of
blood while an angry ANC soldier stood over him, yelling at him
to get to his feet. The loadmaster pushed past Steve to look at the
injured prisoner. "Shit," he said. "Stupid bastard's getting blood
all over everything."

The knife edge of the steel band had slashed a deep incision diagonally across the inside of the man's thigh. He grasped Steve's
shoulder with a clawlike grip as Steve helped him off the ramp.
The blood pumped evenly out between the man's fingers, puddling
in the roots of the coarse grass next to the hardstand. Steve was
not thinking. His head was silent, but he was able to move. He removed a cloth tourniquet and several combat dressings from the
canvas first-aid pouch hanging on the bulkhead in the cargo bay.
Something in his manner frightened the menacing circle of ANC
soldiers forming around the prisoner. Steve had the tourniquet
tightened above the wound when he spoke to the man for the first
time.

"Tu parle français, toi?" he asked.

The voice answering him was a shock. The man spoke perfect,
unaccented French. His manner was calm and dignified despite the
obvious pain of his injury. "Yes, monsieur," the man said. "I suppose I ought to speak French. I taught the language for ten years."

The prisoner was a man in his middle forties. His face was
smooth and devoid of tribal scars. His limbs were very thin, and
his prison uniform stank. "Oh," Steve said, "I thought you were a
Simba. What are you? A political detainee?"

"I am an officer in the People's Liberation Army," the man
said gravely. "I am a prisoner of war." Then, glancing at Steve's
dusty bush shirt and khaki trousers, he asked, "Are you one of the
European *volunteers?*"

Steve finished tightening the dressing in place over the wound.
He directed the prisoner to hold the tension on the tourniquet. He
looked at his watch. Ten minutes and the bleeding should be
stopped.

"No," he said, "I'm from the American Embassy in Léo. I'm a civilian. You *are* a Simba then?"

"Some of our soldiers call themselves Simbas," he said. "I have the rank of captain. I fought against the ANC and the mercenaries in the region of Paulis. I had the good fortune to be captured by the Europeans and not the ANC. That's why I'm still alive. These others are Bamadi tribesmen who were porters for our supplies. The American airplanes dropped the surrender papers on them while they hid in the forest. They came over as a group. I was captured in combat by the South African mercenaries."

Steve looked skeptically at the man. "I heard that the rebels killed all the teachers and *fonctionnaires*—anybody they called an 'intellectual.' "

"There have been very shameful acts committed by both sides," he said. "When I joined the People's Liberation Army there was still discipline. I was mostly in the bush, working with chiefs and moving supplies from our allies in the Sudan. When I heard of the massacres it was too late to stop. I had already taken my oath to the revolutionary government and was a hunted man with a price on my head, so I continued. I led my men the best I could, and I actually prevented several outrages against European hostages. The survivors told the mercenaries. That is why they spared me."

Steve lit two cigarettes and gave one to the prisoner. "Why would a man like you want to join the rebels? That's hardly the place for a teacher."

"It's easy for you foreigners to judge us," he said. "You have never seen the things we have had to suffer since Independence. For four years I kept my school open. During that time I was never paid. All the money went to the politicians and the soldiers. The ANC would raid our villages and steal our crops, taking our wives and daughters. There were no more hospitals, no more books for the schools, nothing that they had promised us, only taxes and the army and the speeches of the Léopoldville politicians. And then"—the man's face brightened slightly—"the revolution began. The first cadres came into our village. They arrested the soldiers and took away their automobiles and trucks. The rest of the ANC ran. That is when I joined. I saw very little of the *dawa* and the murders. I was always in the bush, moving supplies to the troops. I know these things existed, but you must understand the causes, monsieur. All we wanted was to be free of the politicians and the soldiers."

Steve looked down at the man's face. "Well, *mon capitaine,*" he said, "the war's over now. You were on the losing side. I know it's a very hard thing to accept, but at least the killing is finished. There's a new government, you know. General Mobutu is in control now, and he says he's going to change things—no more corrupt politicians. He says he's going to retrain the Army, make it responsible for its acts. Who knows? At least the fighting is over."

"What about the Liberation Army at Fizi?" the prisoner asked. "I have heard that they have made advances against the ANC."

"Well, that's almost cleaned up, too," Steve said. He felt a certain kindness toward the man. He did not want to destroy his illusions. "They put up a good fight, though, but the supplies from Tanzania aren't getting through any more. I'm sure that most of them will come over when they know it's safe to surrender. I think you'll be back in your school before too long."

Steve eased the pressure on the tourniquet, watching the white gauze of the dressing for new bleeding. "Not as bad as it looked at first," he said.

One of Captain Lokosé's men came forward and pulled the prisoner to his feet.

"Thank you for you kindness," the prisoner whispered as he was dragged away.

"Hey, buddy," the pilot called to Steve, "I'm afraid you'll have to translate for us again. We can't sit around here waiting for Léo to come up on the radio. Let's talk to Captain What's-his-name."

Captain Lokosé sat on the bumper of his truck. He belched loudly as Steve, Dubois, and the pilot approached him. Creighton followed several steps behind.

"O.K.," the pilot said, "this is the deal. Dubois gets three men from the Captain here to help him drive the vehicles into the CODOKI garage in town. Then we'll take fifty of the prisoners with us to Kamina. When we get there, we'll arrange for a couple Congolese C-47s to come on up tomorrow and get the rest. That way everybody's happy. Tell him that, O.K.?"

Steve translated.

"What about the guards for the prisoners?" Lokosé asked.

"We've got men to guard them ourselves," the pilot said, pointing to the GIs.

Lokosé looked at Dubois and spoke coldly in Swahili. Dubois stiffened.

"What's all that about?" Creighton asked.

"Nothing especially," Dubois said in English. "An insult." Very quickly, he shook hands with the crew and, taking Steve aside, spoke in a hurried whisper. "I must go, you understand? I can't take a chance of losing the CODOKI vehicles. I think it will all work out. Half the prisoners will go today and half tomorrow with the FAC planes. It's a good solution, *n'est-ce pas?*"

"Will they really keep the other half of them overnight?" Steve asked. "You said they were planning to have a *fête* for the New Year."

"Who knows?" Dubois whispered. "At least half of them will get away. It's better than none, isn't it? You've seen the kind of man Lokosé is."

"They're going to *kill* the others, aren't they?"

Dubois turned away. "It's not our affair," he said. "We're doing the best we can. Half is better than none."

"You were talking before about strength and fairness," Steve said. "This isn't fair—it's murder."

"It's not our affair," Dubois said. He walked away and ordered the three ANC drivers into the armored vehicles. One of the soldiers was dispatched to carry Steve's valpac and briefcase up the porch of the small airport building. Dubois was very businesslike, checking the oil level in the Land Rover engines, cautioning the drivers to watch their speed and keep a proper interval on the road to town. With a ragged cheer from the troops, the little convoy drove away.

"O.K.," the pilot said, "let's get them lined up and counted on. We ain't got all day here."

"Now what the hell is he waiting on?" the pilot asked.

The prisoners had been herded out onto the hardstand and pushed into five ranks of roughly twenty men each. The ANC soldiers took every opportunity to wield their rifle butts and kick the prisoners who did not move smartly enough to please them. When the ranks had been formed, the Congolese soldiers inched nearer the airplane, peering curiously up into the gaping maw of the cargo bay. Steve stood with the three flight officers and Creighton in the shade of the wing.

"Hey, Peters," the pilot called to the loadmaster. "Let's get 'em loaded."

"I tried to, Captain," Peters said, "but they don't understand no English."

Creighton walked up to the ANC sergeant in charge of the prisoners' guard. "Fifty," he said. "Count off fifty and get them in the airplane." He made a fanning motion five times with his ten outstretched fingers and motioned to the loading ramp. No one moved. Then one of the ANC soldiers began an infectious giggle which was quickly picked up by his comrades. Creighton stood in his sweaty flight suit with his hands on his hips. "Goddamn it!" he shouted. "Move! Do something. Don't just stand there like a bunch of grinning monkeys."

Captain Lokosé strolled out to the group, his drunken gait now obvious.

"Come on," the pilot said to Steve. "Let's see what he's trying to pull now.

"Tell him we're in a hurry," he said when they were next to Lokosé. "If he doesn't get his fifty loaded in five minutes, we're leaving without them."

"As you like, monsieur," Lokosé said. "I told you before that these Simbas were the affair of the Americans. We poor Congolese aren't rich enough to fly rebels around the country. We have other means of taking care of them. If the pilot wants his precious fifty, he can count them himself. He can choose the ones he wants to take and the ones he wants to leave."

"What kind of shit is this?" the pilot asked. "What's the big deal about counting them, anyway? The rest are going down tomorrow. What's all the sweat about?"

The voices coming at Steve seemed artificial, distorted as with a badly fitting pair of earphones. He knew the pilot was talking to him, but he could not answer. He stared at the white bandage on the rebel officer's leg. The man stood in the front rank, halfway down the formation. Good, he thought, at least he will be in the ones that get away. There was a silent trickle of sand slowly building toward an avalanche inside his head. He had felt this sensation before, in the schoolroom at Kando Mission when Père André had explained the differences in the milk ration. The inaudible slipping in his skull had become a landslide as he suddenly saw the faces of the doomed children. Now, as he stared down the ranks of prisoners, the same process was beginning. He was lucky to have caught it in time. It would be degrading to faint before these soldiers.

"Listen, Captain," Steve said to the pilot. His voice was surprisingly calm and forceful. "This is very important. Dubois warned me when he went that they're going to kill the ones who are left behind and they want us to count them so it looks like we chose some and sentenced the others to the firing squad. I know you think he's bluffing, but I'm positive he isn't. Look at those guys. If you don't take them all, they're going to be dead at the bottom of that lake up there in less than an hour. Just look at them. It's up to you."

The pilot scratched again beneath his flight suit and bit his lips. "Jesus *Christ!*" he said. "Why the hell does he want us to get mixed up in this mess? If he's going to shoot them he's going to shoot them and that's all there is to it. We're doing the best we can. I'm breaking orders the way it is by taking any of them."

Creighton was about to speak, but Steve cut him short.

"We *are* mixed up in this," he said in the same calm voice. "It was an *American* decision to make those surrender passes. They know that all over the bush because the passes were dropped from *American* planes. It's up to us to get them out of here."

"Oh, bullshit," Creighton said. "This ain't our goddamn war. Those are a bunch of rebels. They're lucky we're taking fifty. We've got nothing in our orders says we have to take any nigger rebels."

"What's your decision, monsieur?" Lokosé said, smiling. "We, too, are hurried."

Steve did not translate, but turned back to the pilot. "Those prisoners aren't really rebels," he said. "I mean they're not dangerous. They were just villagers up north who got caught up in it and were drafted to be porters. They're not going to rip your plane up. I bet they won't even move a muscle between here and Kamina."

"You get ninety-seven of those coons in there in a storm like we had coming up to Stan Sunday and they'll move a muscle all right," Creighton said. "It's a stupid risk to take, Captain. You got to think of the safety of the aircraft and the crew first."

"O.K.," Steve said, his voice increasing in speed. "Maybe it would be too dangerous to fly them through the bad weather. Don't take them to Kamina then. Take them down the lake to Ka-membé. I'll go with you. The airfield is on the Rwanda side of the border. I can arrange with our Consulate at Bukavu to get some of the CODOKI people to take them. You can carry ninety-seven that far at least. It's only about a thirty-minute flight."

"We ain't got no authority to land in Rwanda," Creighton said.

"Then take them down to Albertville," Steve said, "and leave them with the Ops Sud people. I *know* they're using Simba prisoners who came in on surrender passes for repairing the roads. I read a report on it last week. You can fly to Albertville and cut back over to Kamina."

" 'Cut back over to Kamina!' " Creighton laughed. "Mister, you should have been an Air Force colonel the way you got us hopping around. The hell with it, Captain, it ain't our business. Besides, you saw that weather we had coming out of Albertville last Sunday. You get them cells built up over them mountains down there and you're really in trouble. We'd have to get Léo on the radio with a new flight plan. Hell, we just don't have the *time* to fuck around with all of that even if we could."

"*Time?*" Steve said. "They're going to shoot forty-seven men because you don't have *time.*"

"What do you guys think?" the pilot asked, turning to the navigator and co-pilot, who were sitting on the loading ramp behind him.

"I don't know, Bruce," the navigator said in his squeaky, adolescent voice. "We could probably make it to A'ville and over to Kamina the way he says. We'd have to get airborne before we could raise the A'ville tower to get the weather, though."

"It'd be pretty crowded back there with ninety-seven of them," the co-pilot added. Steve watched the pilot's face. He could feel the tension melting inside himself. They were going to take them. He had won. He wanted to laugh, to shake the pilot's hand.

The pilot turned back to the navigator. "How about getting me a tentative flight plan to Kamina via A'ville with, say, a fifteen-thousand-pound load. Figure in head winds just to be on the safe side. I want to see if we can make the whole trip in daylight," he said. "Figure an hour on the ground at A'ville and take-off here in thirty minutes. Jerry," he said to the co-pilot, "see if you can get the WIGMO people in A'ville on the single side band. I got their frequency and call sign on my clipboard. Tell them our problem and get something on the weather en route."

Creighton did not speak until the two officers had entered the plane. "Captain," he said, "excuse me for speaking out this way, but I feel I've got a right to say my piece. I ain't been on your crew very long, but I know other guys who've flown with you. Believe me, sir, you been flying too much. Not just this trip, even though we've all had too much on this one. But this whole year. Out in Pleiku and then all those trips to the Dom. Rep., going around the clock. Then back to Vietnam. You're tired, sir. We're all tired. But it's worse on you, 'cause you're the A.C. When you're tired you let things get to you. The only reason I'm saying this, sir, is 'cause I seen a lot of it before, during the Berlin Airlift and Korea and now with 'Nam and the Dom. Rep. An officer, especially an A.C., has got to think about the whole picture, sir. You got to think about the safety of your aircraft and men. This ain't our problem, Captain. We can't let ourselves get in a bind over it. We're taking a big enough risk the way it is by hauling fifty."

The pilot was silent, staring at his boots.

"Sir," Creighton continued, his voice warming, "there's absolutely no reason I can see why we should risk our asses to carry all them rebel prisoners. It's fourteen hundred already. It'd be fourteen thirty before we got out of here and damn near sixteen thirty out of A'ville. They don't have no JP-4 at A'ville, which means we'd be heading into Kamina low on fuel after dark. You know as well as I do that their Nav Aids ain't worth a damn and Lieutenant Hanson hasn't had that much experience navigating down here. It'd mean flying over those mountains at the worst time of day, over unfamiliar country with no beacons to home in on."

"You could spend the night in Albertville," Steve blurted out.

Creighton ignored him. "Besides, all that, sir," he said, "I really think that it would be a stupid risk to carry that many. Look at them, Captain. They're rebels. What the hell is the sense of us flying all that ordnance over here to fight rebels only to risk our necks to keep them alive? This ain't our business, sir. It's too damn dangerous. They may look peaceful enough, but you never know with these coons. Once you get them in an airplane they're liable to riot. Besides, we don't owe them a damn thing, do we? Shit, they're the ones who raped all them white women and cut their husbands' guts open. Remember those guys from that one-thirty wing out of Evreux? The guys who were carrying refugees down here last year? Remember what they said about those little white girls who'd been gang-banged day and night for months by hopped-up nigger bastards? Why should we take chances to save a few of them when you know damn well they'd slit our throats and cut our balls off if they had half a chance?"

The pilot looked up quickly at Creighton and then at the prisoners. "You're right," he said, avoiding Steve's eyes. "Sorry, buddy. There's nothing we can do." To Peters he said, "Count off fifty and give me a call up front when we're buttoned up. Come on, Creighton, let's get the hell out of this hole."

Steve stood listening to the echo of the pilot's boots on the hot pavement. Then it was quiet. Off in the direction of the Goma *cité* he heard some faint drumming. The blacks were beginning their *fête*. Standing next to him, Peters looked blankly out at the group of prisoners.

"How should I do it, mister?" Peters asked. "Just count off fifty from the end or are there any special ones we should take?"

"It doesn't matter, really," Steve heard himself saying. "They're coming for the rest of them tomorrow. Just count off fifty from the end."

Peters did not move. They stood silently watching a flock of black-and-white ravens alight on a rubbish pile near the shabby airport building. "Big babies, ain't they?" Peters said. Steve nodded. "Down home we have a lot of fun hunting crows," Peters said. "Real tricky bird to shoot. Never seen any of them black-and-white ones, though, till I came on this trip."

"They're called African pied ravens," Steve said. "I looked them up in a bird book once."

The ravens were squabbling over bits of cloth in the rubbish. "Hell," Peters said, "I'd better double-check those tie-downs on them crates. It looks like we're going to get some more weather between here and Kamina." He indicated the prisoners. "Those bastards don't listen to me and I don't speak no French, Captain knows that. Why'd he want *me* to count them, anyway?" He pointed to the Negro PFC standing at his post beneath the cylindrical fuel tank of the right wing. "Hey, Johnson," he called, "come on over here and count off fifty of these dudes. I gotta go check on the way those crates are tied down."

Johnson turned to them, his face drawn. "Captain told us not to leave our posts till he was rolling," he answered.

"Well, goddamn it, Johnson," Peters said, *"I'm* telling you to get your ass over here and count off fifty of 'em. They'll listen to you. They won't pay no attention to me at all. Now move when you get an order!"

Johnson kept his post, staring at the ground, Steve could see his knuckles bloodless gray as he gripped the stock of his weapon. "I ain't supposed to leave my post," Johnson mumbled. "Besides, Captain told *you* to count 'em, Peters. You're loadmaster. That's your business—passengers."

"I *told* you, Johnson," Peters said, "I got stuff to do in the aircraft. You just going to stand there and disobey a direct order?"

"Ah, hell, Sergeant," Johnson pleaded, "don't make me get mixed up in it. Please, I don't want no part of it. Take one of the other guys."

Jesus, Steve thought, looking at Johnson's face, he's just a kid, eighteen or nineteen years old.

"Johnson," Peters said, "I'm telling you for the last time . . ."

"Leave him alone!" Steve said. "I'll do it."

Out in the sun on the hot pavement his cranial avalanche was beginning to rumble. He could feel the cyclone in his head gaining on him. He had to move fast. Like an inspecting officer reviewing troops, he squared himself before the ranks of prisoners. Moving with a scissorlike sidewise motion, he strode down the line, counting aloud, his right hand chopping down to designate each rank of five.

"Twenty-five, thirty, thirty-five, forty . . ." He was almost there. The cold death wind off the avalanche was freezing the dripping sweat on his body. But he was almost there.

Then his feet froze. He saw the big painted numbers on the tail of the airplane. He saw the ravens flying at an odd angle against the sky. He saw the grass-clogged cracks in the concrete. They were watching him, the prisoners in the doomed half of the formation. He saw their faces. African faces, obviously from the same tribe. Simple bush nigger faces, wide of lip and nose, heavy brows, sweat gleaming on their skin. Their eyes were soft, submissive, watching him. He'd seen those eyes before. He had to move, but the eyes held him.

". . . forty-five . . ." His hand chopped down. Only one more rank, but they were all watching him. He had seen those eyes before—where?

His head rose slowly. The sunlight was red against his eyelids. Nothing had changed; he had gone away for a moment, but nothing had changed. They still stood there before him with antelope eyes, silently measuring him. They were dead. He could smell the sewer ripeness of their filthy prison uniforms. Their matted Bantu hair was black, slightly grayed in patches by the lava dust of the long road they had traveled. It was not the chemical yellow fuzz of the children at the mission, but they were just as dead. "They can always run a bit, even when they're dead!" They could stand there watching him in the freezing sunlight, even though they were dead in the deep water of the volcanic lake.

He moved, looking up to face the man before him. An empty black face with liquid eyes stared back at him. To his right he saw the white and red of the rebel captain's bandage. It was his friend, the teacher. The man stared back at him. Steve wanted to say something to explain his presence to the teacher. He was an educated man. He would understand why Steve was there, why he had been forced to count them off, to separate the living from the dead.

He had started to speak when a raven claw slashed him. The prisoner to the captain's right had struck out to grip the bare flesh of Steve's arm. The man's nails were jagged and filthy. They dug into his flesh. *"Moi!"* the man screamed. *"Prends-moi, patron, prends-moi!"*

Steve clearly saw the swarming pack of street boys in the swimming pool parking lot. He saw the black hand tearing at the flesh of Lisa's leg in the back seat of the Peugeot while the mob pressed against the car and the drunken dance music blared out into the hot night. *Why don't they just leave me alone?*

Savagely he broke the man's grip. "Enough!" he screamed. *"C'est assez.* Take them away." He was rooted to the pavement as the ANC guards swept in, snipping off the forty-five prisoners he had chosen from the main formation. Silently he watched the rebel teacher's rank dissolve into a jumbled hoard being clubbed toward the waiting trucks.

And then it all moved very quickly. The chosen prisoners were already in the airplane and the insane screeching of the turbines grew louder. He watched Johnson pull himself through the side door as the C-130 rolled toward the runway. He stood alone in the sun while the soldiers drove off in a plume of black dust. The wings of the plane flashed like an arc light as it banked away and began its climb over the volcanoes. A breeze blew off the lake, clearing the kerosene smell of the plane's engines and the dust raised by the departing trucks. The ravens had returned to their rubbish heap.

CHAPTER **24**

Steve was alone. Tiredly he walked up to the steps of the little terminal. The policeman and the band of curious Africans usually found about the airport had disappeared with the arrival of the battalion convoy. It was two-fifteen. In only half an hour he too would be gone. All he had to do was wait, to sit here alone in the sunny breeze with his eyes closed, not thinking about the peroxide fluff on the children's bulging skulls or the antelope eyes of the prisoners or the grave courtesy of the rebel captain: "Thank you for your kindness." The faces and the colors and even the smell of the prisoners' uniforms were swirling with the blizzard in his head. He had to stand up, to walk around. He was thirsty. The pills had dried him out. His lips were dry, his tongue bloated.

Where the hell was that plane? Why had they stranded him here alone and crazy, thirsty in the sun with nothing to drink? He had to keep moving. As he paced up and down the chipped cement porch of the building, he heard the sputtering static of the airport radio. An African voice spoke somewhere inside the building and was answered by an unintelligible pilot's voice. His flight was coming. The fingernails of his right hand had dug little craters of bleeding flesh out of the palm. His hands ached from the constant contractions. His scalp was dirty and itched unbearably. His mouth was dry. Pacing like a zoo animal, he talked to himself, mumbling curt nonsense phrases simply to hear his own voice. He was moving too fast. He had to slow down. There was too much pressure building up.

He found the little foil-wrapped package of pills in the medical kit in the bottom of his briefcase. He had two of the red tablets nestled among the sores in the palm of his hand. They had to give him something to drink. As he remembered the chalk-dry codeine tablets he had choked down on his hangover ride out to N'djili Field, his stomach contracted violently and he nearly retched.

"Bonjour, patron."

An airport clerk with a purple necktie was standing above him. Steve blinked up at him. The man smiled nervously. "Get me some beer," Steve said in English, "a big bottle of ice-cold beer."

The man smiled again. "The soldier brought your bags to me," he said in French. "I'm the one who has watched them, patron. It's dangerous to leave suitcases where the Army can find them. They will steal anything. I watched them very closely."

"I don't want another speech," Steve said. "Just get me a beer."

"Pardon, patron, je ne comprends pas l'anglais."

"I don't want excuses," Steve said. "Just get me a bottle of beer. I know you've got cold beer in there. You've always got beer. Everybody's got beer in this country. Get me a bottle. Now!"

The clerk backed against the brick wall. There was something wrong with him. He looked stricken. Dirty bastard's holding out on me, trying to bluff me again with another goddamn political speech. They're so full of political crap. Everybody had some horseshit pitch to throw you. Why didn't he just get the beer and shut up? They were always trying to sell me something. Why did they zero in on me? Fucking phony Count trying to blame me for everything. All he really wanted was to look down Lisa's dress, slobbering over her hand, trying to cop a feel. Screw him. Screw all of them. Little piss-ant of a lieutenant making speeches. Those Katangan Gendarme MPs took care of him O.K. Served him right. Just what he deserved.

And Dubois, shit! Just like the stupid Count, only the reverse. Americans were the heroes. Americans were going to save them all. All their shitty little tea plantations; pack of lousy slave drivers. And those stupid native mothers waiting till it was too late to bring their kids in and then blaming the Americans. Poisoned milk, they'd probably say. And that goddamn Captain Lokosé. *"I'm* in command here." Shit! He couldn't command a bunch of Girl Scouts—plenty of speeches, though, and threats. Why the hell did they always come to me with their crazy stories? Bullshit! That guy wasn't any schoolteacher. Just another lying nigger. That fat-assed Creighton, stupid hillbilly, couldn't get a job on the outside. Who the hell would stay in the *Air Force* if he could get anything decent on the outside? And that pilot—yellow, just like a dirty little coward. Michigan State! I can just see him with his crew cut and his pistol matches. *Pistol* matches! Sawed off little squirt like him with his big-deal pistol match; bars full of dollies —he's probably a queer. The way he let that Creighton boss him around.

What the hell is wrong with this guy? Just standing there with that stupid look on his face. I told you to get me some beer, boy! Big-deal necktie. They put on a necktie and they think they're all cabinet ministers or something. I'll fix your purple necktie, boy. I'll fix your political shit.

"I said I want some beer!" Steve screamed, the clerk's necktie twisted in his bleeding hand. "Shit. You made me drop my medicine." Looking down for the two red pills, he saw the heavy pistol in his left hand. He had taken the pistol from the briefcase. He had it in his hand.

"Oh, Christ!" he whispered. "What the hell am I doing?"

"*S'il vous plaît, patron,*" the clerk begged, "don't hurt me. I was only joking. I'm glad you let me watch your bags. We're all proud of the European volunteers. I was only joking."

"I'm not a mercenary," Steve said quietly in French. "I'm sorry I frightened you. It was only a misunderstanding. Look. The pistol is for the ravens there. It isn't even loaded." He broke the action, spinning the empty cylinders against the sunlight. "Here," he said, handing the startled clerk a new thousand-franc bill from his wallet. "This is for watching my suitcase." He took out another thousand francs. "Do you have any beer?"

The clerk had regained his composure. "*Oui, patron,*" he said.

"Give me a bottle," Steve said. "The rest of the money is for your children, for the *fête*. Look, the pistol is empty. It's to frighten the ravens. The birds over there—don't you see them?"

The clerk nodded again, pocketing the money as he slid into the doorway of the radio room.

The beer was warm. Steve belched between swallows, his foot resting on the rusted metal railing of the porch, the pistol wedged uncomfortably in his belt. He took the second pill with a long slug of the warm, gassy beer. He knew that he should put something on the fingernail cuts. He belched again, tasting leeks and the rich antelope gravy.

"Hey," Steve called to the clerk, "I've got another present for you."

The man walked forward very cautiously, his eye on the pistol. Steve unzipped the side pouch of his valpac and removed the plastic-wrapped antelope quarter. "Meat," he said, handing the wet package to the clerk. "Fresh antelope. I shot it myself this morning up in the mountains. Your wife can roast it with pili-pili and you can have a real *fête, n'est-ce pas?*"

The clerk smiled. "*Oui, patron. Merci, patron.*"

"Listen," Steve said, "don't get scared or anything, but I'm going to shoot some of the ravens for you, *d'accord?*"

The clerk frowned.

"Don't worry," Steve said. "I used to be on the pistol team of a large American university."

Clumsily he inserted the shells into the cylinder. "Watch this." He cocked the hammer with his thumb and fired the gun six times in quick succession. The barrel was hot; the smell of cordite made him sneeze. On the rubbish heap one of the ravens lay squawking on its back, the breeze ruffling the feathers of its smashed wing.

"This morning," Steve said to the terrified African, "I shot six guinea fowl with six bullets. That's good shooting, isn't it?" The clerk did not answer.

"Goma, Goma, Goma, Goma, Goma," a Cuban voice burst forth over the radio. "Goma tower, Lima Poppa Charlie, Goma tower, Lima Poppa Charlie, over."

"*Votre avion, patron,*" the clerk said with relief. "Your plane is coming." Steve yawned deeply, then burst out laughing.

"Goma, Goma, Goma, Goma, Goma . . ." he sang. I made it, he thought, I made it! They're coming for me now to take me home to Lisa. "Listen," he said in English to the clerk. "Take a look at this once." He dumped the hot pistol into the briefcase and removed the picture of Lisa in her bikini. "Look at that, will you, boy? That's where *I'm* going. So you can all just fuck yourselves with your political speeches and prisoners."

He sucked the last of the beer and threw the bottle into the rubbish. He saw the C-46 small in the distance, gliding down from the crest of mountains to the west. "It doesn't matter, anyway," he said softly. "What kind of life would they have had hiding up there in the forest—no food, no medicine? At least half got away, didn't they? You saw them. They got on that one-thirty and flew away to Kamina. Half is better than none, isn't it? Damn right it is. Besides, old Lokosé won't shoot them. He's just a bullshitter like the rest of you. He wouldn't dare do it here in a town like Goma . . . too many whites around to report him . . . look at the hotel and the beach. This is a civilized place. He was just bluffing to get Dubois' Land Rovers. He'll be out here tomorrow with the rest of them. You know that as well as I do.

"Christ, am I stupid," he yelled, slapping himself on the forehead. "I never got a picture. They told me to take any pictures I could on this trip for the USIS publications. That would have been a good picture for the wall newspaper—U.S. Air Force plane, responsible Belgian settler doing his patriotic duty, Captain Lokosé representing the 'New ANC,' the repentant prisoners being flown off to be put to useful work. It would have been perfect. Why did I get so screwed up and forget to take a picture?"

He dug again in his briefcase for a piece of Embassy stationery. "Listen," he said to the clerk, "this is of extreme importance. There is supposed to be a Pakistani in town who takes pictures, a photographer." He scrawled a message on the paper. "You take this letter to him this afternoon and tell him to be out here tomorrow with his camera when he hears the Congolese transport planes coming. He must take pictures of the prisoners boarding the planes. I've written the address where he should mail the film. Do you understand?"

The clerk stared at him.

Steve took out another thousand-franc bill. "This is for you," he said, smiling. "You're a good boy. After you deliver the letter, you go down to the market and buy a big sack of powdered milk for your children. They should drink three glasses of milk every day. Understand?"

"Oui, patron, merci."

Steve yawned and smiled happily. The C-46 was turning into its final approach. It would be good to sleep, sleep all the way to Léopoldville. The clerk lugged his heavy suitcase as they walked toward the hardstand. The breeze shifted to the north and Steve looked back at the line of sleeping volcanoes. He would be back up here soon with Lisa. They would climb the volcanoes. He waved, seeing the long-billed yellow cap of the Cuban pilot.

The engines were suddenly silent and he could hear the hot metal creaking and the sputtering of the contracting valves and cylinder heads. The shiny aluminum hatch was opened. There was Charlie. Why was he there in the airplane with his dusty boots and his dirty brass belt buckle? Charlie reached down to help him up. Steve yawned again. I sure am sleepy. The clerk waved; his purple tie was twisting in the sudden wind off the cloud-covered volcanoes.

"Man," Charlie said, "what's wrong with *you?* You must be either sick or stoned or *something."*

The wind was cold.

Steve stood in the open doorway of the plane. "Do you hear it?" he whispered.

"What?" Charlie said. "What's there to hear?"

"Be quiet," Steve said. "Listen."

From far away to the north they heard the faint, dry tattoo of machine guns. Pop-pop-pop in four long bursts. Then there was only the whistle of the breeze.

There was something very wrong with the bed. The sheets were not made of cloth. In the darkness they felt cold and wet. Steve let the fingers of both his hands move freely in the darkness. It was rubber. There were people above him in the darkness. They had him in a rubber bag on the steep-banked shore of a lake. It was night and there was no moon. They were closing the bag around him as he slid toward the dark water. This was the punishment they had chosen for him.

"Leave me alone, leave me alone . . ." he screamed.

Charlie stood over him. "Christ!" he said. "It's O.K., Steve. It's O.K. You were having a nightmare or something. But it's O.K. now. Hey, wake up. It's O.K."

The interior of the old C-46 was noisy bright with the engines thudding and the high-altitude sun pouring through the dirty plexiglass. He sat up on the sweaty rubber air mattress stretched out on the aluminum bench seats. The cabin was heaped with tied-down crates and baggage. He saw Charlie's bulging army duffel bag. Lisa and Henderson were sitting across from him down toward the tail. They were staring at him. Henderson was wearing a uniform and Lisa had dyed her hair darker brown. One of the rebel prisoners had stolen an ANC uniform and was lying dead or sleeping on a gunnysack in the tail.

"You all right now?" Charlie asked. "You O.K.?"

"It wasn't my fault," Steve whispered through dry lips. "Ask Henderson. It wasn't my fault, ask Creighton. He was there."

"Hey," Charlie said, dragging Steve up to a sitting position.

"Wake up, for Christ's sake. You were having a nightmare. What's wrong, anyway? You sick?"

Steve shot another look about the plane's cabin. Then, turning his head to stare out at the passing clouds, he spoke to Charlie in a conspiratorial tone. "What are *they* doing here, Henderson and Lisa?" he said, nodding back over his shoulder at the man and young woman. "How did *they* get here?"

Charlie squatted down next to the seat. "The chick's the girl friend of the French kid who flies the helicopter for WIGMO down in A'ville. She's going to spend New Year's with him. The big guy's a Danish Red Cross doctor from Stan. What's wrong with you anyway, Steve?"

Steve stared at their faces, a long, questing look. Charlie was right. Lisa and Henderson were far away. The African in the rear of the plane was really an ANC soldier. His head was thick from the pills, Steve told himself. "I was having a bad dream, Charlie," Steve said, his voice very childlike.

"Yeah," Charlie said. "It must have been a real winner, all right, the way you were rolling around and yelling."

Steve dragged his legs off the seat and placed his feet on the vibrating deck. In doing so his hands ran over the clammy sweat-dampened surface of the rubber mattress. He shuddered again.

They smoked Charlie's mentholated cigarettes. Charlie was laughing as he explained some complicated story. Steve could hear his voice, but the words made no sense. He was still very sleepy, but he knew the dream was there waiting for him if he succumbed to the drowsiness. "How long was I asleep?" he interrupted Charlie.

"You fell asleep right after take-off. I put you down on this mattress. You seemed like you were dead or something."

Steve nodded and had begun to speak when the thought pierced him: "Was there an Air Force one-thirty there and a bunch of ANC trucks?"

"Where?"

"At Goma."

"No, you were all alone with a Congolese guy from the airport."

It had just been a dream then. It had only been part of the same nightmare. He *had* fallen asleep after Dubois had dropped him off. Incredible how real it all seemed. Christ, I need some leave. I need some rest. It was just a reaction to those poor little kids up at the mission. It's amazing the way something like that can happen in your head, so real. They always talk about those kind of things in psychology class, but, Jesus, they *really* can happen. It happened to me. It was so real.

"That was pretty funny, too," Charlie continued. "The whole airport was deserted. We were carrying a couple crates of radio batteries for the ANC and there was nobody to help unload except that Congolese cat, and he was one of these white-shirt-and-tie boys who wouldn't dirty his hands."

"White shirt and tie?"

"Yeah, you saw the guy. He was helping you with your bag."

"What color tie?"

"What's wrong with you? You were with him. It was a real bright purple tie, with little circles on it."

"Purple tie?"

Charlie nodded. "Jesus!" he said. "Be careful of that cigarette, Steve. Your hands are shaking."

Steve's laughter filled the airplane. The Danish doctor squirmed uncomfortably over his magazine and the girl looked away. They had been in the Congo long enough to know better than to try to help a crazy mercenary. The doctor looked up once more, ascertaining the proximity of Charlie's automatic rifle to Steve, who sat doubled over in laughter.

"*Now* what's so funny?" Charlie asked.

Steve pulled at his face muscles, twisting away the compulsive smile. "Oh," he said, "nothing really. It's hard to explain. I was up at a Belgian's tea plantation last night. We stayed up late drinking. I guess I'm just hungover again. We met some little Congolese kids on the way down to Goma who were really a riot. Very funny kids."

"What'd they do so funny?" Charlie asked skeptically.

"Oh, nothing really," Steve said desperately, "They were just *funny,* that's all. Is there a law against laughing or something?"

They sat without speaking, letting the roar of the engines numb them. Outside, the gray undercast was breaking up and Steve blinked against the sunlight reflecting back from the surface of Lake Tanganyika far below. "Where are we, anyway?" he said.

Charlie glanced out of the window and then at his watch. "More than halfway to Albertville," he said. "Should be coming up on Cape Burton in a minute. Yeah, there it is. See that peninsula there? Well, there's Baraka just to the north of it and Fizi is up in the hills there. That's where they're fighting now, back up above Fizi in all those goddam mountains. Hell of a place to have a war, isn't it?"

As Steve stared out at the jumble of green mountains, the thumblike peninsula slid past them. "That's Lake Tanganyika," he said after a while. "We're flying *south.*"

"Sure," Charlie answered. "See how long and narrow it is?"

"When do we get to Léo?" Steve asked.

"About eight tonight if we don't have any hangups. You in a hurry or something?"

"No," Steve said. "Just wondering."

"It's really weird," Charlie said after they had lit fresh cigarettes. "This was the first place they sent me in the Congo, before I went up to Stan. I had to come out here the first day after I got to Léo 'cause the mercs were pulling that amphibious landing up there in Baraka and some of their radios got smashed up. I spent a week in A'ville working straight through getting their sets fixed. Now I'm going there again on my last day. Really strange."

"Last day?"

"Yeah. Hell, I *told* you about it when you got on at Goma, don't you remember?"

Steve shook his head.

"Got my early release. I got accepted at UCLA for the second semester. They're letting me out three months early to go back to school. Too much, huh?"

"Yeah," Steve smiled. "Great."

"Really weird though," Charlie continued, "coming back here. It seems like ten years ago, wow! You know what happened when I was there in A'ville fixing those sets? I thought the whole goddamn *world* had gone crazy. No shit. The mercs had it pretty bad on the beachhead. They were getting plastered by all kinds of mortars and recoilless rifle stuff from the ridges. The WIGMO planes were working close air support so that's why the radios were so important. Anyway, it wasn't going so well for the mercs, ambushes and really accurate coordinated fire against them. Not at all like the regular Simba kind of deal. One day I was testing some antennas and tuning a set when I hear these Cuban pilots speaking Spanish. Two different planes, two different voices—a B-26 and a T-28 working over the rebel positions. All of a sudden there was a third and then a fourth Spanish voice on the frequency, only they were talking about something completely different, about moving ammunition to a new position. I called in one of the CIA spooks from the WIGMO ground staff and he listens for a while, smiling. 'Oh, yeah,' he says, 'those are the *bad* Cubans, the advisers Castro sent over to help the rebels.' He thinks there's nothing especially funny about *that*. No, sir, just one of your average, garden-variety rebellions in Africa. In the goddamn heart of *Africa,* lost up there in those mountains, you got *good* Cubans flying the spooks' airplanes fighting *bad* Cubans, who are directing artillery fire against a bunch of Johannesburg cabdrivers. Wow, I thought, this is a real sweet little country they got here."

"What did you say?" Steve said flatly.

"What do you mean, what did I say?"

"About good and bad."

"Cubans," Charlie said. "Good and bad *Cubans.*"

"Oh," Steve said. There was a choice between laughter and sleep. Laughter would ruin him with the others, the Henderson doctor and the Lisa girl and Charlie and the good Cubans. The black water was waiting for him in sleep. He lay down again on the mattress. "I'm going to sleep some more, Charlie. Wake me up if I start to act funny. I'll tell you all about it tonight in Léo. We can go to a couple of parties together. Lisa will find you a date. She's got lots of girl friends. Don't worry about anything."

CHAPTER **25**

Pierre Tshipama was hungry. The day had started early, with anger and insults, and he had missed his breakfast. Once again Major Nkutu had dragged him from his straw pallet to torment him, to threaten and ridicule him. There had been nothing Pierre could do in defense. The major was the Intelligence and Security Officer in Albertville, and even the Belgian advisers at the Opérations Sud Headquarters were afraid of the man. It was he, Major Nkutu, who had received the coded telex message about Pierre from ANC security in Léopoldville. It was obvious that it would be Major Nkutu who would finally arrange Pierre's death. He did not seem to be particularly hurried, however.

He was content to continue acting out the charade that Pierre was a real infantry officer assigned to Ops Sud for disciplinary reasons. Pierre had been given the duties of Officer of the Guard, which, in principal, were easy. In reality he had spent the previous week at the ridiculous roadblock on the sagging steel bridge over the Lukuga River two kilometers north of Albertville. Pierre had been kept at the roadblock day and night. Sometimes the rusty Volkswagen truck would come with food and beer and sometimes it would not. The men in the guard squad were, like him, outcasts, soldiers who had deserted or who had shown cowardice in action against the rebels to the north. They were a slovenly, ill-tempered lot. Only the corporal displayed any respect for Pierre's rank. The rest would barely listen to him when he spoke and laughed outright when he attempted to give an order. Like Pierre, they had been selected for the next levy of replacements to the rifle companies being decimated by the rebel ambushes in the forested mountains north of Fizi. For all of them it was only a question of time.

Corporal Ramazani woke up and crawled out from behind the sandbags. The guard position was a wheelless metal freight car that had been dug into the side of the road next to the spur track. The corporal was in a cheerful mood. He stood blinking at the sunshine and scratched mosquito bites along the waistband of his trousers. Pierre sat on a wooden crate with his boots up on the metal girder of the bridge, staring off at the white clouds above the hills to the north. His stomach was rumbling with hunger. Without looking at the corporal, he asked, "Did they clean the machine gun as I ordered?"

"Who?"

"The soldiers, of course. I ordered them to clean the machine gun and arrange the ammunition belts before Major Nkutu comes back."

"I don't know," Corporal Ramazani said. "Are you hungry, *mon Lieutenant?*"

Pierre turned to look at him. "Do you have anything to eat?"

"Yes," the corporal said. "I got some bananas and fish from those women who came through this morning on their way to the market. Peanuts too. I also have some bread from yesterday, and there's still one can of sardines from the Arab merchant. Should I have one of the men make you a meal?"

Pierre looked at his watch; it was almost noon. The crumbling blacktop road stretched toward town, ending in a swamp where the waters of Lake Tanganyika had flooded. To the north the road went flat along the sandy beach leading to the airport. Overhead the wind off the lake hummed among the high-tension lines connecting the town to the hydroelectric plant in the mountains.

"Yes," he said finally. "I don't have any money to pay you for the food, though."

"*Ça ne fait rien,*" the corporal said. "It's my pleasure, Lieutenant."

He heard Ramazani yelling to the others in Swahili. After a while he could smell wood smoke. His stomach churned with the aroma of fish and peanuts bubbling in palm oil. Maybe they would also have some rice.

"Won't you come inside in the shade and eat with the others and me?" the corporal asked.

"It stinks in there," Pierre said. "The fat Katangan vomited last night and hasn't cleaned it up. I'll eat out here in the breeze."

Corporal Ramazani brought him a tin plate of food. They ate their meal with knives, watching the empty road to the north.

"There have been no civilians on the road since early this morning," Pierre said. "Only the whites from the airplanes and some mercenaries. Today's a *fête*. I wonder why more aren't going to town."

"They're afraid," Corporal Ramazani said. "Last night a patrol found some villagers on the railroad tracks carrying rebel weapons. One had a Communist land mine in a box. The villagers said they found them washed up on the beach. Major Nkutu questioned them, but they wouldn't tell him anything."

"What happened to them?" Pierre asked. "Were they really rebels?"

"Oh," Corporal Ramazani said, smiling, "they weren't really rebels. They just found the boxes of weapons on the beach and were taking them to sell, I suppose. Major Nkutu poked out one boy's eyes with a bayonet. The others were kicked to death and thrown in the river."

The corporal laughed. "The major sees rebels everywhere. If people think there are rebels coming back into Albertville, the major can do what he wants and he won't have to go up into the mountains and fight the real *Mulélistes*. The major is very clever. He used to be a corporal in the Force Publique. He knows the Army very well."

"How do you hear these things?"

"I have lots of friends in the Police Militaire. I was in jail here and they all know me."

"Where did you learn to speak French so well?" Pierre asked. "The others cannot even speak Lingala decently."

"Before the rebellion I was at a vocational school in Stanleyville. The priest and the brothers taught us French. I was going to be an electrician. But then I became a soldier."

"Have you fought much?"

"Oh, I fought when the others did, and I ran when the others did, too." He laughed. "It was very difficult last year in Stanleyville, especially for the *arabisés*. You see from my name that I am *très arabisé*. My mother was a Muslim. I know parts of the Holy Koran. Are you a Christian, Lieutenant?"

"I used to be. I am baptized and confirmed."

"The brothers at the school wanted us all to be baptized. But I refused. I was lucky because I had an uncle in the Sûreté. When the *Mulélistes* rebels came, he joined them and they killed many priests."

"Were you also a prisoner of the rebels?"

Corporal Ramazani looked away, across the lake to the mountains of Tanzania where the first of the afternoon storms was building up.

"I was lucky," he said. "My uncle Omar was in the Sûreté."

Pierre heard a vehicle approaching. It was the green-and-white jeep of Major Nkutu splashing through the swampy water down the road. "Quickly," he said. "Get the men to work on the machine gun."

Pierre snatched up a cumbersome FAL automatic rifle and walked to the middle of the low bridge. The Lukuga flowed swiftly past, close to the steel girders. This was very strange country, he thought. The river flowed *away* from the huge ghost-gray lake. The corporal had told him that this was the source of the Congo River, that the waters flowing by beneath his feet drained Lake Tanganyika and Lake Kivu to the north and went out this narrow river to join the Lualaba, which became the Congo at Stanleyville. It seemed impossible.

He heard the brakes of the jeep squeaking with the muddy water of the swamp. Major Nkutu, tall and birdlike, with tinted glasses, stood over the men of the guard detail. They stooped to their work, some stripping the unfamiliar weapon clumsily while others cleaned and rebelted each shining brass cartridge. The mess tins and food had been hidden. Pierre strode briskly down the bridge to salute the major. "This is the second time I have had them strip and clean the weapons, *mon Major,*" he lied. "Perhaps they will get it right now."

The major looked at him sharply. "Did you do well in the weapons classes at Infantry School, Lieutenant?" he asked.

"As well as the other cadets, *mon Major.*"

"That's good," the major said, his manner changed, softening slightly, "because we now have a serious situation to contend with. You heard of the rebel infiltrators last night?" Pierre nodded, and the major continued. "Good. They were attempting to smuggle arms into the *cité*. I have reason to believe they will try something more tonight. The entire situation looks grave to me, *oui, très grave*. Do you understand me, Lieutenant? No? Well, listen carefully." He led Pierre to the middle of the bridge. Pierre saw what was different in the major's face. He had seen that expression often in Makala prison among the prisoners who were able to bribe the guards to bring them hemp. The major gazed at the sunlight on the river before he spoke.

"I have evidence that the mercenaries are involved in this as well, Lieutenant," he said quietly. "Do you understand the gravity of this?"

Pierre stared back at him without answering.

"It's very complicated, but you must understand it if you are to react properly when I need you. Listen carefully. I have made many investigations since I arrived here. I was assigned by the President himself. He trusts me. There is something suspicious here in our sector. Do you understand me?"

Pierre nodded again. The major's face was strange, his eyes flat.

"I have sent for reinforcements!" he yelled, the sudden loudness of his own voice surprising him. "Listen carefully," he continued in a whisper. "There are many elements . . . mercenaries and the Americans and even the ones from South America who fly the airplanes. . . . I think that they are planning a coup against the new Army. . . . I think that it will begin here. I have informed Léopoldville. . . . I have informed the President himself. The Belgians are worried. Only one thing is clear—we must all do our duty as soldiers. . . ."

"I'm not a real soldier, *mon Major*," Pierre said softly. "You know that."

"Before tomorrow," the major continued, ignoring Pierre's words, "we will either be dead or covered with glory. It's victory or death, isn't it?"

Again Pierre nodded, avoiding the major's eyes.

"I have only spoken to a few officers and men about this, do you understand? There are only a few who can be trusted. You are new here, so I am sure you are not part of the plot. Of the others I am not so sure. These are your orders—each vehicle carrying whites must be stopped here. You must carefully count the number of men and the types of weapons they carry. If they are carrying boxes of armaments, they must be opened and counted. Make lists and telephone me at my special office. Your field telephone is operating, isn't it?"

"It doesn't always work properly."

"*Ça ne fait rien.* By tonight my commandos will have arrived. They may arrive by air, they may arrive by boat. That is secret. Do you have any questions?"

Pierre felt an impulse to ask the major how much hemp, how much *bangi,* he had smoked that morning, but instead he nodded curtly and saluted.

The major walked back to his jeep with long, slow strides. He smiled at the men cleaning their weapons and muttered in Swahili. The men smiled back.

"He's been smoking *bangi,*" Pierre said after the major had departed.

Corporal Ramazani grinned. "*Mais oui,*" he said. "The major always smokes hemp. It helps him see things which are hidden. He's in the Sûreté. It's important that he see things clearly."

"Then it's wrong for him to smoke hemp," Pierre said with conviction.

"The priests told you that, didn't they?"

"Perhaps."

"The priests always say that because they don't want you to see things. Did you know that Patrice *Lumumba* smoked hemp? He was Prime Minister and bullets would not kill him. He spit on King Baudouin and the King got sick. Gaston Soumialot can talk to Lumumba in heaven on the telephone."

"Do you really believe that?" Pierre asked, staring at the corporal.

"I was born in Maniema Province," the corporal said slyly. "If you had been born there, too, you would not have to ask these questions. I am *arabisé, très arabisé,* and you are a Christian. Why should we argue?"

Pierre smiled at the corporal. "You're a good boy," he said. "I don't agree with all the things you say, but you've still been kind to me. Major Nkutu, though, he's a difficult one to understand. All week he's been kicking me and shouting, and now he comes to tell me that I'm one of the few officers he can trust. He's afraid of a conspiracy between the rebels and the whites."

Corporal Ramazani scratched at the rust on the girder with his knife. "The major may seem crazy, but he is still the major," he said.

"It's more than a question of *seeming* crazy," Pierre said. "He's talking about a coup here and rebel infiltrators. That Belgian officer yesterday, the one in the parachutist's uniform, he told me that there aren't any rebels within one hundred kilometers of Albertville. I think the major is just making an *histoire* to seem important before the whites."

"Perhaps," the corporal said, "but what is the difference? We have all done something very bad and that is why they sent us here. The major has complete control over us. If he wanted to slit our throats and throw us in the river, who could stop him? So you see that it does not matter at all whether or not he is crazy. We must follow him and do what he tells us."

"Well," Pierre said, "you're right there—we must obey the major's orders. Watch the bridge now and keep the men working. I'm going down to the river to wash. Call me if anyone comes."

Pierre Tshipama stood washing in the tepid river. There was swamp scum and clumps of flood-killed weeds in the shallows. He remembered the clear forest rivers of his childhood. He thought of his father and mother and felt that he was going to cry. Somehow he knew that there would be more trouble, trouble between the insane major and the whites and that he would be involved. The wheel was turning again. Why did they always have to drag *him* into their *matatá*? He was tired of it all and longed to be with the baby and the girl in the quiet little bungalow in Coquilhatville with his mother and father there too, and the bicycle and six o'clock mass and Mama teaching Christianne to sew and Papa with little Henri balanced on his thick leg as he sang the old Tshiluba legends. Pierre no longer wanted Da Silva's diamonds or a big house in Djelo Binza with white girls. He wanted to be far away from this cold gray lake and the hard-eyed whites with their machine guns and that ranting, storklike major. He wanted the sun and the shade of the Equateur and little Henri and the girl and Mama and Papa.

" '*Tenant, 'Tenant, viens vite,*" Corporal Ramazani yelled down from the bridge. "There's a truck coming with white soldiers."

Pierre stood on the bridge, his clean uniform shirt unbuttoned, his boots spongy from the dripping river water. The truck bounced up onto the far end of the bridge as Corporal Ramazani pushed aside the other soldiers to position himself behind the machine gun. Pierre was trembling. He picked up the FAL and stood blocking the exit of the narrow span. The truck was big, covered with dried red mud and dust. The windshield was gone and the cab was protected with a lashed-down row of sandbags. From the top of the cab the snout of a light machine gun stuck over another row of sandbags. In the back of the truck a group of sunburned mercenaries lay on piles of baggage drinking beer. The driver flashed his headlights through their thick coating of red clay and sounded the horn. Pierre stood his ground. The mercenaries stood up in the back of the truck. They laughed at him, waving their beer bottles. The truck kept coming. He closed his eyes as he heard the brakes squeal.

"Wot in the fuck is *this?*" the driver yelled down in English.

"*Controle,*" Pierre said weakly in French. "I must see your papers."

"Get out of the way, you stupid kafir," one of the South African mercenaries called down from the truck. "We didn't come all this way down here for a spot of leave to 'ave no kafir *controle.*' "

Another mercenary jumped from the truck and walked smiling up to Pierre, addressing him in Swahili. The man continued smiling as he pushed the muzzle of Pierre's FAL toward the lake and waved the truck through. Pierre stood impotently aside as the vehicle rolled past the guard post. A small bearded mercenary laughed and spat a full mouthful of beer into Pierre's face. The truckload of white soldiers erupted in laughter. Pierre heard them break into a happy military song as they sped down toward the swamp. Blinded by the stinging beer, he raised the automatic rifle, trying to sight on the moving truck. He jerked the trigger but it would not move.

"It must first be cocked," Corporal Ramazani said. "There must be a cartridge in the chamber."

"Yes, of course," Pierre said. His face was hot with shame and anger. "Why do they act like that? Why won't they listen to me when I order them to stop?"

The corporal stared off at the departing truck. "The whites are often very evil," he said. "They have done many evil things."

"Now I can believe you," Pierre said as he wiped his sleeve across the greasy wetness on his face and neck.

The other soldiers snickered from their hiding place behind the sandbags.

CHAPTER **26**

It was hot in the metal belly of the airplane. Steve awoke desperately thirsty with flies on his face. Someone had turned him end for end on the rubber mattress so that he lay with his feet down the incline as the C-46 rested on its tail wheel. Waving off the flies, he licked his lips and stared vaguely at the cabin ribs above him, remembering in an instant the children at the mission and the prisoners and the nightmare. Instinctively he looked at his watch. Five o'clock. They were still on the ground at Albertville. He recalled Charlie sitting him up for landing and the co-pilot, Chico, frowning and saying something about the port generator. Then they had stretched him out again and he had slept a black, unhaunted sleep as the barbiturate and the alcohol drained his mind of ghosts and memories.

He sat up. Five o'clock and they were still on the ground. They would be late getting into Léopoldville. He must send a radio message asking the Embassy to call Lisa. She would worry about his being late. His lips were like cardboard, his hair still caked with the Kivu lava dust. He dropped warily down to the hot asphalt of the tarmac and saw WIGMO mechanics sweating around a work stand beneath the left wing of the C-46. There were pieces of the aluminum engine cowling and toolboxes strewn about in the sun. Across the shimmering tarmac more ground crewmen were pleating brass belts of machine-gun ammunition into the nose of a green B-26 fighter bomber. A pair of shiny single-engined T-28s sat on their tricycle landing gear near the hangar. Charlie walked out of the shade, carrying two cans of beer as if he had read Steve's mind and sensed his thirst.

"Happy New Year, Sleeping Beauty," he said. "Look's like we're going to be the guests of the CIA tonight."

Steve sucked at the cold beer. "What do you mean? What's wrong?"

"Whole damn generator's burned out on that engine. They're pulling it now and are going to try to get it repaired tonight. Maybe have it back in by tomorrow morning. Their Ops officer, Spencer, just told me to wake you up and get our bags. He'll drive us into town. The doctor and the girl have already gone in."

Mechanics walked past them, carrying tools and boxes of ammunition. From behind the WIGMO hangar he saw the green sparks of an arc welder and heard the chugging of a diesel motor. He could see the water of the lake over the elephant grass bordering the runway. "I'm supposed to be in Léo," he said, shaking his head. "My wife's waiting for me. We're invited to people's houses tonight."

"Well," Charlie said, "I'm sorry about that. Have to take a raincheck unless you plan to walk back, 'cause that's the only way left."

"No," Steve said stubbornly, his mind still thick with sleep, "Lisa will be waiting for me. I'm sick. I think I have malaria."

"Spencer's trying to get the Embassy now on the single side band. He'll give them a list of the passengers and they'll call everybody who needs to know. We're stuck here and that's all there is to it, Steve. It's a hell of a lot better than being down in the bush with an engine out. At least they can fix it here."

"Shit," Steve said. "I promised Lisa I'd be home for New Year's. What about Air Congo?"

"Once a week to Léo. I already checked. Flight's on Thursdays. Today's Friday."

"Goddamn it. What about these other planes? They can take passengers, can't they? They promised to get us home for New Year's. They've got to take some responsibility."

"Those are bombers, Steve. They're not going to send us down in one of their operational planes just to go to a bunch of New Year's parties."

"You don't understand," Steve said angrily. "I *promised* Lisa." He felt Charlie's hand on his elbow. The mechanics were looking at him. "I know, Steve," Charlie said. "Nothing we can do about it, though. We'll have our New Year's party tomorrow night, O.K.?"

Steve stared, hot-faced and bitter, at the toes of his shoes. "Goddamn it," he muttered. After a long pause he followed Charlie toward the waiting car.

Spencer turned his head to talk to them as he drove. It was crowded in the cab of the Land Rover, forcing Charlie to draw his knees up so that Spencer could shift gears. Steve sat slouched against the right-hand door, taking little part in their conversation. They sped along the smooth concrete road from the airport, past abandoned skeletons of fishing boats in the Greek's shipyard on the beach. The three thuggish Englishmen from the ground crew bantered back and forth in the rear of the vehicle in an incomprehensible Merseyside slang.

"Nice thing about having your own aircraft," Spencer said, holding up his can of beer. "We're not hurting for anything here. Got a real Butterball turkey for New Year's dinner. If you guys are still here tomorrow night, we're having a big poker game listening to the bowl games. I rigged up a great receiver at the hotel with speakers on the walls. Sounds just like you were in the States. We get all the pro games, too. Clear as a bell on Armed Forces radio."

Spencer's pressed khaki uniform bore no insignia. His balding head was splotchy with peeling sunburn. He whistled cheerfully as he drove.

"Boy, oh, boy," he said. "Nineteen sixty-six tomorrow. Time really flies, doesn't it?"

Charlie murmured something. There was horseplay and snuffling laughter from the mechanics. Steve watched the thunderheads glowing rosy with the late afternoon sun above the mountains of

Tanzania fifty miles across the lake. The straight road along the lake was deserted.

"That's the FILTISAF plant," Spencer said, indicating a low concrete factory complex coming up on their right. "Biggest textile plant in the eastern Congo. They'll be going day and night again as soon as that shipment of American cotton comes in from E'ville. That's their European employees' compound up there on the hill. They've got it made—swimming pool, hospital, the works. Talk about some of the white wives coming back soon. FILTISAF people are having a big New Year's Eve party and invited a few of our boys out. I don't know about moving around tonight, though. ANC'll be pretty stewed, and they've got another one of their horse's-ass rebel scares on. Lot of new mercs in town, too, and all kinds of boys from the Five Cado are down from the mountains for New Year's. What with the South Africans from the Five Cado and those new hard-case frogs and Belgians from the Six Cado and the ANC, I think it might be just as well to stay close to downtown tonight."

Spencer nodded back at the laughing mechanics. "Of course, my boys aren't exactly angels, either. Can raise more hell than anybody if they get drunk enough. Not so bad in Léo where you got some stray white women around. But these boys have been out in the boonies too long. Stan last year and then Paulis. What a hole *that* place is! And then Goma and now we're here. They get a little horny and I have to send them down to Léo every once in a while. Otherwise they start ripping things up. How you feeling now?" Spencer said to Steve. "Want some more beer? We got a whole case back there."

Steve shook his head, trying to smile. "No, thanks."

"Yeah," Spencer continued, "malaria can really get you down. I've had my share since I got in with this outfit. Guatemala and Laos and Saigon, and now here. I can't take the pills regular, either, the way you're supposed to. They make me forget things"— he tapped his clipboard on the dash—"numbers and things like that. Ever happen to you?"

Steve nodded silently. He wasn't going to be with Lisa tonight. He wanted to scream, to pound something, to kick out and smash some valuable piece of equipment. A vision of Spencer's elaborate radio set broken on the floor floated through his head. He sighed loudly and shifted in his uncomfortable seat.

"Yeah," Spencer said, "that's a shame about missing your New Year's down in Léo. I know how a guy feels about getting back to his family. You kind of count on it, especially when you're sick. You'll feel better, though, at the hotel. They've got really nice rooms there—for Africa, I mean. Hot water and screens on the windows. Plenty of light to read by. We're lucky in A'ville 'cause we've got hydroelectric. Man, I get tired of those Coleman lanterns on hot nights in the tropics. Should be a good night, though. Lots of nice guys in town. Bobby, that French kid who flies the helicopter, took a couple of us up yesterday and we got a whole mess of antelope. Small ones. Not really a dik-dik—little bigger than that. Damn good eating. That's what we're having at the hotel tonight. How does that sound?"

"Sounds good," Charlie said.

"How does that sound to you, Steve?" Spencer asked. "Charcoal-broiled antelope?"

"Great!" Steve said hoarsely. "I love antelope. We have it all the time in Léo. The little ones are best, aren't they?"

Charlie looked at him. "You O.K?" he said softly.

Steve did not answer. They bounced up onto the bridge across the Lukuga River and Steve began laughing. Spencer looked toward him but then saw the obstruction at the end of the bridge. The ANC had dragged gasoline drums across the end of the span. A thin young Congolese officer stood behind the barricade with a rifle.

"Jesus!" Spencer said, stopping. *"Now* what are they trying to pull?"

"Arrêtez-vous!" the lieutenant called. *"Controle, descendez tous."* Lieutenant Tshipama pointed the loaded FAL at the windshield of the Land Rover.

"Out of the way, woggey," one of the mechanics yelled.

"Shut up," Spencer said, "he's an officer." Then, leaning out the window, he addressed the lieutenant in halting French. *"Qu'est-ce qu'il y a, Capitaine?* What's the trouble? You know us. We're from the fighter squadron at the airport. What's the problem? We come through here every day."

"Everyone get down," Lieutenant Tshipama repeated, again menacing the vehicle with his weapon.

"Put up that popgun, niggey," one of the mechanics said, "or I'll get down and ram it up your bleeding arse."

"Be careful with that weapon, Lieutenant," Spencer cautioned, his voice changing. "I'm an officer in the État-Major of Ops Sud. Put that gun away and look at my *laissez-passer*."

"You must all get down for the *controle*," Pierre repeated.

Spencer scratched his head. "Son of a bitch," he said between his teeth. "See what I mean about the ANC?" He opened the door and got out, carrying his clipboard. "Look, Lieutenant," he said, "threatening a superior officer is a very serious offense, even in the ANC. Here's my *laissez-passer*. Take a look at it. You've got thirty seconds to open this barricade. If you don't let us through, I'll go back to the airport and radio the colonel's office and get some military police out here to arrest you. Now put down that gun and look at my papers."

Pierre looked confused. He shot a quick glance back at the sandbagged guard post in the deep shadows of the swamp reeds at the side of the road, then walked hesitantly between the fuel drums to verify Spencer's papers. "Do you have weapons?" he asked.

"That's our affair, Lieutenant," Spencer said coldly. "You can see from my *laissez-passer* that I'm a civilian, but I have the rank of lieutenant colonel. I don't have to answer to a subordinate who shows disrespect to a superior officer. Now get your stupid barricade out of the way."

"The day of white *officers* in the ANC is almost finished," Pierre spat. He called out a command in Lingala and two soldiers pulled aside the drums. "Now, *mon Colonel*," he said in the same tone, "get your hoodlums off my bridge."

"Wot's a matter, Admiral?" one of the mechanics yelled, as the Land Rover lurched forward. "Ain't ya gettin' enough out 'ere? Won't yur boy friend there let ya suck 'im off?"

Pierre spun on his heels to face his tormenter. The long-haired young Englishman laughed as he reached down for a fresh can of Budweiser. Shaking the can violently, he peeled back the opening tab until foam shot out. " 'Ere ya are, Tar Baby," he yelled.

" 'Appy New Year." He threw the foaming can which exploded with a geyser of beer at Pierre's feet, drenching the front of his clean uniform. Spencer shifted into third and they were away safely.

He smiled grimly. "Christ, this has been a real great day, all right. The forty-six down with that generator and maybe no spare; Antonio and Raphael are out there on a long strike and called in saying they want to refuel at Kindu and go on up to Stan for the night. Just go on up to their buddies in Stan like they're driving Mustangs or something. They were pissed off when I told them no. They get up there to Stan and they'll spend the whole weekend. Jesus! And now this crap from the ANC. A real beauty of a day, all right. I could have used a little something stronger than this." He threw his empty beer can out into the wind.

Steve breathed in the suddenly cool swamp air and shifted again in his seat. "Wasn't that the same little ANC guy who rode up to Stan with us?" he asked Charlie.

"Was it?" Charlie said. "I didn't notice."

They drove up the wet detour lane around the flooded stretch of road, emerging from the high grass near the CFL railroad yards. A squeaking locomotive whistle sounded, announcing the end of the workday, and at once lines of workers were dogtrotting past them, hurrying toward their homes in the *cité* before the first ANC and police patrols appeared with the fall of night. The mission church, a massive red-brick cathedral, stood out nakedly against the eucalyptus trees on the hills rising above the one-street business district. Here the rising lake had caused havoc, flooding the main street, which had been filled with gummy laterite clay to become a humped-back ridge rising between two ditches of scummy, backed-up water. The porches of the Pakistani and Arab general stores swarmed with Congolese crowding in to purchase their beer and rice for the evening's *fête*. Everyone was hurrying, their bundles balanced gracefully on the women's heads as they trotted toward the *cité,* the heads of their sleeping babies carried on their backs swinging violently as the mothers leaped giggling across the water-filled ditches. The eucalyptus gave way to a straight line of coconut palms as they drove into the town's center. To their left the CFL yards widened into the port complex, clogged with rusty, half-submerged barges and a shattered lake steamer. Here there were more soldiers on the street, dressed in their holiday khakis, wandering hand in hand as they peered into the barred shop windows at the meager displays of civilian clothes. Spencer swung in before the pink stucco façade of the Palace Hotel where the three young Englishmen hopped down. "See ya layter, alligaytor," one boy called. "Thanks for the lift."

"See you tonight," Spencer answered.

There were other WIGMO ground crew and several Cuban pilots sitting around long tables in the drab ground-floor barroom. Congolese cha-cha music blared loudly.

"They're getting an early start," Spencer said.

They continued to drive up the mound of earth fill past the bullet-scarred Banque du Congo, finally dropping back onto the original pavement. "We've got the pilots and ground crew billeted at the Palace," Spencer said. "The boat and air group staff and most of the Belgian officers from Ops Sud are at the Hotel du Lac. We've got the two top floors. Always keep a couple rooms for visitors."

"Place hasn't gotten any prettier since September," Charlie said.

"Oh," Spencer said, "it's coming along all right—for *Katanga,* that is. You should have seen it last year. Of course the lake flooding up like this kind of messes things up, and there's been fighting here off and on since Independence. Lot of different troops been through here since 1960—Tshombe's mercs during the Katanga secession deal, and then the UN, and then the Simbas. They did a whole lot of damage during the occupation. Of course, the ANC raised hell when they recaptured the place. I'm afraid we did our bit, too." He pointed off toward the fuel tanks and docks of the port. "My boys flew a raid the last day of the rebel occupation. We were worried they were going to try to get away across the lake in boats. The boys kind of outdid themselves on the rocket passes, I guess. The Belgians, especially the CFL people, were pissed off about it. Well, we just gave them the old '*c'est la guerre,*' you know. Nothing we could do about it. ANC wanted an airstrike so we gave them one. Goddamn CFL was trading, 'business as usual,' all during the rebel occupation, regular lake service up to Bujumbura and over to Kigoma. If they wanted to play footsies with the rebels, they had to expect to take a few losses. Really a funny little war here, isn't it?"

"They're all real funny," Charlie said. "Hilarious."

Steve's laughter was explosive. Spencer turned to him, taking his eyes off the road. "Oh, I don't mean funny like humorous," he said. "I mean strange, complicated, all kinds of fucking around behind the scenes. Almost as bad as Laos. It's harder than hell when you're trying to fly airstrikes. Rebels might be in one village, but the tribe in the village is pro-government or the ANC colonel might have a lot of relatives someplace and doesn't want you to hit it even though it's full of rebels. It's a lot better now, though, that we're flying against the ones who are holed up there in the mountains. You *know* that they're all bad guys up that way." He laughed, showing his gray teeth.

"Hey, watch it!" Steve blurted out.

An ANC jeep pulling a trailer piled with beer cases shot out of a narrow driveway between two buildings. Spencer swerved, braking sharply, but was unable to prevent the collision. Steve bit his tongue as his head slammed against the windshield. There were soft snowflakes of light shimmering before his eyes, and he tasted the warm blood in his mouth. He sat there watching the ensuing confusion with a wet smile. Spencer was shouting in his bad French, waving his clipboard at the driver as he gestured at the twisted bumper of the Land Rover. Beer cases were strewn across the pavement, spreading a wide puddle of beer. The street filled with laughing black soldiers who pushed each other to get a closer look at the angry white man. At the sight of the soldiers the few remaining groups of civilian Congolese shied into doorways. Suddenly Spencer was on the ground in a rag tag scuffle with several of the ANC soldiers, and Charlie was among them, pulling and shouting. More soldiers joined in the melee, their eyes now devoid of the original merriment. Steve knew that he should be out there, beyond the spider-web crack on the dusty windshield, but it all seemed so unreal. He saw blood on Charlie's collar.

Whites from the Palace Hotel trotted up the street to join the disturbance; some carried pistols, others clubs. People were yelling in Spanish, Swahili, and English. The Land Rover rocked wildly as ANC soldiers and the WIGMO men scuffled against it. More bottles were broken. Steve leaned out the window to get a better view. Three big French mercenaries from Six Commando charged down the street. An ANC jeep driven by an MP roared up, depositing a tall Congolese major who beat at anyone, black or white, who came within the range of his flailing swagger stick. Spencer had been pushed off to the sidewalk where he stood mopping his nosebleed with a handkerchief, yelling in vain to his own people to break off the engagement so that the major could restore order among the ANC troops. The major struck out, hitting a small Cuban pilot full in the face. The pilot pushed the major into the waiting arms of a mercenary sergeant who threw the Congolese officer to the ground and kicked him viciously in the groin. The confused mass of blacks and whites quickly dissolved to reappear as two lines, one white, the other black, divided by the jeep trailer and the mound of crushed beer cases. Major Nkutu pulled himself up, howling with pain and anger.

Two more jeeps carrying ANC MPs careened down the street with sirens honking. The black soldiers appeared chastened by the arrival of the MP reinforcements and the sight of the armed whites facing them. Spencer walked out onto the street, turning his back on the screaming major, and spoke severely to his men. They protested briefly, but he was soon able to turn them back toward their hotel. Spencer jumped back into the Land Rover, threw the bloody handkerchief out the window, revved the engine violently, and backed the vehicle away from the crushed beer trailer. Charlie hopped into the back of the Land Rover, and Spencer cut the wheel sharply to swing around the jeep. Major Nkutu sprang forward to block the way.

"*Criminels!*" he yelled. "This is a criminal act. You have attacked my men in broad daylight. I shall call a curfew. I will prosecute the guilty parties. This is a disgrace and an insult. There must be a court-martial."

"There *will be,* Major, goddamn it," Spencer yelled back. "There'll be a full report of this incident on the colonel's desk in the morning. Your men attacked me after causing this stupid accident. Look at them. They're drunken scum. Now get out of my way or I'll run you down."

The newly arrived MPs were shouting loudly, gesturing at the damaged jeep and the pile of smashed beer cases. The major stood, congested with rage. One of the lenses of his tinted eyeglasses was cracked. Suddenly Steve started laughing; the same wild laughter he had heard from Charlie in the Reeds' Djelo Binza garden he now felt erupting inside of him. Major Nkutu pointed at Steve with his swagger stick. "Criminal!" he screamed. "Mercenary!"

At that instant a riptide wave appeared to strike the group of black soldiers, throwing them to the pavement. Spencer cringed behind the steering wheel. "Oh, no!" he gasped. For a moment Steve could see nothing through the smashed windshield. Then he saw them. Unbelievably low, only inches above the frayed tops of the coconut palms and insanely close to power lines and buildings, two olive-drab B-26 bombers flying nose to tail came hurtling out of the late-afternoon sky. They flew at full throttle, ripping in over the port and up the main street on a mock strafing run. Steve knew that they would strike a tree or a power line and come down to engulf the street in flames. They were too low. He saw tiny printed numbers stenciled on inspection panels on the nose and wing of the lead plane. With a pounding blast of engine noise they were past them, banking lazily back out over the port, before climbing to make their approach to the Albertville airport. Deafened, he sat in silence as Spencer drove up the street, angrily slamming the gear shift.

"Antonio and Raphael," he said. "God*damn* those guys. Why did they have to pull that crap *today?*"

Looking back, Steve could see the ANC soldiers still flat on the pavement. The gaunt black major had slumped down next to his jeep.

C H A P T E R **27**

Pierre heard the airplanes long before they could be seen. He and Corporal Ramazani stood on the bridge sharing a bottle of beer and a can of oily fish. His anger had cooled. This was not the time for blind rage. He must carefully plan each move. Things were changing quickly, and it was possible that he could save himself through an alliance with Major Nkutu. The major was obviously not a rational man. He had power, however, and he had money. Pierre knew himself to be a rational person. He was educated and he could reason, planning his actions far into the future. He must display these qualities so that Major Nkutu would come to realize he was of more value to him alive than dead. If the major wanted to fight the white men, then Pierre too would fight the white men.

He sucked out the last of the fish juice from the jagged edge of the can, then tossed the can over the side of the bridge to plop onto the fast-flowing surface of the river. The corporal handed him the beer bottle. High overhead two airplanes took shape against the thunderclouds to the north. They looked tiny, but the sound of their engines rolled loudly in the valley of the Lukuga.

"The Cubans," Corporal Ramazani said, pointing at the planes. "They've come back from bombing the rebels."

Pierre nodded, watching the planes grow larger as they began their shallow dive toward the south. "I wonder where they are going now?" he asked.

"They will fly in a large circle," Corporal Ramazani said, waving his knife in the air. "Then they will go out again over the lake and come in very low, just there. That is how they always land."

As the corporal spoke, however, the planes became louder and dove steeply toward the beach. Pierre thought that they would surely hit the water. Instead they flattened out and roared over, just above the beach, screaming past the bridge toward the city. The last of the afternoon sun hit their wings as they tilted like swallows and disappeared over the port. The noise echoed back from the hills.

"They are going to bomb the city!" the corporal shouted.

"Don't be a fool," Pierre said disdainfully. "They are our allies."

They turned to watch the hills to the south and were frozen to the bridge at what they saw. The two planes were coming back at them out of their own echo, low, lower than the power lines, only a few meters above the swamp reeds. They were flying directly at the bridge. "They're coming now for us!" Corporal Ramazani screamed.

The two B-26s passed so low that their engines whipped up choking clouds of red dust from the surface of the bridge, blinding Pierre as he cowered beneath the railing. Even the water of the river danced as if in a violent storm. After they had shot by, he rose and watched them turn back over the lake and settle gently with their wheels lowered at the end of the airport runway.

The corporal was next to him, laughing as he stuck his fingers in his ears. "They missed us," he said. "They tried to get us, but they could not do it."

"They were just playing a game," Pierre said. "They tried to scare us because they think we are stupid, like children. Those airplanes carry guns and rockets. The plane itself cannot hurt a person. It's a *fête* and they are drunk so they want to scare us."

"*Eh bien,*" Corporal Ramazani said. "They were successful then, because they certainly did scare us. Airplanes are supposed to fly up in the sky, not down on the road. They must be crazy."

"They all seem to be crazy," Pierre said. "Where I grew up the whites were different. They were priests and teachers and doctors. They always helped us. Here they are not the same. They drink all day and wave their guns just like Force Publique soldiers after Independence. I think that the good whites are all either dead or have gone away back to Belgium."

"The whites put my father in prison and beat him with ropes," the corporal said. "He would not pay their taxes and he laughed at their priests. When he came back from prison, he was never the same again inside his head. My uncle Omar often told me to study my father if I wanted to see what the whites could do."

"I was lucky in Equateur. We had good whites there."

"There might have once been good whites where you came from, but now since Independence they are all bad, especially the ones called *les Américains*. It is the American airplanes that destroyed the rebels. They carried the Belgian parachute soldiers who captured Stanleyville. All the whites were defeated and running before the Simba Army until the Americans came. I know this is true because I saw these things myself at Stanleyville."

"Were you with the rebels?" Pierre asked cautiously.

"I was there, and my uncle Omar was in the New Sûreté. I had been a soldier, but then I stopped. I will only say that I think the rebels were not all bad. They killed the Bangala politicians and all the bad soldiers who had cheated us since Independence. The rebels had a lot of money and paid for beer and food. They did not hate the *arabisés* the way the whites did."

"All the whites weren't bad," Pierre said. "They did not hate the blacks where I lived. My father worked with the white doctors and priests all his life, and he told me that the whites were here to help us. My father was an *évolué,* and I'm sure that he knew more than your Uncle Omar."

"Did your father go to the church and read prayers with the priests from the special Bible?"

"What special Bible? There is only one Bible. It is the word of God and always the same. It doesn't matter if it's written in French or Lingala or Swahili."

"There are at least *two* different Bibles," Corporal Ramazani said gravely. "Maybe there are more. In Stanleyville we all know this. Why do you think the Belgians always got well when they went to the hospital for the whites, while the blacks so often died when they went to the *dispensaires?* Why did the Belgians and the Portuguese who owned stores become so rich? . . . They said the prayers from the special Bible that the priests kept for the whites."

"This doesn't sound correct to me," Pierre said.

"In Stanleyville among the *arabisés* we all know these things. Once you learn this, everything becomes very simple. Did you know that when Patrice Lumumba went to Brussels, he met white people who were called socialists and who hated the priests, so they gave him the special Bible and taught him how to say the prayers? Didn't you know that? That is one of the reasons the whites and Moise Tshombe killed him—because he had become too powerful with the special prayers."

"I cannot believe this, Corporal, because I was raised with the whites, very close to the church. I know the priests and they were always good to us."

"Then there is no sense talking, because you are already one of them and you must already know about the Bible."

Their conversation was interrupted by the approach of another vehicle, an olive-green Volkswagen minibus bouncing down the darkening airport road with one headlamp shining. It stopped at the far end of the bridge span and a short man in a one-piece flying suit got out. "What is the problem?" he called in French.

"Controle," Pierre said. "You must show your papers and have the car inspected." The Volkswagen advanced to within a few meters of the barricade and the three passengers got out. Two wore flying suits and the third was dressed in greasy shorts and an undershirt. "We're both pilots from the squadron," the short man said. Pointing to the tall man in shorts, he added, "Jorgenson is a mechanic. Here are our papers. Take a look in the car if you want."

Pierre studied the identification cards and *laissez-passers* of the three men. He shone his flashlight into the car. "Are you carrying weapons?" he asked the pilot.

"Only these," the Cuban answered, patting the automatic pistol in the holster under his arm and pointing at the other pilot's gun.

In the light of the headlight Pierre carefully noted the men's names in his soiled notebook and copied the license number of the car.

"Is there anything else, *Chef?*" the Cuban asked cheerfully. Pierre handed back the papers and shook his head. "How many are you here at this bridge?" the Cuban asked in the same tone.

"I cannot tell you that," Pierre said. "Why do you ask? What business is it of yours?"

"Nothing important, really," the Cuban said, still smiling. "It's just that today's a *fête* and we've got some extra beer. It's very good and it's also cold. I can spare six cans. Try it. It's really very good. It comes from America. Would you like some?"

"Yes, thank you," Pierre answered.

"Here you are, six cans, *Bonne fête, Chef.*"

"Bonne fête, monsieur. Merci."

They watched the car's taillights winking off down the road toward the swamp. "We should not drink this American beer," Corporal Ramazani said.

"Why not?" Pierre juggled a can in his hand. "Feel it, it's nice and cold. They were all drinking it—why shouldn't we?"

"It's very hard to explain," the corporal said. "I know that you do not believe in the same things that I do, or perhaps you know all this already and also more powerful things, but you won't admit it to me. How can I explain?"

"Explain what?"

Two of the soldiers came out from behind the sandbags and approached them. "Can we have the beer, Lieutenant?" one asked in his bad Lingala.

"Take four cans. Leave two for us."

"You can have mine too," Corporal Ramazani said. He waited until the soldiers had returned to the guard post.

"What is there to explain, Corporal?" Pierre asked.

"Have you never heard of the powers of certain waters? Have you never heard of *mai Mulélé?*"

"That's rebel witchcraft," Pierre said with disdain.

"Not only the rebels use waters for their spells. Look at the priests! All of them have special waters they use for their magic. Special waters and special prayers. Just like their Bibles, they have special prayers for the whites and others for the blacks. They use waters when you are baptized and when you marry and when you die."

"That's holy water," Pierre laughed, "You can't say that it has anything to do with magic."

"You can call it whatever you want. It is still true that the whites use special waters for their *dawa* just as we do. That is why I do not think that we should drink the beer they gave us. The man said that it was from the Americans, didn't he?"

"Yes, of course. Here, look at the can. It says U.S.A. here in small letters. U.S.A. That's the same as America. Look at it—you can read."

"I don't want to see it," the corporal said, looking away and muttering unintelligibly.

"What's all this about beer, anyway?" Pierre said.

"If you really want to know, then I will tell you. You will not like what I say, however."

Pierre laughed again. "Go ahead and tell me. I'm not a child, you know."

"You have told me things about your life. I didn't ask you these things, did I? You told me because you wanted me to know. We are of the same age group, and that is important."

"Yes, yes, go on."

"I think now from what you have told me and what I have seen here at this bridge that you are in very serious trouble. I think that the whites have a spell on you."

Pierre laughed again, but this time the laughter dried cold on his mouth as he watched the expression on Corporal Ramazani's face. "How could they have a spell on me?"

"With this," the corporal said, pointing to the beer can. "With the *mai*."

"It's only beer."

"The water the priests use is only water, isn't it? Look what magic they can do with their water you call holy water. Think what they could do with beer."

"The whites have nothing against me," Pierre said weakly. "Why should they want to put a spell on me?"

"This I do not know," the corporal whispered. "I only know that twice today these evil white men who have killed so many blacks with their machine guns and their airplanes have wettened you with beer. This is how they use their *mai*."

Pierre glanced away to the west where the sun was slicing into the first row of distant hills. In a moment it was gone and the heavy darkness seemed to rush with a chill wind off the already dark waters of the lake. A night bird he had never heard before began a monotonous squawking among the swamp reeds. The corporal still stared at him.

"I have already suffered much, even though I am still young," Pierre said. "You must not joke with me this way. You may think that I am weak, but if you are trying to trick me with stories of spells and magic, I will make you pay for it."

"Why should I try to trick you? I have said before that we are all outcasts here. We have all suffered. Perhaps you more than me because you have been mistreated by the whites since you were a little child. You told me that you did not even have any uncles with you to teach you about the world the way a boy should be taught—you only had the white priests and brothers. You must believe me. I'm not trying to trick you."

"You really feel the whites can place spells on people this way, by using waters?" As Pierre spoke he suddenly remembered the acid taste of the champagne he had vomited in the taxi.

"You believe that there are good whites who can do good things with what you call holy water, don't you?"

"Certainly. I have often seen the priests give God's blessing with holy water. I have even helped them in the service. They use wine also. It becomes the blood of Jesus Christ just as bread becomes Christ's flesh."

"So!" The corporal smiled. "I see that you recognize all of it —what you call sacraments are really magic just like our *dawa*. So, if the *good* whites can do good with their waters and their wine and bread, why cannot the truly *evil* whites like these who have come across this bridge today, do evil things with *their* waters?"

"There's a big difference between a priest who has been ordained by God and a soldier throwing beer. I cannot believe what you say."

"From what you have told me of your life, you have probably been cursed from the very beginning, for so long that you can no longer see it happening to you."

Pierre stood with the sweating beer can in his hand. It was now dark and the soldiers had lighted the kerosene lanterns to prepare their evening meal. To the south the lights of Albertville looked reassuring with their civilized regularity. Here at the bridge it was black African night where many things could be believed which are not possible beneath the electric lights of a city. He heard the whir of the field telephone.

Major Nkutu's voice sounded far away. "They have already begun," he screamed. "They have attacked my men in broad daylight on the main street. Then they tried to panic us with their airplanes. It is all very complicated, but I can see the purpose. It's all very simple, do you understand me, Lieutenant?"

"Oui, mon Major," Pierre yelled back into the mouthpiece. "Perfectly."

"Good. The pilots who tried to panic us into retreat will cross your post at the bridge. You will arrest them and take them to my special office at my villa. If they resist, shoot them. I trust you to carry out my orders. If you let them through, then I will know that you are a traitor and I will treat you accordingly. I am in direct contact with Léopoldville. Do you know what that means? Good. Carry out your orders without weakness and you shall be rewarded."

The line sputtered once and fell dead. Pierre gazed out into the darkness. He felt hopelessly alone, as he had when manacled to the floor of the MPs' vehicle listening to Christianne's screams as she was raped. Now there were no metal chains, but they had again trapped him just as surely. He wanted to cry, to run away.

The corporal touched his sleeve with a twig. "What did he want, Lieutenant?"

Pierre was silent. After a long pause he turned to Corporal Ramazani. "What did you say before about my life being cursed from the beginning?"

"This seems very probable to me, from what I have seen and from the little you have told me about yourself."

Pierre tossed the sealed beer can slowly from hand to hand. "I do not think that this could be possible," he said with conviction. "I had a baby brother who was born with me; he died after one week. If anyone was cursed, it was he. I have always been lucky. I have had both very good and very bad luck. It seems to move in circles like a wheel. If there was any curse in my family, it fell on my little brother."

"You had a brother who was *born* with you?"

"Yes, of course. Didn't I tell you that before?"

"You were born as a *twin?*"

"Of course, two babies, both boys, both exactly the same. We were very small, born too soon. The white doctor saved my life with a special box. They put us both in special boxes after we were born. They are called incubators. It's the same as a mother's belly. I learned about them at school.

"My mother nearly died. They had to cut her stomach to take us out. Because my father was so good, they treated us very well, just like the whites. I was treated very well. So was my brother, but he died. We were both very small, but he was baptized and went to heaven."

The corporal stepped back and muttered something Pierre

could not understand. The corporal disappeared into the guard post, returning a moment later with a canvas holster and a tight roll of bank notes. He laid the pistol and the money at Pierre's feet. "You never told me you were a *twin,*" he whispered. "You did not say that you had been cut from your mother's belly by the white doctors and placed inside a special box. Now I can see things more clearly. You must take these gifts. In my family we still honor the old ways. We know that babies born as twins are very special, that they should be given gifts. Take them from the ground. I cannot touch you until the spell is broken."

Pierre stooped and picked up the pistol and the money. The heavy revolver felt good clipped to his belt. There were seventeen one-thousand-franc bills in the money roll. With this money he could easily bribe a fisherman to take him across the lake to Tanzania. His luck was changing once again.

"The pistol is from a dead white soldier," the corporal said. "The money I have taken from many places. They are a gift from me."

"Thank you, Corporal. I am pleased with this gift."

"Will you allow me to help you more, Lieutenant?"

"How?"

"I know a wise old man who has also suffered much from the whites. He comes from another tribe far away down the lake, but he has traveled very much and seen many things. He is a sorcerer and he worked with the rebel army here and in the Maniema. He knows the *dawa* of the whites and how to defeat it. Now he lives just here, in that village across the river where you see the lights. Not the first lights, but farther back, there in the hills. I bring him food and money when I can get away. He is a great enemy of the whites and I know that he will help you."

"Perhaps we can go there in the morning," Pierre said.

"We must go *now,* Lieutenant. If anyone asks for us, the others will tell them that we saw something and went to patrol the riverbank. We must see the old man tonight. I am afraid of the white men's *mai.* We should take the beer with us and he will tell us about the spell."

"If it won't take too long, then I will go. How far is it?"

"Just there—you can see the lights."

CHAPTER **28**

Charlie came out of the bathroom wearing a pair of GI under-shorts. "Wow," he said, "that's really good. Just like Spencer said, plenty of hot water. It was about a hundred and ten in the shade today up in Stan and I got all sweaty. Shower feels great." He set his plastic toilet kit on the night table between the two beds and lit a cigarette. Steve sat on his bed, still fully dressed. There were several old magazines and newspapers lying unread before him. "You going to get cleaned up now?" Charlie said, putting his watch on. "Spencer said for us to come on over next door for a drink before dinner."

Steve stared straight out before him without speaking. He picked up an American Army newspaper entitled *Strike Command* and glanced at it. "Go blind trying to read in this light," Charlie continued in a pleasant tone. "Want me to turn on the overhead lamp?"

Steve looked up at him. "What?"

"You going to read? I'll turn the big light on for you if you want it."

Steve looked down at the newspaper and let it drop from his fingers to the floor.

"You O.K.?" Charlie asked. "You take those malaria pills?"

"I don't have malaria," Steve said.

"What have you got then? You said you had a malaria attack or something."

"I think that I've got an attack of the Congo."

"Diarrhea?"

"Diarrhea in the brain, Charlie. I can't stop thinking."

"What's wrong? What happened to you?"

Steve laughed loudly. "Nothing, really. Nothing happened to *me*. That's the problem. Nothing ever happens to *us* in this coun-try. We just swim through it and go to another party. It's not our country. Why should we give a shit? It's not our fault if kids get wrapped up in plastic and a bunch of poor stupid villagers get themselves dumped in a lake. Why should we worry?"

"What in the hell are you talking about, Steve?" Charlie pulled on his Bermuda shorts and a sports shirt, then stood with his comb in his hand, staring at Steve.

Steve laughed again. "It's a long story, Charlie, and we don't have time for me to tell it now. Look, why don't you go on over to Spencer's room and have a drink? Tell them I'm still feeling sick. Tell them I went to church or something. I just don't feel like listening to all their fucking gung-ho stories right now."

"What about dinner? Spencer said eight o'clock. They got a whole bunch of antelope down there barbecuing in the kitchen."

"I'm really not hungry. I had a big lunch."

"You sure? Can I get you something?"

"No, really. Thanks a lot. You go on now. Have one for me."

Charlie stared at him for a moment and then turned to leave. "You sure you're O.K. here?"

Steve smiled, squelching another burst of laughter. "Yeah, I'm fine. You go ahead. I might come over afterwhile."

Steve flicked out the small bedside lamp and sat perfectly still in the darkened room. A steady lake breeze flowed in through the screen door to the terrace. He could hear the clinking of ice-cube trays and the laughter of the men drinking on the terrace of Spencer's room. A dog barked somewhere out on the deserted street. After a long while a car passed by, carrying with it the soprano lilting of Lingala voices. With the fingertips of his left hand he delicately explored the scabs on his right palm. He heard the rippling laughter of a girl speaking French and listened hungrily to her high heels clicking along the corridor. Helicopter Bobby and his girl friend were going down for dinner. Lisa's face and the curve of her body came over him so suddenly that he could almost feel her physical presence, the tickling of her hair along the inside of his forearm cradled on the pillow beneath her neck. His palm sores were bleeding again.

Another round of boisterous laughter wafted in from Spencer's terrace, voices harsh and masculine, empty of compassion. The two CIA officers of the Air and Boat group were swapping Congo stories for the benefit of Charlie and the visiting Special Forces officer from Fort Bragg. There was another, softer voice speaking now; it was George White from the Embassy's CIA Political Section—Poly II, they all called it, as if, Steve thought, it were some sophomore survey class. The breeze shifted slightly and he heard their voices more clearly. "Oh, hell," Spencer said with resignation. "I don't really *blame* Antonio and Raphael. They've been out here a long time, you know, since the beginning. They've probably been flying too many strikes too, you know, those long hauls way up there in the mountains where it's a real chore just to find the target, let alone do a decent job on it, and then all the way back here with the weather always closing down and fuel low. I don't really blame them for wanting to spend a couple of days up in Stan with their girl friends. Can't blame them for buzzing town either. They were just letting off a little steam. They had no way of knowing there was that rumble going on." He laughed.

"Did those niggers finally get their beer back to the ANC camp?" somebody asked.

"Last I saw they were still fucking around out there on the street, arguing with the old Arab to replace the broken bottles," Clayton, the boat group officer, said.

"Almost had a real shoot-'em-up there," somebody said.

"Yeah," Spencer said. "I think a lot of my boys would've liked nothing better than to work over old Major Nkutu. Those new French guys from the Six Cado would have liked to help."

"The big sergeant with the red beret is ex-Foreign Legion," George White added. "Named Serge. Fought with Bob Denard and all those other jokers for Tshombe in Katanga. We've got a file on him back in Léo as long as your arm. He's wanted in France for about nine counts of murder in Algeria during the OAS. The central government here had a price on his head for a while in '62. He used to like to kill any ANC they captured with his bare hands when he was with the Katanga Gendarmes. Same deal for that skinny corporal with the scarred face and the blond goatee. He's a German really, named Schneider, was in the SS when he was about fifteen, the Legion in Indo-China, OAS in Algeria, fought with the Kats during the secession. Now they are right back in Katanga, fighting *for* the ANC this time. . . ." More laughter in the darkness.

"Isn't that pure Congo?" Clayton said. "Hell, Mobutu was on the radio the other day screaming and yelling about sending a battalion of paracommandos down to stamp out Ian Smith's Rhodesian racists, and the same day a *Rhodesian* DC-6 lands at Kamina with a whole gang of new mercs, Rhodesians, South Africans, and all these new Six Cado hoods like those guys."

"Newly developing countries," a voice said dryly.

"Here's to the goddamn Third World," someone said. Glasses clinked.

"Yeah, it's funny," Spencer mused, "all these guys down here wanting to fight. They don't give a damn who they fight, as long as they get paid and there's plenty to drink. I still say that there's going to be a real bust-up here sometime when there aren't enough rebels left to go around and no more bank vaults to blow. Someday they're all going to get together and really mix it up, the ANC and those Katangan battalions and the Six Cado and the Five Cado. It'll be a real meat grinder when it happens. People sure like to kill each other down here."

"Ever see the way the Nungs and the Yards go at it with the ARVN?" someone asked.

Steve did not hear the answers. The wind was picking up off the lake. Lightning flashed soundlessly in the Tanzanian mountains. He shivered, very much alone in the night. Pressures were mounting dangerously in his head. He had to stop thinking.

In a rash of unaccountable panic Steve reached down to pick up the Army newspaper. "STRIKE," it read. "Swift Tactical Reaction in Every Known Environment." The lead article proclaimed the record number of troops carried in record time during the American intervention in the Dominican Republic. The bottom of the front page displayed a photograph of a parachutist in free fall. As he ripped open the paper, his glance fell on a column:

Focus on MEAFSA

The Congo . . . in Review

Editor's note: This is a continuing series of thumbnail sketches highlighting countries located in the U.S. Strike Command's overseas area of responsibility—the Middle East,

Southern Asia, and Africa South of the Sahara—commonly known as the MEAFSA area. These condensed country profiles are designed to give Strike Command personnel a broad factual overview that might be helpful should their service in the MEAFSA area be required.

He read down three paragraphs slowly, pronouncing each word to himself, trying to find some comfort in the dry military prose. The words were senseless.

He reread the last paragraph. He could find no meaning. On his feet, alone in the dark room, a sudden idea overcame him. He would ask Spencer for the use of the single side-band radio. There was always a duty clerk in the Embassy communications section. The clerk could contact Lisa at home and they could spend the night talking. He would tell her about the mission children and all the rest.

They would laugh at him—all of them would—call him a weakling and a crybaby. It did not matter. He wanted to hear Lisa's voice. Let them laugh with their Swift Tactical Reactions and murderers' files and their WEEKAs and MEAFSAs. He did not want any more of it. He was finished with it. They could write their surrender passes and host their shitty cocktail parties. He and Lisa were finished with them. He and Lisa were leaving it behind. There were better things to do with their lives. Life was so fragile, so short. It was New Year's again and the years were blurring past like a shuffling deck of cards. He did not want to grow old in hotel rooms with these hard-eyed men clinking their cynical whisky ice cubes between bombing raids and street battles. He did not want to be responsible for rubber bags and political surveys and surrender passes in the Middle East, Southern Asia, and Africa South of the Sahara. He did not wish to ride in airplanes with French killers and write wall newspapers about the glories of *La Nouvelle Armée Nationale Congolaise*. He never again wanted to see the bloody bandage on the leg of a rebel.

It's so simple, he thought, lacing up his desert boots. Dubois had said it so clearly. They can always run a bit, even when they're dead. *Ils peuvent toujours courir un peu, même quand ils sont morts.* We're all of us dead. We're all going to be down in some lake somewhere, sooner than we realize. Someplace out there in the future they were going to wrap him and Lisa in plastic and put them in the red ground. Why should he choose to fill the road between this room and that hole in the earth with clarification on a priority basis so that interests would not be compromised to the detriment of wider policy considerations? He had no policy. Lisa was his only consideration. He had come to Africa to help people, not to laugh at them and shoot them and to abet the treachery of their politicians. If this was diplomacy, then he did not want it. This was diplomacy. The Swift Tactical Reaction. This was the road they wanted to lead him down.

What did they sing over morning coffee and the *Courrier d'Afrique* in the frigid brightness of the Political Section, in their little club in Poly I? "They're rioting in Africa, tra-la-la-la." They could sing their songs and have their topless parties. He and Lisa were leaving that life. Fuck their airgrams and their immediate cables and their reception lines. Fuck the Credit Union. He and Lisa were going someplace quiet to live their lives with each other.

His head felt strange and light but very clear as he walked through Spencer's room to the terrace, noting on the way the huge operations map of the eastern Congo filling one wall and the radio gear and the African teakwood gun rack, bolted with a shiny padlock, containing two mean-looking automatic rifles and a gracefully long sporting gun. On the night table beside the bed was a picture of a fat red-haired woman surrounded by three fat red-haired children. The little girl wore teeth braces.

The men on the terrace looked at him oddly as he went silently to the card table and filled a glass with whisky, soda and ice. He drained it in three long swallows and filled it again.

"That's *spit* you're drinking, you know," the Special Forces major said with a mischievous smile.

"What? What did you say?" Steve said, his voice thick with annoyance.

The major stared back at him with a flat expression and the disappearing barroom grin still pinching his mouth.

"The major was just going to say that the soda there, they call it Spit," Charlie said nervously, pointing at the wooden case of soda bottles. "That's actually the name of it. They make it up in Bu-

jumbura. The CFL ships bring it down. Comes in about six fla-
vors, you know—cherry, lemon-lime, like that. They really call it
Spit—look at the bottle."

Steve swayed slightly as he gazed at the bottle. "Isn't that something?" the major asked. "I'm taking a couple bottles back with
me to the boys at Bragg." The officer's voice was warm, Southern,
and his nice-to-meetcha-fellow smile had returned. Steve glared at
him, taking in the well-tailored khakis and the smooth glow of
the toes of his jump boots. "Spit," Steve said. He attempted a
smile, but managed only a grimace. "Real hot-selling little number
down in the *cité,*" Spencer contributed. The obligatory round of
chuckling was abortive as the drinkers stood watching Steve.

"You feeling any better?" George White asked.

"Spit, is that anything like MEAFSA?" Steve asked the major.

"Beg pardon," the major answered. "Say again."

"It must stand for something," Steve recited. "S.P.I.T., the ini-
tials, anything like MEAFSA?"

"Don't follow you, I'm afraid."

"It doesn't matter."

Silently they all refilled their glasses. "Well," Spencer said, "last
one before chow. I can smell that barbecue from way up here."

"Finish telling us about the Montagnards, Major," George
White said in an effort to restore the previously jovial tone of the
conversation.

"Oh, yeah," the major said, "where was I? Right. Anyway, we
had a regular A-team operation right near the Cambodian border
where the Trail branches off all over the place. There were a
small bunch of Nungs for perimeter defense and the mortars and
two companies of Yards for the recon patrols. Pretty snug place,
really. NVA moving all around the camp, but they didn't bother
us much 'cause they didn't want to show their hand and bring
down the B-52s on top of them." Spencer grunted approval at the
mention of air power.

"So it was a pretty good place as those camps go," the major
continued. "To make a long story short, the ARVN moved in an
engineer company over in the next valley to repair an old French
airstrip, and while my Yards were off on a long patrol, some of
the Yard women and kids and old folks from our camp went on

over there to see if they could trade chickens with the ARVN and generally do a little scrounging. Those old Yards are the best sneak thieves in the world, and you *know* there isn't any love lost between them and the regular slopes. You think these black apes here got a tribal problem. Wow! Naturally the ARVN engineers steal all our Yards' chickens and trading goods and mess around with the women to boot. So, first thing when the companies get back from the patrol, the shit hits the fan and the old headman— Captain Bligh we used to call him—comes around and starts talking French to me. Always spoke French when he was pissed off at the lowland slopes. Says the boys in the company are going to borrow some mortar shells and one of the machine guns and go over and pay a little neighborly call on those ARVN engineers who messed up their women. Hell of a note. Couldn't have my Yards going over and wiping out a company of our loyal Vietnamese allies, even though half the ARVN company had already gone over the hill to the VC. Wouldn't do for good P.R., you know. Old Captain Bligh wouldn't be talked out of it, though. Those Yards are stubborn buggers about something like that. Finally landed on a compromise. He could select two platoons of his best boys and put on regular slope black pajamas and go over and take out a few ARVN people, providing he didn't dig up the airstrip too much and he didn't lose any weapons. Civilian Irregular Defense Groups fighting their own allies wouldn't do, I said, but who could control what the VC did?"

They laughed loudly at the major's contrite smirk. Steve laughed longer than the others.

"What happened?" Spencer asked.

"Well, funny thing," the major said, allowing the Southern military idiom in his voice to thicken. "That old ARVN company got pretty chopped up next night by a real mean old bunch of VC. Captain Bligh came back with a stringer full of ears and gold teeth and some pretty good power saws to pay for the ammo he used— just the kind of saws I'd been trying to get out of Nha Trang for a couple months. So everybody was happy, 'cept the ARVN who contributed the ears and teeth."

Everyone except Steve laughed. Charlie's grin was forced, obviously painful. Ice cubes were sloshed in the bottoms of glasses.

"Well," Spencer said, grinning, "it *has* been a long day. One more for the road won't hurt us, will it? Can't let all that good Spit go to waste."

"Ears?" Steve whispered toward the dark port. "Teeth?"

"Yeah," the major said. "Gotta remember to get a picture of me tomorrow drinking a bottle of that. You know, with the label showing an' all. New Year's hangover in Albertville, suckin' down a bottle of Spit."

"They should probably call it piss," Steve said without turning away from the terrace railing. "They could make up little candy bars and call them shit. Then you'd really have something to laugh at the coons about, wouldn't you? Go over great at Fort Bragg. You could put it right up there in the trophy case between the ears and the teeth. Ears and gold teeth and piss and shit. Swift Tactical Reaction in Every Known Environment. If the piss doesn't get the wogs the shit will. There's some more beauties for your goddamn trophy case up there in that lake at Goma. One of them even has a bandage on his leg. You could stick a bottle of spit in his mouth and hook a bottle onto his cock marked 'piss.' Just the thing for Fort Bragg."

The major squared his shoulders and stepped forward. "Just exactly what *is* your old problem, buddy-boy?" he said, squinting at Steve.

"It's not an old problem and I'm not your buddy, Major," Steve said.

"Don't they teach you kids anything about courtesy these days at the Foreign Service Institute?" George White said.

"Oh, yeah," Steve said, breaking into his laugh. "Plenty of courtesy and a lot of protocol and also proper drafting style. They don't teach us enough about Swift Tactical Reaction or rubber bags or prisoner counting, though." Steve laughed out at the circle of angry, embarrassed faces and the shaggy tops of the coconut palms along the deserted street.

"Why don't you come on back to your room and lie down a while, Steve," Charlie said. "I'll bring you up some dinner."

George White mumbled something to the major, and they both turned their backs on Steve and walked to the far end of the terrace. Spencer and Clayton lit cigarettes and stared at their glasses.

Steve allowed Charlie to turn him by the elbow. He felt his feet shuffling beneath him. They were leaving the terrace. He stiffened and broke away from Charlie.

"The only trouble is that I'm not crazy," he said, his voice surprisingly calm. "You wanted to know what my problem was, Major. Well, I'll tell you. You people just all bore the shit out of me. You're robots. You're all just robots. You don't have any human feeling left. You're neither good nor bad, you're machines. None of you gives the smallest damn in the world about people. They're just spics or niggers or slopes to you. They're something to fuck around with, something to laugh at and plan air strikes against and make up lies about in your horseshit reports. It doesn't matter where they send you. It'll always be the same, doesn't matter if it's Cuba or Laos or the Congo. You just follow orders. You're no more responsible for your actions than one of the major's power saws. That's *my* problem, old buddies. I can still feel something about these people we're fucking around with all over the world. I haven't turned into a robot yet."

George White walked up briskly from the end of the terrace and stood in the hexagon of yellow light falling from Spencer's room. White's crew cut was absolutely symmetrical, as if sculpted with a laser beam.

"Why don't you shut your whining mouth," White said. "If you think we bore you, Sherman, you ought to look in the mirror. This isn't some college kid freedom ride meeting, you know. This is the real world. You're just a punk and a snot-nosed loudmouth. I *know* you've got problems down in Léo, but they're not our problems. These guys have all risked their asses time and time again protecting kids like you. Why don't you just take your beatnik coffeehouse theories and go away. We don't want you here. You're lucky somebody hasn't pushed your teeth down your throat. If you think you've got any career left after all that shit in Léo and this little stunt you've pulled here tonight, you can forget it. You won't get a security clearance for a pay toilet in Red Square when I'm through with you. Just beat it while you're still in one piece."

The four officers gazed at Steve with easy, somnolent expressions of distaste.

"I beat you to it," Steve said. "I wouldn't stay in this business to save my soul from hell. I decided to get out a long time ago. I'm just glad to have had the chance to see for certain what you people are really like. You can keep it. You can take your murderers' files as long as your arm and your good Cubans and your bad Cubans and rubber bags and surrender passes and lump them all together and ram them up your collective robot ass, sideways."

Striding out through Spencer's room, he spit a long, stringing gob of phlegm at the little red pins stuck into the large map.

CHAPTER **29**

The stars were bright now, giving the foot-polished path a faint sheen as they walked between the walls of brush. Pierre followed several meters behind the corporal, who led the way to the old sorcerer's hut. They crossed open fields of manioc and detoured around dark banana groves. Dogs snarled at them and roosters crowed raucously, upset by their passage. Crickets and frogs sounded as they came down a grassy hill and followed the path through a stand of papyrus near the river. Then they climbed again, threading between thorn trees. Neither man spoke. Far away to the right, on a higher hill overlooking the Lukuga, were the lights of a Catholic mission school, but the reassuring street lamps of Albertville were hidden. On the crest of the hill ahead of them was a row of huts. The corporal stopped, touching Pierre with a twig.

"You must wait here," he whispered. "I will talk to the old man. I am sure he will help you, but first I must talk to him. I will need two thousand francs from the money I gave you. No, put it here on the path. I cannot touch you."

Pierre lay the bills on the smooth dirt. The corporal touched the four corners of each bill as he muttered between his teeth. Holding the money in his cupped hands, he walked into the village.

Pierre waited on the path. The damp was falling, and he wished he had worn another shirt. The beer can was still cold, chilling his leg through the cotton fabric of his fatigue trousers.

"Come," Corporal Ramazani called. "It's this way. We go to the left, past the other houses, in back of the cane hedge."

Unlike the large tin-roofed mud-and-wattle houses in the rest of the village, the old man's hut was small, with reed walls and a steeply sloping roof of palm thatch. It was isolated from the rest of the village by the cane break and the wall of a banana grove. The corporal still leading, they stooped low to enter. Pierre paused in the doorway, choked by the stench. At the far end of the small room the old man sat, half hidden in the shadows thrown by a smoky oil lamp fashioned from a dog's skull. All about him hung the implements of his profession: musty sacks with bones protruding, decomposing bits of animal entrails, and shiny uniform buttons caked with dried blood. At the foot of his low, three-legged stool a stillborn goat lay wrapped in a putrid fish skin. The old man glared at Pierre out of the shadows, pointing a green branch at a mat before his stool.

"Sit," the corporal whispered. "He tells you to sit before him."

The corporal squatted next to Pierre. Together they gazed up at the old man's face. He was toothless and deeply scarred, not in any recognizable tribal pattern, but with hideous, overlapping welts, as if he had been badly slashed or beaten years before. He wore a mantle of brown and gold monkey skins and a pair of threadbare European trousers. About the wrinkled folds of his neck hung a *dawa* necklace of shells and beads.

The sorcerer spoke softly in Swahili.

"He asks if you came to him of your own will or if you have been forced," Corporal Ramazani whispered, translating the old man's words.

"What shall I tell him?"

"I will tell him for you that you have heard of the old man's powers and that you have need of them, that you are in danger from the whites."

Corporal Ramazani spoke a long while, and the old man listened impassively. Then the old man answered.

"He wants you to tell him the story of your life. Start with your birth. Leave out nothing." The corporal paused, frowning. "But I think perhaps you had better not mention learning from the white priests how to cut babies out of women's bellies. The old man has suffered much from the whites. The white doctors near his village south of here killed his only daughter. She was sick and they put her on a table and killed her with shining knives. That was many years ago. He burned the house of one of the doctors, so they put him in prison and beat him. He escaped and the whites chased him for many years. Tell him everything, but do not say that you were learning from the whites in Léopoldville how to cut women."

Pierre smiled. This is ridiculous, he thought. If the corporal, who has himself been to mission schools, cannot understand about studying medicine, then how can this old *féticheur* help me? Still, I must try. Perhaps he really will change my luck.

Pierre began speaking slowly in French. After a while the corporal touched him with the twig and translated for the sorcerer. They fell into a regular pattern and slowly progressed through the story of Pierre's birth and childhood in Coquilhatville. As he spoke, the old man squinted at the flame of the oil lamp, puckering his toothless mouth in concentration.

"He wants to hear again about how you were cut out of your mother with a brother and about the special boxes that the white doctor made to put you in," the corporal said. As Pierre repeated the story, the old man rummaged behind him in the shadows, retrieving a gourd of liquid and a chipped enamel cup.

"You must drink this," Corporal Ramazani said. "It will help you remember things."

The liquid was deep brown, like coffee, and tasted bittersweet as Pierre swallowed. The old man carefully filled a gourd pipe with a finely chopped grassy substance and lit it from the oil lamp.

"Smoke," the corporal said. "This too is good for memory."

Pierre sucked at the mouth of the pipe. As he spoke the cloying stench of the hut dissipated. He was soon unaware of the corporal next to him on the mat. The only thing he saw was the face of the old man, clothed in the flickering lamp shadows. His tongue was thick as he spoke, but the words came rippling past his parched lips.

He paused again to listen while the corporal translated for him. The pipe was refilled and he smoked. The story came back to him.

He could see his mother bending low to change the gauze dressings on his back as he lay stinking with the boils and the fever. He saw again the crowded deck of the riverboat taking them to Léopoldville after his father's death. The kind young priest returned, and the inspector from the Sûreté who had blocked his entrance to the university. He went back to the crowded pen of the Central Commissariat and to the trial at which the white United Nations mechanic pointed across the courtroom to identify him. He smiled at the memory of his comfortable cell in Makala prison and the easy regularity of his job in the dispensary.

As the corporal translated, Pierre savored the memory of Christianne, and the baby, little Henri, the son he would never see again.

The pipe was filled again and Pierre told of the sham trial in the paracommando camp after Da Silva's betrayal. He explained the loss of all his savings and the humiliations to which the American airmen had subjected him on the trip from Léopoldville. Finally he told the old man of Major Nkutu's strange behavior and the indignities he had suffered from the white soldiers passing through the roadblock.

There was silence. Pierre's mouth was dry, but his head was ringing clear and bright as the lamp flame. Whatever the old man had given him to drink had surely helped him to remember. Perhaps there *had* been magic in the liquid. Corporal Ramazani was right. It was not only the white priests who possessed holy waters. It had been as if his entire life had been shown to him again. There were things he wished he had forgotten and things he was happy to remember.

The old man spoke again. "Show him the beer the white man tried to make you drink," the corporal translated.

Pierre placed the can of beer at the sorcerer's feet. With elaborate caution the old man examined the can. "How does it open?"

Pierre peeled back the aluminum opening tab, loosing a fine spray of beer foam. The old man hissed, kicking the can aside and shaking his green branch over it. He spoke excitedly as he dug again behind him to produce a brass cartridge filled with fine red powder. This he shook vigorously over the beer can, which lay gurgling in a puddle.

Pierre laughed. The stupid old man was actually afraid of a simple can of beer.

"Do not laugh!" Corporal Ramazani said. "Listen to what the old man says."

Pierre fell silent while the corporal translated. The old man touched the beer can lightly. "This is well-known *dawa,* used especially by the white soldiers. Often it takes the form of a smoke which chokes you and makes you cry like a woman. The old man has seen it used in Kindu and in the big prison when the Nations Unis soldiers came and the prisoners all ran away."

Pierre laughed again. "He's talking about a gas which the whites use. They call it tear gas because it makes you cry. It is not *dawa.* It's simply a gas they throw when there is trouble. I also saw the United Nations soldiers use it—once in Léopoldville when the people got excited and tried to take all the flour and milk powder the soldiers were giving out in Kinshasa Commune." Pierre laughed again. This old man was a stupid bush *féticheur* who knew nothing of the whites.

The old man spoke sharply. "He says that you do not believe him, that you laugh at his wisdom."

"He is wrong about this beer, that's all I know," Pierre said. His head felt very good. It was funny how the old man had shaken his *dawa* on a beer can.

Again the old man spoke in angry tones. The corporal disappeared and returned with a screeching rooster. "You must be shown the old man's wisdom if he is to help you."

The sorcerer took the rooster by the wings, avoiding the pecking beak. Savagely he seized the bird's head and neck and twisted until the rooster lay dead at the foot of his stool. Pierre and the corporal watched silently as the old man took another pouch of powders and shook them twice over the bird's body. Then he touched the bird with the branch and dropped more powder. With a clumsy flapping the rooster got to its feet and shook itself. Its bright eyes shone in the lamplight. The old man spoke to the bird softly. The rooster pecked at a singed moth flickering in the shadow near the lamp, then squawked and ran through the open door of the hut.

"Now will you listen to what the old man says?"

Pierre gravely nodded his head. This was nothing the priests could explain. This was real *dawa*. The lamp flame rose again so that Pierre could see the wisdom in the old man's face and eyes. He also saw the suffering. *All these long years it had been a spell.* How simple it all seemed now.

"Are you ready to listen to your story?"

Again Pierre nodded.

The old man began speaking, slowly at first, but with increasing speed until he fell into a rhythmic chant, punctuated by the slapping of his branch against his open hand. Pierre listened in fascination to the long story. The old man was not simply talking, he was re-enacting Pierre's life. He was speaking the words spoken long before by Pierre's father and the priests and doctors.

"Now you will hear the real story of your life, the truth that has been hidden from you since you were a baby." As he spoke, the corporal frequently reverted to Swahili to verify a point in the long narration with the sorcerer.

"The old man has seen the truth," the corporal said. "It is as I suspected. The whites have had a spell on you since you were a baby. He sees many things which I never guessed, however. Do you want to hear?"

"Of course, that is why I came here."

"The old man says that he will tell you what he sees only if you promise to follow his instructions. He will show you things that are secret and also powerful. If you learn these things and then tell them to the whites, this would be a great evil and dangerous for us all. Do you promise to obey him?"

"What will he ask me to do?"

"He will only tell you what you must do to break the spell which they have on you."

Pierre felt another smile forming on his lips, then he thought of the rooster's broken neck and the red trickle of blood dripping from the corner of its beak. The bird *had* been dead, yet the old man had brought it back to life. "I will obey him."

The corporal spoke and the old man waved his branch once again. "The sorcerer has listened carefully to your story and he is worried for you. You have been under the white men's spell since before you were born. This is clear to him. As you have told us, your father was always with the white priests and doctors. He spoke their language, even in his own house. The woman he married, your mother, was trained by the white sisters who are as evil as the priests. These things are sad to learn, certainly. It is sad to learn that your own mother and father were *wafumu,* working the evil *dawa* of the whites. This is obvious, however. Why else would your father leave his family and village to study with the whites and then take his wife far away from her village to live among strangers? He was taught the white man's *dawa* and did what they told him. For this he was given a special house just like the whites. For this he became rich. These things are true, aren't they?"

Pierre frowned. He wanted to speak, but the words were locked in his mouth. He could feel the upper half of his body slowly separating itself from his legs. The old man handed him a second cup of brown liquid and he drank in silence. The pipe was refilled. He smoked as the corporal continued the old man's explanation.

"Your father was a powerful *mufumu.* This is why he worked so closely with the white doctors and the priests. From them he learned how to make twins in your mother's belly. Everyone knows that twins are not normal, that they are the spirits of ancestors returned to earth inside human bodies. When your father made the twins he angered his white friends and they sent him away on the river so that they could cut you and your brother from the belly of your mother. They put you inside special boxes just like our little *dawa* huts. You they gave back to your parents, but they kept your brother inside the *dawa* box until he was completely white.

"The priests worked with your father to train you in their *dawa* in their churches and schools, but your spirit rebeled. This is why you were sick and have had so much trouble in your life. Inside your body there is a spirit which hates the whites and their evil *dawa.* They have tried to trick you and to kill you. They have put you in prison twice. But they are not strong enough to stop you. The old man says that only the twin who was born with you can do this. Today you have been touched by their *dawa* water. The old man says that the twin is here . . . close by. It is a *fête* for the whites. They have sent many new soldiers here. They have brought your white twin. If he can kill you tonight, it will be a great sacrifice for their new year."

Pierre's head floated slowly from his trunk. The solid flesh of his neck had dissolved in the oil flame. His face rose as a bubble in a viscous liquid and hung in the pool of light just before the old man's eyes. His brain was clear, but his body was gone, below him, silent and insensible. "What can I do?" he croaked.

The old man dug again in the shadows for pouches and bottles. He mixed a new liquid in the same chipped enamel cup.

"You must find your white twin, the evil one who has come to kill you. When you find him you must kill him. When he is dead you will cut out his heart and liver. You will eat one finger of the heart and one finger of the liver while they still are warm and bleeding. The rest you bring to the old man who will make a special *dawa* from them which you will also eat. Then you will become very rich and very strong. The woman and baby will be returned to you."

"How will I find my twin?"

"The old man is making a powerful *mai*. You will drink this and take an oath. Then the spirit inside of you will open its eyes and you will be able to see your twin. The *mai* will also protect your body from the white men's bullets."

Pierre drank the glutinous, bitter liquid. He placed his hands on the old man's chest. The flesh was chill and flaky beneath the monkey-skin robe. The words of the oath were strangely musical, a language he had never heard before, but which seemed to come naturally to his lips. This was the language of the spirit. This was the tongue spoken before the first white church was ever built in the Congo forest. The cup was refilled and he drank again. A cap of monkey skin was placed gently on his head. Pierre removed the gold watch that Da Silva had given him and laid it at the foot of the old man's stool. Monkey-skin bracelets were clamped onto his arms. He dropped the roll of thousand-franc notes next to the watch. The lamp flame turned blue like morning river water. The rooster stood in the middle of the mat and stretched its neck to crow. With surprising strength and dexterity the old man swung a long-bladed knife and decapitated the rooster. Blood squirted green into the lamp flame to rise in a reeking cloud of gray smoke. The headless rooster was thrown into the shadows.

The cup was filled with a mixture of the beer and hot rooster blood to which three powders were added. As Pierre drank, he saw that the old man's scars were countless twisting snakes, his necklace a colony of bright-eyed crabs, each with its pincers locked to the next in line, forming a living collar.

Pierre lay the pistol and holster at the foot of the stool.

"No," the corporal said. "This gun was taken from a dead white man. The old man says that you must use it to kill your white twin."

The holster was back on his hip, dangling toylike so far below him in the orange light. The old man dropped powders into the lamp flame and began a chant from deep within his chest. The rooster appeared out of the shadows, its eyes nervously bright in the light. Twice it pecked at the mat before Pierre's feet and then it crowed, breaking the rhythm of the old man's chant with snatches of Latin liturgy. Pierre answered as he had in church so long before. The old man spoke to the bird and it tucked its new head beneath its wing and slept.

"Do you see now with the eyes of the spirit?" the corporal asked.

"It begins."

"Then we must go."

Pierre bent low and the old man touched a greasy liquid to his forehead, tapping the monkey-skin cap with his branch. The corporal was very small in the doorway of the hut. Together they followed the rooster out into the darkness.

C H A P T E R **30**

"I feel like a pig," Randy said, reaching across the table for more oysters.

"Well," his wife answered, "you certainly *act* like one."

"No, really," Lisa said. "Go ahead. I can't eat any more, and I've saved back more than twenty for Steve. I'm sure he won't eat that many."

"Well, O.K.," Randy said. He put the last five oysters on his plate and doused them liberally with vinegar, adding pili-pili sauce from the cut-glass bottle in the middle of the table.

They sat by candlelight at the window end of the long Danish modern table. Frangipani and bougainvillaea lay in a loose centerpiece. The oysters were served on Moroccan earthenware plates. Randy took some more pumpernickel and refilled the champagne glasses from the ice bucket next to him. In the distance the bedroom air conditioner chugged with a sudden drop of current.

The breeze from the open terrace windows flared the candles as thunder rumbled. "We'll probably get drenched tonight," Emily said.

"You will," Lisa said, smiling. "Not me."

"You're sure you won't change your mind?" Randy asked. "I hate to think of you just sitting alone up here on New Year's Eve."

"I really had enough partying at Christmas," Lisa said. "As a matter of fact, this champagne is the first liquor I've had all week."

"Well, we had enough to last us awhile, too, Christmas night," Emily said soberly.

"Oh, hell, it's New Year's," Randy said. "Let's have another bottle of this duty-free champagne. We'll never have it so good anyplace else—better take advantage of it while we have it. This stuff costs ten bucks a bottle in the States."

"Should we have another if we're going to Larry's?" Emily said.

Randy stopped halfway to the kitchen. "Come on," he said. "It'll be 1966 in two hours and Lisa's barricaded herself in this apartment just because Steve got stuck in Albertville, so we've got to get her sloshed enough to come with us."

Lisa remembered the cold gin and the candles on Judy Pringle's terrace. "No," she said. "I really don't feel like going out without Steve tonight. Everyone's going to be drunk and in couples and I'd just be in the way. You go ahead now—you've stayed keeping me company too long. You're going to miss all the fun."

"One more bottle," Randy called, "then I can recite Shakespeare all the way up to Parc Hembise and Emily can't laugh at me. I was an English major, you know. Lot of good it does me writing press releases and wall newspapers."

"You're invited to Larry Mitchell's too, aren't you?" Emily asked Lisa.

"Yes, there and about fifty other places. How about you?"

"We turned down all the dinner invitations because it's more fun to party-hop—everybody's got a buffet anyway. As it is, we'd better make an appearance at Larry's and Sal and Betty's and our neighbor's down the road—you know, from the French Embassy."

Lisa nodded, finishing the champagne in her glass. The night had not cooled as expected. If they stayed, she would have to close the terrace windows and start the living room air conditioner.

"Do you know if the Hendersons will be at Larry's?" Lisa. asked.

"I really don't know," Emily said. "Why?"

"I wanted to ask Michelle about a dessert soufflé she made last month . . . I couldn't find it in the *Gourmet* cook book."

"Oh, she's not here. She's skiing someplace in Europe. Must be nice, huh? All that snow and ice."

"Voilà," Randy called, popping the champagne cork as he came through the kitchen doorway. As he filled the glasses, he began to sing "The Night They Invented Champagne."

"Oh, please!" Emily said. "Poetry I can take, but spare us your singing."

"Philistine!" Randy laughed. "Absolutely no appreciation of the aesthetic side of my nature."

Emily reached out to pinch the bulge of stomach beneath her husband's embroidered African dashiki. "I appreciate your grosser talents."

They were such a nice, uncomplicated couple, Lisa thought. We really should start seeing more of them. They were so much nicer than Robert's friends. Randy and Emily were happy with each other. They had beautiful children and scrupulously avoided the Embassy gossip circle. This was how she and Steve should be: relaxed and happy with each other, satisfied. She sighed.

"You're lonely," Emily said. "Don't worry, he'll be home tomorrow."

Lisa smiled, walking with her glass to the open terrace door. The thunderheads were putting on a spectacular display over the western hills. "I'm O.K., really," she said. "It's just that I know Steve'll be so disappointed. He was looking forward to the parties."

Randy's face was flushed as he bent to refill her glass. She saw him staring at her body. I certainly can't wear this dress if I go out alone to any parties, she thought. Do I really want to go out? They'll all be drunk and the men will slobber all over me and I'll have to keep pushing them away. It was fun on Sunday, but I was drunk and didn't really care. I'm getting drunk again, have to watch myself. This champagne is so good, though. If I go with Randy and Emily up to Binza, I'll have to get a ride home with someone and I'll probably end up having to beat off some drunken husband. It's better just to stay here.

"Did you make that dress *yourself,* Lisa?" Emily asked.

"Heavens, no. I ordered it from the French Boot Shop. I've got their catalogue here. Things come right away through the APO, and they're not at all expensive."

"Are they really wearing skirts that short?" Randy asked.

"Some of them are even shorter."

" 'Bout time those faggy fashion designers started thinking about what *men* like to see," Randy said.

"I'm afraid I'm a little old-fashioned," Emily said.

"I'd buy you a dozen dresses like that one if you'd wear them."

"I think it's better for a person who looks like Lisa to wear a dress like that."

"Thank you," Lisa said. "It came in the APO mail Wednesday. I was going to wear it as a surprise for Steve."

Randy glanced at his watch. "Jesus, we'd better get going, honey. There're going to be a lot of drunks on the road and I don't want to have to speed."

"Sure you won't come with us, Lisa?" Emily said.

"No, I'm fine. Happy New Year. Thanks for coming."

When they had gone, Lisa drained the last of the champagne into her glass. Unexpectedly the breeze was picking up, cooling the living room nicely. She put down her glass, walked unsteadily to the far end of the apartment, and opened the doors to the bedroom terrace so the soft air blew straight through the apartment. The last LP record on the stack clicked down to play, and *The Messiah* filled the candlelit room. It wasn't really so bad to be alone. Steve was alone, probably just a bunch of soldiers and mercenaries for company. I can perfectly well be happy sitting here in the breeze and listening to this nice music. The champagne was so delicious. Probably give me a headache in the morning, though. Have to remember to take some aspirin before I go to bed. She hummed with the chorus on the record. Lightning was lovely out there, orange and yellow. One more hour until the New Year. Have to make a resolution. That's silly, I suppose. Not really. Things like that can be important. O.K., what resolution then? That I'll be a good wife and maybe even a good mother. That would be something, wouldn't it? A baby. This is kind of fun, really. Waiting for Steve. Saving myself for him. I haven't even done it with my hand all week. I really shouldn't go out, not when I've had all this champagne and I'm feeling this way. I'll just get in trouble wearing this dress.

If I do go downstairs to a party, I'll really have to change my dress. That would be just begging for trouble—to show up at midnight alone wearing *this*. No, I'll stay home and drink a toast to the New Year and go to bed. Steve will be happy. I lost *four* pounds this week swimming so much. Hardly ate, either. It's such a bore to eat alone. It's going to be so pleasant now, playing tennis in the evenings and not drinking so much. Steve will understand about Robert. I'll just have to explain it the right way. Really, it didn't have anything to do with *him*. It was *me*. I was just curious, that's all. We got married too young. I know he'll understand.

Would *I* understand if he were doing the same thing? Of course. Really? Why, of course I would. Be honest, what if he were screwing some other woman, somebody interesting and rich who'd

been around and knew much more than I do? How would I feel if
he told me that? Well, he isn't. That's not the point. How would I
feel if he told me that? I don't know. But he isn't doing it. What if
he were? Why would he want to go with an older woman when
he's got me? So why did I want Robert?

Well, I've *got* to tell him. I've already decided that I'd tell him,
not about the others, Carlo and Paul. There's no sense in telling
Steve about them. But what about Robert? What if Steve just says,
"I'm leaving you. You're a whore and I'm through with you"? He
couldn't do that. Why couldn't he? Look at it, this is serious. This
is adultery. Stop it, we've been over this all before. He won't leave
me. We can't live without each other. We've always been married.
So what if I made a mistake? It's not that bad. There's not even
anything to forgive. It didn't concern him. It wasn't like I did
something against Steve himself. I did it because I wanted to try
it, just once, just one time before I get too old. All right, did I
enjoy it? Yes. Then why complicate things by telling him now? I
can always wait. Maybe in a few years when we have children and
we're far away from here I can just one day tell him that I was
with Robert. I don't have to go into details. That would hurt him.
I'll just say that once in the Congo I got drunk and slept with
Robert Henderson because Michelle was gone and we were both
lonely and it will be years in the past and it won't hurt him and he
won't call me a whore and maybe we'll even laugh about it.

So I'll stop worrying about him leaving me. He loves me. He's
lucky to have me. Drink the champagne and stop worrying. It's all
gone. Should I open another bottle? A small one. There are three
left. We'll have to eat the oysters tomorrow morning or they'll
spoil. I'd better save two bottles for tomorrow. It's so cheap when
you buy it by the case. I'll just open another little bottle and drink
what I can. There will still be two for tomorrow.

The wire's all rusty. I'll break a nail. No, be careful. I really
don't need any more. But I have to have a toast for New Year's.
Pop. Oh, catch it in the glass, stupid, it's flowing all over. There,
forty-five minutes. Have to drink slowly. I should have gone with
Randy and Emily. It's silly to sit up here alone on New Year's
Eve. What am I afraid of, anyway? I'm an adult. Just because I go
to a party doesn't mean I have to go to bed with every man there,

does it? Of course not. I should have gone with them. I could always have gotten a ride back downtown with some couple.

I can always go downstairs to Allison's. All the young kids will be there, the communicators and the secretaries. They're really better than the old fogies. At least they dance. Maybe I should just go down for a minute and drink a toast for the New Year and then come back up and sleep. Steve'll probably be in early tomorrow. I'll take the bird of paradise and another bottle of champagne. Nobody'll mind if I come late. I'll have one bottle of champagne and give Allison the centerpiece flower. That will be nice. Just one drink and then I'll come back upstairs. It's silly to feel so lonely with a party going on.

C H A P T E R **31**

Steve must have slept. His watch had stopped at ten. He must have slept because the arm he had curled beneath him was dead asleep with faint pins and needles just now beginning to tingle as he raised himself to a sitting position. There was someone sitting on the terrace of the hotel room. "Charlie?" he called.

"Yeah, I'm out here."

Charlie sat smoking on one of the canvas deck chairs on the terrace.

"What time is it, Charlie?"

"Almost midnight, I guess. Twenty-five to twelve. Almost 1966. You get something to eat?"

"I ate a couple cans of *C* rations before I went to sleep. How was dinner?"

"Too much, wow! Barbecued antelope and sweet potatoes and champagne. And ice cream. Can you believe that? Ice cream. Too much. This whole night has been too much. Last nights are really something else. What a meal. Just like my last night in Saigon. Hey, you want to smoke some of this? It's my third one and I really do believe I'd better not smoke all of it 'cause it's the new shit that Boniface gave me right before I left Stan. It's too much! I went to say good-bye to him and brought him some presents—you know, some old clothes I had and a flashlight and pots and pans and crap I had laying around my room there—and, man, was he ever happy, so he sends one of his sons back to his stash he keeps in his hut by the river and gives me this big bag of grass. Fantastic stuff. Very happy stuff. Light, it takes your brain up in the sky just like a bird. It's definitely superior stuff. Want some of this?"

Steve shook his head. "I'd better not."

"Well, look. I made up a whole pack of joints here. Same as Jerry used to make with Salems. All grass, no tobacco, but you still get that menthol taste. I'll put them there in the top of my duffel bag and you just help yourself if you want one, O.K.? Only I think you should definitely smoke one because you're probably still feeling down and this stuff is very happy and'll make you feel great. It's funny how some stuff is very visual, and some makes you hear music better, and some gets you sort of freaky. But this stuff is all happy. I been sitting out here laughing for a couple of hours."

Steve glanced cautiously at the terrace of Spencer's room. "Where are the others?"

"Oh, they're all still downstairs drinking up a storm and talking about the good old days in Korea and all that bullshit. Man! You really ought to try some of this stuff. I kid you not, it's the best I ever had."

"Were they very upset, you know, pissed off at me for spouting off the way I did?"

"I don't know, I guess so. Who cares? I'm getting out and you're getting out, so screw them. I was right in there with you, you know that, don't you? That was beautiful the way you put them down. I wish I could have helped you out some—you know, moral support. What could I do, though? They've still got me by the balls. I'm still in the fucking Army. About two weeks from now and I'd have really let them have it too. Stupid bastards. I had to keep my mouth shut, though. But that was beautiful, the way you did it." Charlie tipped the long ash from the end of his cigarette and smiled at the glowing ember. "Yeah, I guess they were pissed off, but Spencer sort of told them to cool it 'cause you were sick with malaria. Only I told them you weren't sick at all, just pissed off, and they didn't like that one bit. Spencer told me I was crazy 'cause he'd been all the hell over the tropics for years and he's seen a lot of guys who get that way when they've got malaria coming on. That way, you see, they wouldn't have to think about what you told them about being robots and zombies and all that, which was beautiful, but, man, they don't want to *hear* that kind of shit about themselves. That messes them up too much. Try one of these babies, once. It's the best goddamn grass in the world."

"Will it make me feel funny the way I did before? You know, scared of things like I was up there on the river at Stan?"

"No, no. Not freaky. This stuff is all different, and besides, we ain't been drinking the way we were last week. Here, take a couple of joints and stick them in your pocket. Smoke them now if you want or wait and smoke them with your wife tomorrow. This stuff really makes you want to screw, wow!" Charlie got unsteadily to his feet and stood smiling out at the night. "Listen," he said, "there's a Portuguese cat downstairs named Antonio, works for the CFL. Met him here in September. He's got a couple of mulatto girls in his apartment in back of the SEDEC store. Real clean girls, he says, almost white, from Angola. He asked me to come on up there with him. He can't really set up shop with the chicks 'cause he's afraid of a riot or something with all these mercs and WIGMO guys in town. Says these girls are semi-pros or something, but clean. You want to go up there with me and screw one?"

"No, I don't think so, Charlie. I think I'll stick around here until midnight and then just go to sleep."

"Well, listen. I think I'm going up there with him and screw one of those chicks. I'm really horny as hell and this stuff makes you want to screw. It's beautiful, you can screw for hours. Save one to smoke with your wife. It's great when you're fucking."

Steve cleared his throat, shaking off a vision of the Tutsi girl.

"Oh, Jesus," Charlie said, "I'm sorry. I mean, I don't have any right to talk that way about your wife. I'm sorry. I guess I'm pretty stoned."

"That's O.K., Charlie. You go ahead if you want to. I'm fine right here. I'll listen to the radio."

"Yeah, well, if you change your mind just come on over to the SEDEC building down the street there. The apartment's right in back. There'll be some kind of a light on."

"O.K., Charlie. Happy New Year."

"Yeah, happy New Year. Wow, am I stoned. Can hardly see the floor. Just like Saigon that night with Jerry, only much happier. Wow!"

Charlie stumbled out of the room, leaving the door open to the lighted hallway. Steve leaned against the terrace railing and watched the red and green channel lights at the mouth of the port. The streetlights stretched down between the coconut palms, illuminating the blank storefronts. Leaning out, he saw a Volkswagen bus stop before the lighted porch of the Palace Hotel and several obviously drunken WIGMO men unload wooden cases of beer. The breeze stopped abruptly and he heard the sound of dancing drums very clearly from the direction of the *cité.*

He yawned. So sleepy. Be a shame to sleep through the New Year, though. Wonder what Lisa's doing. Probably sitting at home lonely and disappointed. Maybe Randy and Emily came over to help her eat the oysters and have a glass of champagne. It didn't really matter. They could have their party tomorrow. It sure will be a new year, all right. A new year and a new life. Must be almost midnight.

He lit one of Charlie's cigarettes and coughed violently as he drew in the hot smoke. Menthol doesn't help all that much. Have to take smaller drags. It was easy after that. Short and even pulls, filling his lungs and counting to ten slowly in his head. The mission hospital and the prisoners and the scene on the terrace drifted back into the past. Why brood on those things? They just happened and they weren't my fault anyway. I was lucky to have seen them and learned from the experience before I was too old and trapped in this business. Don't think about past history. Think about tomorrow with Lisa and the future.

The cigarette head burned his fingers. He pinched it and watched the slow trajectory of the spark as he released the butt. The breeze off the lake was soft.

"Sherman, you awake?"

There was somebody tall standing in the lighted doorway.

"Out here. Who is it?"

George White walked out to the terrace and stood facing him. His crew cut looked even more clipped and angular as he stood silhouetted against the hall light. He looked like a priest. Why did he look like a priest?

"I was wondering how you were. May I sit down?"

"Please," Steve stuttered. "I mean, sure, go ahead. Want a drink?"

"No, thanks, I just came to see how you were. I was on my way to bed."

"Is it midnight yet?"

"In ten minutes. I didn't feel like staying for the toasts. I decided to go to bed, and I saw your door open."

He paused and watched Steve's face. I must look pretty silly if I look the way I feel inside my head, Steve thought.

"Look, Sherman. What I want to say is that maybe I spoke a little rashly earlier. I realize that you're very upset, and I guess I would be too in your position. I don't think you really meant all that. I talked it over with the major and Spencer, and they're willing to forget about the whole thing if you apologize to them in the morning. I spoke too quickly as well, I guess, when I talked about you ruining your career. We all realize that you're upset and we want to help you."

Steve let the words echo through his brain. They were as hollow as the paragraphs in the *Strike Command* newspaper.

"Apologize?"

"Yes. You know, nothing formal. Just shake hands all around and we'll all forget that it happened. You've got enough problems and we don't want to add to them."

Steve laughed. That's why White looked like a priest. Of course. They all spoke the same bullshit. They were all missionaries, even the Green Beret, even Major Nkutu and the flight engineer.

"I don't want to shake hands with you people," he heard his voice say. "I meant what I said and I'll say it again. Please just go away, because I was enjoying myself here until you came."

"I can understand your bitterness, but why single us out for your insults? Hell, you don't even know any of us."

"Nobody knows you people. That's the problem, that's what I was talking about. You don't have any souls left. You're all robots. You're not even immoral because if you were you'd have to be individuals. Real people. My problem is that I'm moral and can still feel guilt and remorse for the things we do. No, I don't want to shake hands with you."

"You seem to have a rather strange definition of morality."

"Well, that's just the way it is. I've got mine and you've got yours, only I think yours stinks like shit. All you people going around the world writing surrender passes and bombing the hell out of people and stuff like that. It's O.K. as long as you say they're Communists. Those poor bastards up there in that lake weren't Communists. Why the hell do *we* always have to decide who gets bombed and who gets the milk powder? No, don't interrupt. Don't try to tell me about milk powder. I'm an expert on that. I had a long lesson on that one. I know we carry milk and wheat and rice all the hell over the world for those poor people and we feed them and take a picture and stick it on a wall newspaper, I know all about that one too. Well, we carry a hell of a lot more armored cars to keep guys like Dubois in business than we do milk, I can tell you that. And then we even bullshit ourselves, writing our stupid reports, telling the Department whatever they want to hear. That's the secret of this business, isn't it? Figure out what they want to hear and then tell them. If they want to hear Tshombe's a rebel and a traitor, then we tell them that. If they want to hear that Tshombe's the savior of his country, out pops an immediate telegram . . . 'Tshombe proclaimed savior of country. Keep C-130s coming.' . . . I'm not saying this shit doesn't have to be done. It's not a question of that, I guess. I know somebody's got to do it—if the Russians and the Chinese and the good Cubans and the bad Cubans are doing it, then *we* have to do it too. All I'm saying is that I don't want to be part of it. I don't want to turn into a zombie like all of you. I know all the arguments about war being a dirty business and there have to be civilians involved to control the thing, so we all shouldn't just pack up and leave and let the military creeps run everything. I've heard that one too. The fact is, though, that we're no better than the major there with his ears and teeth. We should know better. Well, I don't want it any more. My wife's a teacher and we're going back to America and teach people. We're not going to make a lot of money and have commissaries and houseboys and diplomatic passports, but we'll still have something left inside, which is more than I can say for all of you."

George White sat with his teeth clenched and his hands set squarely on his knees.

"You finished now?"

Steve was trembling with anger and excitement. It was so unreal to say these things after smoking grass. He slid down the railing to the end of the terrace, turning away, lit the second cigarette. The breeze carried the pungent smoke off over the terrace of Spencer's room. He sucked hard on the minty filter. "Yeah, I'm finished," he called back to White.

"I don't have the faintest idea what you're babbling about— surrender passes and milk—all I can say, Sherman, is that I wish you luck, because with the problems you've already got at home and that attitude of yours you can sure use some. Maybe you ought to go out to Berkeley. Your politics and your so-called morals would fit in pretty well out there just now. Maybe your wife *could* do some teaching. You could teach political science to all those goddamn beatniks and she could teach physical education. She could give those kids a real good education, all right."

"What the fuck are you talking about?"

"You don't have to try and play stupid now, Sherman. You're the one who brought up all this morality crap. I really felt sorry for you at first, but now I couldn't care less. You certainly don't give a person much of a chance to help you. All that half-baked morality might go over really big with your Peace Corps pals, but just don't try to hand it out to us. Not with your wife back there fucking half of Léopoldville."

The hemp was finely chopped and had been loosely packed in the tube of cigarette paper. Steve inserted the filter between his lips as White spoke. He sucked the smoke in a thin stream directly into his lungs as White's words ricocheted inside his brain. He felt amazingly calm. His brain was working very well. The parties. Of course, he's talking about those stupid pool parties where the girls took off their tops. Fucking CIA's got nothing better to do than spy on a bunch of bored European business creeps getting drunk up in Parc Hembise. He thought it was a real orgy. Let him believe what he wanted, probably gave him some kind of a cheap thrill, probably wished he and that flat-chested wife of his would get invited to a party like that themselves. Typical reaction, people are naked so it had to be an orgy. Probably queers deep down inside anyway. Always talking about guns and fighting and all that he-man shit. They can't understand anything outside of their own little compartment in life. Why stand around here arguing with this guy, listening to his slanderous bullshit?

"You don't know what you're talking about, White," Steve said. He drew the last drag on the cigarette and tossed it over the railing. "That doesn't stop you from shooting off your mouth, though. That's the trouble with you people, you've always got to talk about things you don't understand. Everybody's always got to have an opinion. Can't be caught at a committee meeting without your opinion. That wouldn't do, no, siree, might look bad for your efficiency report. Everything's got to be spelled out in black and white. Rebels get Communist weapons so the rebels are Communists. People get drunk at a party and so the women are all whores. Same stupid robot thinking."

White got to his feet and placed his hands on his hips. "You poor son of a bitch," he said. "It just dawned on me that you really *don't* know what's going on in Léo." He turned to leave. The hall light polarized through the fringe of his razor-sharp haircut. It was incredible: each hair *was* exactly the same length. Must take hours for the bastard to get it cut that way. Like machining a block of steel, no tolerance, plus or minus .000000000000001 millimeters. Look at the ring, too. West Point? The Air Force Academy. What's the difference? Good-bye, Mr. Machine Head White of Poly II.

Steve and White laughed out loud in unison. White shook his head. He was in the hall doorway.

"Tell Henderson that he could sell some of those Polaroid pictures of Lisa that he keeps there next to his bed, with her dancing panties, to the few guys from the oil lift who haven't fucked her yet. But he'd better hurry up if he wants to find any customers."

Steve leaned forward at a strange angle to the floor. White was transfixed in the lighted doorway just as Charlie had been silhouetted against the river sunset. He was speaking the Truth. He had become the *Commentator*. White hung there in the light.

"She really ought to get some color film and start turning out postcards for the boys. You know, 'a souvenir of your stay in the Congo'—that kind of thing. I'm sure Henderson would be glad to help her out. God knows she's done a lot of little special *favors* for him. You wouldn't think looking àt her that she knew so many tricks. Takes some girls years and years to learn that kind of thing. Of course, most girls aren't as *morally* equipped as your wife. You're a real lucky guy, Sherman. One thing she goofed up on, though—I'm sure she'd want to correct it. Next time she's doing that little rock-'n'-roll dance for Henderson in front of your bedroom mirror, tell her to turn down the volume just a bit because it raises hell with our microphones, especially on the base notes."

Steve suddenly remembered the frequent visits of the "incompetent" Embassy electrician. Out in the dark port a boat whistle honked loudly, rising in pitch to a steady, insane screech. Two locomotive whistles followed it. A cherry-red star shell popped above the mercenary billets toward the *cité*. Several car horns joined the salute. A yellow parachute flare glided magically up to burst above the Palace Hotel. Then a green and another red star shell floated up from the mercenaries.

"Happy New Year," White said. "Let me be the first to wish you a happy and peaceful and *moral* New Year, Mr. Sherman."

"Lisa and Henderson?" Steve said weakly.

"And Lisa and a pilot from the oil lift. Maybe there're more. I left Léo on Tuesday, so who knows where the count's at now? We've been keeping close tabs on Henderson since September. That's how we found out. I suppose you'd say it's *immoral* to bug your apartment, but that's where Henderson spends a lot of his time, and as you also say so eloquently we're just robots and not capable of making moral decisions. Do you mean to tell me that she and Henderson have been fucking like that right under your nose for almost three months and you didn't even begin to guess?"

"Lisa and Robert Henderson?"

"You wanted to hear it. You kept harping on that morality bit. Don't blame me. You practically forced it out of me."

Downstairs they were singing "Auld Lang Syne." The flares from the mercenary and WIGMO billets glided up in a regular stream, red and yellow and blue. Steve sank to his heels beneath the terrace railing.

"Don't worry," White said, his voice softening slightly. "There are only two people in my section who know about it. We didn't even tell the security officer or the Ambassador. As far as we can make out there's no security problem. We had to keep tabs on Henderson—he's involved in a lot of things. But he's straight with *her* at least. The oil-lift boys are not our problem. They seem to be fucking half the women in Léo anyway, married or single." He turned finally out into the hallway. "Don't blame me for telling you. You're the one who asked for it."

CHAPTER **32**

This rum and coke was a stupid idea, Lisa thought—too sweet on top of champagne. Why couldn't they just have given me a straight coke? Had to try to get me drunk. Didn't have to try hard. I should stick my finger down my throat and be sick and go to sleep. This is ridiculous, a charade. To take along my drink so it looks like I'm coming back down to the party, and him with that silly plastic ice chest as if we're just going upstairs for ice cubes. These elevators are impossible.

"Push the button, the light's gone out. It's empty now."

He's actually not bad looking and certainly better behaved than he was on Sunday, not so much the big-deal pilot. He was a real jerk at Judy Pringle's party, sticking his thumb under my dress and breathing whisky breath in my ear. What should I do? I'm drunk again, damn it. Look, there's still time. Just tell him that you're sorry, but you don't feel so well and why doesn't he go to somebody else's apartment for ice? That's the truth. I certainly don't feel very good. Oh, damn, here's the elevator.

I really shouldn't have had all that champagne. Ugh! Somebody
threw up in the elevator. The least they could have done was clean
it up. 1966. What a dumb party. She shouldn't have tried to make
it so Hawaiian, all those vines and flowers hanging everywhere.
Couldn't even dance with those palm fronds scratching my legs.
He's not as drunk as Sunday, not mean like he was at Judy Pringle's.

O.K. Now what do I do? Should I ask him to come in or should
I just have him wait out here while I get the bag of ice from the
freezer? What do I want to do? He was such a boor on Sunday,
but he's nice enough tonight. That's because he's not as drunk.
Still, he's a little drunk, look at the way he's staring at me. Well, I
shouldn't have worn this dress. It was for Steve.

Do I want it now? I feel like I'm going to be sick any second
from this stupid drink. Look, do I want to sleep with him?

No, not really, just go in and give him the bag of ice cubes and
say good night. Stick your finger down your throat and go to sleep.
It's after one, I've got to be up early because Steve's coming
home.

"Hold the elevator, Greg. If we lose it again we won't get it
back for hours, not with all these parties in the building."

"That's O.K. with me."

"No, really, just keep your foot in the door and hold it open.
I'll get the bag of ice."

The freezer light's out again. I called the Embassy twice about
that. They're just impossible. Can't blame them, really, always
having to chase up to all the COMISH houses to unclog the toilet
some snotty little kid has stuffed full of lawn cushions. We're all
like children here, sucking on the Embassy for everything. Steve
was right about that, it's like living in a diving bell. Where did
François put those ice cubes? There were three big bags of them.
My hand's freezing. Oh, damn, I really did break a nail this time.

"Oh, Greg. You let the elevator go. . . . Stop it, you'll rip my
dress. . . . No, wait, close the door."

Don't be a fool, just tell him to leave. You got rid of Robert.
Just don't give in, be cold, don't press against him. Stand still,
perfectly cold. He won't try to force me.

"You're hurting me."

"Let's go to the bedroom, Lisa."

"No, really, Greg, I think you'd better go back to the party."

"Come on."

"You'll rip my dress, it's new, stop acting like an animal."

"Come on to the bedroom."

"Wait. Let me lock the door."

It doesn't matter. He's drunk. What's the difference. It's better than being alone. He's so cruel, though. Could I like that?

"No, don't turn on the light. I feel a little sick. All right, just leave the door open and the hall light on. . . . Wait! You'll rip my dress!"

CHAPTER **33**

George White was gone and the door was closed. The only light on the terrace came from the reflected street lamps and the tinsel illumination of the flares. No, no. Not Lisa and Henderson. That was not true. Oh, a red one under a little parachute. And now she's with Robert Henderson. . . . No. Ah, two green ones together. What a fantastic color, like a Christmas tree bulb. No, she wouldn't just lie down there in *our* bed and let him lick her body and put her head like that down between his legs. No. It can't be true. But what about that time I came home early to change for a cocktail at the DCM's and Lisa was there in the bedroom with the records all stacked on the player and she was so sexy and did that dance and I pulled her down and was just going to put it in her and she pulled away and went into the shower? She said she was too hot, but she was really still all wet inside her from him. No. And then she came out from the shower and licked me with her tongue, tickling me all down inside my legs which she had never done before to *me*. No. *He* taught her to do that. No. What did he say about guys from the oil lift? No. Maybe with Henderson. Think, use your head. Be calm inside like before and think about it. No. Not with Robert Henderson. It could happen. Think about it. Look at that red one. It's falling on the palm trees there. What's that? It's tracers. Look.

The mercenaries are shooting their guns in the air. How pretty they are, red and orange. Tracer, just like in the John Wayne movies.

It could have happened. She was alone so much and stuck up there in the apartment all day with only those Embassy wives' teas that were really not teas at all. They should call them Embassy wives' whiskies or gins, but they certainly weren't teas. And she's become so sexy down here. Why shouldn't she give in? She's just human. Yellow now. The WIGMO boys are still on flares. The mercs have beat them. They've got real tracers and the WIGMO boys are still fucking around with flares. But all those times I'd call and she wouldn't be there and then later she'd say she was at the pool. She was at Robert Henderson's posing for Polaroid pictures. No. Oh, the WIGMO boys have got tracers now, too.

This is a nice hotel, but the stairway is slippery. And hot. That smells good. The antelope. Stay away from the dining room. They're still in there. Look at Spencer. He's drunk. They're drinking brandy. Look at the cigars. Big fucking deal.

They're looking. The major will come out here. I don't want to talk to him about ears and teeth and powdered milk. I'll go for a drive, that's the best thing. I'll borrow Spencer's Land Rover and go for a drive.

No keys in it.

More flares now. That's a big one from the mercs. It's cooler out here. SEDEC. That's where Charlie is. I'd better talk to Charlie about it. What a crummy store window. Nothing in it; just sardines and soap powder. Jesus, I'm still all dirty. My hair's full of dust. Should have taken a shower and shaved. Feel all grubby. Henderson always looks so smooth with his tropical white shirts and after-shave lotion. I should have washed these cuts on my hands. They'll get all infected. Oh, I'd better go talk to Charlie. He's been in a war and he'll understand. POP-POP-POP, popopopopopop. That must be a burp gun, the little one. Jesus, they're really shooting now. What a dumb thing to do. Just like jagging off, shooting all those guns in the air.

Why would she do it? Does she hate me? No, she *loves* me. Then how could she do it? No, she couldn't have done it. She did it. That's too loud. I can't think with them shooting their stupid jag-off guns in the air. Listen, they're cheering like at a football game. Just like little kids. Of course, it's a contest between the mercs and WIGMO. Who's going to shoot the most. What a stupid game. Bastard White with his microphone. Lisa probably had a party with some of the kids from the building and played a lot of music and Lisa made a pizza and everybody danced. That's what they heard with his microphone. How could they do that, put a microphone in my bedroom?

Look, two tracers hit each other. *That's* what they're trying to do, make their tracers hit the mercs' tracers. Like flashlight tag at camp. Stupid, too noisy, can't think. The flares are nicer, pretty green. Henderson and Lisa. She did it and she still loves you.

Bored. That's why. She was just bored. What the hell kind of life does she have down here, anyway? Yes, but she actually sucked his *cock*. She's going to do it again tonight. Think about *that*. Yes, but it's just with their bodies. So what? We eat and shit and vomit and come and it's only our *bodies,* it's not us, not really us as people. It's just our bodies.

A person isn't just his body. . . . That's what they teach you at church, isn't it? That's why they have body bags, right? No. Don't start in on *that* now. What was I trying to remember? . . . Can't think with this stupid grass in my head. My head's my body too, isn't it? Yeah, so that's wrong, she did it with her head, too. It wasn't just her body. Think about that once. She did it on purpose.

Like I did with the Tutsi girl. No! Christ, that's too loud in there. Why can't they stop that noise? No, it was an accident with the Tutsi girl. That was just a misunderstanding, Dubois was trying to be nice to me by sending the girl with the towel. The girl couldn't help it. She's a refugee, Dubois said so. So I just *had* to fuck her, right? Yeah, but it *was* just bodies, I don't even know her name, I couldn't even talk to her. I sure could screw her, though, couldn't I? I *came* the same as Henderson comes inside Lisa.

"Stop this shit! It's only bodies. It doesn't matter. Ask Charlie, he knows."

Jesus, I shouldn't have smoked two of them. They're too strong.

Can't think. What was I saying? Oh, yeah, so it's only bodies. She loves you. I wish they'd stop that noise.

Screw it. Go and see. Don't try to think about it now. I wish I could vomit this shit out of my brain so I could go someplace quiet and think. You can't vomit it up and get sober like whisky. I wish you could vomit with your *brain.* Go in there. Look, they're all inside the courtyard shooting again. So loud. There's really *fire* shooting out of those guns. They never show that in the movies, do they? The fire. They don't have the noise either the way it hurts your head, or the fire like when Charlie scared away the ANC, or the puddles of gut shit and the real blood, and nobody screams. And they don't show the green bags either, do they? And they don't show the little girls whose legs you can practically see through. And they could never get that yellow fuzz with techni-color. They couldn't show that on their television screens. They couldn't show Henderson and Lisa either, could they? Oh, Christ! Hang on to it. It's all slipping inside. Why can't I just puke this stuff out of my brain? It's too damn loud. Don't go in there. It's too loud. Where can I go? See Charlie about it. He'll fix you up. He's had this before and he can help me with it.

Here come Spencer and the major. They're drunk, look at the way they run with their elbows up like that. Stupid shits, double time. Everything they do is by the numbers; can't even run like real people, just a couple zombies. Don't talk to them. They're just robots.

Steve followed the two officers in through the bottle-strewn bar-room of the Palace Hotel and out onto the edge of the courtyard. The WIGMO pilots and ground crew stood about with their weap-ons and liquor bottles, taking turns in the center of the court. A little Cuban was kneeling there, the butt of his captured Chinese automatic rifle braced against his thigh as he loosed a ragged burst of tracers up into the sky. Inside the enclosed court the pounding of the weapon was deafening. The air burned with powder stench. Brass shell casings tinkled underfoot. The men were dressed in a hodgepodge of uniforms and civilian clothes ranging from a gan-gling Swede barefoot in dirty tennis shorts and singlet to one of the Cubans who wore a flashy sports coat and tie. They all carried guns. On the flimsy metal tables at the sides of the courtyard spent magazines and cartons of ammunition were piled. Men were drinking vodka and whisky straight from the bottle.

The Cuban's long burst was over. Steve tried to yawn in an effort to clear his ears. The Cuban accepted a bottle of bourbon. In the square of night sky above the courtyard a pencil line of orange tracers arched up from the mercenary billet. One of the English mechanics stepped unsteadily forward to answer the challenge.

"Hold it!" Spencer yelled, pushing through the crowd. It was too late. The Englishman flipped off the safety of his FAL and sent a shocking burst of red tracers up into the darkness. Spencer flinched away from the muzzle. Steve saw a man in Levis and a short-sleeved bush jacket toss something down from the second-floor balcony which ran the length of the courtyard. With a whoosh and a faint hissing audible between bursts from the FAL, the courtyard was filled with choking clouds of pink smoke. It rose in gaudy billows, like balls of cotton candy until it was impossible to see across the court. The men cheered and sucked at their bottles. The fiery muzzle back flashes lit up the pink fog like extraterrestial lightning. Men were laughing and choking. Someone with a Very pistol joined the Englishman and began arching yellow star shells up through the smoke from the grenade. Spencer yelled again but was ignored. Suddenly there were three lines of tracers coiled about themselves magically in the darkness above the pink atmosphere. People jostled each other to join the final salute. The noise was impossible. Steve drew back to the stucco wall beneath the balcony and forced the heels of his hands tightly against his ears. It was too loud.

The big Swede stumbled down the balcony stairs next to Steve, carrying another grenade cupped in a huge red hand. He swayed forward toward the center of the court to stand just at the edge of the firing with a slack-jawed drunken grin on his face. A mechanic lurched forward to pull him back to the edge, but the Swede jerked out of his grasp. Holding the grenade with his long arms extended before him, he delicately plucked out the pin, flicking it away into the smoke like a cigarette butt. Holding down the fuse handle, he swayed again, waiting for the firing to abate before releasing the second grenade. The men around Steve screamed with an orgiastic frenzy as the tracers Roman-candled and the casings clattered on the cement floor. Again, the Swede strode forward on beanpole legs, the grenade thrust out in front of him. Then, like a terrier dashing in to snap at a larger dog, a Cuban ran through the smoke in a crouch to seize the mechanic with both arms about his chest. The Swede tried to free himself. The firing ended with one uneven burst. The Swede pushed, laughing at the Cuban. "Frag! Frag!" the Cuban screamed, pointing at the grenade. "Not smoke, it's a frag."

The Swede gazed wall-eyed drunk down at the Cuban and then slowly shifted his eyes to the grenade. He frowned, pursing his lips.

"Bent, for Christ's sake," an English voice boomed out of the smoke, "that's a fragmentation grenade. Put it up, man. It's not smoke."

The mechanic stood swaying with his arm still thrust out before him. The smoke was clearing slightly and the men who had a moment before been screaming and firing were now either frozen into paralytic fascination or scurrying for cover at the far end of the courtyard.

"Put the pin in, Bent," the Cuban said, still grasping the mechanic by his torn undershirt.

"Pin?"

"Where's the pin? Put the pin back in."

The Swede's frown deepened. "Pin?" he repeated. He had the smooth-skinned grenade firmly clutched in his traplike hand. Spencer stumbled out of the smoke and took the mechanic's free hand.

"Come outside with it, Bent," he said. "We'll take it outside where it can't hurt anyone."

Escorted by Spencer on one side and the Cuban on the other, the Swede passed by Steve through the swirling pink smoke, holding the grenade straight out before him like some ancient ikon. They walked gingerly out through the smoke-filled corridor to the barroom, followed by the others who fell silently into a procession behind them.

On the broken sidewalk in front of the hotel entrance the Swede stopped to gaze vaguely across the street. Spencer's face was pouring sweat; his eyes bugged out in the effort required to think soberly. "We'll put it in the ditch over there," he said, pointing. "There's two, three feet of water. Come on, we'll put it in the water."

The mechanic, still guided by Spencer and the Cuban, struck out toward the opposite ditch across the hump of the laterite road. The doorway of the hotel was crowded with faces as the men pushed to watch the spectacle. Pink smoke snaked out in bright wisps between their legs.

As they reached the center of the road, they were illuminated by the headlights of a vehicle bearing down on them from the right. A battered green-and-white jeep with five black MPs in it swerved to miss them and skidded to a halt crossways in the road directly before the hotel. The firing from the mercenary billet behind them rose suddenly with a cloud of red and green tracers and then abruptly stopped. The strange trio on the road continued on their way in silence, the Congolese MPs turning in their seats to watch them. When Spencer had led the Swede fifty yards up the road he stopped; then, gingerly tugging the man's free hand, he indicated the water-filled ditch and backed away. He and the Cuban dashed back toward the hotel, turning after thirty yards to watch the mechanic. They all heard the splash as he dropped the grenade into the water. The tall man in shorts walked slowly back toward them with the same vacant grin on his face. "Down!" Spencer screamed. "Get down!" As if genuflecting, the Swede lowered himself to the muddy road just as the grenade exploded with a slapping, watery bang that rattled the hotel windows and sent a white geyser spouting up to the tops of the coconut palms.

The echo of the blast bounced back from the hills above the town. On a curt order from their sergeant, the MPs jumped from the jeep with their rifles and took cover behind the vehicle, facing the crowd on the porch of the hotel. The men pushed out of the smoky barroom now to stand in the cooler air of the porch, their weapons slung across their backs and cradled in their arms. The MP sergeant yelled something in Swahili, pointing his club at the porch as his men leveled their weapons.

"Wait," Spencer yelled, running up to the jeep. "There's no

danger, Lieutenant. It's all over. He thought it was smoke. It was an accident, that's all." His French was slurred by the liquor he had consumed over the long evening.

The sergeant's eyes were reptile-flat as he stared back at Spencer. The MPs crouched lower behind the jeep. "My men have just drunk too much, that's all. It's a *fête*. Soldiers always drink too much on a *fête*, you know." Spencer forced a grin onto his flushed face. "They were just having fun. They'll stop now. I wasn't here before. They got too excited, but now they'll stop and go to bed. There's no danger, really."

The sergeant was silent.

"Get me a bottle of Scotch and some cigarettes," Spencer called over his shoulder in English. Several fresh packs of Winstons and an unopened bottle of Johnnie Walker were passed out from the barroom.

"Here, Lieutenant," Spencer said, laying the goods on the hood of the jeep. "It's a *fête*. Soldiers should always share with their comrades, *n'est-ce pas?* There's no danger now. My men are putting away their guns and going to bed."

He faced the porch. "Get those fucking weapons out of sight and stay inside, all of you. Don't point them this way. Just move inside, slowly."

The sergeant reached warily across the hood to take the cigarettes and bottle. His men still had their weapons pointed at the porch, which was slowly being cleared of onlookers. "Here," Spencer said, reaching very carefully into his hip pocket and removing several thousand-franc notes. "You must be going off duty soon. Why don't you take your men down to the *cité* and buy them a drink?"

The sergeant's eyes brightened at the sight of the money and his soldiers relaxed, standing upright to watch the transaction.

"*Merci, monsieur,*" the sergeant said.

"Think nothing of it, Lieutenant. We like to help our friends. *Bonne fête.*"

"*Bonne fête, monsieur. Merci.*"

As the sergeant started the jeep's engine, a doomsday crack whiplashed from the direction of the mercenary billet, followed instantly by a high-pitched screech as a bazooka rocket ripped past over the hotel toward the lakefront. Still on the porch, Steve watched the sparking trajectory of the missile falling across the road. It was a long, well-aimed shot that would have surely landed in the lake had it not been deflected by the crown of a palm in the railyard. The rocket, a white phosphorus round, exploded in a dazzling pinwheel of white smoking fire, spiraling out in all directions. Blazing flakes of phosphorous fell hissing into the ditches. One landed on the canvas top of the jeep. An MP dropped his weapon and ran off into the darkness. The sergeant managed to start the jeep after twice stalling it. He drove off wildly to the left, leaving behind a brilliant trail of orange sparks from the burning canvas roof. In the railyard grass fires had started and were burning brightly in the fresh breeze off Lake Tanganyika.

"Jesus!" Spencer said, sagging visibly. "Now we're in for it. Everybody get inside." As he spoke, the row of streetlights blazed up unnaturally and then faded inexorably to complete darkness. A single red flare popped above the town.

In the hotel barroom the scene was frantic; men milled about in the darkness, laughing and calling each other in a babel of languages. Flashlights cast pink beams in the smoke, bottles smashed, and weapons clattered to the floor. Spencer banged the heavy metal-and-glass door shut and bolted it. "Get some fucking lanterns down here," he yelled from a table top. Two gasoline lanterns were lit, casting garish shadows in the smoke. A Congolese cha-cha record roared out from the portable behind the bar. "Stop that fucking noise!" Spencer screamed. The speaker was silent. His face looked even more strained in the light of the lanterns. "Listen to me, goddamn it!" he yelled. "You stupid shitheads have really done it now. Put down those fucking weapons and listen to me." Slowly the laughter and raucous drinking noises subsided. Spencer wiped his hand across his red face in an effort to clear his head. He swayed on his perch. "Everybody get those weapons unloaded, right now. No, you stupid bastard, point it at the ceiling. Unload 'em right now. I'm not kidding around any more."

Subdued somewhat by his tone, the men sheepishly removed the magazines from the weapons. "Check the chambers, too. Get every round out." Ejected cartridges sounded on the floor and metal table tops. "O.K.," Spencer continued in the same hoarse voice. "Everybody's going to bed, right now. The bar is closed. You stupid shitheads have caused enough damage for one night. No arguments. That's an order. I said you could shoot off a couple flares at midnight, but I didn't say anything about weapons. You act like a bunch of juvenile delinquents and that's the way I'm going to treat you. There's a plane going down to Léo tomorrow and a couple of you birds are going to be on it, contract or not. I've got a pretty good idea who started this crap, and you're going to pay for it, so help me. Any of you guys who want to join your buddies on that flight and kiss your bonuses good-bye, just start complaining or fucking around again. Now get up to your rooms and don't hang out the windows. The ANC is going to be out in force now. Right in the middle of one of their fucking rebel panics you guys start this crap. They're scared shitless by all this shooting and they're drunk. I'm not going to have another goddamn incident with them. This door's going to stay locked and you guys are going to stay in your rooms with your weapons out of sight. I don't want to hear any crap or back talk. As far as I'm concerned, you're all responsible. Now move!"

The men shuffled slowly out of the room, carrying their weapons and an assortment of bottles with them. No one spoke. At the far end of the room Spencer sat with the Special Forces major. The remaining gas lantern cast rainbow reflections from the puddles of spilled beer on the floor. The overturned tables, broken glass, and the last swirls of cotton-candy smoke added to the aura of a deserted battlefield which clung to the room. Steve stood up and walked toward the door.

"What the hell are *you* doing here?" Spencer croaked.

"Nothing," Steve said. "I mean, I just heard the noise and came to see what was happening."

"You drunk or something?" the major asked.

Steve shook his head. His ears were ringing painfully from the firing.

"You'd better get back to the hotel before the ANC come back," Spencer said.

Steve did not move. He stood in the hot glare of the lantern staring at Spencer's sunken eyes.

"What are you waiting for? Gonna make some more speeches?"

Steve shook his head slowly and unbolted the door.

"Go straight back, kid," the major said. "These dudes are going to be pretty pissed off about all the firing. You don't want to get caught alone by them out there in the dark."

Steve paused in the open doorway. He wanted to speak, but he did not know what to say. "Good night," he finally blurted out and disappeared into the darkness.

CHAPTER **34**

Outside the old man's hut in the starlight the night birds sang the Easter mass. Pierre stopped to answer them, collapsing back to his normal height from high above the banana groves.

"No," the corporal said. "We must not stop. Do not speak. It will weaken the *mai*. Count numbers. Count to seven nine times and then to nine seven times. Do not think and do not speak. Count your numbers."

They came down the hill in silence. The dogs tempted him with their Lingala catechism. Their eyes were burning yellow. He looked past them, saying his numbers.

In the papyrus stands the frogs chanted a Kikongo prison song. It was wrong not to join their singing. Prisoners should always help each other. He must not weaken the power of the old man's *mai,* however. Soon he would meet his twin and then he would need the protection of the oath and of the *mai.* Traveling with his spirit legs was easy, his spirit brain needed no air, and, even though they trotted, his lungs and heart lay silent in his chest.

Coming down the last ridge he saw another living necklace—the city lights. Magically, the distant streetlamps split themselves once and then again, so that there were four strings of light where there had been one. The points of yellow changed to a soft green as they pulsated in the distance. The eyes of the spirit were powerful. They could see things hidden to normal men.

He wanted to stop and watch the dancing lights and their answering reflections in the river. He started to speak, but then remembered his numbers. He must not forget the *mai.*

The corporal stopped him when they reached the paved road. "Wait," Corporal Ramazani said, touching him with the twig. "I must warn the others or they will shoot when they see us."

When the corporal had disappeared into the darkness, Pierre spread his arms, raising them stiffly to lock like the metal wings of an airplane. He sped down the road, feeling the lift of his wings. He was a passenger in his new body, an airplane to carry him wherever he wanted. His mind climbed smoothly above the fetid air of the swamp. He was not one of the lumbering old transports he had flown in so often on the monotonous trips to the Kasai. He was a huge jet, powerful engines slung beneath his wings sucking the fuel from the tanks deep in his belly. He turned slowly above the city. It would be easy to kill them all, the whites who had laughed at him, his twin, and Major Nkutu. If he used the heavy bombs hanging from his wings, though, the twin would be destroyed so completely that his heart and liver would be lost. The old man had insisted on the heart and liver. He must leave the airplane and attack the city on foot. It did not matter. With his speed and strength no one could defeat him. He turned out over the lake, preparing for a landing as he had seen the two bombers earlier that day. A red flare burst over the city, followed by the faint metallic honking of boat and locomotive whistles. They had seen him in his flight and were spreading the alarm. It did not matter. He had taken the oath and drunk the *mai*. No white man could hurt him.

He landed softly on the road and taxied toward the spot where the corporal had left him. More flares popped above the city— red and green. Then the first of the machine guns began to fire. The strings of tracers looped up above the town to intertwine like fiery snakes. More flares. He laughed; they had heard him as he flew so high above the city. Now they were searching for him, shooting blindly into the darkness. It was very funny.

"Hurry," the corporal called. "Major Nkutu is on the telephone."

The metal of the bridge rang with colored music as they pounded across the span with their heavy boots. The soldiers looked so tiny and afraid, huddled wide-eyed in the darkness of the guard post as the tracers and the flares fountained up over the city. He would protect them. They were his men and he was now a powerful officer. They would build a new army, destroying the white men and their slaves. Major Nkutu would die. He would sweep the paracommando camp on Mount Stanley clean, sparing only those who would take the new oath.

"It has started." The major's voice was squeaky, faintly yellow in color as Pierre held the cold plastic of the field telephone to his ear. "Can you see the firing? Can you hear it? They have begun just as I said they would. Can you see it?"

"I can see everything."

"Good. These are your orders. You will hold the bridge. If the whites try to get to their airplanes, you will hold them at the bridge. Your post is solid and you have a machine gun. Do not hesitate to fire when they come. If they attack your post, you will send the corporal and two men to the airport. They will burn the white men's airplanes. I will coordinate the defense from this sector. We have them in a trap. It's very easy, isn't it?"

"It will be very easy."

The major's voice turned green as it faded from the earpiece and sucked back into the wire. He watched it running weakly down the line, a small halo of color, ghostly among the swamp reeds.

"Prepare the rifle," Pierre said to the corporal.

Corporal Ramazani stared at him.

"Load the rifle with the colored bullets, just like those whites are shooting."

"With tracers?"

"Yes, there is a box of them inside the crate of machine-gun ammunition."

His own voice was red, hot red like the squirting blood of the rooster.

The corporal quickly loaded a magazine and inserted it into the FAL.

"Make it ready to fire."

The corporal cocked the weapon, checking to be sure the safety was engaged.

"Do the same for the pistol," Pierre said, handing the pistol to the corporal, who checked the magazine and cocked it.

"There are no colored bullets for the pistol, Lieutenant."

"It doesn't matter, the pistol has been blessed by the old man's *mai*. It will kill without the colored bullets."

"Do you have a knife?" the corporal asked.

"I have a knife."

He stood watching the firing in the city, the bridge rippling slowly beneath his feet. Filling his chest with the blue river air, he rose and towered above the guard post. When he had swelled many meters into the air, so that he floated near the singing power cables, he spoke. "You will stay here to guard the bridge. If the whites attack, you will shoot them. I'm going now for the heart and liver."

CHAPTER **35**

There were faint shadows rippling across the hotel façade as the grass fires burned down in the railyard. The lantern's glare and the grass fires provided the only light. The lake breeze waxed, causing the fires to flare. Somewhere back toward the hill a dog was howling pitifully. Steve looked down the stretch of darkened road leading back to the Hotel du Lac. There was something lying in the mud: the MP's rifle.

It's an FAL just like Dubois had. That's what I shot the antelope with. Christ, why do I feel so *sad?* I feel like crying just like a little kid. That's what the Special Forces major called me, he called me "kid." How *tired* their eyes were. They've been through scenes like this too many times. Stuck out in some crummy place with a bunch of drunken guys shooting off their frustration. What kind of a life is that? Spencer's got a family. He can't help it if the little girl's got braces and the boys are fat. They'll grow out of that—all kids do. He didn't want to come out here in the first place. He just follows orders. Why did I have to talk to them that way before? What the hell's wrong with me, anyway? It's not their fault. They didn't make the crummy war here. They didn't start

Vietnam or Laos or Santo Domingo. Why should I blame guys like that? They're just regular hard-working guys who have their jobs to do and do them without complaining like crybabies.

They don't just play at this, coming on a trip for a week. They live this way. They spend their whole *lives* out in these places. The way Spencer's eyes looked, he doesn't enjoy this crap. He'd like to be back with his family. What the hell's wrong with me, anyway? I should go back and shake hands and apologize like White said. No. I'll do it in the morning.

It wasn't the pilot's fault, either. He had orders just like the rest of them do. Why should I blame them? Creighton was only doing his duty. Nobody told them anything about surrender passes. Hell, the passes were a good idea. They worked, didn't they? The rebels came over and the ANC actually tried to get them shipped down to Kamina. Why should I blame guys like White and Spencer for the prisoners? It wasn't their fault. You know what I am? I'm a snotty little crybaby who doesn't know his ass from a hole in the ground. There's a war going on here, and there are a lot of ugly things. Kids starve and prisoners get shot by mistake. Why did I have to blame my *own* people for it? Why do I always blame other people for things? So what if I have to do the Bio File for a year? I'm learning the ropes, aren't I? A person just can't walk in fresh out of the Peace Corps and expect to know it all. What the hell do I know about the Congo, anyway? Nothing really. All I've ever seen is airports. That doesn't stop me from shooting off my mouth, though, does it?

O.K. So what? What the hell do you mean, so what? My life's a real mess. I whine all the time about things I don't even begin to understand, and then I practically kick my wife into another guy's bed and then I smoke all that crap to ruin my brain so I can't even think straight when I have to. That's so what. O.K. But what am I going to do about all of it? What the hell can I do? Well, for one thing, I can just go to bed tonight and not try to think any more, and then in the morning I'm going to apologize to those guys for shooting off my mouth the way I did, and I'm going to go home and talk to Lisa and see if I can't make things work. And then I'm going to write my report and not care if anybody reads it or not and go to work and keep my eyes open and maybe actually learn something, that's what I'm going to do.

Yeah, well, all right. But where the hell am I? Fucking streetlights out—just like the Congo. When you need something, it doesn't work. Look, I've been walking the *wrong* way. I've been walking *away* from the hotel. I'm past the mission church already. For Christ's sake, what a stupid thing to do. It's not my fault, though. Stupid Congolese can't even keep the streetlights running. Must have been that bazooka rocket, hit a power line or something. No, it was the fucking stupid Congolese. They got scared and panicked from the noise and probably ran away from the power station, and too much current came down the lines from the mountains and burned out the whole transformer. This country is really a mess. Face it. It's really just a hopeless mess. All that crap I've been peddling about man in the tropics is just horseshit. Face facts. They're just a bunch of savages. They can't run their own country. Hell, they can't even keep the lights working. They're just a pack of superstitious savages. Look at Dubois. He was born here. He knows these people. He speaks their languages as well as he does his own. Why didn't I listen to *him?* Look at the Count. He's been here thirty years. Who was I, trying to tell *him* things about the Congo?

He was wrong about one thing, though—it's not the Americans' fault. It's not the Belgians' fault either. It's the fault of the Africans themselves. They wreck everything they touch. Look at that little bastard who spilled the picnic basket. All they can do is drink and argue and slaughter each other.

The trouble with this country, it's filled with little murderous pimps like the lieutenant and that captain and Major Nkutu. Somebody ought to just go out and round them all up and shoot *them.* Do this country a hell of a lot of good. It really would.

Where am I *going,* anyway? Look, stop right here and throw away this stupid rifle and go back to the hotel and sleep. O.K. Better not throw away the gun, though. Better take it back and give it to Spencer. Right. They've got some lanterns back there now. Must be at the Ops Sud headquarters. Jesus, I walked a long way. Stupid thing to do. O.K., just cool it and walk back. Wonder what time it is. O.K., so she's fucking him now. So what? That's going to stop, right? O.K. You understand why she's doing it, don't you? Right, it's nobody's fault. Just this goddamn country and those loudmouthed niggers who think they know so much.

Yes, but how could she really do it, taking off her dress and bra and everything for *him?* But I don't *own* her. She's not my slave. I didn't sign a paper to buy her body when we got married. Yes, but while I was out here trying to save those poor damn prisoners, she was back there in *our* bed with his cock all up inside her. Christ, what are you running for? Stop. Stop running like you're crazy. Don't run in the dark, you asshole!

One of the Pakistani merchants had cut a narrow canal across the laterite road to drain the water collected in a stagnant pool in front of his store. As he ran blindly, Steve's left foot hit the far edge of the canal, sprawling him headlong through the air. He fell. The heavy FAL unslung, casting out before him with the web sling twisted about his elbow. The gun's muzzle struck him sharply in the right temple. For the second time that day he tasted blood and saw glimmering snowflakes before his eyes.

C H A P T E R **36**

Pierre's long spirit legs moved beneath him and he was away from the bridge, striding stiffly through the brown cloud of insect noises. As soon as he was gone on the dark road, the corporal and the other soldiers dropped their weapons and ran, heading quietly toward the paths among the banana groves above the river.

The white fools still fired at the sky, wasting their ammunition in their vain search for his airplane. It would be easy. He continued through the swamp, ignoring the false pleas for help sung out in a variety of languages by the water creatures. The old bullfrogs begged him in Tshiluba to release them from the fishermen's traps. The crickets sang in French, evoking him as their master. These were tricks. He must not talk to them. The whites were strong and treacherous. It was not easy to enlist the aid of these creatures. If he had not heard them with his spirit ears, he would not have believed the whites were this clever. Once he had rejoined the paved road, he stopped. He kicked the balled mud from the soles of his boots and studied the city lights just ahead. Those were the lights of the mission. Would the twin be there? It was probable that he would be with the priests and doctors. Perhaps he should go there and kill the priests in any event. With the priests dead, his twin would be deprived of powerful allies.

He kept to the shadows beneath the iron trees bordering the railyard, then passed the red brick compound of the old hospital. This was a very evil place. He could smell the sour pink of the whites' evil *dawa* flowing out of the crumbling wards into the night. His father had indeed been evil to have spent his life serving the doctors. They had almost succeeded in transforming him into one. He shuddered—all the shining knives. At last the truth had been shown him and now his life would be made good again. All he had to do was kill the white twin. He stopped.

He must kill another man this night and eat his heart and liver. Surely this too was evil. It was evil to kill, and, still worse, cannibalism. He had been taught that as a child. The savages in the bush killed in blood feuds and ate their victims at hideous ceremonies. This was against everything he had been taught. But the old man had been clear in his orders. *You will kill your twin and bring me the heart and the liver.*

Pierre stood teetering in the dark. What if it had been the *old man* and not the whites who had tricked him? What if the *mai* he had drunk was not magic at all but simply a drug to warp his brain? He had a good brain. He had wanted all these years to become a doctor and now he was going to kill a man and eat his flesh. He sat down clumsily on the root of a tree. He must think carefully. It was hard to think with the noise of the firing. It was hard to think with the colors constantly rippling before him with strange music. These were his spirit eyes. He must try to think with his own brain. What was his brain? What belonged to him and what to the spirit? Were the spirit and the soul really the same thing? Was this possible? The rooster had twice been killed and twice the old man had brought it back to life. This had been no catechism story from a book. He had seen it happen. He had felt the spirit within him wake and had seen the city so far below him as he flew on his spirit wings. This was the truth. He must now do his duty. He must break the spell or the spirit would die.

The grenade blast echoed down the street. Dimly he saw the column of water rise from the ditch. He got to his feet. His enemies were in the center of the city. They were waiting for him. He should not have thought so much. Thinking weakens the *mai*. He must say his numbers to bring back the power of the oath. The night birds were talking again. They would help him with the numbers. He knew that they could be trusted. He unslung the rifle and walked unsteadily forward. The white phosphorous rocket exploded in a flaming pinwheel far down the road. This was something evil, fiery and very evil.

He sat down again. As he watched, the electric streetlamps grew tired, fading from a bright red, like the blood color of his spirit voice, to a pus-yellow. Then they died and he was alone in the dark. Fires were burning green and blue in the railyard. He must not wait any longer. He had thought too much and the *mai* had weakened. The road was muddy here and badly rutted from the trucks. He peered ahead into the darkness. There was something moving among the green fires. It was coming at him, blowing flame and blue sparks.

It was a fire machine the whites had sent for him. He dropped to one knee, trying desperately to hold the careening jeep in the pulsating rifle sight. The car swept past him, laying down a trail of smoke and sparks as the roof flamed off in strips. Again the rifle was frozen. Their *dawa* was too strong. He could not fire. Coughing in the pall of smoke, he stood again. This was very evil, worse than the killing of his twin. That had been a machine from *hell* itself. His finger touched the safety catch. He had been tricked. Violently he pushed the little button. They would not fool him again. His twin was close. He felt sapped by the thinking and the hell machine. Now he must stand here and say a complete series of the numbers while he waited. His twin would come soon. He must not think of his father or his mother or the soft mornings on the river after mass. Such things were evil. They were part of the spell. They had to be forgotten. Think of the whites who must die. First, the twin and then Da Silva and the priests who had tricked him. They were all evil.

He had completed the third circle of numbers when the grass fires blazed up again. There was someone running toward him on the road. It was a man with a rifle. The green fire spread in the railyard, gleaming back at him from the windows of the mission church. The road between the stores was visible now in the firelight. The man had disappeared. He was out there in the darkness waiting. Pierre Tshipama finished the last of his numbers and walked forward to meet his *twin*.

C H A P T E R **37**

"Merde!" Serge yelled, braking the jeep hard on the muddy side lane. "What the hell was *that*?"

There were three men in the stolen Five Commando jeep— Serge, hulking like a buffalo in his camouflage smock behind the wheel, and two other mercenaries, men like himself, killers, ex-Foreign Legion, ex-Organisation de l'Armée Secrète, ex-Katanga Gendarmerie, men who had spent their entire adult lives fighting and killing, first for the honor of France and later for the honor of their regiment and still later for the promise of easy money and now simply because they had grown to enjoy the killing and knew no other life.

The flaming ANC jeep swept past them trailing a plume of smoke and sparks down the road toward the swamps. The small, unshaven man in the back seat sat up, steadying himself as he took a long pull at the half-empty bottle of Scotch. "ANC *Police Militaires,*" he laughed. "Must have gotten hit by that white phosphorous the Sud-Afs let off."

Serge snatched the bottle from his hand and gulped down three mouthfuls. "Wonderful!" he exploded. "Fantastic! Remember in '52 when we booby-trapped the pagoda the Viets were using and all the monks came running out with their pretty saffron robes on fire? Remember that?"

"Oh, spare us your goddamn *war stories,"* Schneider answered, laughing sarcastically. His French was thickly accented and his words snapped out with brittle quickness. "You broken-down, drunken old fart, if you were such a hero in the First *Paras* why can't you ever set foot back in France again? It's amazing how half a bottle of that rotgut can transform a thug like you into a patriotic warrior."

"Shut your Kraut mouth," Serge said quietly with deep bitterness muffling his voice. "Your trouble, Schneider, is that you're not even French. You're a queer Nazi dope fiend, and all these years you've hated France and the French Empire."

Schneider made a sloppy attempt to palm two more amphetamine capsules into the corner of his mouth, but his fingers shook so badly that he dropped one. "Why don't you just use a needle like you did this afternoon?" Serge said coldly. "One day I hope you give yourself too much of that and your brain pops like a grape."

"You won't be there to see it happen, *mon Sergent,"* the other answered. "You'll be floating in a coffin full of that horse piss you can't stay away from. I like my pills all right, especially when I'm going to have a woman, but you can't even tie your boots in the morning until you've had half a bottle of whisky."

The small mercenary in the back seat threw up his hands in exasperation. "For Jesus Christ's sake," he laughed, "this is a little bit stupid, don't you think? We steal a jeep and get that Portuguese pimp to come through with his two little half-white whores and all you two want to do is sit here and trade insults. If you don't want to fuck, that's fine with me. I'll drive you back to the billet. I told him we'd be there right after midnight, and he said he'd wait till one o'clock. We've got about three minutes to get there."

Serge and Schneider joined him in intoxicated laughter. With a great flourish Serge put the jeep into gear and turned smoothly onto the main road. "It's been three weeks since I've even *seen* a white woman," Serge said. "As long as they're not fat-assed and platter-lipped and don't stink of manioc and they've got just a couple drops of white blood in them, I'll give them the best fucking they ever had."

The purple glow of the jeep's headlights blossomed behind Pierre like the dawning of an alien sun. He heard the wheels on the dried mud. The road before him was illuminated in a rippling spray of colors. Twenty meters ahead he saw a white man lying in the mud, a heavy automatic weapon cradled in his arms. The power of the *mai* numbers had stricken the *twin,* but now, he knew without even looking, that the hell machine had returned to take him. The whites had used the twin as a bait so that he would turn his back on the fire machine and he had been snared by their trick like a stupid goat caught in a forest trap. Now the *mai* must save him or he would drown forever in the lake of fire just as the priests had warned him so long ago in catechism class.

"Our Father," he mumbled, "send me your *dawa* and hallowed be Your name. . . ." He dropped flat on the muddy road and, protecting the rifle with his body, rolled to the shallow drainage ditch. The patternless screen of light from the onrushing jeep blinded him like the sunlight through the stained glass of the big church by the riverbank. "Holy Mary, blessed be the *mai* of thy womb. . . ." This time he could not miss. The rifle butt slammed against his shoulder. The rope of tracer bullets lashed into the jeep and it toppled to its side into the opposite ditch. The whites were *very* evil. They had restored the canvas roof of the jeep which only moments before had been in flames, and they had transformed the black soldiers into *whites.* These were evil creatures, not men with souls, but spirits like himself. Now two of them lay grotesquely sprawled, blood spattered, dead in the yellow-and-green glow of the one remaining headlight. Pierre floated easily to his feet. He must kill the third, and then he must use his knife to take the heart and liver of the twin.

Schneider's head was clear. He knew that his right arm was shattered at the elbow and that he would probably bleed to death before help came. He'd been hit by bullets and shrapnel so often before that he knew the pain would not begin for several minutes, that the nerves were still deadened by the impact of the bullet. Serge and little Philippe were dead. The water in the ditch stank of feces and his own blood. With his good arm he reached gingerly into the tilted cab of the jeep and removed Serge's FAL. He braced it against the gearshift and cocked the action. A small, crazy-eyed native dressed in monkey skins and the remnants of an ANC officer's uniform was stumbling toward him on the road. *"Also, mein kleiner* nigger . . ." Schneider whispered. The blast of the FAL caught Pierre in the legs and groin, sommersaulting him backward into the drainage ditch.

"Schön, sehr schön." Schneider grinned happily. He pulled himself slowly out of the watery ditch and braced his left side against the fender of the jeep. The native lay a few meters away across the road, his head and shoulders just inside the pool of light from the jeep's headlamp, his eyes glowing like bicycle reflectors. Schneider reeled slowly, his chest heaving from the exertion of raising himself, making it difficult to sight down the barrel of the weapon. Dryly his precise mind clicked through a calculation. . . . That was very amateurish. I'm losing my touch . . . must have used fifteen in that long burst and only hit him with three or four. Hit him low, too, so he can still shoot back. Switch now to single shots because there are probably more than one of them. Rebels, do you think? *Nein,* probably ANC renegades. Fire single shots now and stop when you hit his head. . . . I'll need a belt for a tourniquet. . . . All these years I've been at this and I never learned to shoot left-handed. . . . He's hit badly, but look at those eyes. . . . There he goes for the pistol. Stupid animal. He can't shoot a pistol into the light. Go slowly, there're bound to be two of them. They're just animals, just like the Viets and the Arabs, misguided animals who must be destroyed. Not so high, my friend, you shot right over the ditch. Look at all that blood coming out of Serge. They always say that alcohol thins the blood. Big fellow like him must have twenty liters in him. . . . That's better, got him in the shoulder. Must have been smoking hemp, doesn't seem to feel it. Just a bit to the right and I'll have the head, and then I can do the tourniquet and flush out the other one and maybe I'll even live to see the sun come up. Very slowly now, need the head shot before I can get another magazine from Serge's belt and put on the tourniquet and wait for the other one. . . . Right, I said, you idiot, not left . . . you're wasting ammunition. Have to kill this animal before he gets the range with that pistol, but they're hard to kill when they're doped like that. . . .

It was good mud, warm and wet. Steve lay on his side, smiling. He had never fully lost consciousness, the blow of the rifle barrel only stunning him free of the cascade of wild emotions that flooded his brain as he ran blindly on the darkened road. He was tired; his mouth was very dry.

I'll just go back to the hotel and drink some ice water. They've got plenty of ice cubes there—Spencer said so. There isn't any sense in trying to think this thing out tonight. That's one thing I've got to learn, and this is just as good a place as any to start. I don't *always* have to figure *everything* out. So what if the Africans can't handle things? That's not my problem. That's their problem. They'll learn. It'll take time and we've got to help them and it's not going to be easy. Nobody ever said it was going to be easy. It won't be easy getting back together with Lisa either, but I'm going to do it. And then I'm going to work at really trying to *help* these people. White and Spencer and the major can do whatever the hell they want to, but Lisa and I are going to really begin helping people. What was it that the Count said to Lisa, about her visiting the black mamas and reminding them to wash? O.K. That's not a bad place for *her* to start. I'll do their fucking Bio File for them, but I'll do a lot more too. It's going to be all right. . . . We're going to make it. I've just got to learn to take one thing at a time.

Steve reacted instinctively to the glare of the jeep's headlights. He was on his feet in mid-stride across the drainage canal when Pierre's weapon spouted the stream of red tracers from the shadows of the palms at the side of the road. Time slowed, taking on a viscous, elastic texture as he watched the huge mercenary topple from the vehicle.

Time stopped as the droplets of blood were sucked along with the tracers whipping out of the chest of the little mercenary in the jeep's back seat. The blood hung there suspended in the yellow glare of the headlight as the jeep turned on its side, careening into the water-filled ditch on the opposite side of the road.

Steve's mind was clear of conscious thought. The uncontrollable flood of words was gone. He could only stand there rooted to the muddy road, silently watching the spectacle before him as Schneider dragged himself from the jeep and with great patience worked to steady the weapon on the advancing figure of the native in the monkey-skin headdress.

Then time started again for Steve, accelerating wildly as he watched Pierre's body, clouded in its own bloody aura, flip backward before the muzzle blast of Schneider's weapon. With the shock of the firing Steve's brain began to function again. Words would not form, but a jerky collage of images smeared across his consciousness, quickening with the insanity of the action he witnessed. He saw Charlie's blacked-out street in Saigon and the wounded Viet Cong sapper limping through the darkness. He clearly saw the impact of the bullet striking Pierre's shoulder and at that moment recognized Pierre as the young ANC lieutenant beneath the monkey-skin *dawa* regalia. He watched as the mercenary sighted again, aiming at Pierre's head as he lay sprawled at the edge of the headlight's perimeter.

"No!" Steve screamed, suddenly seeing Charlie again, leaping from the hood of the jeep on the muddy road outside of Stanleyville to disperse the gang of ANC renegades with a burst of fire above their heads.

The butt of the MP's automatic rifle was against Steve's hip. He knew that he must help them. Both men were wounded. Another bullet spouted water in the ditch behind the lieutenant's head. He had to stop them from killing each other. There was no reason for this. He had to help them *both*.

Schneider felt the heat of the bullets passing over his head. So, he thought dryly, there *is* another one up the road. These animals are so predictable. Very good. I'll stay down here now behind the jeep. Let the fool come up now, I'll stay here as if I'd been hit again. Watch the shadows from the headlight. There, he's coming up. Think this one out very clearly, Horst. You're a trained German soldier and these two are subhuman primates. Draw on your experience. Remember when the FLN ambushed the convoy outside of Souk el Kebir in the Kabalia? You got yourself three weeks' leave in France for that action. Wounded in both feet that time, but you stayed there in the lead vehicle and waited until they came in to clean up, and you got six of them with grenades. They were even white, Arabs at least, much whiter than these apes.

Schön. Listen to him on the mud. He's staggering like a sleep-walker. Watch his shadow. One grenade or two?

The pins will be a problem with only one hand. Use your knees to hold them. So that's the way it should be done. These are NATO grenades, American really. Three-to-four-second fuses. Don't worry about that, these animals wouldn't think of throwing them back at you. So the fuses don't matter, just don't drop them. *Roll* them. Just a little toss so that they'll roll. *Ganz gut,* there's one and there's two. *Now* we can think about a belt for a tourniquet.

Pierre's blood was surprisingly cold on Steve's fingers, the body surprisingly light as Steve stooped to drag it fully onto the road. Oh, Jesus, Steve thought, he's going to *die.* Look at how his legs are bleeding. *Why the hell do we have to do these things to each other?* He's just a kid, but look at what they've done to him. Look at what he's done to those men on the road. It's not his fault and it's not theirs either. O.K. then, whose fault is it? I don't know. But, God, I wish I did. This poor bastard's going to die on me right here in the road, and those two others are already dead, and what I want to know is why they did it. There's got to be an answer. . . . Maybe *that's* what Lisa and I can do, maybe we can try to figure *this* out.

The first grenade bounced past Steve's feet and rolled a few inches into a puddle where its fuse sent fizzing bubbles to the surface. The second grenade landed with a thud on the surface of the road next to Pierre's head. Steve felt his mind and bowels and genitals suck uncontrollably inward with futile, self-protective instinct. No, he thought, this is stupid. Wait. I can explain. Wait. There's no reason for this.

C H A P T E R **38**

After the dimness of the bedroom, the fluorescent glare of the bathroom blinded her. Lisa knelt naked on the cool tiles watching the toilet bowl and the tub and the bidet move in a flat circle. The chunks of oyster and the sour champagne splashed against the porcelain. It was awful, it would not stop. She retched so violently that her toes cramped. It just would not stop. She sweated. Breakfast avocado came up. Her hair was down there in the reeking bowl.

She pulled herself up to the sink. Maybe Greg would leave her alone now. Twice he had tried. He's too drunk. It wouldn't stay hard. He couldn't come, just banging away at her as she lay with the pressure band of sickness tightening mercilessly about her head. Now it was better. She had nothing more to throw up. She washed her face with the tepid brown water from the cold faucet, rinsing her mouth and again weakly attempting to clear her nose of the acid mucous. I should take some aspirin now. It will help my head in the morning. No, codeine, that's better.

The crowded shelves of the medicine cabinet were bewildering. Codeine? Steve's got the codeine bottle. I dropped it to him last week. Only a week? Steve would tell him to leave her alone. I don't want to do it. Not with this headache. Why does he keep trying? He can't come. Can't even keep it hard. It just twists and bends. He shouldn't butt that way. Does he think that's nice for me? Maybe he's asleep now. Maybe we can both sleep and then he'll go away.

Lisa tiptoed unsteadily through the shadowy bedroom to fall on her stomach on the far side of the tangled bed.

"Greg, don't pull like that so hard. You're hurting me."

"Come on."

"No, don't be silly. Let's just wait till morning. We drank too much."

"Come on, damn it."

"Wait, don't push so fast. You'll hurt me."

"There. How's that? How do you like that?"

"It's still all soft. Let's wait till morning. We'll get all rubbed sore. It won't work like this."

"No, now."

"I feel sick, Greg. You're hurting me. Please, I feel sick."

"No, damn it. I didn't come up here to wait till morning, so shut up and lay down there."